LAST AT BAT

MARK DONAHUE

White Dog Books

ISBN 978-0-9842351-0-0

First Edition: October 2009

Art for cover design from Dreamstime.com

Printed on Acid Free Paper

To Mildred (Millie) and Merle Hough whose lives defined the spirit of Blossom.

ACKNOWLEDGEMENTS

Not unlike the children that need a village, a book needs a community of people to make it grow and develop – a group that sees potential, renders support, provides criticism and demands discipline. My community consisted of family and friends who did not laugh at the idea. Instead, they took time, offered insight, hope and encouragement.

Janet Aiello, Dr. Jane Badegian, Susan Davis, Laura Dempsey, Gary Donahue, Steve and Carol Elson, Frank and Edie Kennedy, Larry Hamblin, Joanne Houston, Helen Jackson, Rick Johnson, Beth Kimbler, Elizabeth Lehman, Glenn Levitas, Demian Lichtenstein, Steve Obert, Kevin Riley, Dave Schultz, Mark Smith, David Workman, Mike Wolf and Dayton Young, you were all there when I needed you, and I sincerely thank you for your commitments of time and attention.

I also want to thank Beth Duke, Jeffery Ledford, Kathy Marazzi, Julie Reasoner, Erin Spears, George and Tari Steberl, J.J. Tiemeyer and Maestro Dino Zonic. You all helped bring the characters of *Last at Bat* to life in what I will always remember as the long awaited comeback of the Belmont Players.

To John Woods at Words That Work, Cathy Pearson at White Dog Books, Denise Fraile at Verati Design and Judy Lammers, editor extraordinaire, your combined knowledge and expertise was the lifeboat I needed when I got in over my head.

I want to thank Bart Zeller and my teammates of the Chicago Fire who allowed me to keep playing baseball, when I needed baseball far more than it needed me.

Finally, I want to thank my son, Matthew, for being the kind of person I always wished I could have been, and the writer I will never be. To my wife Marsha, I marvel at your love, intellect, insight and most of all your patience in all things. To Angie, Tammy, Schaeffer, Maggie and Carly, I only hope heaven is a place where dogs rule. If invited, I'll bring the Milk Bones.

Prologue

Cooperstown, New York

The sign on the door of the ivy-covered O'Reilly's Stone House Tavern read "Closed." A graying man wearing a Dodger baseball hat, Hawaiian shirt, and wrinkled khaki slacks decided the sign did not really mean closed to him. He pounded on the thick wooden door. When that did not elicit a response, he pounded again.

From inside a voice said, "We're closed 'til 4:00 o'clock. Come back then."

"That's four hours from now," he said. "I'm meeting some folks here later and have no place to go 'til then."

"Sorry Pal, no can do."

"I'll give you a hundred dollar tip plus the cost of a bottle of your best scotch."

The resulting silence from the other side of the door indicated that someone was doing the math.

"Hold on a minute."

A clunk of the door's lock was followed by it being opened six inches and the face of a young man in his mid-twenties peering between the door and the jamb.

"You serious about that C-note, Pops?" he asked.

"As a heart attack," said the older man holding the hundred dollar bill up to the cracked door.

"Hey Pops, you can't say anything about this to anybody."

"Why would I want to do that?"

"Alright, come on in."

1

Last At Bat

The man in the Dodger hat smiled as he entered the cool, dark bar. It had the essential aroma of an old tavern.   It smelled like spilled, stale beer was forever embedded in its wooden floors, mahogany tables, chairs, and stained bar. He figured there was even beer on the ceiling.

Slapping the hundred on the table the older man said, "Glenlivet, neat and turn on ESPN, if you don't mind."

Picking up the remote, the young man said, "Don't mind at all. You want to watch the Hall of Fame induction?"

"Yes, I do," he said.

"You a big baseball fan, Pops?"

"First of all, I am not, thank God, your Pops. Nor would I want to be. Secondly, I am a baseball fan of sorts and would like to sit here quietly, sip my scotch and watch the induction ceremonies. Any problem with that?"

"Nope, you paid the fare."

On the wall mounted flat screen, the year's lone inductee into the Major League Baseball Hall of Fame was being interviewed by several reporters prior to the commencement of the ceremony. Video replays showed highlights of the player's illustrious career. There was a seemingly never ending stream of home plate celebrations, teammates pounding his back in elation after yet another game winning hit or defensive play. There were scenes of locker room craziness immediately after a game and fans in the stands waving red and white banners.

The young bartender washing glasses in the sink behind the bar said, "They're sayin' he was the best of all time. You buy that, mister?"

"How would I know? You think I have seen every goddamn ball player since 1869?"

"Well, all my friends and I think he was the best we ever saw, and the numbers don't lie. You really think one of those guys from the old days was better than Matt Wolf?" he asked.

"Numbers do lie, kid. In fact, they lie like hell," he replied.

"So? Who was better?"

For a split second, a smile flickered across the old man's face. Then, he remembered and began to speak.

Last At Bat

1. Still Hurts

Twenty Three Years Earlier
Cincinnati, Ohio
Thanksgiving Day

On the banks of the turgid Ohio River, a light fog mixed with a cold, misty rain shrouded the signature smoke stacks behind right center field of the Great American Ball Park. On the river, only a few feet away, a small tugboat strained as it pushed a barge filled with coal upstream. Its horn blew a needless warning to a deserted downtown Cincinnati.

The stadium's reflection in a rain puddle on Pete Rose Way in front of the ball park was shattered as a yellow cab splashed through it. A young man, looking older than his twenty five years, exited the cab. He pulled up the collar of his leather coat to shield himself from the rain and biting November cold.

"Please wait here, I'll just be a few minutes," the young man said to the cabbie chomping on an unlit cigar.

"Take your time, son," he replied

The young man, with his hands in his pockets, felt the familiar pain in his back and moved slightly stooped in an effort to find some comfort. He walked slowly around the ballpark, the area deserted, as a cold, stiff breeze blew the rain into his face. As he moved around to the east side of the stadium, he came to a locked metal gate which afforded a view from the left centerfield area all the way to home plate. He grasped the metal fence and placed his face against the cold, wet bars and stared in at the empty stadium.

Last At Bat

He remembered that night. He heard the crowd roaring so loud that the air vibrated. He remembered how warm it was for an October evening. How he saw the fastball all the way. He remembered that micro second before anyone else on the planet knew where the ball was heading off his bat, he knew.

He also knew the game was over. Standing there he could feel the pounding he took from his teammates as they rushed to meet him between second base and the pitcher's mound. The seven- year- old memory was as fresh as the day it happened. Looking out at the field, remembering, his pulse raced and sadness engulfed him.

Pushing himself back from the bars of the fence, the young man put his hands in his pockets and walked slowly back to the waiting cab. Before re-entering the cab, he turned and gazed back at the stadium for a last look.

"Thanks for waiting," he said. "Guess we better head to the airport."

"That damn back still bothering you after all this time?" the cabbie asked.

"Only when I walk or sit or lay down," the young man replied with a forced laugh.

"Man, I was sure sorry about all the bad shit that came down on you. Really sorry. I don't mind sayin', even for a white guy, you were my favorite player, seriously. That was a hell of a team you guys had, maybe not as good as that Bench, Morgan, Rose and Perez bunch, but damn good."

"Thanks, I guess we were pretty good," he said.

"Pretty good? Hell, man, you guys was great. It's all just a damn shame. A damn cryin' shame," he said.

As the cab made its way to the airport, Dylan Michael sat back and wondered how it all came down the way it did. In the end, he blamed himself and that made it even harder to take.

"Good luck young man, the cab ride is on me," the cabbie said.

"Hey, thanks anyway," Dylan replied. "But I won't be in need of a whole lot of cash for awhile." He handed the cabbie a fifty dollar bill.

"Thanks, young man and good luck," he said, pocketing the cash.

Carrying a small gym bag, Dylan Michael walked toward the door marked "Departures." He was stopped by a familiar voice.

"Dylan, wait up. It's me, Arthur."

Arthur Robbins was in his mid-forties and a writer for the LA Times covering the world of Major League Baseball. Despite his popularity with his readers, some ball players thought he was an arrogant prick. Others really didn't like him at all.

"Arthur, I can't believe you came all the way from LA," Dylan said.

"Well, I was in the neighborhood and all…"

Dylan chided, "Yeah, I know, I know. Anything for a story."

"Hey, you're news," Robbins replied.

"Old news, now."

"How are you doing?" asked Robbins.

"At this point I just want to get everything over and done. I've been dreading this day for a long time, but now it's here and I just have to deal with it."

As the men talked, several people recognized Dylan as they walked past, but none stopped.

"Is your attorney going to be here?" Robbins asked.

"Yes. He and Drew are going over some paperwork. I have to sign a "Surrender Form" and then it's off to sunny Georgia."

An awkward silence interrupted the men's conversation as neither could think of anything to say.

"Oh, there they are now. Hey guys, this is Arthur Robbins. He's a writer for the LA Times and he came to see me off. Arthur, say hi to Drew, my stepdad and Bob, my attorney."

Both men ignored Robbins' extended hand, and Bob snarled, "How the hell did you find out Dylan was leaving today? We sure don't want a bunch of damn press and fans out here making it tougher than it already is."

"My sources are confidential," Robbins replied.

"Fuck you and your sources. You guys are a royal pain in the ass."

"Yeah, well, it's a livin'. I guess we're all just opportunistic bastards, eking out our miserable existences, eh, Bob?"

Dylan interrupted, "C'mon guys, knock it off."

Bob turned his glare from Robbins and said, "While you guys catch up on old times, I'm going to go inside and see if I can find that deputy who is going to escort you down to Atlanta."

Drew ignored Robbins and pulled Dylan a few feet away. "Look Dylan," he said, "Bob got us a good book deal. We're going to write a book that, you know, tells your story. Everything that has happened. We just need your approval."

"Is that what you have been on the phone with Bob about the last few days?" Dylan asked.

Drew, defensive, replied, "So what? It's a way for all of us to make some money. Since you went and fucked everything up, we don't have lots of options. Besides, with all this bullshit, the legal fees and my time, you owe me. "

Incredulous, Dylan replied, "Owe you? For what? You've made millions off me then spent it on booze, strippers and hookers. As for the legal fees, it was my money, and you wasted that by hiring your idiot friend Bob, who I'm sure put more than half of it back in your pocket."

Drew ignored the accusation and snarled, "I made you a goddamn superstar and you go and piss it all away."

"That's right, Drew. I fell on some ice and hurt my back just to spite you. Then I got hooked on painkillers, got in trouble with the IRS, lost my wife, got seven years in jail just to piss you off. It's all about you, Drew."

Through clenched teeth Drew hissed, "You sign these papers or you are on your own, pal. I'll be done with you once and for all. I mean it."

"On my own?" Dylan huffed. "Oh, I get it. If I sign, you intend to go to prison with me. Is that it? I'm not signing anything that is going to make you and Bob money while I'm in jail. You're the one on your own and I mean it."

Drew took a menacing step toward Dylan. Dylan straightened up ready for whatever Drew might try.

"You ungrateful prick, I should kick your ass right here."

"Careful Drew, I'm not twelve anymore."

Drew stopped, looked at Dylan, and realized he was not twelve anymore.

"You don't scare me," Drew bluffed.

"Then that would be a serious mistake," replied Dylan.

Suddenly realistic and pragmatic, Drew changed his approach. "Aw, c'mon kid. We're all upset over this. I'll leave these papers with you, and when you calm down, you can sign them later and send them to me. We'll make sure you get a big piece of what we make, and it will be waiting for you when you get out."

Dylan took the papers, looked at them and tore them in half.

"Fuck you, punk. See you in seven years," said Drew as he stormed past Dylan, just as Bob returned.

"What's wrong with Drew?" Bob asked. "Did he tell you about our book deal?"

"There is no book deal, Bob. I'm not signing anything."

"Why not?"

"Because it's my story, not yours or Drew's."

"Shit. Alright. Well, this is Deputy Tom Martin and he's going to be your traveling companion."

Dylan shook Tom's hand. Tom, a former Junior College linebacker morphed into a star struck member of law enforcement when he met Dylan. "Hey, Dylan. Man, I have been a fan of yours for a long time, ever since you came up with the Reds. Yeah, buddy, I went down to the stadium seems like a hundred times to see you guys play. I remember one night against the Cubs…"

Checking his watch Bob said, "Hey guys, I really don't have time for old home week."

Dylan replied, "You can go, Bob. I think I'm in good hands with Tom here."

"Yeah, well, alright. I do have some things to do in the city," Bob said. "I guess I'll take off then. Take care. I'll let you know about the appeal, but like I said, it doesn't look good. Don't forget to sign those papers Tom has."

Without shaking Dylan's hand, Bob turned and walked away from him.

Arthur walked up to Dylan and said, "Sorry, I could not help but hear all that. Those guys are real sweethearts."

"Yeah, rats leaving a sinking ship, I guess," Dylan mused.

"Was he the best you could find when you went looking for an attorney?"

"Drew found him and my accountant years ago."

"Not the same accountant who..?"

Nodding, Dylan replied, "Yes. Same guy. But it's all water over the dam now."

"One hundred mil lost and seven years in jail is a big dam."

"It was my own fault. I was a fool. I should have paid attention."

"Sounds like Drew was a little pissed too," Robbins said.

"If I didn't do things his way, he had a habit of doing that," Dylan replied. "It got worse after mom died. When I was about thirteen, he was told I might be able to make some money playing baseball. So, he took over as my business manager, and I was too young to understand what that all meant, until it was too late."

Arthur changed the subject. "I see your back is still hurting you."

Ruefully Dylan said, "I'm sure a prison bed is going to do it wonders."

Standing to the side of Dylan and Robbins, Tom the deputy pulled out a pair of handcuffs.

"Hey Dylan, we'll need to get going in a few minutes."

Dylan, saw the handcuffs and looked around, embarrassed. "Never thought about this part."

"Deputy, is that really necessary?" asked Robbins.

"I am honest to God sorry about this, but if I don't put these things on Dylan and somebody sees it, I'll lose my job sure as hell. Look, I'll just wait inside and we can put them on in there. Ten more minutes?"

"Thanks Tom, I appreciate it," said Dylan as he and Robbins watched the deputy walk away.

"Dylan, I don't know what to say except as I was coming over here today, I thought about the first time I ever saw you play."

"I remember that day. It was about nine years ago in Ventura. Not sure if I got any hits, but I do remember that afternoon."

"You hit two home runs and threw a guy out at the plate," Robbins said

"Wow, great memory for an old guy," Dylan teased.

Silence again interrupted the men's conversation. Uncomfortable, Robbins finally said, "Well, Dylan, you take care.

When you get out, I will help you anyway I can. By the way, I want you to know I will be doing a little story about you but I think you will be okay with it."

"Thanks, Arthur, I appreciate that. And I appreciate you coming even though it was a slow news day."

The men shook hands.

Dylan turned and walked toward the "Departures" sign. Arthur watched Dylan walk away and was surprised to see a young woman appear just as Dylan was reaching for the door to enter the terminal. She looked familiar.

Dylan, surprised, said, "Cara! I asked you not to come...but I am sure glad you did."

Dylan's soon to be ex-wife was her usual stunning self. Dark raven hair, with cobalt eyes that Dylan used to say, "would glow in the dark."

"I would have come over sooner but I saw you talking to Bob and Drew and decided to wait my turn. I don't like either of them, and I hated the way they treated you. Like you were some kind of product they created. I was surprised they weren't going through your pockets looking for loose change," she said.

"It's all over now, no use going over that stuff again," he replied.

"You okay?" asked Cara, as she moved a piece of Dylan's hair back into place with her hand.

"I'm just "peachy," he said. "Get it? Going to Georgia. Peaches."

Cara shook her head, smiled and said, "Always the joker."

"Maybe I'll work on a stand up routine in the Big House. So, how are you doing?"

"Alright," said Cara. "I feel better since I decided to move back to Cincinnati. I missed my old job and friends."

"And after today, you won't have to worry about running into me again," he said.

"That's not the reason I moved back and you know it. Look Dylan, I really hate to bring this up now, but my attorney will be sending you the final divorce papers in a couple weeks."

"So soon? Who's the hot date?"

"You know better than that, too. I am sorry about the timing, but I thought he was going to get the papers to you before, you know, before today."

"It will give me something to read. Did you come here today just to tell me I would be getting some mail?" asked Dylan.

"No Dylan, I came here to tell you how very sorry I am about everything. What happened to you. What happened to us, all of it."

"You could have called and told me all that."

Exasperated, Cara replied, "You still don't get it do you? You hate me because I left you, but you don't understand that I couldn't bear to see what was happening to you anymore. After the injury, I couldn't stand how Bob and Drew kept telling you to take all that medicine even when they saw what it did to you. And you listened to them and not me. Then I told you they were stealing from you, but you never believed me. Why? You changed Dylan. When I first met you…"

Interrupting, Dylan took Cara's hand. "First of all, I don't hate you and never could. I know it's too late now but over the last six months, I came to realize you were right about a lot of things. Things I couldn't see before."

She sighed. "Dylan, what hurt me most was just as Drew and Bob made you a product, you tried to make me a trophy. The blonde hair, the push up bras, the parties, the magazines; all of that. That wasn't me and it wasn't us. Or at least the us I thought we were."

"I'm sorry for all that," he said. "I listened to Drew and Bob and shouldn't have. They were trying to package both of us and I let them. I was an idiot."

Deputy Tom peeked from the terminal door and said, "Dylan, it's time to go."

Nodding to Tom, Dylan said, "Cara, tell your folks I said hello and thanks again for coming today."

Cara leaned her head into Dylan's chest. Her tears left wet marks on his shirt. "I will. They always loved you, you know? Carly too. Funny, you were the only man she wasn't afraid of."

"Good bye, Cara. And give Carly a Milk Bone for me."

"I will, good bye."

From a nearby cab, Arthur Robbins, hard ass LA Times writer, watched Dylan disappear into the terminal and shook his head. "What a fucking waste," he mumbled.

2.   Thanksgiving Day

Sonny and Gwen's Lake House
Southern Kentucky

Two men in their late sixties traded several long, drawn out yawns. Doc Watson, relying on six years of medical school, three years as a military doctor, and thirty-five years in private practice said, "It must be the tryptophan from all that turkey."

Sonny Cook, next to Doc in an identical, black Lazy Boy, mumbled a drowsy second opinion based on some time tested personal experience of his own, "Or, it could be those five Budweiser's."

Doc, acknowledging his friend's plausible, well articulated hypothesis, replied, "Yep, could be that, too."

They'd polished off the Thanksgiving's fare along with the Bud's, before collapsing onto their leather thrones two hours earlier to watch some football. After forty years of friendship and watching hundreds of games together on TV, they had established a pattern that worked just fine for them and neither would consider changing it.

"Sonny, I told you we need more firewood." While reaching the firm stage, Gwen's voice coming from the kitchen did not have that *final tone* to it that would have meant Sonny had better get off his butt that minute. Though she had reminded Sonny at least five times the firewood was low and more bad weather was coming in the next few days, Sonny ignored her, yet again.

Less than three minutes later, both Gwen and Annie came into the family room, positioned themselves directly in front of the Panasonic and assumed "the position." Hands on hips, they glared down at their two semi-comatose, beer and turkey filled husbands, who finally realized that there was no place to run and no place to hide.

Annie asked, "Are you two deaf?"

She'd made an unfortunate choice for a question. It prompted both men to launch into an impromptu skit which included cupping their hands around their ears and saying, "Eh, what's that again?" They then looked at each other and pretended to use sign language all the while talking in loud incoherent voices. Both men were soon gasping for breath from laughing. Their wives rolled their eyes in unison and cleared their throats.

Their wives' distinct lack of respect for sophisticated male humor forced them to accept the inevitability of their situation. The men reluctantly threw on their jackets and within two minutes went outside into a cold, face-stinging rain.

Facing the woods with the rain at their backs, Sonny asked the obvious, "Doc, why does it feel better to pee outside?"

"Some things in life just need to be enjoyed and not explained," Doc replied in earnest.

Sonny nodded his understanding of a mystery unsolved.

After zipping up, the men began loading kindling and already broken up firewood into Sonny's rusted wheelbarrow.

"Load it up, Sonny. I sure as hell don't want to come back out in this crap," Doc said. The cold, bone-chilling November wind promised to get worse before it got better.

"My knees hurt. I think it must be all this damn rain," complained Sonny.

"Could be you're just an old bastard," said Doc.

This time it was Sonny who carefully considered Doc's alternative diagnosis and said, "Yep, could be that, too," and both men laughed.

As their laughter died down and the force of the rain increased, Sonny asked, "What's that?" as he looked up into the leaden sky toward the west.

"What's what?"

As the words left Doc's lips a deafening sound from the west was now almost directly overhead. Both men instinctively dropped into a crouch next to the wheelbarrow following the ear-splitting hissing noise. They strained to see through the rain for what was, at that moment, scaring the hell out of both of them.

All either could make out was the pastel blue and red lights shrouded in clouds on the underbelly of a huge jet as it moved at what they later estimated was nearly 200 miles per hour only 150 feet above them. The speed and mass of the jet created powerful eddies of spiraled rain and wind currents that looked like mini-tornados in the gray mist.

Slowly rising from their crouched positions, Sonny whispered, "My God, there ain't no place for a plane to land in that direction."

Seconds later, an explosion could be heard followed by a series of smaller impacts like when a race car crashes, then tumbles down the track in a seemingly never ending series of roll-overs. The sound of the crash echoed through the surrounding hills and valleys like the repeating thunder of a summer storm. Seconds later, black smoke rose in the eastern sky and with it an orange/red glow appeared within the thick gray cloud cover.

"That looks like it's over near Deer Valley," gasped Sonny.

Both men ran toward the house. When they burst through the kitchen door, Gwen was already on the phone having called 911 seconds after hearing the jet scream over their house followed by the subsequent crash and explosion.

"Tell them it looks like it hit over near Deer Valley," said Sonny. Gwen nodded and relayed the location to the 911 operator who requested Gwen stay on the phone in case more information was required to find the crash site.

Sonny moved quickly to the Panasonic and turned to CNN to see when the network would begin reporting the crash. "Doc, could you tell if that was a commercial jet or not?" Sonny asked.

"No, but given the size, I would guess it was," Doc said.

The first report of the crash came within ten minutes as a "crawl" at the bottom of the screen during a political news story. It said there had been "reports" of a plane crash in the hills of southern Kentucky although there had been no confirmation of the type of plane.

After a few more minutes, a "Special Report" interrupted CNN's programming:

"CNN has received a report of a crash of a commercial jet in a remote area of Southern Kentucky. Details are sketchy but the FAA has confirmed a flight from Cincinnati on its way to Atlanta has been lost by radar and presumed down. There have also been several reports of a loud explosion. CNN will continue to monitor this breaking news."

"I keep telling you it crashed over near Deer Valley. Are you sending emergency crews?" The exasperation in Gwen's voice was obvious. She'd been told that the deteriorating weather and impending darkness was preventing emergency crews from reaching the remote crash site and it could be hours before help would arrive.

"Let's take the Polaris over there and see if we can do anything," said Sonny.

Doc put his coat back on and said, "Let me grab my bag out of the RV. Gwen, you and Annie round up some blankets and any medical supplies you have around the house. Also, get me some sewing materials and don't forget alcohol, flashlights, and anything else you think might help."

Sonny climbed onto the ATV and started the engine. "I'll bet Potter Road is closed with all this rain," he said. "We'll need to take some back trails, so hold on tight, Doc. It might get a little dicey up in those hills."

Loading the large gym bag the women had filled with supplies onto the back of the ATV and tying it down with rubber cables, Doc said, "Just get us there."

"I got my walkie-talkie and I'll call you when we get there. We'll wait until the emergency crews arrive," Sonny said as he hugged Gwen good-bye.

The risk the men were taking in trying to get to where they thought the jet had gone down was significant. Though both were aware of the danger, neither said anything. They took off into the darkening November afternoon toward the black smoke that continued to spiral over a tree line two miles away.

"Tyler Creek might be a bit of a problem," said Sonny of the normally placid five feet wide and twelve inches deep rivulet about quarter mile from Sonny's house. At the bank of the creek, they could see it was now at least fifteen feet wide and over three feet deep and moving at a clip that could turn over the ATV. "We need to stay in our seats. Hopefully our weight will keep us upright," Sonny wished out loud.

Doc nodded and gripped the roll bar above his head as Sonny slowly entered the churning water. Several times the rushing current pushed the ATV up onto its right two wheels. In response, Doc and Sonny leaned left, and the ATV regained its footing. After several seconds of seeming to flounder, the powerful ATV virtually exploded out of the water after Sonny gunned the engine and its knobby tires bit into the creek bed, found traction, and clamored out onto the far bank.

For 30 more minutes the rugged ATV slid up and down rain soaked rocks, past fallen trees and slopped through five-inch deep mud paths. After following the black smoke that could be seen between water laden pine trees, the two men found themselves approximately 100 feet above the crash site.

"Oh, my Dear Lord," Sonny whispered.

What they saw did not look like a jet plane. They stared at a debris field that extended nearly half a mile down the valley floor with few pieces larger than a subcompact car. The huge jet looked like it had been placed in a gigantic blender and turned on high.

With the gym bag full of supplies looped over Sonny's shoulder, the men made their way down slippery gravel and mud toward a nightmare. They saw things they would never share with anyone else. Smoldering corpses and body parts were mixed up in seat cushions, luggage, blue blankets, carpet, plastic, and miles of electrical wire. A blue-gray haze produced by burning oil and jet fuel mixed with rain and created a thick halo of smog that hovered over the crash site.

"Doc, everyone is dead. They're all dead."

The men ignored the near freezing rain that continued to fall as they walked down the valley floor. The hellish sight was juxtaposed against a soft orange glow created by a raging fire that burned 200 feet in front of them engulfing what had been the center section of the jet. They were not aware that what they were seeing was the section of the plane where over 150 passengers had been incinerated.

Smaller fires scattered for hundreds of yards down the valley and created a lighted path that seemed to never end. When the freezing rain hit the fires and the white hot metal they were consuming, it sounded like bacon sizzling in a hot skillet.

The men threaded their way through and around the dead in what they were sure was a fruitless search for survivors. But Doc suddenly yelled, "Over here!", sprinted to his left and headed for a pretty blonde girl still strapped in her seat. Her head rested on her left hand with her legs crossed. She was leaning against what was left of a window seat in what was clearly the first class section. The girl looked casual and relaxed and appeared to be taking a nap.

Bending on his left knee, Doc took the girl's wrist and searched for a pulse. Finding none, he laid her on the wet ground and discovered her neck was broken. "God dammit" was all Doc said. The young girl's face would haunt Doc for years afterward.

For the next several minutes the two men, who only an hour before had been watching college football on a 52" big screen, sat side by side in the mud, blood, and ice cold rain and silently cried for people they had never met.

A crackle from Sonny's walkie-talkie jolted both men.

"Sonny," said Gwen. "I just talked to the 911 operator, and she said the rescue teams were not going to be able to get to the crash before morning because of the flooded roads and rain."

"Tell them there's no hurry. There is no one left alive up here. No use getting somebody else killed trying to get here at this point," Sonny answered.

"Oh my God, Sonny, I am so sorry you and Doc had to see all that. You boys come on home now, you've done all you can do," Gwen said softly.

"Alright, darlin', we're on our way."

Sonny put his arm on Doc's shoulder and said, "C'mon, Doc, we've seen enough of this. Gwen's right, there is nothing we can do and it's going to be a rough trip back to the house."

"All those people gone," said Doc.

After another minutes of silence, Sonny stood up and helped Doc out of the mud, and both men started walking back up the rain-slicked hill toward the ATV. As they began their ascent, both noticed for the first time the acrid smell of burning oil that stung their noses and burned their throats. Doc also detected a familiar odor that reminded him of Viet Nam when he had to treat men burned by napalm. He kept the recognition of that awful smell to himself.

About half way up the hill Sonny thought he heard something coming from the only recognizable section of the plane.

"You hear that?" he asked.

The men stopped their climb, turned toward the tail section of the jet and listened. After a few seconds, the sound of what appeared to be scratching came from the very rear of the huge vertical stabilizer that was still intact even though it had been ripped away from the fuselage on impact with the mountain side.

"I'll bet it's some damn varmint trying to get to some of those people," said Sonny.

He then grabbed a four feet long piece of aluminum, began walking to his left and worked his way to the area near the rear of the plane where the sound was coming from.

As he walked toward the ruptured tail section, Doc said, "You be careful, Sonny. That section doesn't look all that stable. It might come sliding down on you."

Ignoring his friend, Sonny waited until he heard the sound again and swung the aluminum piece at the back of the plane hoping to scare off whatever critter was inside the piece of aircraft. The metal on metal clang created an echo that bounced off the valley walls and repeated several times before finally fading, allowing the sound of the incessant rain to return.

"Dammit , Sonny, I said be careful," growled Doc.

But Sonny was mad at something. He kept slamming the piece of metal into the side of the plane until Doc came over, grabbed his arm and softly said, "That's not going to help, Big Boy."

Standing in the rain next to the huge section of the plane, both men simultaneously had an overpowering urge to be with their wives. Sonny threw the piece of aluminum down and said, "Let's go home."

They turned to walk the final 50 feet up the hill when another sound froze them in their tracks. Scarcely breathing, they strained to make out what was now both movement and sound coming from inside the fractured plane.

A muffled groan overcame the sound of the rain hitting the ground and metal. Both men ran to the ripped open tail section and, using their flashlights, peered into the blackness.

"Anybody in there?" yelled Doc.

For nearly a minute there was no answer. Doc was about to shout again when they heard the sound they had heard moments before. Only louder this time.

"We have to go in there, you know," said Doc.

"I know." Sonny grimaced.

Last At Bat

3.   Aft Lavatory Occupied

Inside the tail section, the heavy rain created a staccato background noise that, coupled with the flickering of the fires through the windows of the jet, produced an otherworldly effect. The sensation led the men to break out in sweat despite the rain and cold.

Both had faced gnawing, paralyzing fear before when they were in Viet Nam, and both had seen and been close to grisly death. Yet what they were now seeing and hearing gripped them like neither had ever experienced.

Their flashlights bore into the darkness revealing no passengers in any of the roughly dozen rows of seats that led to the rear of the plane. What they could see was more wiring and oxygen masks hanging from the ceiling along with little TV sets, carry-on luggage, briefcases, and clothing strewn around the cabin. Black trails of scorch marks and soot discolored the top of the seats, walls, floor, and ceiling of the fuselage.

"Looks like this was hit by a blow torch," said Sonny as he covered his nose, trying to escape the putrid smell of seared flesh.

After passing the first row of seats, they realized why they had seen no passengers when entering the plane. Upon the violent impact with the rock, the supports holding the passenger seats had snapped off at their base, throwing the passengers to the floor of the jet.

Doc stopped as his flashlight lit on two men and one woman lying nearly prone with their legs broken at the knees. It was also clear that their necks had been compressed by the force of the crash as their heads sat on top of their shoulders. All three faces had second degree burns that produced red, raw skin that had already formed blisters. Most of their hair had been scorched off.

Doc and Sonny slowly made their way to the back of the plane. Doc stopped at each row. Unless it was clear the passenger was dead, he checked the pulse of each person to make sure it was not one of them making the moaning sound he and Sonny had heard.

Sonny followed Doc down the aisle of the jet and saw images that were branded into his brain. Row after row of death ranged from what appeared to be peaceful sleep, to gruesome carnage. A young man's severed head was in the lap of the woman seated next to him with no visible injuries. An elderly couple had died in an embrace, her head against his shoulder, each of their legs having been cut off at the shin bone. A business man in a blue pinstriped suit had a ball point pen stuck deep into his chest, his eyes open wide in shock.

Each contortion of death leapt out at the two men from the darkness. The stark glare of their halogen lights moved from body to body and produced ghastly snapshot images that in several instances made Sonny gasp.

Only once did Doc stop and appear to re-coil from what he was seeing. Near the rear of the cabin he had come across a little boy, maybe a year old with a pacifier in his mouth, lying face up in the aisle. He looked neither injured nor burned. Doc picked him up and gently laid him in a seat, praying it was he who was making the sound they were hearing. He checked for a pulse and put his face next to the little boy's mouth, hoping to feel a breath or a heartbeat. Finding neither, Doc reached down, picked up a blue blanket and covered the little boy like you would when you tuck in a child at bed time.

As the men silently stared down at the little boy, their depression was palpable, but they were brought back to reality when they heard another moan, this time much louder, almost impatient. They were at the last row of seats and could not tell where the sound was coming from.

Sonny said, "We're here to help but we can't find you."

Seconds later they heard a light rapping sound, followed by a painful scream from the aircraft aft lavatory. The door was slightly ajar, revealing a toilet that had been dislodged from its normal position; it was nearly upside down with the top of the bathroom laying in the direction of the front of the plane. The bottom of the commode was at a 45 degree angle, slanted toward the ceiling.

Doc pulled with all his strength on the handle but the door was jammed.

"Let me try that," Sonny said. He moved in front of Doc and grabbed the upper part of the door which had been pulled four inches from the frame. Using all of his 6'5'' and 255 pounds, Sonny yanked until the tendons in his neck popped out like rope. The door sprang open exposing what the men's brains could not, at first, comprehend.

This time it was Sonny who re-coiled from what he was seeing.

The glare of the flashlight distorted what was inside the lavatory. Before their eyes could adjust to the incongruity, their noses detected a new cacophony of odors that were unmistakable. It smelled like an outhouse.

A bright blue color, mixed with brown and dark red, covered what was an indistinguishable mass inside the bathroom. Then, the mass moaned.

Doc and Sonny realized they were looking at a man's body that was crumpled downward toward the roof of the john. A leg stuck straight up into the air and bone was sticking out above the left ankle. The blood seeping from the crushed body was mixed with urine, feces, and blue toilet bowl cleaner.

"What the hell do we do now?" Sonny asked Doc.

Doc stepped in front of Sonny and said, "Clear away this door and make some room on the floor. Then, go grab as many blankets as you can from up front and bring them back here."

Doc identified the body he was looking at as a male by the clothes being worn. He also knew by the labored breathing, the amount of blood loss, and external injuries, that the man would likely be dead within minutes.

The first challenge was to get him out of the lavatory without killing him on the spot. Unfortunately, the position the man was in made it nearly impossible to lift him without causing even more injury.

"We're going to have to knock down the three walls to be able to get him out," he said.

"I got that, Doc," Sonny replied as he began to tear the john apart piece by piece. After three minutes of kicking and smashing, the walls of the bathroom were gone and what looked like a young man lay on the floor of the plane.

Doc carefully stretched him out. Despite Doc's gentleness, the young man screamed in pain.

"He didn't…he didn't just die, did he?" Sonny asked.

Doc checked the man's pulse. "No, he just passed out. Better for him."

Doc used the man's unconsciousness to conduct a preliminary examination to determine if there were any more obvious injuries that needed immediate attention. He was particularly concerned about massive bleeding but discovered none.

What Doc did discover was the young man's face was destroyed. The left ear was missing and it appeared the jaw was broken or dislocated or both. There was a six inch flap of skin that dangled below his chin that at one time had covered his cheekbone. Fifteen to twenty cuts and gashes covered his ruined face from scalp to chin; some so deep that muscle and bone could be seen. Over a dozen pieces of mirror were imbedded into his face. There was a severe laceration from where his left ear had been continuing down his neck. Doc feared this wound may have cut the man's jugular vein.

His body was just as bad. The right arm was broken above the wrist as were several fingers on his left hand. The worst injury was a compound fracture of his left leg where two bones stuck out from his shin and ankle.

After 15 more minutes of examination Doc said, "This young man has no right to be alive, and he won't be if we can't get him some help real quick."

"Hey Doc, look there." Sonny pointed to handcuffs that were attached to his left wrist.

"Yeah, I saw those. Looks like this boy has had a real run of bad luck lately," Doc answered.

"What do we do, Doc? There aren't going to be any EMTs or rescue teams here for the next 10-12 hours."

"Well, we got to do something," Doc decided.

"Then let's try and get him back to our place on the Polaris and do what we can there."

"It'll probably kill him, but I guess we don't have any other options," said Doc.

Over the next 15 minutes Doc and Sonny carefully wrapped the young man in blue blankets. They used pieces of nylon seat belts to secure him, and created a make-shift gurney from the bathroom door that Sonny had ripped from its hinges.

"I hope he stays unconscious until we can make it back. If not, he might die of shock from the pain he will have," said Doc.

Without saying it, Sonny was more than a little worried the three men would even make it back at all. The storm had worsened. Freezing rain slapped their faces and forced them to squint to be able to see. The wind had also increased, and it howled through the valley like a locomotive.

Of immediate concern was getting the strapped- down body of the young man up to where he could be loaded onto the ATV.   The ATV would never make it down the steep rocks and then back up the muddy hill.

They decided to carry the gurney as far as they could. At the base of the hill they tied the nylon rope Gwen had put in the gym bag to the ATV.   With Sonny at the wheel, they slowly pulled the gurney up the last several feet to the path. Nearly an hour after finding his broken body, they strapped the young man onto the back of the ATV and he was on his way to Sonny's - if they could get through Tyler Creek.

As the overloaded ATV slowly began the trip back to Sonny's house, Doc looked down at the crash site one final time. He was struck by the sight of the huge tail section that rose above the valley floor in sharp relief to the rest of the broken, smoldering small pieces of the plane and its contents. For some reason he was reminded of a movie where the remains of the Statue of Liberty rose up on the beach. For the life of him, he could not remember the name of that damn movie.

4.   Butt Saved

"No frickin' way we can make it through that," yelled Sonny through the wind and rain as he looked at the creek that was now a raging river nearly 20 feet wide and four to five feet deep.

"Well, we sure as hell can't stay here all night, either," Doc snorted. Three minutes of heated debate failed to produce a viable option.

"Hell, let's just try and walk through the creek, unless you're afraid of getting a little wet," Doc concluded.

"I ain't scared of gettin' a little wet, but I'm a tad concerned about gettin' a little drowned," reasoned Sonny.

A plan was finally hatched. They eased the ATV as far into the creek as they could without it being washed away. Then, using it as an anchor, they laid large fallen tree limbs from the ATV to the far shore. They pushed and pulled their patient over the ATV and the tree limbs, working slowly toward the other side.   The plan almost worked.

The creek was three to four feet too wide, and Doc, after making sure the gurney and the supply-filled gym bag had made it to the other side, lost his balance and was washed downstream. The nylon rope that they had used to tie off to one another snapped tight and held. Had it not been for Sonny's weight, both men may have ended up in a river in Tennessee.

"I saved your butt again," said Sonny as he hauled a soaked, cold, and exhausted Doc to the shore.

"Bull shit. I had it all the way," was all Doc could gasp.

After 15 minutes of rest, the men began the quarter mile trek to Sonny's house carrying what both felt sure was a dead body.

Sonny had wanted to call Gwen and tell her what they were bringing home. He also wanted to ask her to call 911 and let them know that there had been a survivor, but his walkie-talkie had been washed away in the creek.

After 20 minutes, Sonny and Doc finally climbed the steps to Sonny's front porch and entered through the front door.

"Girls, we're in here," Sonny announced.

"Sonny?" Gwen yelled. "I tried to call you for over thirty minutes, but the walkie-talkie must be dead…"

Gwen and Annie, who had both been running from the kitchen, stopped in their tracks as they saw their soaked and mud covered husbands standing over a mummy lying on the living room floor.

"Oh, my Lord," Annie whispered.

"Gwennie, we need to get this boy onto a bed. Go get some hot water and some dry towels. Take this gym bag of stuff you gave us earlier and put it all in the second guest room," said Sonny, not wasting time on explanations.

"Annie," said Doc, "I'll need to wash up before I can examine this boy. Get me some soap and run some hot water in the guest bath sink."

In less than five minutes the women quickly and efficiently completed their tasks. Sonny and Doc carried the boy, still attached to the bathroom door, to the back guest room and placed him onto the bed. They slid the door from under him and Sonny slowly cut away his wet, bloody, foul smelling clothes.

After washing his hands four times with Lava Soap, Doc came back to the bedroom and for the first time saw a body more dead than alive.

Annie and Gwen had also sterilized their hands. The three of them gently washed away all the blood, mud and fecal matter that covered most of the body so Doc could determine the visible external injuries. The women had been nurses in Viet Nam when they first met Doc and Sonny. They kept the hot water, alcohol, and towels coming without being told to do so and didn't flinch when they washed and scraped off the vile stuff that covered their patient.

Several times during Doc's examination, the young man gasped in pain, and his eyes flickered in consciousness for a few seconds, then he'd pass out again. Each time everyone in the room thought he had died.

As Doc silently cleaned and examined his ravaged patient, he thought of all the hundreds of other young men he had seen in this kind of shape nearly 40 years earlier. As a graduate of the United States Air Force Academy and Yale Medical School, he was sent to Viet Nam as repayment for the education he'd received from Uncle Sam. The experience changed his life.

For his entire tour of duty, Doc believed he'd never make it out of alive. That fatalistic view turned him into a legendary risk taker who treated the maimed and dying under enemy fire and earned him a large cache of medals. After being summoned to Washington, D.C. to receive yet another award, Doc stopped at the 14th Street bridge and threw that medal and all the rest into the murky water below.

Dr. W.W. Watson and Annie, jumped at a program that matched physicians to small, rural areas needing their help. This despite the fact, they had been warned by many that they would be considered "outsiders" in the small Southern town. Yet Blossom quickly embraced "Three-Dub" and Annie as their own, even though 84 year old Jeb Berk said after meeting Doc and Annie, "well, there was time this kinda thing would have never happened here." Soon a small clinic was born, and the childless couple adopted the Blossom community as their family. Doc's seminar work at Duke University and Internet studies made him a pretty damn good doctor, though his poker buddies now called him an "ole, broke down, small town hack who should be put out to pasture before he tried to give someone with the hiccups a warm water enema."

Doc's standard reply was his trade-mark laugh, followed by, "Yep, time's a gettin' short."

Blossom was damned lucky to have Three Dub and knew it. What they didn't know was how lucky Doc felt to have Blossom.

5.   A Red

After 30 minutes of cleaning up the broken young man with alcohol and warm soapy water, Doc was better able to see the extent of the injuries. What he saw offered little hope that the young man on the bed would make it through the night.

"This boy needs intensive care, or he'll be dead by morning," Doc said.

"Doc," Gwen explained, "the emergency crews won't get up the mountain 'til around noon tomorrow and they'll go directly to the crash site. I doubt they'll be able to get here 'til late in the day with Potter Road being closed. If this wind and rain continue, no helicopter can make it up here either."

Sonny added, "Doc, all you can do is try and keep him alive until tomorrow. No one will blame you if you can't."

After a minute of silence, Doc said, "Well, the best I can do is to make sure he stays asleep and try to get some fluids in him. He lost some blood, but I think we can sew up the worst cuts. I should set his arm and fingers while he's passed out and put his nose back into place so he can breathe better."

Dumping the contents of his black bag onto the side of the bed he took inventory of the supplies they'd gathered. What he saw was not comforting. Except for a stethoscope, blood pressure cuff, half a dozen syringes of morphine and eight pieces of candy for the kids who received house calls, the rest of their medical supplies could be found in an average home medicine cabinet.

"God dammit," Doc mumbled to no one in particular when he saw his meager stock.   After sticking a piece of the candy in his mouth, Doc used the morphine as a sedative on the young man and quickly set the broken fingers, holding them in place using tongue depressors as splints. Though the young man would occasionally moan with the pain, he repeatedly relapsed into a drug induced sleep.

Doc sewed up all the major cuts and gashes with regular black thread from Gwen's sewing box. He snapped the young man's nose into place and sewed up the flap of skin that had hung down the side of his face. He even tried to sew the left ear back on which Sonny had found on the floor of the jet, but the tissue was too damaged to deal with.

"At some point, this boy is going to need some major plastic surgery," said Doc.

"Sonny, you need to hold that left shoulder. I have to determine where the break line is so I can put this arm back into place." Without an x-ray machine, Doc poked and prodded then found what he was looking for and jerked the left wrist while grasping the arm above the break. With a resounding "crack," the bones realigned. He then used a *National Geographic* magazine as a cast that he wrapped in tape and gauze to keep the arm in place. The left leg's compound fracture and severe facial damage were impossible to treat, so they would have to wait.

After three hours, Doc, Gwen, Annie, and Sonny collapsed from the strain onto the nearest furniture. They silently shuffled from their patient's room, trying but unable to ignore his shallow breaths and groans.

"I suggest we take turns staying up with him tonight to make sure he doesn't wake up or choke to death," said Doc. "I'll take the first watch for a few hours and maybe one of you can take over then."

"Nonsense," said Gwen. "You go get some sleep now and be ready to get up and help if we need you. Annie and I can keep each other company 'til morning. After all you two have been through tonight, we'll take the first shift."

Before the words escaped Doc's open mouth, Annie put her foot down.

"Don't you argue with us now. Just go to bed." Doc went to bed.

Sonny dragged a blanket from the closet and was quickly snoring on the living room couch.

As the night wore on, the wind and rain turned to a horizontal howling sleet that beat against the windows for hours. Twice the lights flickered, and Gwen thought for sure they'd lose power. The women spent the night checking on the young man's pulse and blood pressure while daubing the seeping blood escaping from his facial cuts and broken leg. Around 4 a.m., the young man moaned loudly, obviously in pain. Annie gave him another shot of their precious morphine to keep him groggy until morning.

At 7:15 a.m. Doc lumbered into the room and saw Sonny, Annie, and Gwen standing around the bed. Hearing Doc enter the room, Sonny turned and said, "He's worse."

As Annie, Gwen, and Sonny stepped aside, Doc blew an exasperated sigh from his cheeks. The battered body was now swollen and grotesque. His head was half again its normal size with the missing ear and broken nose adding to the monstrous visage. Blood had oozed and then clotted from the more than 20 cuts and gashes across his body. The shoulders and back were so bruised that they appeared black and the ankle below the exposed bone on his leg was dark blue.

After a brief examination Doc said, "He may look worse but the body is just trying to heal itself and won't be able to do that until we can get this boy to Knoxville. Any news from the emergency crews?" Not getting a response Doc said, "Well, what have you guys heard?"

"The weather is clearing up and they think they can get to the crash site by noon today," said Sonny, "but we might want to think twice before bringing them here to work on this boy and taking him to Knoxville."

"Why, you damn fool. It's a miracle this boy has survived and you don't want to take him to a hospital? That is the dumbest goddamn thing I have ever heard…"

Doc was just warming up and about to detail how really goddamn dumb Sonny's suggestion was, when he was handed what looked like a credit card from Gwen. At the top of the card, he read: "Cincinnati Reds Player Identification." Below on the left, was a picture of a handsome young man with dark hair, and a big smile wearing a Cincinnati Reds uniform top. On the right side it said "Dylan David Michael." The card described him as "24 years old, 6'3" tall, 190 pounds, green eyes, brown hair, address: Cincinnati, Ohio."

"Remember hearing about that young ball player up in Cincinnati who got in some big trouble?" Sonny continued. "That's him. He had what everybody thought was a minor injury and then got hooked up on some kind of drugs. Then he got into some IRS trouble and was sentenced to prison down in Atlanta which explains the handcuffs."

Doc had heard the story, but it was hard to believe that what they saw on the bed was the smiling, handsome young man on the ID card.

"It seems to us that it would be a damned shame to turn this poor kid over to the authorities just so he could get fixed up by some half-ass prison doctor and then spend the next seven years in jail."

Gwen, who was a big baseball fan, said "This boy was the best player in the game for four or five years, then got hurt somehow and lost everything. Story was, some tight-assed lady prosecutor running for re-election was hell bent on making an example of him and refused to plea bargain. The result was he was sentenced to seven years in prison. Sounds like he got railroaded to me."

Sonny added, "I'm not much of a baseball fan like Gwennie here, but I remember hearing this boy was something special on the field and a pretty good kid, too. Looking at him and knowing what he has already gone through is sad for all of us.

After a few minutes of staring at the swollen face and then the identification card Doc said in an exasperated voice, "Listen to me now, this kid should have died on that plane, but didn't. He should have died on the back of that damned ATV, but didn't. Then he should have died last night and didn't. I am telling you all right now, his luck has run out. He has no chance of surviving, zero chance, if we don't get him to a treatment facility within the next few hours. If he were in intensive care right this minute, the odds would be, at best, 95-5 against him."

Sonny shook his head. "The three of us think we ought to try and stabilize the boy here for a couple more days, play dumb if the authorities come by, and then let the boy make the decision when he gets better if he wants to go to jail or take a chance..."

This time Doc exploded.

"Gets better?!" he roared. "Are you three crazy? Gets better? He won't get better. He can't get better unless he gets to a hospital, today! He will die right in that bed at anytime, any minute. If he wakes up now, he'll be in agonizing pain, and we're down to our last dose of morphine. He has a severe compound fracture that could throw a blood clot. His heart rate is erratic; his breathing is shallow and he will more than likely go into a coma. It's better for him if he's taken to a hospital, even if he has to go to jail, than to die in this damn bed."

"Doc, you ever been in jail?" asked Sonny, arms crossed and jaw set.

"Hell no, I haven't been to jail!" yelled Doc.

"Then you don't know what the hell you are talking about when you say something about spending seven years in jail, do you?"

reasoned Sonny.   Doc mumbled something incoherent and unquestionably profane that Sonny didn't quite catch.

Doc turned to Gwen and Annie, pleading, "You two should know this boy has no chance unless we get him to a hospital right now. This minute."

Gwen's arms were crossed too.   "After we found his ID card a few hours ago, I got online and read what happened to this young man. It broke my heart. He has lost everything and now even his body has been destroyed. All I know is, maybe his surviving, after all he has been through, is some kind of a second chance for him. You are right. Dylan may die in the next five minutes. But, based on what I read about him, I'll just bet he would prefer to die here than end up in some jail for the next seven years. Like Sonny said, let's try and get him to the point where he can make his own decision and do what he wants."

Doc's face contorted with frustration as he started to argue his case again but, seeing the looks on the faces of Gwen, Annie, and Sonny, he just shook his head. He stared down at the broken young man for several more moments and then said quietly, "When the roads open, we need to get into town and get some more supplies."

"No need to wait. I went down to the creek at sunup and fished out the Polaris. She cranked right up and we can be in town at Walgreen's in 30 minutes," said Sonny as though the plan was already in motion.

"God dammit," Doc said.

6.   Oscar and Felix

Sonny Cook and Doc Watson were an odd match. One was a Yale educated physician while the other barely made it out of high school where he had been a bruising All- State tight end from West Virginia. They first met in Viet Nam. Sonny had been drafted and proceeded to get himself shot in the leg and chest after only three days in the country. Doc had initially gone to Viet Nam as an officer and felt very strongly the war was "just and honorable." Sonny thought the war was horse-shit and even before he got shot, had inquired into the punishment for desertion.

Doc had treated Sonny's wounds and immediately took a liking to the raw boned, opinionated young man with "peace" and "love" tattoos on his back and arms. Doc also discovered that Sonny's act as a big, loud, country bumpkin was just that, an act. In reality, Sonny was sensitive, intelligent, witty, funny as hell, very well read, and knew more things about more "stuff" than anyone Doc had ever met.

During their tours of duty in Viet Nam, Doc and Sonny formed the basis of a friendship that would last the rest of their lives. Doc even introduced Sonny to Gwen right before Sonny was released from the hospital. After one date Sonny declared, "I'm gonna marry that girl."

After the same date Gwen said, "I'll never go out with that big oaf again."

Months later, Sonny bragged, "I just charmed that girl to the altar. She couldn't resist."

Months later, at their wedding reception, Doc told the guests, "I've got reliable information that he drugged her."

Doc came to believe that Sonny's view of the war was correct. He'd seen over 1500 young men die brutal deaths. And for what? Even the ones he saved, and he saved thousands, were in many cases destroyed physically, mentally, or emotionally after they were declared "fit for duty" and thrown back into the jungle. Any time he could get away with it, Doc would rule a soldier "unacceptable for duty", hoping the young man would be given a medical discharge and sent home.

Sonny and Doc became acquainted in Viet Nam. They became friends in Blossom.

When their tours were done, Sonny and Gwen came back home and decided to tour the country on a Harley. They became part of the counter-culture and moved from town to town in the early 70's, stopping to work odd jobs when they ran out of food, gas, and grass money. For three years it was fun. By the fourth year, it wasn't. Gwen enrolled in college, but Sonny was adrift.

Doc and Sonny kept in touch by mail for a couple of years, and Doc told Sonny that he ought to settle down somewhere and stop being a road warrior.

"Come on down to Blossom for a visit. It will do you good." Doc wrote.

Sonny's reply was one line on a postcard. "Doc, you just don't know how to have any fun."

In late 1975, Doc went down to the clinic on a Monday morning and found Sonny in a sleeping bag in the parking lot under his Harley.

"Hey Doc, what's up?" said Sonny squinting up and looking at Doc with blood shot eyes framed by a beard and pony tail.

"I think the line is 'What's up, Doc?'" Doc answered as if the conversation had happened before.

"Yeah, I think you're right. How you doin', man? Damn good seein' you," Sonny said, getting to his feet.

"Good seeing you, too, Sonny. What the hell are you doing here?" Doc laughed as they shook hands and gave each other bear hugs.

"Well, I got myself in a little trouble up in Ohio and decided I better hit the road for awhile and let things cool down," Sonny said in a brief confession.

"What does 'a little trouble' mean exactly?" Doc asked.

"It's kind of a long story and I'll tell you about it someday. Do you think I could crash with you for a few days?" Sonny already knew the answer.

Doc never hesitated, "I have a guest room just waiting for you. Annie will be real glad to see you."

"Oh man, that's great. Like I said, I'll only stay here a few days and then I'll hit the road," Sonny said.

After two months in Blossom, Sonny sent for Gwen. That's when Doc got the details about the "little trouble up in Ohio." When a campus cop had grabbed Gwen by the hair to break up a peace rally at Ohio University, Sonny picked him up and threw him 12 feet into the air. It took five other officers to subdue Sonny and finally haul him off to jail. After serving 60 days waiting for his court date, Sonny was given a choice by the judge: either leave town and don't come back or spend a year in jail. Sonny headed for Blossom and his old friend.

Much to the surprise of Doc and to the horror of her parents from Ohio, Sonny and Gwen got married in Blossom.

Gwen went to work as a nurse with Annie at Doc's clinic. Sonny bought a 35 acre farm and decided to grow peaches and apples. To everyone's shock, Sonny turned out to be a pretty damn good farmer. His business grew over the years, and he ended up owning a one hundred and thirty acre spread right outside Blossom and was known as a "gentleman farmer." Whenever he heard the description, Doc would burst out laughing.

Last At Bat

"Well," he'd reply. "You've got that half right."

7.   ESPN

After spending $600 on medical supplies at the local pharmacy, Doc and Sonny made their way back to the house passing scores of emergency crews that had finally made it to the bottom of Deer Valley and were beginning to make their way up to the crash site. Overhead, three helicopters criss-crossed over the wreckage providing directions to men on ATV's and those who were walking up the valley floor, on how to best access the remains of the jet.

The weather had cleared considerably, but it was still cool with a forecast for more rain later in the day. Gwen and Annie met Doc at the front door.

"There's no change in Dylan, except he's a bit more restless," Annie said.

"He seemed to regain consciousness for a few seconds a couple of times," Gwen added.

"We need to keep him sedated until we can get him some help. If he fully wakes up, the pain could put him into shock," said Doc. Compliments of Walgreens and his physician's credentials, Doc hooked up an IV drip that would hydrate Dylan as well provide nutrients and the sedation he would need over the next 24 hours – if he survived that long.

Everyone in the house stayed glued to the TV and saw live video feeds of the rescue crews that had finally reached the crash site. Teams swarmed the site looking for the black boxes and recovering bodies, while cameras from the local TV station, as well as national cable and network channels, gave wall-to-wall coverage. Each story reiterated that among the dead was twenty- five- year- old Dylan

Michael, former two-time National League MVP and National League Rookie of the Year. They reported that his body was burned beyond recognition, followed by shots of his first World Series Championship Ring that had been found at the crash site, and continuous loops of the highlights of his career.

Watching the videos of Dylan on TV, even a non-fan could see the power and grace he possessed on the field and how often he was photographed with a wide smile. At one point Gwen said, "He sure seemed like a happy kid."

Later in the day ESPN did an hour long Special Report on Dylan Michael entitled "Greatness Lost." A newspaper reporter named Robbins who had known him before he signed with the Cincinnati Reds was among those interviewed from the crash site.

ESPN Host.

"He was young, rich, other worldly talented, movie star handsome, funny, self depreciating, and humble. He gave to charities, married a Miss America runner up, was on a Wheaties Box. It seemed like he would be the poster boy for major league baseball for the next 20 years. And then it all fell apart. Arthur Robbins, you knew Dylan Michael as well as anyone in the press, what happened?"

"The kid got screwed; that's what happened."

"Care to elaborate?"

"Everybody knows the story. The injury, the painkillers, the IRS. But the real problem was Dylan trusted the wrong people, and in the end it killed him. It's all a damn shame."

The ESPN interview with Robbins wrapped up with even more highlights from Dylan's brief career. It showed him playing baseball like no one had ever played before. His power, speed, arm strength, and grace separated him from every other player.

As the last frames were playing, The ESPN reporter's voice was heard over the cheering crowds.

"As Tiger Woods redefined the ancient game of golf and Michael Jordon literally and figuratively rose above his peers in the NBA, Dylan Michael was, after only seven years in the major leagues, the greatest talent in the game's history. Had he been able to play the next 15 years, his objective statistics would have confirmed the subjective evaluation of his talent. But there can be no doubt that the loss of that talent and the loss of Dylan Michael, will forever be the biggest "what if " in sports history. All because of a piece of ice."

The final image on the screen moved from the scene of the crash site to a picture of a beaming Dylan being mobbed by his teammates after the biggest hit of his career. At that moment, Gwen, Annie, Sonny, and Doc made a collective decision that what they had decided to do with Dylan was now a plan carved in stone. There would be no turning back, no second guessing, no matter what the consequences.

Within two minutes that vow was tested when the FAA and NTSB officials rang Sonny's door bell.

Last At Bat

8. "No...No...No"

After saying goodbye to Dylan at the Cincinnati airport, Cara returned to her condo in Mt. Adams just northeast of downtown Cincinnati and only minutes from her parents' home. She was a few doors from her home, taking Carly, her Soft Coated Wheaten Terrier for a walk. Deep in thought, she did not see her father's familiar inferno red Jeep pull up to the curb.

"Daddy, what are you doing here? I was going to call you guys when I got back home…"

"Honey, get in. We need to go home."

Cara instinctively backed away from the Jeep. A feeling of terrible dread fell over her.

"No, no, no," she said. Carly sat at Cara's feet and looked up with concerned eyes.

"It's Dylan, isn't it?" Cara cried.

"Come on, honey, get in," her father said softly.

At her parent's home, Cara sat between her mother and father, cradling Carly on her lap and sobbing as they watched the news and heard the grim details of the crash that kept repeating; "No survivors."

Three days later, Cara attended Dylan's memorial service at the same church where they had been married. It all seemed surreal.

"…a young man who had lost his way…" said the minister.

Cara didn't hear him. She was lost in other times…

She filled the aluminum pot with ice cold water and crept into the steamy bathroom to launch a sneak attack. The running water from the shower and Dylan singing "Joy to the World," at the top of his lungs, were all the noise camouflage she needed. She threw the cold water over the top of the shower door and burst out laughing when Dylan shrieked like a little girl.

Dylan erupted from the shower, covered with shampoo. But Cara beat a quick retreat through the house and ran out the screen door, into the presumed safety of the front yard. She smiled sweetly at Dylan as he walked onto the porch.

"C'mon superstar...c'mon out here," she taunted him. "What's the matter? Afraid your fans might see the "Big Red" with no clothes?"

After strategically positioning the thick shampoo over his body, Dylan accepted Cara's dare and moved into the front yard, hands on hips and proud.

"You know I suddenly feel very free out here like this," he grinned. "Who needs clothes"?

"Oh, my God!" Cara gasped, appalled at a situation that had suddenly turned very, very wrong . "Get back in that house right this minute before somebody sees you!"

"Who cares what people think," he said, walking purposely toward her. "I feel free, I tell you and unencumbered. I think you should join me," he said as he grabbed her sweatshirt and pulled upward.

"Don't you dare you pervert," Cara giggled as she broke away and ran back to the house with a naked man chasing her. He caught her.

From another world, the preacher continued, "...we will never know what greatness Dylan would have reached if..."

Cara sat in a box seat at Great American Ball Park. She wore a Reds' cap backwards and yelled at Dylan to "do something." Dylan did something and the crowd roared. Cara cheered and whistled like a man, two fingers to her lips, as she high fived those sitting around her.

The drone continued, "…his greatness on the field will never be forgotten…"

Cara sat in the audience at University of Kentucky. She listened to a surprisingly articulate Cincinnati Reds player give an inspirational speech to UK athletes. She was there only because it was a class requirement on her way to a Masters Degree in Communication. She did not like baseball and had never heard of the speaker.

"I would like to thank the University for inviting me to speak this evening. I would be happy to answer any of your questions."

Dylan looked over the dozens of raised hands in the audience. Cara's hand was not raised, but Dylan, whose eyes had returned to her repeatedly after making brief eye contact during his speech, pointed toward her.

"You there, Miss, in the blue top. What is your question?"

Cara looked to either side of her, flushed scarlet and declared softly, "I didn't raise my hand."

Dylan smiled and addressed the crowd. "Let me repeat the answers to your questions for those in the back of the room. I am 23 and attend Stanford University in the off season. Hobbies? Well, I like old movies, muscle cars and all kinds of music. No, I am not married. What's that again? Why sure, I would like to get married someday but really never found the right person, if you know what I mean. Yes, I do have a good job although the travel can be rough at times. Yes, I do like kids and dogs. In fact, I'd like to have two of each someday. Miss, your questions are getting a little personal. Perhaps I could answer some of those later over coffee."

The audience cheered Dylan's performance. Cara shook her head and laughed.

Later, in the hallway outside the auditorium Cara said, "You should be an actor not a pitcher."

"A pitcher? You've never heard of me, have you?"

"Should I have?"

"Well, not really I guess. Are you at least a baseball fan," asked Dylan hoping for the best.

"Sorry, kind of slow for me. I prefer basketball."

"Well, that's OK, we can talk about other stuff over dinner tomorrow night after the game."

"Dinner? Who said we were having dinner?"

Undeterred, Dylan forged ahead. "I figured the way you were staring at me during my speech, you know, basically undressing me, you would at least want to have dinner before just rushing back to my place and ..."

"Undressing you?" laughed Cara. "Does this act always work?"

"Usually, it does. It did fail once though in Chicago, but it's been pretty reliable."

"Well, said Cara, "It has now failed in Lexington."

"What's the matter?" asked Dylan. "You don't believe in love at first sight?"

Cara reached into her purse, pulled out a business card and handed it to Dylan. "If you don't fall in love again before you get back home, call me sometime and maybe we can have dinner. Maybe."

Cara smiled at her memory as tears streamed down her cheeks. Her mind returned to the church and she heard the minister's final words:

"...let us pray for Dylan Michael."

Cara had moved back to the town in which she and Dylan had shared so much. Her friends and family warned her that all those familiar sights would create painful memories, but, instead, they comforted her. She and Carly often walked down from her Mt. Adams condo and traced the path where the three of them had walked years before. At times she found herself talking to Dylan as if he was right beside her. She wondered how many people had seen her talking to herself and thought she was crazy.

As the months progressed, her friends told Cara that things would get better, she'd heal and move on with her life. To a certain extent, they were right. Yet, in her dreams, she would be with Dylan. While his face remained vague and indistinct, she knew she was with him. Sometimes they would just be talking or walking. Other nights they would be laughing or playing with Carly, at a game, or even making love. But it was Dylan in those dreams, and the realness of those nighttime trysts was comforting and reassuring to Cara. Then she would awake and the ache would come crashing over her like a dark wave.

At other times, she was sure Dylan was still alive no matter what she knew to be the truth. She never told anyone but Carly, fearing they'd think she needed a padded cell. She started many of their walks by saying to Carly, "Let's go find Dylan." An actual search would have been difficult, since Carly was afraid of men and pulled on her leash in the opposite direction if she saw a man coming toward them. But Carly knew the name "Dylan" and was always up for walk just in case he was out there.

There were other times that Cara was sure she had seen Dylan or at least someone who looked like him. Then, she would get a closer look and the illusion disappeared. She made up fantasies that created a temporary reality that would always have Dylan returning to her. Cara knew she was testing the limits of her sanity, but the mind games she played worked. They made her feel better for some reason.

Last At Bat

9.   "Difficult"

(Three Weeks After Crash)

The twenty-one- year- old journalism major from UCLA waited patiently for Arthur Robbins, a crusty veteran baseball writer, to complete his interview with the new Commissioner of Major League Baseball. Jon Wagner had been looking forward to this lunch meeting with Robbins for weeks because it could mean an opportunity to work for Robbins as an intern and follow the "legend" around through the upcoming spring training and into the regular season. There was also always the chance a full time job might be offered after graduation if Robbins liked his work during the internship.

The only problem was Robbins had the reputation of being "difficult." In fact "asshole" was also a term Wagner had heard more than once when he had asked some friends who knew of Robbins.

The lunch meeting, scheduled months earlier by UCLA's placement office, was considered a "plum" opportunity and was arranged through a *Los Angeles Times* program to recruit top journalism students into the field.

After seeing Robbins wave good bye to the Commissioner, Wagner sidled up to Robbins, took a deep breath and extended his hand.

"Hello, Mr. Robbins, I am Jon Wagner. I was told to meet you here at the hotel at 11:30."

"By who?" Robbins growled.

"Ah, well… it was actually my school's placement department. I was told to meet you here…," the young student started to explain.

"You already said that," Robbins cut him short.

"I am in the intern program and ..." Wagner began, again being cut off mid-sentence.

"I know, I know, you were told to meet me here at 11:30. I don't have time for lunch today, and to tell you the truth I really don't have time to spend giving you or anybody else a fucking class in Sports Writing 101. So, why don't we just sit here in the lobby for a few minutes, you can ask me a few questions and I can get the hell out of here," Robbins said, displaying his customary charm.

"Well, OK," said Wagner and concluded the term "asshole" was far more accurate than "difficult."

Robbins dropped into one of the Biltmore Hotel's straight back chairs and motioned for a server. He ordered a double scotch with a twist for himself and, without asking, a Coke for Wagner.

"So what do you want to know?" Robbins asked.

"Well, I dunno... I thought we were going to talk about journalism and careers and..." Wagner attempted before being shot down for the third time.

"Look kid, I am willing to answer some questions, but you should have come prepared," Robbins lectured.

"OK... ah...how much money do you make?" Wagner tried.

"None of your damn business. Next question."

"Well, ...ah, do you like what you do?" Wagner stammered.

"Stupid question, one more swing, kid."

After 15 seconds of awkward silence Wagner asked in a defeated voice, "Who was the best baseball player who ever lived?"

For the first time, Robbins lifted his eyes from his drink and looked at the young man across the table. To Wagner's surprise and relief, Robbins actually seemed to be pondering the question.

"Be more specific. Do you really think I am so old that I would have seen every fucking baseball player since 1869?"

"No, I don't think you are that old...well then, ah, who was the best you ever saw?" Wagner rephrased.

"The best I ever saw may not be considered the best of all time because he didn't play long enough. So your question is another stupid one, but the best I ever saw was Dylan Michael," Robbins offered.

"That was sure sad when he died."

"Yeah, that was sure sad alright," replied Robbins.

"What made Michael so great?"

"Kid, don't you ever run out of stupid questions? If you have to ask, then you never saw him play or don't know a goddamn thing about baseball. Let me make it easy; he was a legitimate five tool player. He hit for power, average, could run, throw, and catch. Not much else you can do on a baseball field."

Trying to avoid another stupid question, Wagner tried again. "When did you last see Michael?"

"I saw him at the airport right before he got on that plane three months ago in Cincinnati. Within a few minutes his stepdad, attorney and even his ex-wife all turned their backs on him. The kid was about as alone as anybody could be."

"Then I saw him turn himself over to a sheriff's deputy who was going to accompany him to prison in Atlanta. I didn't think I could feel any worse for a kid than I did for him. But when they announced he had been killed, I found out I could feel worse. A whole lot worse."

Genuinely curious, Wagner asked, "How long had you known Michael?"

"I first met him when he was a sixteen-year-old high school 'phenom' living up in Ventura and I was writing for a small paper in Encino. My editor sent me up to see this kid who was hitting everything 400 feet, could run, throw, yadda, yadda, yadda. Same bull shit I had heard a hundred times before."

Last At Bat

Robbins ordered another scotch, sat back in the armless chair under the plastic palm tree and remembered the afternoon in Ventura nine years earlier.

"Hey, Coach, I came to see this kid Dylan Michael. Is he playing today?"

"Can't play if he's not here."

"Is he sick or something?"

"Who knows, said the coach disgustedly. He shows up when his old man thinks a scout is in the stands. Otherwise he might have Dylan hit for two hours in a batting cage instead of playing in a game. His old man is a prick."

As the two men spoke, a red Porsche pulled up in the parking lot. A tall, dark haired young man jumped out of the low slung car, trying to stuff his baseball jersey in his pants while running toward the field carrying his glove and spikes.

"Sorry, I'm late coach but my dad.."

The coach interrupted, "Get loose, you'll pinch hit for Joey next inning."

Dylan nodded and ran directly into the dugout.

"You're going to let him play? Why put up with that crap?" Asked Robbins.

"Not really the kid's fault. Did I say his old man is a prick? Besides it hurts the other kids when Dylan doesn't play."

"Is he really that good?"

"You're kidding, right? You never saw him play?"

"No." Said Robbins.

"Stick around," laughed the coach.

Batting right- handed, Dylan swung at the first pitch he saw and sent the hanging curve ball 425 feet over the left field fence for a three run homer. Hitting left- handed, his second at bat, he hit a fast ball a foot off the plate, over the centerfield fence to ice the game.

Hoping to interview Dylan after the game, Robbins hung near the dugout, when the coach approached and said, "That's why we play him."

As Dylan and his teammates left the field, the skinny shortstop said, "Way to go, Dylan! Hey, we're all goin' over to Pizza Hut to celebrate. You comin'?"

"Well, yeah, I'd like to…"

"No way, Pal," said Drew, Dylan's stepdad, who had finally put down the cell phone he had been on the entire game. "We have to meet with an agent tonight."

"But…"

"But my ass," said Drew. "You shouldn't be eating pizza anyway. You want to end up looking like the rest of these lard asses?"

Dylan dropped his head and walked toward the Porsche.

The coach, having heard the exchange, sidled up to Robbins again and said, "Did I mention his old man is a prick?"

Robbins returned to the Biltmore, another sip of scotch and an enthralled Wagner.

"What was Dylan like off the field?"

"He was different. Most jocks are just jocks. Dylan was kind of shy, quiet and smart. Good musician, read the right books, said 'Yes sir/ No sir', that kind of thing. His biggest problem was his parents both died young; his dad in a car wreck when Dylan was seven and his mom from cancer when Dylan was twelve. That was soon after she had re-married a guy named Drew Johns, the prick I already told you about. I doubt Drew would have stayed around if he hadn't seen Dylan was going to make some money in baseball."

Robbins took a sip of his scotch and continued. "The Reds selected Dylan number one in the draft and signed him two days later for more money than any high school kid had ever before received from a major league contract. I remember Drew high-fiving his attorney when Dylan was drafted, figuring he would get his hands on that money sooner rather than later. It was sooner.

"After being away from baseball nine months because of college, Dylan tore up the minor leagues setting records everywhere he went. The tougher the competition, the better he played. It was like he always had another "gear" when it came to his reservoir of talent which I often wondered if he ever fully reached the bottom of.

"When he had just turned eighteen, the Reds brought Dylan to Cincinnati as a September call up, and he hit .383 with six home runs in twenty-five games. The son of a bitch could play. The next year, at nineteen, he made the big league roster, and that put him in a position for the biggest hit in the history of the Cincinnati Reds."

Robbins relived the game in a crystal clear memory. The Yankee manager had two bad options. With runners on 2nd and 3rd and two outs in the ninth, he could either face Nash, the Reds number four hitter or walk Nash and bring the rookie Dylan Michael to the plate. Problem was, walking Nash put the winning run on first thus producing a second guesser's dream.

After a slow walk from the dugout the manager met with his right hand closer and catcher amid the deafening roar of the crowd at Great American Ball Park. "What do you want to do, Skip?" asked Carl Yost, the Yankee catcher.

"I'd rather be fishing. But since I'm not, let's put Nash on. I don't want to fuck with that guy. Look, throw Michael hard stuff inner half, and the change outside. Wish the hell the bastard at least looked nervous."

"OK guys, what's the story?" asked the ump who had joined the meeting on the mound.

"What's your hurry? You're on national TV," said the Yankee manager.

Watching the mound meeting, Dylan swung a lead bat in the on-deck circle, trying to look cool and use all the baseball nonchalance he could muster. He assumed the Yankees were going to walk Nash and take their chances on a rookie. He then had an idea and walked back to his dugout.

"Skip, I think I should go up right handed against this guy. It will take away his changeup and he won't get his fastball by me."

"Dylan, this is no time to experiment. Go up left handed and…"

"Skip, he won't get his fastball by me."

Looking in his rookie right fielder's eyes and seeing something, Burt Shelton hesitated and asked, "Is this what they teach you at Stanford?" Not waiting for an answer, he simply nodded to Dylan.

After the intentional walk, Dylan stepped into the right hand batter's box. " You forget who's out there throwin', Rook?" asked the catcher, Yost.

Dylan silently dug in his cleats, waiting for what he felt sure would be a fastball on the outer half of the plate. Then, he suddenly called time, backed out of the box and reconsidered. The experienced Yankee battery would surely realize why Dylan went to the plate right handed against the right hander. It was to take away a filthy changeup that would break down and away from a left hand batter but directly into a right hand batter's sweet spot. They might figure Dylan would be leaning over the plate looking for the fastball away. Dylan decided he would take a chance that the Yankees would try to fool him by throwing the change up anyway, assuming Dylan would not be looking for it.

He was right.

The first pitch came out of the pitcher's hand looking like a fast ball but then seemed to slow down like it had on air brakes. It headed for the middle of the plate, but only a few feet away started to move to the inner half and would have continued all the way to Dylan's hands.

But he had kept his weight back, refused to over stride, and swung his 35 inch, 33 ounce bat inside the ball, 'quick, not hard' as his high school coach had taught him. He caught the pitch on the sweet spot. The ball rocketed toward the left field corner like a two iron shot, rising toward the left field bleachers at Great American Ball Park in Cincinnati. As the ball rose, so did the sound of the crowd which produced a high pitched wail as it realized the ball was going to easily clear the left field wall.

As the ball curved toward the left field fair pole, the crowd roar suddenly dissipated and became a collective "oooo aaahhh" as the left field line umpire motioned the ball foul.

"Good guess there, Hoss," said the catcher to Dylan as he strode back into the batter's box.

"Yeah, a little too much top hand though," was all Dylan said, while wondering if he had looked like Fisk trying to keep the ball fair back in '75.

At that point, Dylan knew he was going to hit the Yankee right hander. Hard. It may not be a base hit but he had seen everything the reliever had, and he had nothing that was going to get past him.

As the crowd roar reached another ear splitting crescendo, Dylan calmly prepared for the next pitch which he *knew* would be a fastball down and away. Again, he took a chance. He moved two or three inches in toward the plate so he could cover the outside corner a little better and hoped the catcher would not notice. He was right again. The right hander threw a 92 mile per hour fast ball, intending to waste it, six inches off the plate. It was only three.

Again, Dylan swung hard but under control, squared the fastball and put himself into baseball history.

Robbins now had the cheeseburger in his hands, but every time it looked like he was going to take a bite, he would continue to tell his story.

"That three run double by Dylan to right center field in the bottom of the ninth inning of the seventh game of the World Series, was a moment that the folks in Cincy have talked about for six years. It's likely they will talk about it for another hundred. Like Bench's home run off Blass , Rose's hit off Show for 4192, Perez' shot off Bill Lee, the sweeps of the Yankees in 1976 and the A's in 1990, it was a game I never forgot either and I have seen thousands of fucking games."

Scooting up to the literal edge of his seat, Wagner wanted to hear more. "How did Dylan get hooked on drugs?"

"See, that's the bull shit kind of question that is based on not knowing the fucking truth about what happened to Dylan. He got hooked on prescription pain killers. This was shit his doctor, under the orders of Drew, gave to him to try and get him back on the field. Dylan wasn't on coke or heroin. It was medicine, for God's sake, he got from a doctor he trusted. It still fucked him up though.

"The people in Cincinnati were heartsick when Dylan got injured but even more devastated when he was sentenced to seven years in jail. Many called his mistakes misdemeanor crimes. That tax thing was really nothing more than the result of some people stealing from him when he was drugged out on the meds. The city was outraged, and even the mayor made a personal plea to the prosecutor's office. But some attorney bitch who was running for office wanted to 'make an example' of a pro baseball player."

"What happened with his wife?" asked Wagner.

"The medications began to have an impact on his personality and put a severe strain on his marriage. Cara told him to forget about baseball for awhile, get better and come back when he was healthy. He wouldn't listen, feeling he had an obligation to the Reds and his fans. The more he tried to work through the pain with the meds and shots he took, the worse he got.

"Cara tried her best to get him to come to his senses, but it didn't work. Finally she had enough and told him she loved him too much to see what he was doing to himself and she walked out. I think she thought that would jolt him into snapping out of it.

"Anyway, six years after "The Double" and two years after his new contract was signed, he was alone, broke, sick, sore, and depressed. He had been informed by the IRS that he was to begin a term in a federal prison for tax evasion and illegal drug use. He was twenty-five- years- old and his life had turned to shit. Then his fucking plane crashed. Yep, he was the best I ever saw. Hell, he may have been the best there ever was. It was a goddamned shame."

For nearly a minute Robbins was quiet as he stared at his yet to be tasted cheeseburger. Jon Wagner became more and more uncomfortable as silence lingered, and he saw the emotional toll telling Dylan's story had taken on Robbins.

Finally, Robbins bit into the cheeseburger but quickly returned it to the plate then summoned over the waiter and growled, "This goddamned cheeseburger is cold. Can't you guys do anything right?" To Wagner, he asked, "How about another Coke, kid?"

10.   Felons

(Day After Crash)

Sonny turned toward the door, following a triple knock from the outside.

"Wait a minute," Doc stopped him. "Just so you all know the facts here, if we don't tell the Feds that Dylan is in the bedroom, we are aiding and abetting a convicted felon."

Sonny stopped for a moment, looked at Gwen and Annie, then smiled back at Doc and said, "Yeah, we get it" and opened the door.

Two men, dressed in navy blue windbreakers, stood on the porch. "Hello, sir, I am Phillip Crandall with the National Transportation Safety Board and this is William Harris with the FAA. We would like to talk to Mrs. Gwen Cook. She was the person who contacted the 911 operator about last night's crash, and we want to confirm a few facts with her as part of our investigation."

"Sure, gentlemen. C'mon in. I'm Alfred Cook but everybody calls me Sonny. Gwennie, these gentlemen are here to ask you a few questions about last night."

The federal officers spent nearly two hours asking the four friends questions about the night before. They were particularly interested in what Doc and Sonny had seen as the jet passed overhead and what they had seen at the crash site before the rescue teams had arrived. Sonny, Gwen, Doc, and Annie patiently answered their questions thoroughly and cooperatively. They told them everything they could remember, except for one small detail. The Feds left them with their sincere thanks.

Taking turns for the next 24 hours, they stood watch over their patient round the clock. Though nothing improved, he was, miraculously, still alive.

"We have got to set the bones in that left leg, and I can't do it here," said Doc after examining the ugly limb that still had two bones protruding through the skin.

"OK, then we'll load him into the RV, take him down to the clinic and bring in the gals to help you tend to him," Annie ordered.

"First of all," said Doc, "it will take us six or seven hours to drive down there. And what am I going to tell all my nurses about what we are doing with this beat up boy? Are we going to get them involved in our crime? That's not fair to them. And even if they would agree to help work on this boy, the chances are he will die on the trip and then what do we do, dispose of a body?"

"Good idea Annie," Gwen ignored Doc's protest. "I'll pack some clothes and food so we won't have to stop on the way. Sonny, go gas up Doc's RV while he's tending to Dylan and put some of the supplies next to that bed in the back of the RV."

"OK," said Sonny, and moved past a startled Doc and out the door.

Doc, who was not used to being so totally ignored, started to rejoin the debate with Gwen and Annie when his patient screamed in pain.

Dylan had awakened before, but now with eyes wide, he flailed his arms as if trying to protect his face from whatever he was seeing in his nightmare. His attempt to sit up produced an anguished wail that reverberated off the bedroom walls. Dylan's scream stopped, followed by gagging and dry heaving brought on by the medication and pain that wracked every part of his body.

Annie and Gwen joined Doc at Dylan's bedside trying to find an uninjured part of his body to try and restrain him. Dylan's violent movements had broken open several of his wounds and blood now flowed from gashes on his face and chest.

"Get me a sedative. We need to get him stabilized before he kills himself," said Doc as he tried to hold Dylan's waving arms against the bed.

Over the next hour Doc toiled over Dylan and his efforts paid off. "The next time he wakes up could kill him, but if we keep adding more and more sedation he may never come out of it. Without x-rays I can't tell what his internal injuries are. He could have a punctured lung, or a back injury. It's likely he has some internal bleeding. I just don't know. If we are going to take him down to Blossom we need to leave right away."

For the previous 14 Thanksgivings, Annie and Doc had driven their 35 foot RV the 350 miles from Blossom, South Carolina, to Sonny and Gwen's lake house in southern Kentucky. After a few days of fishing and gorging themselves on turkey, they'd store the outdoor furniture, winterize the lake house, and leisurely drive back to Blossom. It had become a tradition they all looked forward to.

Now, the drive back to Blossom took on an entirely different meaning. Not only were they racing back to get Dylan the help he needed, they were also increasing the group felony they were committing by taking a convicted felon over a state line.

As they drove south on I-75 through Jellico and crossed from Kentucky to Tennessee, Doc said sarcastically, "By the time we get home we will have violated four state and at least that many federal laws. Hell, by saving this boy seven years in jail we will probably get 10 years each and all die on a prison work farm wearing those orange jump suits."

"Honey, that's OK," said Annie. "We are all so old that in a few years we won't have any idea where we are anyway."

Watching their speed for fear of getting pulled over by the highway patrol, it took the loaded RV nearly eight hours to make the trip through Knoxville, then east to North Carolina and finally to Blossom, South Carolina sitting forty miles north of the Georgia border.

When they were two hours out of Blossom, Doc called his head nurse, Alice, and told her to get hold of two more of his nurses and meet them at the clinic at 8 p.m. that evening. After working for Doc for 23 years, Alice asked no questions. The three of them were waiting patiently in the clinic's lot when the big RV rolled in.

Before helping Sonny carry Dylan into the clinic, Doc motioned the nurses inside for a brief chat with three friends who just happened to be experienced medical professionals.

"Ladies, we have a beat up young man in the back of the RV that is surely going to die if he doesn't get some medical attention right now. You are going to notice he is wearing handcuffs and the fact is, he was on the plane that crashed up in Kentucky. He was the only survivor and was on his way to jail when that damned plane went down. Sonny, Gwen, Annie, and I decided that we were not going to turn him over to the feds and see him sent to jail. See, this boy is a former major league baseball player who…"

"That's not Dylan Michael out there, is it?" asked sixty-three-year- old Alice.

"You heard of him?" Doc sounded surprised.

"My Lord, that poor boy went through something awful, said Marjorie. Of course you couldn't send him off to jail."

The third nurse, Florence, said, "He hit .374 his last full year and missed the Triple Crown by only two home runs."

All the shocked Doc could say was, "Well, OK, I guess you have heard of him. But you've got to keep this news quiet, and if you can't, at least help us stabilize him over the next forty-eight hours and then do what you have to do."

The three nurses simply nodded. But Doc should have known better. Flo, Alice, and Marjorie would have sooner cut off their own arms than betray a confidence with Doc, even if it meant they were part of an ever expanding crime ring evolving around Dylan Michael.

After putting Dylan on a wheeled gurney and bringing him into the clinic, Doc ordered a full set of x-rays and had Flo hook him up to an IV drip that would keep him sedated for at least forty-eight hours. Marjorie pulled a vial of blood from Dylan's other arm for typing if a transfusion became necessary. Dylan's body still looked like he had been in a plane crash, but there were some encouraging signs. His heart beat had stabilized at sixty-four beats per minute and was regular. His blood pressure was also within a normal range, and there did not appear to be any internal bleeding when Doc examined the x-rays.

The biggest immediate challenge was setting the compound fracture of the left leg. That surgery took nearly three hours and required Sonny and the three nurses to help Doc reposition the tibia after an incision of twelve inches was made from the ankle to just below the knee. Doc placed five pins into the bones to keep them in place and had to suture the ligament that runs down the leg into place. There was also some muscle damage to the calf from the bone penetrating it and to the skin but Doc felt that both injuries would heal on their own, over time.

After the surgery the three nurses dressed the leg and wrapped it in a soft cast that would need to be removed and changed every other day to prevent infection. Once they were sure that healing was underway, they would place the leg in a hard cast.

While the nurses finished working on the leg, Doc and Annie cleaned and re-stitched the cuts and gashes on Dylan's upper torso and head. Removing Gwen's sewing box thread, they replaced it with surgical thread and with the help of the improved lighting of the clinic operating room, smoothed out the skin to reduce scarring and stiffness. Doc also put the jaw back into place and re-broke the nose before straightening it and stuffing it with cotton.

Despite their best efforts, Dylan's face still looked like a Halloween mask. The scalp had been pulled away from his skull and needed to be reattached. More than the missing ear, broken nose and cuts, the biggest deformity was the piece of skin that had been ripped from his right cheek. Doc had stitched it back in place the night of the crash, but he realized that this wound would require the skill of a plastic surgeon, and even then there would be significant scarring and scar tissue. The handsome smiling face on the Reds Identification Card was gone.

After six hours of treating Dylan, seven weary people found they had done all they could and simply stared down at the former MVP and wondered if they could have done more.

The adrenaline that had kept Doc going over the past 48 hours suddenly left his body and fatigue gripped him like a vise. For a brief moment, he thought he might pass out but found his balance by grabbing the side bed rail and holding on until he was able to say, "Well, it might not be enough, but it's as good as we can do."

Seeing him struggle, Annie put her arm around her husband's waist and said "Honey, you were wonderful but you need to get some rest or you are going to end up in the hospital yourself. Go lay down in the back room and go to sleep."

Not arguing, Doc said, "I'll lay down for awhile and just rest my eyes." He collapsed in his bed and slept for 10 hours.

11. Sonny and Gwen

While Doc slept, the remaining six people worked out a schedule that would keep three of them in the clinic to look after Dylan and any other patients that would show up over the next few days. While Annie and Gwen were no longer full time nurses, they could take care of the usual colds and cuts and scrapes until Doc returned the next day.

Sonny decided to stay at the clinic. Sitting in the examination room drinking coffee and reading *Sports Illustrated*, Sonny swelled with pride at how Gwen jumped in to help the other nurses. But, he had always been proud of her.

Blossom, South Carolina, was going to be a temporary stop for Sonny and Gwen but nearly three decades later, they were still there. They had come to grips years earlier with the painful reality they could not have any kids, although Sonny was quick to point out it wasn't for a lack of trying. They accepted that fact, and their devotion and loyalty to each other was clear to all who met them.

Their friends felt that Gwen and Sonny had built a damned comfortable life for themselves. They had a nice, although not extravagant, house, a Ford Pickup, an ATV, a van and a Buick. Their two big screen TV's allowed them to indulge in their respective interests in the Financial News Network and ESPN and their common interest in old movies. Sonny also had a Fat Boy Harley that he and Gwennie used to tool around the South Carolina countryside.

There were some things about Gwen's and Sonny's lives that very few knew. When Gwen's parents died years earlier, they left her a nearly $3 million estate. She decided to keep that little bit of information from Sonny. Over time, he found out about it anyway but never let on that he knew anything about the money. Sonny figured Gwen was a lot better at dealing with money than he was so he just let her handle it all.

Gwen had a business degree in addition to her nursing education. Over the years, she'd invested well, usually in Blue Chip stocks paying dividends which she reinvested. She also got into and out of the technology sector early on and did even better. Sonny never really knew for sure, but he figured that Gwennie had put away something around $4 million over the years. It was closer to $14 million.

Gwen had almost totally financed the clinic in Blossom. She did so on the promise from Doc that he would tell no one about her donation. But after a year, Doc figured since the clinic was built she couldn't take the money back. So he told Sonny about Gwen's generosity just to let Sonny know the kind of woman he was married to.

Sonny was so proud of her he almost told her he knew the whole story about the clinic, the $4 million, everything. But that would have blown "the family secret" so he left it alone. He continued to do his farming and made some extra money doing odd jobs and building picnic tables that he and Gwen sold each summer at flea markets around the Southeast.

They had a good life; good friends, a comfortable house built back in the late 1800's on 130 acres that included a lake. Their farm produced corn, apples, peas, strawberries, and watermelon in addition to providing Sonny with lots of hunting and fishing out his back door. As he told Doc more than once, "To tell you the truth, I am a pretty lucky son of a bitch."

12.   "…wata"

The plan for Dylan was simple. Doc and the nurses would stabilize him at the clinic and slowly reduce his sedation. When he awoke in two or three days they would allow him to make a decision relative to accepting his jail sentence and getting some much needed further surgery or staying under the care of Doc at the clinic. The problem with that simple plan was Dylan did not wake up.

After 10 days of round the clock care for Dylan including redressing his stitches, x-raying the set bones, and looking for signs of infection and internal injuries, Doc Watson and his team had done all they could do. Doc told the rest of his staff Dylan's true identity and asked them to keep the news quiet from the rest of the town.

The news reported the crash's cause was a "catastrophic hydraulic failure." Shortly thereafter, other tragedies replaced the plane crash in the headlines. However, everyone at the clinic did read a moving account of Dylan's life in *USA Today* from the sports writer named Arthur Robbins who had been interviewed by ESPN the day after the crash and had known Dylan as a teenager. But then life went on.

Except for Dylan. His injuries were not healing as Doc had hoped. There were undoubtedly more internal injuries that, absent invasive surgery, could not be detected.   And, his healing and misshapen face was a testament to the hasty surgeries. To add to the mess, Doc had shaved Dylan's head in an effort to treat the deep cuts in his scalp.

But Dylan didn't care. He did not fully wake. With reduced sedation, he would move in and out of consciousness several times a day, only to drift off again and, hopefully, feel nothing for hours. Fearing that Dylan's body would never heal if he stayed sedated, Doc slowly began to further reduce the pain killers. While his broken bones were slowly healing, they still produced unremitting pain if Dylan moved too quickly or awoke in a start.

For weeks after arriving at the clinic, Dylan did not utter an intelligible word. He would moan and mumble from time to time, but could not respond to any questions from Doc or the nurses. Doc surmised that Dylan had suffered a serious concussion along with swelling of the brain, and as a result, there was the possibility he would never awaken. But a week before Christmas, Dylan finally spoke.

"Ken I have a gloss of wata?" he said. And drifted off again.

This prompted Doc to convene his staff, Gwen, Annie, and Sonny in the clinic waiting room after hours and revisit the issue of Dylan's condition and the group's collective criminality.

"Folks, Dylan has improved over the last few weeks, but you all need to know that what we see now may be as good as he gets. It is likely he has had some brain damage. It is possible he may stay the way he is now, forever."

"Well," said Flo, "then we will just have to keep doing all we can until he gets better."

"I appreciate everything everyone has done, but I want to remind you all that what we are doing is against the law. The longer we do it, the more problems with the law we could have," Doc continued.

"Doc," said Sonny, "everyone thinks this boy is already dead. The press doesn't even talk about him anymore. With the exception of Dylan's face, it looks like he is getting better. We all know what we are doing and I don't think any of us want to even think of turning this boy in. He's better off here than in some damn jail."

"Maybe, maybe not," said Doc, "but I thought he would have completely regained consciousness by now and he hasn't. Except for a mumbled sentence now and again, he stays unconscious."

"Why don't we agree to keep things as they are for now. If he doesn't come around in a few weeks time we re-visit the issue then," suggested Annie.

Everyone in the group seemed to think that idea made sense except Doc who said, "That's fine but what about the criminal aspect of all this?" Doc could not understand why everyone in the room laughed.

Slowly over the next two weeks Dylan did improve. The pain appeared to lessen when he awoke although he was not able to talk coherently or stay awake for more than a few minutes. As a result of his improvement, Doc was able to remove most of the pain killers and rely on Extra Strength Tylenol. At the end of January, nearly two months to the day after the crash, Dylan suddenly emerged from his fog as he was being bathed by Marjorie.

"Where am I and what the hell are you doing?" Dylan asked in a clear voice as Marjorie washed his left arm.

"Oh my God! Doc! Flo! Come in here!"

Rushing to Dylan's bedside, Doc calmly said, "Hello young man, my name is Dr. Watson. My staff and I have been taking care of you for awhile."

"Taking care of me? What's wrong with me?" Dylan asked

"Well, you were in an accident…"

"What kind of accident? Where am I?"

"Calm down now…I need to ask you some questions," Doc said.

Dylan tried to sit up, and as he did, he felt stabs of pain in his broken arm and leg and nearly dislodged the IV's than ran into both arms.

"Flo," said Doc, as he nodded to the IV running into Dylan's right arm. She responded to Doc's cue and injected a small amount of sedation into Dylan to calm him.

"Young man, you have been in an accident and badly injured. I want you to stay awake, but you need to calm down so you don't hurt yourself further. Do you understand me?"

"Yes", said Dylan.

"Can you tell me your name?"

"Ah, ah, what's going on? No. What's going on?"

"It's okay. Are you in any pain?"

"My leg, my arm, my wrist. What's going on?"

"Do you have any head pain?"

"No. Why can't I remember my name?"

"Son, you've had a head injury. Your brain has been damaged. It will take some time for it to heal."

"How long?" he asked.

Doc shook his head. "I'm not sure."

"What's my name? What do I look like? I can't feel my face," Dylan's voice rose with each question.

"Your face was damaged in the accident," Doc replied. "At this point you've not had any plastic surgery. But you will. In time your face will improve."

"Let me see."

Doc nodded toward Flo again, and she fished a mirror out of a drawer next to Dylan's bed and handed it to Dylan. Doc and Flo were surprised there was no reaction by Dylan to the ravaged face that stared back when he looked into the mirror.

"What did I look like before?" he asked.

"We don't know," Doc replied.

Dylan continued to look at the mirror searching through the red scars, bruising and welts, hoping to find a sliver of recognition. He found none.

"Like I said, plastic surgery will improve your face and help get it back to normal," Doc said.

"If you don't know what I looked like before, how do you know what normal is?" Dylan asked.

"Good question," Doc smiled. "I guess we will just have to do our best. But your question indicates your brain is working and that's even better. You ready for some hard work?"

"I guess. Yes. I'm ready," he said.

Doc walked toward the door, stopped and looked back at Dylan.

"By the way, about your name. The night you were brought in, you were semi conscious. When we asked you your name it sounded like you said "Matt." Is it okay that we start calling you 'Matt?' I think it's better than "Hey, you.""

"Did I say my last name?" Dylan asked.

"No. And we're not real sure you even said 'Matt' but we need to call you something."

"Yeah, I guess Matt is okay. For now."

"Fair enough," Doc said. "Matt it is. Get some rest cause we're gonna' start working your butt off tomorrow."

Later in Doc's office Flo asked, "Doc, why do you think he had no reaction to looking at his face in the mirror?"

"I noticed that too. I figure that since he did not remember who he was or what he had looked like before the crash, the reflection in the mirror, awful though it is, was just a face. He had no frame of reference."

Over the next ten days as Dylan's mind slowly cleared, he was able to ask and respond to simple questions but he became agitated when he could not remember who he was. Doc and the nurses continued their charade.

In early March, Dylan was able to sit up in bed. By mid-April, he was getting around in a wheelchair. His recovery over the next three months was interrupted by various surgeries that required the re-breaking of bones in his arm and shoulder. He was also visited by a plastic surgeon, an old Viet Nam buddy of Doc's, who improved the shape of Dylan's nose, eye orbit, and some of the scarring from the initial facial surgeries. The surgeon also took some cartilage from Dylan's rib cage and fashioned a small ear although he did not have the equipment to do as good a job as he would have liked. Still it was an ear of sorts and certainly better than having nothing attached to the side of his head.

The plastic surgery improved Dylan's face. But it did not return it to its original appearance. The crushed bones, scars, repositioned jaw line, new ear and brow line which needed to be rebuilt using surgical plates around the orbits of the eyes, would allow the face to look more symmetrical and natural but could not make it look like Dylan Michael before the crash.

By mid-summer Dylan was no longer on any medication, and the severe pain that had haunted him for months was, for the most part, gone, replaced by dull aches in his legs and left shoulder. Eight months after the crash, Dylan walked for the first time without the aid of a nurse, a walker, or a cane. "I never thought he would walk again," said a tearful Gwen after she saw a smiling and somewhat unsteady Dylan wobble across the floor of the clinic's waiting room.

After Dylan had returned to his room in the clinic, Sonny said, "I think it's time we get Dylan out of the clinic and move him into our place. We have the room, and the time to devote to his care and it looks like we could leave him alone for a little while if need be. What do you think, Doc?"

Doc nodded. "I think that is a good idea. He has been cooped up in here for a long time now, and a change in scenery would do him good."

Last At Bat

13.   Matt

Doc and Sonny were sitting in a booth at Millie's Diner after ordering two chicken fried steak platters, with mashed potatoes, green beans and apple sauce.   Doc looked at his friend and said, "Dylan is a damn tough young man. His rehab is going well, but we need to work on a story to tell him and the rest of the town about who he is and how he got here."

"Yeah, I've been thinking about that, too," said Sonny. "He's been doing so well I don't want to do anything that might set him back. The better he gets, the more he is going to want to know."

"Well", said Doc, "we can't keep lying to him indefinitely. At some point we have to be prepared to tell him the truth about everything. But I am not sure when that time will be. We tell him too much, too soon, and he could have a huge emotional setback that could hurt him physically."

Over cherry pie, the men created a story for their wives, the nurses and themselves to tell Dylan, at least for the time being. They would tell Dylan that he apparently had been hitchhiking and been hit by a car on a country road near Blossom. The story went on to say he had been brought to the clinic late at night with no ID on him by a passerby.   The next day, Sonny and Doc sat down with Dylan and told him the events they had conjured up the night before. While none of it was true, it was plausible and addressed what Matt and the rest of Blossom needed to know.

After listening carefully to what he was told, Matt was surprisingly quiet. His only question was somewhat strange, "What was I wearing when I was brought here?"

Taken off guard by the question, Doc hesitated and said, "You were wearing jeans and a plaid shirt."

"Did you keep my clothes?" he asked.

"No, Matt, we had to cut them off and we threw them away."

For two weeks Doc and Sonny were surprised there were no further questions from Matt. But eventually the dam broke, and Matt began to ask for more details about what had happened to him over the past year. "Was the driver of the car that hit me ever found?" he asked.

Doc told him, "No."

"Who found me? What did they see?"

"They were strangers in town who just happened to come across you in the road. They said they saw nothing at the scene of the accident. They then left town as soon as they dropped you off here at the clinic." Doc stuck to the story.

"What was the color of my shirt?" he pressed.

"Red."

"I thought you said it was plaid," Dylan responded.

"A red plaid", said Doc.

There were dozens of other questions over the next few weeks, but Doc and Sonny made sure their answers led nowhere. They also made sure the rest of the team knew exactly how to answer each question so if asked again, their stories would be consistent.

After one particularly long series of questions answered with an equally long series of lies, Sonny told Gwen, "Lying to that boy every day is gettin' to me. I know we all said we would make up these stories because we are just protecting Dylan but flat out lying to him makes me feel guilty as hell."

But, almost overnight, Matt simply quit asking questions. He also began responding to the name Matt easily, as if it were a familiar name.

82

Doc and his nurses went back to the care of their regular patients at the clinic, tasking Sonny and Gwen with the day-to-day tending of Matt at their home. They made him comfortable, taking short walks with him around the farm with Sonny supervising the rehab. Gwen became a housekeeper and cook. In short, their life revolved around the battered former right fielder.

Gwen went on-line and read everything she could about Dylan Michael both on and off the baseball field. She felt profound pity for the young man who had it all and because of one literal slip, lost it all. It seemed all the more tragic because of how Matt responded to his physical, emotional, and mental injuries over the last year. He never complained. He never lost his temper. He never cried. He never asked for anything; except his past.

Sitting on the back porch swing watching Dylan complete his daily walk around the lake, Sonny said, "It will be a year next week."

"I know" said Gwen, "but that's not the kind of thing you celebrate, is it?"

"Why not? That boy has been through a lot in a year and come a long way. We should celebrate," Sonny said.

Matt walked toward the porch, shirt in hand, with a pronounced limp.

"I did the route twice today," he said with a smile on his face.

"Damn good" said Sonny. "How do you feel?"

"Not too bad. Might go for three tomorrow."

"Hungry?" asked Gwen.

"You have to ask"? laughed Matt.

"How about heading down to Millie's. Today's "Chili Day," said Sonny.

"Chili? It's too hot for chili," said Gwen.

"Never too hot for Millie's Chili. Matt, you like chili"?

"I think so," said Matt, not real sure.

"Matt, you care if it's 80 degrees?" asked Sonny

"I don't care," he replied.

"See Gwennie, Matt don't care if it's hot either. Let's go."

****

Bonnie Poteet had worked at Millie's Diner for nearly ten years. She had lived in Atlanta, but other than that, no one knew much about her. It was clear Bonnie was smart, pretty and the guesstimate around town was that she was in her late thirties. She also possessed what the high school boys in town called "The BOD" or the "Body of Doom." Many of them would come to Millie's and order anything on the menu just to see Bonnie walk by. What people did not know about Bonnie was that she had a degree in Philosophy from the University of Georgia and a husband… somewhere… although she was in no hurry to find him after the last time he beat her up for burning his toast.

Bonnie had come to Blossom to escape. She stayed because she had no need to go anywhere else.

"Hey Bonnie. Got any chili left?" Asked Sonny.

"Sure do, darlin'," she said.

"OK then, we'll take three chili's and three ice teas."

"Gwennie, why do you always let this big ole' man order for you?" Bonnie asked.

"It makes him feel like he's in control," Gwen smiled.

Looking at Matt, Bonnie asked, "How about you, young man? You really want chili on a hot day like this?"

"Yeah," said Matt. "I think I'll try some."

"Oh, Bonnie, I don't think you were ever introduced to Matt here. He's staying with us, healing up from his accident," said Gwen.

"Good to meet you, Matt. I've seen you around town the last few months. Looks like you're gettin' better every day."

"Nice meeting you too," Matt said. "Yeah, I think I am getting better."

"Alright then, three chili's and three ice teas," Bonnie called as she walked away. Sonny watched every move until he was elbowed by Gwen.

Sonny winked at Matt and said, "It's okay to look, ain't it Matt?"

Matt smiled.

****

Later in the week at Doc's for a checkup, Matt asked a question that had been nagging him for weeks. "Doc, who's paying for all my medical bills?"

"Don't worry about it," said Doc as he looked at Matt's improving left leg.

"What do you mean, don't worry about it?" Matt pressed.

"I mean, the State of South Carolina has this fund set up for uninsured people, and we just send all the bills in every month and get paid," Doc lied with aplomb.

"Oh, OK. I was just kind of worried that's all," Matt said.

The real truth was, even though deeply discounted by Doc, all the bills were being paid by Gwen and Sonny. As the bills continued to come in, Sonny went to Gwen and said, "Honey, I know taking care of that boy is costing us a lot and may cost even more later on. It was my idea to bring him here in the first place so if you think I need to start working at the mill for a shift, I'll do it. I just don't want you to worry about money."

Gwen replied, "I'm not worried, just make a few more tables this winter, and we should be alright. Maybe Matt will be strong enough to give you a hand by then." After thirty-five years of marriage to Gwen, Sonny smiled inwardly at their shared deception.

Last At Bat

Through her research of Dylan, Gwen learned that in his last year with the Reds, he had packed 192 pounds of well toned muscle onto his 6'3" frame. Naturally strong with a long swimmer-like physique, he had never lifted weights in high school or college and relied on his natural strength, exceptional eyesight, and bat speed to generate his power at the plate. He possessed exceptionally strong hands and forearms. While he eschewed weights, he was seldom seen without a spring loaded hand and wrist strengthener that he constantly flexed, much to the chagrin of his teachers. Gwen wondered how he had been able compete with players who appeared so much more muscular.

Unlike most tall rangy athletes, Dylan also possessed speed. He had won the state high school track championship in the 220 meter dash and finished third in the 100.

He was big, strong, and fast, and those characteristics led him to be recruited by colleges for football as well as baseball. But he never embraced football like he did baseball. He really loved baseball. He loved the competition. He loved the pace of the game with its slowly building drama and how his natural talents made the game his. He loved how others, even at an early age, respected him for those talents. Baseball, in a way, formed who he was on and off the field.

Every time Gwen read something about Dylan's past she would say to Sonny, "It's just so sad what happened to that boy."

That wasn't the only thing that had changed in Matt's life. His body, which had played the game so well, so effortlessly, was strikingly different. While still 6'3," he seemed shorter. He walked bent over because of the pain in his legs when he tried to walk too far or too upright. He had also lost nearly forty-five pounds and looked gaunt through his shoulders and chest. He still limped noticeably although the long walks around the lake were helping his overall health. His face still bore deeply rutted scars and some structural deformity though the various surgeries had helped.

Mark Donahue

Matt was only twenty-six-years old, but looked like a man in his early forties who had lived hard and lost. His physique matched a middle aged coal miner or hard laborer who had given up his body to feed his family. He looked beat up.

His second winter in Blossom started the same. Matt helped Gwen around the house with some chores, went for walks or slow jogs in the hills and fields around the farm and then did light yard work when he felt like it and he felt like it, more and more. In the house, Matt liked to play Sonny and Gwen's old record collection of 45's from the 60's and 70's. He had an eclectic taste in music that ran from the Beatles and Stones to Frank Sinatra. One afternoon, Sonny came into the kitchen and thought he heard Gwen playing their old grand piano nestled in the corner of the living room. He had not heard her play in years. When he walked into the room he saw Gwen sitting on the couch and was surprised to see Matt playing a beautiful rendition of "Something" by George Harrison followed by several 70's rock and roll songs.

"I didn't know you could play," said Sonny.

"Me neither," said Matt.

From then on Matt would spend at least an hour each day improving his piano skills and playing requests from Gwen as she worked around the house.

In December, nearly 13 months after the crash, Matt wandered out to the tool shed. He watched Sonny work on putting together the wood, preparing to make some new picnic tables. Matt had watched before, and they both enjoyed the light banter that went back and forth between them. Every once in awhile Matt asked Sonny if he could help, but there was little he could do since he could not lift the wood or cut it without fear of injuring himself. In fact, he quit asking Sonny after being turned down for the tenth time. He finally decided he would just enjoy their time together and watch Sonny work. Sonny liked having him there.

But there was another reason Matt liked the tool shed. He liked how it smelled. He said the freshly cut wood "reminds me of something." A fragrance he could not put his finger on. He also liked the smell of the lacquer Sonny would put on some of the tables.

As Matt's body began to mend more rapidly through that second winter, he found he had more energy. He ate better and discovered he had gained back nearly seventeen pounds of the forty-five he had lost after the crash. He started watching an exercise show on cable featuring this semi-weird guy on the beach doing stretches and aerobic exercises every morning at 6:30. At first, Matt's body rebelled against even the slightest exertion. But over time, he found he could keep up with most of the things the weird guy was doing and slowly began to increase the difficulty of some of the exercises.

He also began a regimen of longer walks. By February of that second winter, he was up to three miles a day. He tried jogging only to find his right knee and left leg ached for days afterward. Each day after helping Gwen around the house, doing his exercises and his walk, he stopped by the tool shed and spent a couple hours with Sonny. They would shoot the breeze while Sonny worked and then head to the house at 1:00 for one of Gwen's big lunches. Matt's portions grew ever larger as the months went by.

By late April, Matt was back to a solid 185 pounds and walking with only a slight limp. His left leg had straightened and his right knee, with the help of some anti- inflammatory medicine from Doc, no longer pained Matt when he jogged. In fact, Matt was now able to run three miles without stopping. Except for twinges in his left shoulder and collarbone from time to time, he was beginning to feel "normal" again, if he was only able to remember what normal was. The irony of all he had been through physically was that he now had no back pain.

Mark Donahue

What bothered Matt the most was no longer physical pain, it was the frustration of his memory loss. He would sometimes doze off watching TV or reading a book, and he was somewhere else. He was someone else. But when he came to, it would all go away. He simply could not bring the memories back with him. One dream was particularly haunting. It was a dream of a woman. Her face was never clear, yet he could see her smile. He could see her dark hair and deep blue eyes. But it was what he would feel, not see, in his dreams that created an ache that at times was overpowering and lasted for days.

When he was awake, he found he liked watching sports on TV. He liked college basketball, pro football, and Major League Baseball. He wondered if he had played any of those sports in his "other life" as he called it. He vowed he was going to try one of those sports some day.

In early May, Matt was in the tool shed helping Sonny pick up pieces oak and ash that Sonny had worked on earlier in the day. Matt picked up a thin piece about three feet long and began swinging it absent mindedly, like a golfer. Then he lifted the piece of wood to waist level and swung the piece of wood very slowly, like a baseball player.

As he swung the piece of wood, Matt continued to talk about something else, but what he was doing was not lost on Sonny. The smoothness in Matt's movements, the connection between his hands, forearms and shoulders, how the piece of wood moved fluidly from shoulder to shoulder as he casually talked, made Sonny tune out what Matt was saying and focus on what he was seeing. But then Matt simply flipped the piece of wood away and asked, "You ready for some lunch?"

That night, Sonny told Gwen what had happened in the tool shed.

"Do you think anything clicked with Matt when he was swinging that wood?" she asked.

"I don't think so but you never know," he replied. "I do know I wished it would have triggered something. We both know it's only a matter of time until we have to tell him about his past life. He seems to be getting along so well I hate the idea of doing anything that would set him back."

Gwen agreed and said, "He is such a nice young man. I don't want to see him hurt again." Then she said, "You know, if we ever had a son…" then her voice trailed off.

"I know, honey, I know," Sonny said.

A week later Matt entered the tool shed as normal after his run and saw three baseball bats leaning up against the saw horse in the corner of the shed. Sonny was working on a fourth using his power sander to thin down the grip. When he was done he said nothing and placed the fourth bat next to the other three and began some small talk with Matt about how hot it was. Matt seemed to ignore the bats at first and agreed it was damn hot, especially for running. As they continued to gab, Matt sidled over to the bats, sat on the saw horse, and asked, "Who are these for?"

"I made them for a men's baseball team over in Greenville. They order a few dozen a season."

"Oh," said Matt. "Let's go eat."

14.   No Coincidences

Matt had dreamed of her before. The dark eyes and dark hair were now familiar and yet her face remained in shadows, he would call out to her. She wouldn't answer.

Moving to his bedroom window, Matt dreaded another sleepless night. Too many nights before he would dream, awaken and then lay in bed for hours trying to put together a mental jig saw puzzle with a thousand pieces of all the same color. This night he decided to break the cycle.

Throwing on his jeans, t-shirt and running shoes, he opened his bedroom window and jumped into the clear moonlit night. He walked into town two miles away trying to forget the dark- haired woman.

Blossom's small downtown area looked different at night. The traffic light in the center square would tint the old buildings and tall trees in red, yellow and green. Each time the light would change color, it would buzz and then make a clicking sound that would create a small echo amid the deserted town.

Matt walked along the sidewalk and peered into the empty shops. He would see his still damaged face and quickly turn away. Looking into Smith's Pharmacy window, he was startled when the reflection of a woman appeared over his left shoulder.

"You always do your shopping at 2:00 in the morning?" she asked.

Matt turned quickly and saw Bonnie smiling at him. Like the town, Bonnie looked different at night too. Her hair was tied loosely with a red ribbon on top of her head. She wore jeans, sandals and a low cut sleeveless tank top.

"Whoa, you scared me, there," said Matt.

"Sorry. Didn't mean to. I was just out here walkin'. I come out some times and stroll through town when I can't sleep," she said.

"I couldn't sleep either," said Matt. "Maybe it's the full moon."

"Maybe," agreed Bonnie.

Bonnie and Matt began walking down the middle of the deserted street as they talked.

Haven't seen you for awhile. You doin' OK?" she asked.

"Yeah, I'm feeling pretty good, I think," he replied.

"What do you mean, 'you think?' Either you feel good or you don't."

"I mean, I don't really know what feeling good used to feel like," said Matt.

"I wouldn't worry about it. If something feels good just go with it and be thankful you don't hurt."

"Guess you're right."

"You know," said Bonnie, "You've been given a gift we'd all like to have."

"What's that?" Matt frowned.

"You don't remember your past," she said. "Whatever bad things are there don't bother you."

"What about the good things?" Matt asked.

"For most people there is more bad than good," Bonnie said. "To be able to start over like you can, is like a second chance. Like being reborn."

"I never saw it that way. I keep wanting to find out about who I was. I keep having dreams of people, and I don't know who they are."

"A woman?" asked Bonnie.

"Yes," he answered. "All I see are her dark hair and eyes. Maybe I made her up, I don't know."

"Maybe you will find her someday. Or she will find you. Whatever happens is already planned," she said.

Matt stopped walking and turned to Bonnie.

"Already planned?" he asked.

"There are no coincidences in life," Bonnie explained. "It's all a plan. One thing happens and that leads to another thing and so on and so on. We're all just part of a plan."

Pointing to her house, Bonnie, said, "Well, this is me. I better try and get some sleep to be ready for my stimulating job in the ever exciting food service industry. If you ever want to talk, just knock. I'm always home. Even at two in the morning."

"OK", said Matt.

Matt watched Bonnie walk slowly to her house. She stopped on the porch, looked back at Matt and waved. Matt, feeling unsure about something, waved back.

Last At Bat

15.   Snap Your Fingers

As usual, Cara's friend Marie was late for their lunch date at McCormick's and Schmick's in downtown Cincinnati. Bouncing in with her usual flair, Marie saw Cara in a corner booth and made a beeline to the back of the restaurant carrying several Sak's packages.

"Oh, it's so good to see you. It's been weeks. How you doing?" she asked.

"I'm fine. Keeping busy," Cara replied.

"Well, you look beautiful. Are you still seeing that pilot?" Marie asked.

"No, he was just a friend anyway," she said.

"Oh my God, he was gorgeous. What happened?"

"Nothing happened. I just wanted to be friends and he wanted…"

"Cara, you didn't see anyone after you left Dylan, and now it's been eighteen months since the accident," Marie said. "You're allowed to have a life, you know."

"I've   tried," she sighed. "Several times. But being with someone I don't care about or find impossibly boring is worse than being alone."

"Well, you can't just stay home all the time. Anyway, with the way you look you could have any guy in town if you just snap your fingers."

"Maybe I'll snap my fingers someday. But for now I would rather stay at home with Carly and read a book. Dylan Michael is a tough act to follow."

"Cara, I love you like a sister, but you need some help. You were going to divorce the guy. Had he not been killed, you would still not be with him," Marie reminded her.

"I know, but at the airport that day, he was different," Cara replied. "Like the old Dylan. Maybe my leaving him had shaken him up, or maybe it was being off the meds, I don't know. Later, I wrote to him, saying I still loved him and would wait for him. I was going to put the divorce on hold. He never got my letter. He never knew how I felt."

"Ok, I understand, I guess. But you are too young and beautiful to be alone. So when the time is right, I know this really cute guy who works in my office who…"

Cara, shook her head and smiled.

16.   July 4th

For two weeks, the bats Sonny had made remained leaning against the saw horse. Matt ignored them every time he entered Sonny's work shop.

In preparation for the annual Blossom Fourth of July Picnic Country Music Karaoke and Pantomime Festival, Sonny had a question. "Hey Matt, you like picnics?"

They had not attended the previous year because Matt had been too ill. But Sonny and Gwen wanted to formally introduce him to the town and some of their friends. The story around town was that Matt had been a stranger who had been hit by a car while hitchhiking and Gwen and Sonny had taken him in and nursed him back to health. As far as the folks in Blossom were concerned, that was just about all they needed to know. They all liked Gwen and Sonny, respected their privacy, and Blossom residents didn't ask a lot of questions.

Besides, many of them had run into Matt over the last year at the Ingel's store or down at the Shell station and commented on what a nice young man he was. That was about the only litmus test needed in Blossom. Was he a nice guy or not? He was, so that was that. That his face was clearly damaged did not matter. There were no movie stars in Blossom.

"I think I like picnics," answered Matt.

"Oh Lord", moaned Gwen as she rolled her eyes.

"I mean a picnic sounds like fun."

"Don't mind her none," said Sonny. She just don't know how to have a good time. By the way, Bonnie told me she was going to be there."

Last At Bat

Matt smiled.

A large red, white and blue banner proclaimed "Welcome" to the Blossom Park and Picnic Grounds on the edge of town. Matt toted a large picnic basket and heard the loud country music in the background.

"Let me check this one," said Sonny as he kneeled down to check underneath the picnic table. "Yep, we're OK, it's one of mine."

"Thank goodness, the picnic table police have done their job," said Gwen, ignoring Sonny's scowl.

After a few minutes, folks from Blossom who didn't know Matt went out of their way to come over to Sonny's picnic table just to say hello and drop off some cookies or apple pie. Matt was a bit shy at first about meeting so many people. But the openness and genuine kindness of these people put him at ease. He was soon talking to everyone who came over to, "Say hey."

Around 4:00 in the afternoon, a few of the guys came over to the table and announced that a softball game would shortly commence. They made it clear that Gwen, Matt, and Sonny were not only welcome but would be looked down on as community malingerers if they did not join in.

Gwen said, "Go ahead, you two. I'll clean up this mess while you go play."

"What do you think Matt? Wanna play?" Sonny asked. Matt could not hear Sonny as he had already started walking toward the grass field that was laid out with flat canvas bases and an empty Coke 12- Pack as home plate.

After the teams were chosen by two players on the local high school baseball team, the game began with Matt and Sonny on the same side. Matt was told to play left field and Sonny played second base. Their team took the field first.

Sonny wondered if Matt was as comfortable as he looked out in left field, tossing the ball around to the other outfielders. Matt told Sonny later that for some reason he was actually "excited" about being out there in left field - a feeling of excitement that was not worthy of a Fourth of July softball game with a group of men, women, and children. All Matt knew was he liked what he was feeling.

After a ground out back to the pitcher, the second batter hit a high fly ball to left center. Matt instinctively yelled "Mine!", moved to his left, caught the ball one handed and lobbed the ball back to the infield.

"Two hands for beginners," yelled the shortstop good naturedly. Matt smiled and it was clear he wanted another ball hit to him.

The next batter hit a double to right center and stood on second making fun of his uncle who had been forced to chase the ball down. The fourth batter of the inning then lined the ball between third and shortstop. The runner took off from second and was laughing as he rounded third with what he assumed was the first run of the game.

Without knowing why, Matt began moving toward the left field line even before the batter had swung. By anticipating where the ball was going, he was able to field it on the second hop. He then turned and threw the ball on a line to the catcher, Mary, a fourteen- year- old junior high softball player. She stood her ground as the ball and runner came to the plate at the same time. She caught the ball without having to move her glove. Even though it stung like hell when it came in like a rocket from left field, she tagged out the startled runner.

At first no one said anything. They simply looked at Matt. He was already headed back to his bench and said to his catcher, "Good hands."

She said, "Good hose," and they both laughed. Then Matt's teammates began pounding him on the back and laughing their asses off.

Last At Bat

As a shrewd evaluator of talent, and recognizing an old guy when he saw one, Matt's fifteen-year- old manager designated Matt to hit ninth on the team. The fact that Matt struck out his first time up did little to fill his manager with confidence. When Matt came to the plate for a second time, the bases were loaded with two out and the "bad guys" leading 6-4.

"Just try and meet the ball and get on," said the young John McGraw to Matt. "We got Mary on deck if you can just get on," he pleaded.

Matt swung at the first pitch. The bat smashing into the ball was a sound that no one on the field had heard before. As for the ball, it landed roughly 350 feet away over a chain link fence, over a road, a creek and into the woods. The good news was Matt's team won the game. The bad news was he lost the ball.

"Holy shit," said the pitcher.

"Fuck me," said the catcher.

"I'll be goddamned," said the first baseman.

Most everybody else just laughed at the sight of the leftfielder climbing a fence and disappearing into the distant tree line.

That night, watching the fireworks, several of the softball players came over to his table and congratulated Matt on his hit. He laughed and thanked everyone. Sonny knew Matt had figured out he had played the game before.

As the evening wore on, Matt was becoming more and more comfortable. The friendliness of the people of Blossom, the easy laughter and good natured banter between old friends, had a calming effect on him. He realized what he was seeing were folks who were happy.

Country music drifted over the crowd, mingled with lots of laughter and an occasional hoot and holler. As "Thank God, I'm a

Country Boy" was ending, three men in bib overalls came rushing up to the table and said in unison, "Hey Sonny, it's time to do Charlie!"

"Oh, my gawd, not again," said Gwen rolling her eyes.

"Darlin', my public is demanding that I do an encore from last year," said Sonny in a voice dripping with self sacrifice.

"And the year before that and the year before that…"

Ignoring Gwen's less than enthusiastic support, Sonny said, "Gentlemen, I accept your invitation and unlike my wife here, your encouragement. I submit to your request and bow to your obvious knowledge and appreciation of true musical talent."

"Don't go pullin' a groin up there," said Gwen

For the next five minutes and twelve seconds, Sonny pantomimed Charley Daniels' "Uneasy Rider" including putting his hair *"up under my hat."* The folks from Blossom knew talent when they saw it and saved their loudest cheers for Sonny who, when finished, gave a deep bow and blew kisses to his "fans."

Matt watched from the edge of the crowd and laughed out loud at Sonny's gyrations on stage. He took in all the people gathered around the makeshift stage, laughing, yelling, and generally having a great time with family and the friends they had known for a lifetime. They cared about each other and it showed.

From behind him, Matt heard a voice say, "He does this every year."

"Hey", said Matt. "Where have you been? I was looking all over for you."

"Oh, I just got here," said Bonnie. "Wasn't gonna come but decided I couldn't miss Sonny's act. Besides, I wasn't sure you would want the whole town seeing you talking to an old married woman."

"You know I like talking to you, and I don't think anyone would care one way or the other."

"Maybe, maybe not", said Bonnie.

"You hungry?" Matt asked. "We have lots of food left."

"No thanks. I just came over to say hey. Tell everybody I said hello to them too," she turned to leave.

"Don't go. You just got here."

"I gotta make my rounds and say "hi" to everyone. You know, Millie's Diner marketing. What are you doing later? Much later?" Bonnie asked.

"Like around 2:00?"

"Make it 1:00," said Bonnie.

"See you then."

Matt was quiet on the way home from the picnic.

Gwen asked, "You feeling OK, Matt, or did that last hot dog do you in?"

Matt laughed and said, "I feel fine. I'm just thinking about how much you folks have done for me and how nice today was."

Sonny said, "Hell, boy we're just glad you're getting better. We're glad to help. It makes us proud that so many folks seem to take to you so quick, like you have been around for a long time."

"You know it was fun playing softball today. I think I may have played it before," Matt offered. Gwen and Sonny said nothing.

The next day Matt came by the tool shed as usual, but this time he seemed to be looking for something. "I guess you already sent that team from Greenville those bats you made for them, huh?" asked Matt almost nonchalantly.

"Why?" Sonny replied even more nonchalantly.

"Oh, I was just wondering," Matt trailed off.

Without saying anything else, Sonny nodded to a closet on the west end of the shed. Matt opened the closet door, and the smell of lacquer and wood seemed to have a physical impact on him, as if he were inhaling a memory. But then it was gone.

Standing in the corner of the closet were four 35"- 33 ounce bats, made of hard, white North Carolina ash. Sonny had flame treated them and then dipped them in two coats of lacquer. He'd read that was the size bat Matt had used with the Reds.

"Those teams from Greenville never picked up those damn bats. I was just gonna give them give to the high school, unless you want them," Sonny said.

Matt didn't say anything at first. He simply picked up one of the bats and swung it slowly like he had done with the piece of wood weeks before. But this time he increased the length of the arc he was making until he made the air in the room hiss with the power of his swing. He swung the bat right handed like he had when he batted at the softball game the day before. But then he effortlessly switched to a left hand position and swung the bat with the same smoothness and power. Matt was silhouetted by the sun streaming into the tool shed. A fine dust hung in the air, and it distorted his face and body, creating a surreal image. Sonny was transfixed by what he was seeing and not sure how to react. Finally it was Matt who said, "Yep, I think I may have played some ball in my day."

Later that week, Paul Able, of Able's Bar and Grill fame, came out to visit. This visit was very unusual since he had never been all that friendly to either Gwen or Sonny over the years. Sonny had heard he still referred to them as "outsiders" after decades of living in Blossom.

"Hi Sonny. I just stopped by to say hello."

"Hello, Paul," said Sonny.

Eschewing any further social niceties, Paul said, "By the way, is Matt around? 'Spose he'd be interested in playing softball for my team?" Paul sponsored a local team that played for beer and bragging rights in a league made up of seven small communities around Blossom. The winning team went to Greenville for the state championship in early September. The league had started in May and Able's Bar and Grill was in fourth place. Paul decided he needed some outfield help and, after the picnic, hoped Matt could be recruited.

"Well, I guess you will have to ask Matt that question," Sonny said. "Then if he wants to play, Matt will have to ask Doc if it's okay."

"I'd like to play," said Matt as he stood in the doorway taking in the conversation. "I'll go see Doc tomorrow and see if alright with it." Then he abruptly turned around and walked up to his room.

"I guess he'll play," Sonny said. Since there was very little else Paul Able could think of to talk to Gwen and Sonny about, he stayed another minute and left.

Matt saw Doc the next day.

"It would probably be good for you," Doc told him. "But don't go sliding into bases. One small mistake could tear up your leg. No softball game is worth that."

"Whatever you say, Doc," Matt replied. He smiled all the way home.

17.   Slo Pitch

The rest of that second summer, Matt began to look forward to those softball games so much that he had trouble sleeping the night before each one. His team played on Tuesday and Thursday nights and every other weekend. He showed outstanding defensive play at center field, but Matt hit poorly initially. It was a slow pitch league, and the arc of the pitch actually worked to the disadvantage of a hitter with a level swing.   He struck out three times in the first three games, something no other player on his team did.

But it was his outfield play that set him apart in the league. In his first few games Matt was afraid to run at top speed for fear something might "break." But after awhile, any ball hit between right center and left center was gobbled up by Matt. After he had thrown out four runners in one game trying to take an extra base, the league quit trying to run on his arm.

The highlight of the year defensively was a catch Matt made "Willy Mays style" against the fence in centerfield, 300 feet from home plate. He caught the ball, gathered himself and threw the ball on a line to third base cutting down the runner tagging up from second, who was stunned when the ball beat him to the bag.   Even the opposing team from up the road in Danton gave him a standing ovation.

Despite a slow start offensively, Matt began to hit after the fourth or fifth game. He learned how to uppercut his swing and, as a result, began launching incredible drives into the trees beyond both the right field and left field fences. He discovered he could hit both ways and enjoyed going up to the plate and deciding at the last second which way to hit.

Eventually, the pitchers in the league decided it was a good idea to pitch around Matt especially after one game when batting left handed he hit a laser shot right at the first baseman. The guy somehow caught the ball before it took his head off. However, he then began howling, threw his glove in the air and discovered the ring finger on his left hand had been nearly severed by his wedding band from the force of the ball hitting his hand. After that incident, Matt tried harder than ever to hit the ball high. He was afraid he might kill someone.

Despite playing softball in a league with twenty to forty year olds only three days a week, Matt was still sore the morning after each game. He kept the pain to himself for fear Doc might get wind of it and make him quit. Sonny and Gwen could see his soreness by the way he gingerly walked the mornings after his games.

The league gave Matt the incentive to increase his exercise routine. For the first time in his life he began lifting weights, running harder and faster, and with Sonny's permission, chopping trees down to make firewood for the winter. The axe striking the wood jarred Matt's shoulder and left him sore for days. But soon he was hitting trees with amazing force, and Sonny would count out loud how many strikes of the axe it would take, for him to cut down a tree sometimes as much as 24 inches in diameter.

As he worked with the axe, Matt's body began take on a new shape. His waist thinned, and his arms, shoulders, and back developed ripples of muscles that were not there the year before. His legs, toned from his long daily runs, were becoming so developed around the thighs that Gwen had to let out his work-out shorts.

Watching Matt from the window as he broke up a few cords of wood, Sonny was amazed at the physical transformation Matt had undergone. Gwen and Sonny had read about his well publicized back problem but he certainly showed no sign of that as he sliced his axe through tree after tree.

As his strength and endurance improved, so did his play on the softball field. In one game alone he came to the plate six times, hit three home runs left handed, one right handed, walked once, and nearly de-balled the third baseman who actually tried to field a ball Matt ripped right at him.

Thanks to Matt's performance on the field, Able's Bar and Grill captured the league championship and were to leave on a Wednesday for a four day, twelve game tournament in Greenville. Disappointed, Matt told his teammates he could not go when he learned that each player had to come up with $189 for a new shirt, gas, food, and rooms at the tournament. He was not going to ask Gwen and Sonny for anything after all they had done for him.

When she heard about it, Gwen said, "If you want to go and play up in Greenville then go ahead and go. And don't worry about the money, you can afford it. I have kept track of all the hours you have worked around the farm, and I opened a little savings account for you in my name months ago. You have over $4,500 in the bank, so you can afford to go on your own money, if you want to."

Matt was so touched by Gwen's kindness and generosity he was more convinced than ever not to go to Greenville. It was only after Sonny insisted to the point of raising his voice for the first time in Matt's brief memory that Matt agreed to pack his things and go.

Though Matt had traveled around Blossom for months, leaving for that tournament was strange and a little unnerving. He was not sure why. On the bus ride to Greenville, he kept thinking how great the Cook's had been to him. He also wondered, as he often did, about his own family. Did he have a mother and father or even a wife and kids who were looking for him somewhere? What was his real name?

Everybody called him Matt because they just couldn't keep saying "hey you" all the time, but he missed having a real last name.

Earlier in the summer there had been a little contest over a last name for Matt (winner bought ice cream), and Doc kept insisting Dylan should be known as Matt Wolf.

"It's a good last name," Doc explained, "Easy to remember and it sounds..." he paused for effect "...animalistic." When he finished with a growl, Matt laughed with his friends. From that time on, he was known to all as Matt Wolf. But Matt still privately wondered what his real last name had been.

While Matt would be eternally grateful for all the Cook's had done for him, he decided on that bus ride that when he returned from Greenville, he was going to make a focused effort to find whatever family he had. He was becoming comfortable in the life he was leading but there was something missing. His dreams of another life were now nightly occurrences. When he awoke from his dreams, the sadness and sense of loss was palpable. It scared him because that sadness and feeling of regret was starting to carry over into his day-to-day life. As he leaned back against the bus seat and watched the white lines of the highway slip past, he did not at first see Steve Obert, his team's shortstop standing next to his seat.

Steve said, "Hey Matt, mind if I join you for a minute?"

"No, man, not at all."

"I just wanted to give you a heads up about a baseball league that I played in a few years ago that's here in the Greenville area. It's a fall league that has just started up last week and runs until mid- December. It's made up of former college and pro players, but it's a little bit over my head," Steve admitted. "As good as you are, you must have played baseball at some point, and I think you might do well in that league. Like I said, their season just started last week, and if you want to play some hardball for the next month or so, I can hook you up with a tryout."

"Yeah, if my leg holds up after this weekend, I might take you up on the offer. Thanks for the heads up," Matt said appreciatively.

For the next four days Matt forgot all about the conversation with Steve. During the softball tournament in Greenville, Matt put on an offensive exhibition that was talked about for years. He came to the plate 62 times during the 12 games and hit nearly .800. He hit 16 home runs and drove in 36 runs. His stats would have been even better if he hadn't been intentionally walked 17 times.

Had his team been able to catch the ball more than they did, they would have won the tournament. Their defense was pitiful and even Matt made two throwing errors trying to nail runners at the plate. But he also threw out six base runners who tried to stretch their hits going for an extra base.

After the tournament, when Matt was given the MVP trophy, he acted like he had been in the limelight before. Not cocky, just experienced with the accolades. Matt was one of the more popular players at the tournament given his quiet approach to the game and the genuine humbleness that permeated his personality. He was clearly the best player in Greenville that week, but by talking to him no one would have ever known it.

Perhaps one reason people were so taken by Matt was the pity they felt for the accident victim. He had the body of a serious athlete now, but his face, despite the round of plastic surgery earlier in the year, seemed to be deteriorating. Large masses of scar tissue seemed to be enlarging across the right side of his brow. His hair line had receded almost a full six inches on the top, left portion of his scalp, which led to Matt shaving his head totally. Where his redesigned ear had been placed, a nasty red discoloration had formed that ran from the left side of his skull down the side of his face to his cheek bone.

His broken nose was still somewhat misshaped even after surgery, and his broken jaw had not healed correctly causing his lower jaw bone to protrude an inch and a half beyond his upper jaw. It gave Matt a *stupid* look.

At least that was how a couple of guys on a team from Pickens described "that great player from Blossom." The comment earned the Pickens team a pretty good ass kicking in the parking lot outside the hotel where the teams stayed. Matt's teammates made sure he never got wind of that little incident.

His facial appearance didn't seem to bother Matt, who often entertained his team with jokes he made about himself. He was funny as hell. His deadpan humor had teammates laughing in the dugouts, restaurants and back in their rooms during the nightly penny ante poker games.

Uncharacteristically, Matt was quiet and appeared depressed on the bus ride back to Blossom after the tournament. He was happy his team had played well, and happy with his performance, but he felt as if something was wrong. A few of his teammates picked up on his disposition and tried to get him to talk. While he was polite like he always was, it was clear Matt wanted to be left alone.

Halfway through the trip, the bus pulled into a truck stop restaurant, and twenty hungry softball players invaded like a bunch of locusts. As they devoured their food, several noticed a baseball game and saw the Cincinnati Reds taking on the Chicago Cubs on WGN. As the leftfield camera moved from the hitter to the pitcher and back again, Matt realized The Great American Ball Park looked very familiar to him. But it was more than that. When a line drive was hit into the Reds' dugout, it scattered some players. As the camera showed some Reds waving white towels and laughing, a doorway appeared at the home plate side of the dugout for a split second and Matt said to Obie, "I know where that doorway goes."

"You do?"

"Yes, there's a tunnel and I know it leads to a red carpeted area," he insisted. The image and the familiarity faded, and a dangerous depression fell over Matt. He successfully hid it from his teammates, but he knew something was wrong. And he suddenly hurt all over. Ninety innings of softball had taken a toll.

Matt was relieved when the bus let him off at the Blossom High School and he was able to be alone. Except he didn't exactly want to be alone. Instead of walking back to Sonny and Gwen's, Matt decided to stop in and see Bonnie. It was the first time he'd gone to her house uninvited. As he shuffled up her walk, it appeared all the lights were out. He wondered if she may have gone to bed early or maybe was away for the evening. He almost turned around and headed home when he heard the familiar squeak of her front porch swing.

"Hey," a voice said from the darkness.

"Hey," said Matt still not seeing Bonnie in the moonless night.

"You win?"

"Yeah, we won most of our games."

"Were you the star?"

"I did okay."

"Want something to drink?"

"No thanks, I'm fine. Want to go for a walk?"

"Why don't we just sit here for awhile. I won't bite."

"Okay", agreed Matt.

Matt dropped his gym bag on the porch and eased into the rhythm of the slowly moving swing. In the silence and darkness of the night he began to unwind and relax for the first time in days. But he had a question.

"Remember the 4th of July picnic?" he asked.

"I remember," she said.

"You didn't want folks to see us talking. And over the last few weeks you never want to go anywhere people might see us together. Why is that?"

"It's because you are a single young man and I am a married middle aged woman. People would talk," she replied.

"So what? You haven't seen him in years."

"You must have never lived in a small town."

Turning to Bonnie, Matt asked, "Is that really it?"

"What do you mean, 'really it'?"

"I don't know. Maybe you don't want anybody to see us together because of other things."

"What other things?" she insisted.

"Never mind," said Matt.

"You're not talking about your face, are you?" she asked, sounding hurt. "You think I don't want to be in public with you because of how you look? That's an awful thing to say to me. I thought we were friends? Who could have put such an idea in your head?"

"I'm sorry, he said, but I know how I look. I've heard guys on the other teams we play make jokes, and I can look in a mirror. Doc said I am going to get more plastic surgery, but I doubt it will help all that much."

Taking Matt's hand and putting it in her lap, Bonnie said, "First of all, Matt, your face has gotten better over the last six months, and it will get better in the future. But I like you because you are smart and funny and, at the risk of sounding like a dirty old lady, you have a beautiful body. Got it?"

"Yeah, I got it." After several moments of silence Matt then asked, "so, you like me, huh?"

"Yeah, I guess, a little", said Bonnie.

"And you like my body, huh?" he grinned

"Yeah, I guess, a little," said Bonnie.

"Hmm, so what do we do now?" Asked Matt. "I mean, I like you, you like me, we're sitting all alone on a beautiful summer night, nobody is around..."

"That depends on how discreet you are," she said.

"Discreet? Oh, anyone can tell you I am, above all, discreet."

Bonnie unfolded her long tan legs she had pulled up under her on the swing and placed her bare feet on the porch. She rose from the swing and took Matt's hand. "You better be," she said and led him into her unlit home.

Two hours later, Matt walked into Sonny and Gwen's living room surprised to see them both still awake.

"There he is," said Sonny. "How'd you do tonight?"

"I did great," said Matt.

"That's more than your usual 'okay'," said Gwen. "You hungry?"

"No thanks. We grabbed a bite on the way home. Think I'll just turn in early. I'm kind of tired. G'night," he said and quickly headed for his room.

"'Night, Matt. See you tomorrow," said Sonny.

Hearing Matt climb the stairs, Gwen said, "Matt seemed upbeat tonight."

"I think that softball is helping Matt", ventured Sonny.

"Well, something is," said Gwen.

On the way to their room later that night, after watching Casablanca for the hundredth time, Sonny and Gwen could hear Matt's distressed voice as they passed by his room. They listened quietly for a moment and eased open his door. They could hear him mumbling in his sleep but could not make out any of the words. He was tossing and turning in his private nightmare. Whatever it was continued throughout the night.

Sonny stumbled into the kitchen the next morning, looking like something the cat dragged in. A half-hour later Matt followed and said, "I really don't feel like running today. Is it okay with you guys if I go back up to bed for an hour? I think that tournament wore me out a little bit."

"Head back to bed and get some rest", Sonny said. Matt slept 'til 4:30.

"Matt is not acting right," Gwen said to Sonny that night. "I know he said he was just tired from the tournament, but I think it is more than that. I'm worried about him."

"I think you might be right. Something is wrong, but I guess we could expect that after all he has been through. Maybe we should talk to a psychologist or therapist and get some advice," Sonny suggested. They both decided that they would keep a close eye on Matt's behavior and also talk to Doc about their options.

18.   "I want to play..."

Matt's body quickly recovered from its first real test on the softball field, and he resumed running, stretching, and weight training. He also played in a dozen or so baseball games up in Greenville and did very well, though Sonny and Gwen had to hear of his exploits from folks in town because Matt would never give them any details.

The only thing about the baseball league Matt disliked was having to bum rides with fans and teammates to make as many games as he did.

The last game Sonny and Gwen attended, Matt hit a couple home runs, had four hits and looked like he was having a whole lot of fun, at least on the field. Away from the field he still seemed "down in the dumps" to Gwen.

When the fall season ended, Matt began helping Sonny build furniture on a daily basis. Together, they actually opened up a small retail shop in town and were making a decent profit. Of course, any money Sonny made ended up in Gwen's capable hands. Gwen didn't have the heart to tell Sonny or Matt that she had already salted away more money than they would ever need and neither of them really had to work. She was afraid Sonny might just keel over at the news, plus his work kept him out of the house. She didn't want Sonny to know they were rich.

Doc's plastic surgeon friend also worked on Matt a half dozen more times when the baseball league ended. In the second round of procedures, the surgeon removed scar tissue and calcium deposits around his forehead and cheek bones and smoothed down some of the scaring that had remained on his face. The most invasive procedure involved moving Matt's jaw bone back into place. That surgery, though painful, did the most to normalize Matt's appearance even though he lost 10 pounds during the healing process since he could not eat solid foods.

From the neck down Matt was healed, actually, more than healed. He was in the best shape of his life. Not only could he run six minute miles and sprint a quarter-mile in 62 seconds, (he asked Sonny and Gwen to time him at the high school track), he could bench press over 225 pounds 10 times and would routinely do 50 arm curls with 60 pound weights in one workout session. But the key to his strength was his flexibility.

Doc insisted that he do stretching exercises daily. Matt obliged by watching a cute young girl on TV teaching yoga every morning at 7:30. After just a few months Matt could put his hands flat on the floor while standing and could contort his body in ways he never dreamed possible the year before, or ever, for that matter. Doc said that stretching would help the reduce scar tissue around his broken bones and prevent further injuries.

After the crash Matt had not played ball for nearly two years and had been unable to work out while his body mended. As a result, he lost muscle tone and mass while his body fat increased from 11% to 20%, leaving him with little stamina. By that third Christmas twenty five months after the crash, Doc measured his body fat and found it was under 10% even though his weight was up to 221 pounds.

By late winter, the final round of plastic surgery had changed Matt's appearance significantly. While he would never again resemble the handsome young man Sonny and Gwen had seen on the Internet or on his ID card, he looked better. Much better. His face finally looked "balanced" although he did look significantly older than his twenty-seven years. Perhaps it was his new found physical prowess and better looking face that gave him the confidence to do something he had not really wanted to do before. He wanted to go somewhere. Alone.

"I am not sure where I want to go but I want to go somewhere. I want to take a trip, visit a big city, do something," Matt announced over breakfast in early January.

Gwen and Sonny were somewhat taken aback by his statement because there was really no way Matt could travel without some kind of ID.

"Well, you are going to need a driver's license to drive or even fly, and that's going to take some time since you don't have a birth certificate, a social security card, or any other ID," said Sonny. "That's going to be a bit of a hassle."

For the first time in twenty-six months, Matt let his frustrations erupt and slammed his hand against the breakfast table, "I don't care if it is a hassle or not. I want... I really need to go somewhere. I need to find some things out."

Trying to placate Matt, Sonny suggested, "Why don't we load up the van or borrow Doc's RV and go to Atlanta or even up to Atlantic City for a couple weeks."

Staring down at the table Matt quietly said, "I really want to take a trip on my own. I checked my bank balance with Gwen and I have over $12,000. I would like to take some of that money and go somewhere. It's not that I want to leave you guys, especially after all you've done for me, and I won't be gone for more than a week or two. But being on my own for awhile is something I need to do."

Finally, Sonny said, "You don't need to explain, we understand. You have been with us 24/7 for over two years, and it's only natural that you want to have some freedom. Give me a couple days to work on how we might be able to get you some ID so you can travel."

"Thanks, Sonny," Matt sighed.

Last At Bat

Sonny and Gwen understood what Matt wanted to do and why. They also realized it was all part of the healing process. They were actually happy that he felt good enough physically and mentally to want to move on in his life. But they were torn about how Matt could survive in a world that thought he was dead. And if the world found out otherwise, they could put him in jail for years. After all Matt had been through, and what Sonny and Gwen had learned about him, they did not want him to end up in some jail cell rotting away for the next seven years.

Later that night Sonny told Gwen, "It's time to tell Matt the truth. There is really no alternative. What if he goes out into the world and gets a job requiring fingerprinting or some other background check that would reveal his identity. He would have no chance to escape prison. If he knows the truth, perhaps he could, with our help, cobble together a life that would not only be fulfilling but also keep him free."

Gwen agreed, "I know you're right, but telling him the truth scares me to death. How's he going to react when he finds out we have all been lying to him?"

The next morning Sonny and Gwen asked Matt if they could join him on his morning walk. Matt smiled and said "Well, it's usually a morning run, but I guess I can walk this one time."

"Thanks," said Sonny. "Our running days are sure behind us." As the three of them walked toward the woods, the cool morning air was filled with the smell of pine trees. A light fog hung in the air and blanketed low lying areas around the farm giving it a "Brigadoon" appearance.

After nearly a half mile in silence Matt asked, "You guys know who I am, don't you?"

Stunned by the question, Sonny and Gwen both stopped and turned toward Matt. Gwen said, "How long have you known that?"

Matt said, "Well, I guess I really never knew for sure until this second. But there were too many unanswered questions, too many things that didn't add up when I would ask you guys about things. At first, I believed what you told me, but over the last six months or so I figured you weren't telling me everything. Since I knew how you cared for me, I thought there must be a good reason why you were holding back."

"There is," said Sonny. He then told Matt the whole story; who Matt was, what had happened to him, the crash, everything. As they walked Matt said nothing for nearly a mile. Soon he began to ask detailed questions trying to fill in the remaining blanks. Some things Sonny and Gwen had answers for, some they did not. But they held back nothing. While they were relieved to get the burden of the secret off their chests, their biggest concern was how Matt would react. Would he hate them? Would he leave Blossom? Would he need psychological counseling? Would he be depressed? Even suicidal?

After another silent mile Matt said, "I want to play baseball again."

Last At Bat

19.   Dylan Michael

Over the next week Matt Wolf spent hours on the Internet studying Dylan Michael. His memory was inching back with each article and film clip. The images of him were familiar, yet removed, but the pictures of Cara were torture. The ache for her was worse than all the physical pain he had endured.

Knowing that Cara was the dark-haired woman in his dreams solved the mystery, but destroyed the comfort he'd come to anticipate each night.   He stopped at a close-up of her and reached for the screen. As he ran his finger over her cheek, his memory returned in tactile form; he knew the soft silky smoothness of her skin and the gentle touch of her fingers on his.

Glancing from the handsome face in pictures of his former self to the reflection in the windows by his desk made him cringe. He self-consciously rubbed the side of his head where his real ear had been, and for the first time since the crash, he wanted to hide his face.   But the photos did give him one consolation; the body he now inhabited was much bigger, stronger and more muscular than Dylan Michael's body. And, though it didn't show, far more flexible.

Watching the videos of games from years before made his heart rate race. He actually broke out in a sweat watching himself dive head first into third base or run down a line drive in the gap. The video of "The Double" gave him chills each time he watched himself round second, knowing that it had produced the game winning run and had electrified an entire city.

His excitement at reclaiming his past was soon overshadowed by a deep, dangerous depression. It started with a series of sleepless nights when he would lie in bed with a million unrelated visions exploding in his brain. He told Sonny and Gwen of familiar faces or snippets of events that filled his nights with elation or an overwhelming sense of loss. Many times he woke, bathed in sweat and overcome with nausea.

Watching the depression deepen, Gwen decided to act.

"Doc, we need your help," Gwen said when Annie handed him the phone.

"Just ask," Doc replied.

"It's Matt," she said. "Knowing his past was great at first, but he's so depressed, I'm starting to worry. I hope I'm not overreacting."

"You're not the overreacting type, Gwennie. Deep depression can paralyze or kill him as easily as that plane crash. Let me give my old hunting buddy Bill Sheppard a call. He's retired now, but he was one of the best I've known at treating post traumatic stress syndrome."

"Thanks, Doc," she said. "I'll sleep better tonight."

For the next few weeks, Matt worked with Dr. Sheppard. When he learned the extent of Matt's injuries and the collective losses that had been thrown at him in such a short period of time, he was astonished that the depression wasn't more severe. In fact, had he not been depressed, Dr. Sheppard would have said that Matt was either seriously brain damaged or terminally stupid. After ten minutes into their first session, he knew that Matt was neither.

In his early sessions, Matt was not as talkative as the doctor had hoped. Slowly, he accepted Dr. Sheppard's assessment of the normality of his reactions. Matt intuitively agreed with the doctor, but still had trouble accepting what had happened to him.

The sleepless nights and the therapy continued for two long weeks before the changes began. Then, he woke one morning without having dreamt of the plane crash or of going to jail. Soon, his dreams of Cara included walks with Carly down their favorite streets and time together in their Cincinnati home. And, many nights were filled with playing ball with the Reds. He was surrounded by the smell of the ball park, rounding first base and counting the twelve steps to second and his teammates pounding the air with their fists when he beat the throw by an eyelash.

He began to share his progress with Sonny and Gwen and, eventually, with the medical team responsible for his miraculous recovery. He made peace with the loss of his former identity and cracked jokes about his damaged face. He even began to accept the loss of his wife. He reveled in regaining baseball as part of his life, but his friends tried to lower any expectations he had of returning to professional baseball.

A couple of nights after the sessions with Doctor Sheppard ended, Sonny, Gwen and Matt surprised the clinic conspirators who were working late, with pizza. Matt appeared to be his happy self again as he poked fun at himself and his extended family.

"My shrink tells me that I need a plan; something to work toward with 'tenacity and focus,'" Matt explained. "I told him I wanted to be a Chippendale dancer, but he wasn't very enthusiastic."

"Hell, boy, I not only like that idea, we could be a team," Sonny said, jumping to his feet. Matt joined him in an impromptu chorus line amidst the cheers of their appreciative crowd.

"God, Sonny, you've ruined him," Gwen said as they took their bows and fell into their chairs.

"So, what's plan B?" asked Doc.

Matt became serious. "I'm going to play major league baseball again."

Flo was the first to recover her voice. "Now, Matt, it would break our hearts not to watch you play around Blossom. With all you've been through, why not aim your sights a little lower so we can cheer you on."

"But I can still play," he said, jumping to his feet. "Look," he said as he paced in front of them, "I'm only twenty-seven years old. I survived a plane crash that killed nearly three hundred other people. I'm in the best shape of my life. Even my bad back is healed."

"But you could go to jail," Annie said.

"I know," Matt replied. " But, it might take them a few years to figure out who I really am, and by the time they can prosecute me, I could have played for maybe two or three years. Even if I end up in jail, I was headed there anyway."

"But you could really hurt yourself," Gwen said.

"I know that could happen, but I really don't care, Gwennie. The only thing that does concern me is you guys. If I did play and the truth came out, what will happen to all of you?"

"Don't worry about us," said Doc. "We already talked to an attorney, and we might get into a little dutch, but we got the resources to fight, and there are extenuating circumstances here. But Gwennie and Annie are right, you could go to jail and you could get hurt. I am not sure your body is healed to the point you could play professional baseball again."

In a near whisper Dylan looked at a roomful of people who cared deeply for him and said, "playing baseball again is all I really want. The rest of the stuff I can deal with. I can't deal with never playing again. I just can't. If I have to go to jail, then that is a risk I am willing to take. If I were to get injured again, I want to do it on a ball field. I mean that. I really do." He turned and left the clinic, leaving behind a silence that filled the room with the emotion of his words.

Those remaining in the clinic stared quietly at each other, dabbing at their eyes and softly coughing.

It was Doc who broke the silence. "What the hell? The boy is right. He might go to jail, and he might get hurt, but that could happen even if he stays here in Blossom. But if they catch us, we'll all be trading our clothes for orange jump suits and picking up trash along I - 85."

The room erupted in laughter.

That night a bunch of senior citizens from Blossom, South Carolina, decided to become full-fledged, willing and unapologetic, big-time felons. They also realized that they had to enlist a bunch of other felons as well.

"I'm in!" said Flo. A chorus of 'me too's' rang out, and they high-fived each other feeling twenty years younger and more determined than ever to help the former Red.

Last At Bat

20.   Truth

"Haven't seen you for awhile," said Bonnie.

"Did you know the truth too?" asked Matt.

"Oh, when did you find out?"

"Couple days ago."

"I knew the basics."

"Being lied to by the whole town is.."

"Is what?" asked Bonnie.   "Is it hurting your feelings or something? Don't start feeling sorry for yourself now. Sonny, Gwen, Doc and Annie all went out on a huge limb for you. They could still get hurt if the truth ever came out. They did it because they love you like a son. Then they got damn near everybody in town to join in and protect you."

"I know. I know they care for me," he said.

"Then act like it."

"It's just the idea of finding out so much about a life I never knew I had.   It was like reading a book about someone else."

Bonnie asked, "What did you learn?"

"It seems like I was a fool," he replied.

"Yeah, I guess you were. But we're all fools from time to time. The difference is you have a second chance. Very few of us ever get that."

"I had a wife," Matt said.

"I know," Bonnie replied. "Was she the one with the dark hair?"

"Yes. It was her."

Turning to Matt on the front porch swing and putting her arm on his shoulder, Bonnie said, "Be careful, Matt."

127

Last At Bat

21.   The Team

Doc began to formulate a very specific plan that would require as many as a dozen more felons to insure its success. He knew the more people that were involved, the greater the risk would be of someone slipping, talking about the plan and the whole thing going to hell in a hand basket.

Doc gave each member the same speech. "I'm going to ask you to do something illegal. We're going to try to give Matt the second chance he deserves. I'll understand if you think the risk is too much."

Doc worried that someone would not only turn him down, but blow the whistle on *the plan* before they even got started. What Three-Dub didn't realize about the folks of Blossom was that they would have done a whole hellava lot more for him than he was asking.

When he asked Tom Carr, the former Blossom High School principal to join the team, Carr said, "That's all you want? The way you were talking I thought maybe you wanted us to kill somebody. But before I would do something like that, I would need to know if they actually needed killing."

Most of the team had only one concern: was Matt actually good enough to play baseball at the professional level again? Pounding the snot out of the local boys was a far cry from competing in the big leagues.

Doc recruited Dutch Brown to do the initial evaluation. Brown managed the local high school team and had a history with the St. Louis Cardinals' as a career minor league player and hitting coach. He'd actually played in 32 Major League games one year and had "Cardinal" as a vanity license plate. Brown agreed and asked Matt to take batting practice against his star left-handed pitcher who was being scouted by a dozen big league teams and figured to be a first round pick in the upcoming amateur draft.

After fouling off three ninety-mile-per hour fastballs, Matt began to zero in on the young lefty's pitches and rifled them all over the deserted high school field. The sound that emanated from Matt's bat meeting the ball was something Brown had not heard in years. It became obvious to the teenager that he was not going to get a fastball by Matt, so he went to his slider. That, too, was smashed. He tried a change-up, back to the fastball, and even a knuckle ball. Each pitch was seemingly hit harder than the last. Brown was surprised to find that Matt wasn't swinging hard. He had a very short stride and a quick compact swing that generated tremendous power.

Brown had studied video of Dylan Michael before the practice. Dylan had held the bat high, while Matt held the bat much lower. Matt's stance was different, too, from both sides of the plate. Brown wrote this off to Matt's compensating for his injuries.

But then he thought there was perhaps another, more obvious reason for the differences in the stance. Matt was clearly much stronger than he had been in his last year with the Reds. As a result, he could wait longer on the fast ball and did not need to take the long stride into the pitch that had been a trademark of his swing. Brown saw that long stride on the videos and knew despite all his success with the Reds, that long swing had led to Matt's propensity to swing and miss more than he should have. Finally Matt had his feet spread further apart in the batter's box than he had previously, which also cut down on his long stride. That would explain why Matt didn't miss a single pitch thrown to him by the young lefthander. Not one.

After a 10 minute break, Brown began hitting fly balls to Matt and found it nearly impossible to hit one over his head or in front of him. Matt's anticipation of where the ball would land was uncanny which made up for some of the speed he may have lost from his injuries. When Matt let go with a strong throw, he could bounce the ball on one hop from anywhere on the field to Brown, who was hitting from near the pitcher's mound.

The last test was the most risky; timing Matt's running speed from home to first, first to third, and then from home plate to home plate. At first, Matt seemed afraid to "bust it" from home to first. Both Doc and Sonny were concerned that a pulled hamstring or ripped Achilles' tendon could put an end to Matt's dream before it started. After a few tries, Matt increased the speed on each attempt. On the last run to first, he burst out of the batter's box and sped down the line in 3.97 seconds.

After the last plate to plate dash, Sonny walked over to a sweating, panting Matt who was bent over at the waist with his hands gripping the bottom of his Nike shorts. Waiting for him to catch his breath, Sonny saw a small smile come over Matt's face.

"God, that was fun," Matt said.

Gwen, watching from behind the backstop, cried openly at what she had witnessed, while the other founding members of the team looked at one another in stunned silence.

It was Doc who finally said, "Well, boys and girls, seems like we got some work to do."

Over the next week Dylan Michael officially became "Matt Wolf." The name also belonged to a stillborn infant who died years ago. His unwed mother, who also died three days after the child's birth, belonged to a family of migrant workers who disappeared after the deaths to avoid impossible medical bills. Doc remembered seeing the name on a headstone in the small cemetery. "Matt Wolf" was anything but a coincidental choice. Since the first days of the conspiracy, Doc had been planning a way to give Dylan a name.

Last At Bat

Doc enlisted Harry Hughes, the Blossom undertaker, and asked him to retrieve the old death certificates from his files. Harry did as asked and burned the records. A dead Matt Wolf was suddenly very much alive following the creation of a new birth certificate that Doc prepared by backdating an old form he still had in his office files.

Coach Brown typed up a couple dozen articles on Matt Wolf describing his exploits on the baseball field; game winning hits, record breaking batting averages, and home runs by the score and posted them on the Internet.

Former principal Tom Carr spent a weekend reconstructing a permanent record file for Matt Wolf and decided, if he was going to make up an academic record, it might as well be a good one. Matt "graduated" with 3.80 GPA, with exceptional marks in math and science.

Gwen put together a work history for Matt that included pay stubs from over the last three years and applied for a social security number. She even filed a belated income tax return for Matt and paid back taxes including interest and penalties. Mary Lester, who worked at the license bureau, had Matt come in on a Sunday, took his picture, gave him an eye test, and got him his driver's license.

The real kicker was getting the mayor and Blossom's only two policemen to join the team in case state or federal cops ever got curious. They not only enthusiastically joined, but were also somewhat pissed that Doc had not gone to them in the first place. After a flurry of activity, Matthew David Wolf was born, grew up, went to school, and worked for several years all in the space of eight days.

"One more day than the good Lord needed to build heaven and earth," reminded Gwen.

Sitting around the Cook's kitchen table having some Bud's, the 14 members of "Matt's Team" were laughing their butts off about

Matt Wolf who could hit for power, hit for average, field, run, throw and was only eight days old!

All he needed now was to be discovered.

******

Maps and papers were strewn over the kitchen table as Matt, Sonny and Gwen scoped out options regarding Matt's first tryout camp.

"The Braves are having a series of camps starting in late April through May in the Southeast," suggested Sonny.

"Too close. If one of the fellas Matt played with around here shows up, it could raise some questions," said Gwen.

"That's true. What do you think Matt? Where do you think you should go for your first tryout camp?"

"How about out West?" he suggested.

"You mean like KC or St. Louis?" Sonny asked.

"No. I was thinking way out West like California."

"That might make some sense", said Gwen. "Besides it would be fun to take a nice long drive and relax."

"OK with me. Look here, the Mariner's are having a camp in Portland in late April. The Giants, A's and Dodgers are holding camps the following three weeks. We could start in Portland and work our way south, then head back," said Sonny.

"Sounds great to me ," said Matt.

Last At Bat

22.   The Plan

Matt's excitement over going to Portland and trying to re-build his baseball career was tempered by leaving Bonnie. Matt was fond of her and respected her advice, humor, intellect and serenity. The night before he left, he visited Bonnie and told her what he thought was a great idea.

"I want you to come with us to Portland. I know Sonny and Gwen won't mind. They like you."

"And what am I supposed to do in Portland, Matt?" Bonnie replied.

"We could spend time together and see the country. When was the last time you had a vacation?" he asked.

"Matt, I can't tell you how touched I am that you want me to come along, and I would love to see you try out for all those teams. But my life is here. I know you care about me, and I adore you, but us being together is not part of the plan."

"How do you know, Bonnie? Maybe it is the plan. Maybe we're supposed to end up together. Maybe the crash, coming here, all of it, *is* the plan. I don't want to leave you here. I may not be back for months. Won't you miss me?"

"Of course, but the plan is for you to take advantage of this second chance. Maybe even find your wife. At least try. If you turn your back on this second chance, I'll never forgive you. It's time for you to leave here and follow the plan. It will all work out somehow."

"But what about you?" he asked.

"Don't forget," said Bonnie, "I'm now part of the plan too. Don't worry, it'll all work out, Sweetie."

Last At Bat

Bonnie leaned over and kissed Matt before taking his hand and leading him into her house.

23.   Number 21.

Dew clung to the grass and glimmered like diamonds on green felt on a Saturday morning in late April in South Carolina. The air was sweet with lilac, apple blossoms, and hyacinth. The sky was baby blue and free of a single cloud.

"C'mon darlin'," said Sonny. "You're gonna make us get behind schedule."

"What schedule?" said Gwen. "We're gonna be gone for a month."

"Alright, I warned ya. Let's go Matt. We'll make this a man's trip."

"I'll man trip you," said Gwen.

Twenty-nine months after surviving a plane crash, Matt Wolf (aka Dylan Michael) and Sonny packed up Gwen's GMC van and all three began the six day drive to Portland, Oregon. Matt would have enjoyed the chance to get out and see the world, even without the possibility of baseball. It was not the "alone" trip Matt had requested but he enjoyed Sonny and Gwen's company. Peering out of the front passenger window like a ten year old, Matt watched an unfamiliar world move past him at seventy miles per hour.

They planned to attend a Mariners' tryout camp outside Portland scheduled the following week, then hit the Giants' camp in Sacramento, and an Oakland A's camp in San Jose before going to Bakersfield for a Dodgers' camp. They figured if they were 0 for 4 in this approach, they would go to "Plan B" even though they had no idea what the hell "Plan B" was.

Last At Bat

At Matt's request, they drove west via Cincinnati, stopped late the first day and stayed at the Westin Hotel only blocks from the downtown stadium. Around 9 a.m. the next morning they had some breakfast, walked around the city and finally wandered over to the Great American Ballpark. The impact of walking up to the stadium had a profound physical impact on Matt; his breath became labored and shallow, and the closer he got to the ball park the dizzier he became.

"Could we stop for a minute?" he asked. "I need to catch my breath."

"Maybe this was not such a good idea," Gwen frowned. "Let's go back to the hotel."

"Maybe you're right," Matt said. But then he saw a line of flags on light poles along Pete Rose Way. They looked familiar. Each flag had a name and number: Johnny Bench "5," Joe Morgan "8," Tony Perez "24," Ted Kluzewski "18," Sparky Anderson "10," and Pete Rose "14." The last one in the row read Dylan Michael "21".

"That was me," said Matt.

"That *is* you," corrected Gwen.

Except for the Major League Baseball Hall of Fame in Cooperstown, New York, the Reds Hall of Fame and Museum is the largest baseball museum in the country as befitting the oldest franchise in major league baseball. With photos dating back to 1869, the Reds' Hall of Fame brought the team's history to life.

Among the large displays was a tribute to the "New Red Machine," the team on which Matt had played, and been a major contributor, helping his team win three World Championships. A huge banner dominated the room entitled, "The Double." Within the space, was the famous shot of Dylan Michael. It captured the moment that changed his life. It was 15' high and so detailed that "Louisville Slugger" could be clearly read on his bat.

A bronzed plaque below the photo eulogized Dylan:

"While only 19 years old, Dylan Michael had arguably the biggest hit in Cincinnati Reds history when he connected for a bases clearing double to win the seventh game of the World Series against the New York Yankees. Michael's brief but brilliant career with the Reds ended five years later when he was injured, never to return to the field. Tragically, Michael's young life was cut short when he died in a plane crash in the hills of Kentucky. Below is Michael's first World Series ring that was recovered from that accident."

As Matt stared at the ring, the synapses in his brain surged to life. In a flood of visions and feelings, Matt's memory was instantaneously and completely restored.

Last At Bat

24. ”I am afraid we are in for a rough time...”

Dylan had taken a cab to the airport alone even though many of his friends and teammates offered to go with him. He met his attorney and step dad there and officially turned himself over to a court appointed sheriff who was going to accompany him to Atlanta and then on to the prison in southern Georgia. They had tried to keep the exact time and date quiet, but Arthur Robbins, the writer from the *Los Angeles Times* used his network of sources and found out when Dylan was leaving. He had flown all the way in from California and cut short a vacation to wish Dylan well. Dylan was genuinely touched by Robbins' presence.

"Arthur, I can't believe you came all the way from LA. Must be a slow news day," he had teased.

Cara had also shown up at the airport that day to say goodbye. It was devastating to Dylan. Only months before, Dylan had finally awakened from the veil he had lived behind caused by too many pain killers. Seeing Cara at the airport made him realize how much he had truly lost.

Tom Martin, the court appointed sheriff accompanying Dylan on the trip to Georgia, was a burly former high school line backer and Reds fan whom Dylan had seen several times during his trial. For forty-five minutes while they waited for the flight, the deputy talked continually about baseball, about "The Double," about what a great team the New Red Machine was, and about what a fan of Dylan's he was.

Once they got on the plane he even asked Dylan for an autograph which was hard to give since Dylan was in handcuffs. The guard undid the cuff on his right hand so he could sign: *"To my long time fan and short time seat mate, Tom Martin, the best guard I have ever had the pleasure of going to jail with. Your friend, Dylan Michael."*

Dylan actually liked Tom and shocked him by asking, "How about holding this for me for about seven years? I won't be needing it." He then handed the guard his first World Series ring.

"Yeah, right," Tom said, but, seeing Dylan's face, he realized that Dylan was serious.

"Dylan," he said, "I couldn't take your ring. It's your World Series ring, for God's sake."

"I was going to leave it with Drew, but he would have sold it. I really don't want to leave it in some jail house filing cabinet for seven years. Besides, it looks like it fits you just fine. Just hold onto it for me. When I get out, maybe you could send it to me," Dylan smiled.

"My God, it really is beautiful," said Tom. "I swear on my kid's lives, I will get this back to you." Dylan believed him.

A couple minutes after the plane took off it flew over the Great American Ball Park, but Dylan couldn't bear to look down into it. Instead, he put his seat back and tried to sleep. But he felt the stares of passengers as they walked toward the bathrooms at the back of the plane just to get a glimpse of him. He could hear the camera phones clicking away. He could hear the whispers, and there were even a few cheers that erupted, but he really did not know how to react. After all, there was little precedent for a "former baseball star going to jail" protocol.

The federal prosecutor who represented the government in its case on both the tax and controlled substance charges against Dylan was not a baseball fan. In fact, she had never heard of Dylan Michael. To the contrary, when she had discovered who he was, she decided to hold him out as an example of what too much money and, in her opinion, substance abuse, albeit prescription medication, was doing to American youth. At least that's what Dylan's attorney said.

She was also running for a congressional seat in Ohio which led her to view this high profile case as a stepping stone toward election. Dylan never knew why she refused to plea bargain his case.

In the end, Dylan was convicted. Since there were mandatory sentencing guidelines in place, he was given jail time and a big fine. The harsh penalty came even though several witnesses testified that his actions were the result of pain medication that rendered him semi-comatose for two years. The judge agreed, but his hands were tied. The public also agreed and refused to elect the prosecutor to the seat she coveted.

Through it all... the lost wife, the lost money, the lost career, the shame, and the humiliation, Dylan missed one thing more than anything else: playing baseball. He still had dreams of the game itself; the smells of the grass, the leather glove, pine tar, and the lacquer from his bat. But most of all, he missed the feel of hitting a baseball hard, which ironically, had very little feel at all. It had been two long years since that career-ending injury. Eight months earlier, he had taken three swings in a batting cage and could barely walk for a year. The rigid position in the plane reminded him it would be a long, painful flight.

Instead, it was short painful flight.

Dylan got permission from his guard, friend, fan, ring keeper Tom, to use the bathroom as the choppy air over the Smokey Mountains began to rattle the jet. He had just shut the bathroom door when he heard the announcement from the captain to all passengers. "Please return to your seats, ladies and gentlemen. We're expecting some rough air ahead," he said.

"What are they going to do, arrest me?" Dylan said aloud. He remained where he was, sitting with his pants up on the closed toilet to enjoy what little privacy the 3'x4' airplane bathroom provided.

"Sir, you must return to your seat," the flight attendant said as she banged on the door.

"I'm throwing up in here, for God's sake, " he lied and the knocking ceased.

What happened next was a blur. The plane hit an air pocket at 23,000 feet and plummeted. Dylan was thrown upward, hit the ceiling of the bathroom and was knocked nearly unconscious. He could vaguely hear the screams of the other passengers as the jet nosed downward, seemingly out of control. But as suddenly as the dive began, the plane leveled out, the whine of the engines abated, and it appeared the pilots had regained control of the huge jet.

The jet was not under control. The report from the FAA would later say the hydraulic controls within the vertical stabilizer had been damaged by the fall. From the rear of the plane, Dylan could feel the tail section oscillating back and forth, foretelling the damaged jet's doom.

The cockpit crew had struggled valiantly to avert disaster. The pilot cut the jet's speed then used throttle controls and flaps to do his best to keep the plane airborne. He nosed the wounded aircraft southwest toward Knoxville. After 10 minutes of fighting a losing battle, the jet began a steady descent over the mountains of Southern Kentucky. The crew contacted Knoxville Air Traffic Control and declared an emergency. They then requested an alternative landing site. They were advised the only option was to head for an abandoned military runway that lay 30 miles ahead. At that point, the captain knew there was no hope for the stricken jet. Their ground speed was still 190 miles per hour when the captain wiped sweat from his forehead and announced in a calm, professional voice that later captivated the nation when the FAA released the cockpit voice recorder tapes.

"Folks, this is the captain.   Please tug on your seat belts once more. Flight attendants, please prepare for a crash landing." Except for a few wails of fear, most passengers remained eerily calm.

Despite his dizziness, Dylan instinctively knew he had a better chance back in his seat with a seat belt pulled tight, than where he was. He wanted to move but his body would not respond when he tried to rise off the bathroom floor. He shook his head to clear the fog, but that caused pain to scream from the place on his head that had hit the ceiling. He could also feel blood trickle down his cheek and saw it drip onto his shirt. So, with no options, he sat on the floor of the bathroom with his knees tucked into his chest and waited. Resignation also gripped the rest of the passengers. There were no more cries. The only sound was a hissing noise as the jet cut through the clouds and rain.

Later, the FAA's report explained what the pilot had been aiming for. Looking at topography maps, the captain located a reasonably flat valley between two mountain ridges and decided this was the best he could do in terms of a potential landing site.

He cut the power completely, and the jet made a swooshing sound no one would have heard over the normal whine of the jet's engines. Seconds before impact, the plane banked twenty degrees left, and the pilot went to full flaps on the right wing to compensate. It was too much and the jet lurched to the right, its right wing tipped at nearly 90 degrees.   A wing-over-wing roll was stopped when the plane's right wing clipped rock and everything went dark inside the jet.

Last At Bat

25.   The Ring

Staring at the ring he had given to the guard Tom Martin, that was now in a velvet lined display case, Matt got light headed and nearly passed out. As he did, he began to sink slowly to the shiny oak floor of the Reds' Hall of Fame. Before he hit the floor, Sonny's strong right arm shot out and caught Matt around his waist. Matt reached out and put his arm around Sonny's shoulder and then leaned into him for support.

Over the previous several weeks, Matt had regained a hazy, incoherent memory of the crash. But now vivid details suddenly came surging back. He saw the face of the cute dark haired flight attendant who had given him a kiss on the cheek when he had entered the plane. He saw the young mother with a little baby in her lap sitting across the aisle from him. He saw the inside of the bathroom where he should have died.

He now remembered Tom Martin's face in vivid detail as he stared at the ring he had given Tom for safe keeping.

Seeing Matt in trouble, a Reds' Hall of Fame employee rushed up and said, "Are you okay, sir? Do you need any help?"

"No, thank you," Matt said as he regained his balance with Sonny's help. "I'm okay. It's just that I knew that guy once, and I guess it just sort of got to me seeing all this."

"You knew Dylan Michael?" the museum guide stepped back and asked, "What was he like?"

Matt knew he had slipped. He improvised as best he could. "I just met him a few times. He wasn't really a close friend or anything."

"Well he sure was a great player and a good guy. What a tragedy so many bad things happened to him," the guide said with sincerity.

"Yeah, that was too bad, alright," Matt replied.

"Hey, if you're a Dylan Michael fan, check this out." The guard led Gwen, Sonny and Dylan to an area that would leave Dylan speechless. Inside a specially designed room were life-sized bronze statues paying tribute to many Reds' Hall of Fame members. Matt paused and looked eye to eye with a '6'3" replica of Dylan Michael.

The guard ambled away, and Matt moved among the exhibits reading everything about himself and the team he had been a part of, reliving the past as part participant and part spectator. Sonny threaded his arm through Gwen's and slowed their pace, allowing Matt to wander the Reds' Hall of Fame at his own speed. An hour later, they all walked outside, moved over to the Great American Ballpark and peered through the locked gate. They could see all the way to home plate from their position beyond the left center field fence. Matt clearly remembered standing in that same spot in the cold wind and rain on the day of the crash.

The last waves of excitement over regaining his memory deserted Matt, and he was left with a numbing comprehension of how much he had lost in his life. The realization plunged him into a sadness so profound, it nearly felled him. He'd lost everything and it had all been his own damned fault. As Matt's head dropped to his chest, Gwen took Sonny's hand and gently pulled him aside leaving Matt alone looking into the empty field.

As he stood staring into the Great American Ball Park, two things solidified in Matt's mind. First, he realized that he now remembered everything, all of it. He could recall his past, starting with "The Double" until that day in the jet's bathroom. He remembered his time in Blossom, his recovery, and Cara. He remembered Cara, and the memory staggered him. Second, he silently swore an oath that whatever it took, he would play major league baseball again. He even swore to himself he would play on this very field again, even if it was for only one last at bat.

As he walked back to the hotel with Sonny and Gwen trailing behind, Matt thought about Cara. He wondered if she still lived in Cincinnati? He thought about driving up to Indian Hill and going by their old house to see if she was still there. Then he saw his reflection in a store window and realized that if he knocked on her door he would probably scare her to death in more ways than one. He decided that was one part of his past life he simply had to forget. At least for awhile.

He dreamt of Cara that night.

Last At Bat

26.   Portland

For the first 30 minutes after leaving Cincinnati and heading northwest on I-74 toward Indianapolis, no one said a word. Matt finally broke the spell by asking, "Did anyone notice that the guide looked right at me, standing right next to my statue and didn't recognize me?" Gwen and Sonny had noticed, but that lack of recognition filled them with both relief and sadness.

"You were a lot skinnier back then," offered Sonny.

"You saying I'm fat now?" Teased Matt.

"You ain't fat. It's just your body is a lot different than it was. Not just your face."

Teasing some more Matt said, "You mean I used to be pretty and now…"

"I'm just sayin' you look different that's all. Just sayin' it ain't likely anybody's gonna recognize you since your body and face are different. That's all I'm sayin.'"

"So are yours," said Gwen.

"Sonny, were you pretty, back in the day, too?"

"Damn right," said Sonny. "Still am. That's why Gwennie stays with me. That and my other talents we won't get into in mixed company."

"Oh, my Lord," moaned Gwennie.

By the time they hit Indy, the talk had turned to baseball and the first tryout camp that was still 2,200 miles and five days away. After what Matt had been through over the previous 29 months, it seemed as near as the next exit ramp. They made their way across the country in three days and arrived in Portland two days before the Mariners' tryout camp which was to take place on a high school field on the south end of town. After a good night's sleep, Matt and Sonny got up late, had brunch, and took a slow five-mile walk around the city.

Later that afternoon, about three miles from the hotel in which they were staying, Matt found a batting cage and spent the next hour hitting over 250 pitches in the cage with "Very Fast" stenciled above the door. By the time he was finished, about a dozen skinny high school players, with varying degrees of bad skin were peering into the cage. They'd been drawn by the loud clang of Matt smashing ball after ball with the aluminum bat.

Sonny had seen Matt hit on many occasions, but what he watched that day was different. Matt was focused like never before. His swings, always smooth and powerful, were now almost vicious in intensity. Ball after ball was squared on the bat and flew off it like a laser.

Matt was drenched. His baseball undershirt stuck to his arms and shoulders as sweat ran down his face in streams. He was oblivious to the growing crowd of high school players and coaches who were now surrounding the batting cage watching him in awe. The bright yellow rubber balls were smashed flat against the metal bat by the force of his swings. One ball actually broke apart near the end of the hitting exhibition, leaving his audience dumb struck.

After using up the last of his tokens, Matt searched his pockets for more. Finding none, he turned to Sonny with a look that said, "More, please."

Sonny shook his head and said, "That's enough Matt..."

With that, Matt seemed to wake up and realize over 50 people were clapping and cheering. As he opened the batting cage door, one of the coaches came up and asked, "Who did you play for?"

Matt just smiled as he walked away. "Nobody, yet."

On the drive back to the hotel from the batting cages, Sonny and Matt rode in silence for several minutes. Matt spoke first.

"I remember times in high school and even on the Reds, when I would be at the plate and knew for an absolute fact I was going to hit whatever the pitcher threw," he began. "I knew he had nothing that would get by me. It wasn't ego or anything. I just *knew* I was going to hit the ball on the screws. It must have been that way for Bonds when he was hitting everything out of sight. He must have had that feeling, too. I couldn't really tell that to anyone because it would've sounded like I was bragging. If a pitcher had heard it, he'd have knocked me on my butt. But in my head, I knew it."

Sonny remained quiet and let Matt talk. "I wonder what would have happened if I had felt that way for an entire year?" The rhetorical question hung in the air for the rest of their drive back to the motel.

The second day in Portland dragged out like a kid waiting for Christmas as Matt anticipated the next day's tryout.

"I think I'll head on down to check out the field," he told the Cooks. Matt took the van to the field where tryouts would take place the following morning. He sat alone in the metal bleachers watching the grounds' crew rake and line the field. As he imagined what he was going to do on that field in less than twenty-four hours, his heart began to race.

After a few minutes, he noticed a group of a half dozen men standing behind the backstop in Seattle Mariners' jackets and hats, looking over a clipboard one of them was holding. He thought one of the guys looked familiar and decided to move over to get a closer look.

As he neared the group, he recognized the short guy as Glen Layton, a former left handed pitcher for the Reds. Layton had won a few games from the bullpen for one of his World Championship teams. He looked at Matt, nodded and then went back to his conversation with the other guys. It confirmed Matt's "invisibility" which was something of a doubled edged sword. Not being recognizable would keep him out of prison. But the former "beaten boxer" visage made him appear older than he really was. Thanks to the repeated plastic surgeries, Matt's face was no longer as misshapen as it had been for months after the crash. Instead, he had a Charles Bronson look, and his grown out hair now covered most of the scars above his forehead.

Dylan Michael's face was completely gone, replaced by one that looked ten years older than it actually was, sitting atop a body that was twenty-five pounds heavier than the last time Dylan had set foot in a major league park.

Matt nodded back at Layton and asked, "What time do the tryouts start tomorrow?" He already knew they started at 9:30 a.m.

Without looking up from the clipboard, Layton said, "Have your guys here by 8:30, We actually get started at 9:30, but need to make sure all the American Legion players and high school guys have their written approvals OK'd."

Stopped in his tracks, Matt, said, "What about those of us out of high school and college."

Finally peering over his glasses and looking at Matt, Layton said, "Tomorrow's tryout is for 17-23 year olds only," and went back to his clipboard.

Matt became physically ill. "I am over twenty-three, but I came a long way for this tryout camp and I was not aware there was an age limit."

"Sorry," said Layton, "if we didn't put an age limit on these things we would have several hundred old guys out here taking up our time and..."

"I said I came over 2,000 miles for this tryout and never saw anything on the Internet that there was an age limit," Matt insisted.

The tone in Matt's voice had an edge to it because all six men looked up at him at the same time.

"Again, I am sorry, pal," Layton reiterated, "but we're looking for young men who we can draft in high school and college, and I would say that you are well beyond that stage of your life."

Matt would not give up, saying, "Maybe, but I thought these camps were designed to find guys who could play ball and help the Mariners."

"I think the Mariners will survive."

After several moments of silence Matt said something he could scarcely believe, "I am better than anyone you will see tomorrow."

"I said no exceptions and I mean it," said Layton.

Matt was relentless. "I am better than anyone you will see tomorrow. In fact, I am better than anyone you will see the rest of the year."

"I don't care if you are Babe Fucking Ruth. I said no exceptions. If you show up I'll have security escort your ass off the field."

"That's not necessary. Let me try out right now. Give me 10 minutes of hitting and 10 minutes on the field," Matt pleaded.

"We can't be giving individual tryouts."

"Sure you can, it's done all the time with the top draft picks."

"You sure as hell aren't a top draft pick…" Layton muttered.

"Maybe not, but your last number one pick is still in rookie ball, hitting .221. I know I could do better than that and for a helleva lot less than the $3,100,000 you signed him for. You were the scout that found that 'gem,' right?" Matt said

As Layton wheeled around, one of the other guys, Greg Beck Chief Mariner Scout interjected and said, "Go get your gear. We will give you 10 minutes of hitting and 10 minutes on the field. Take it or leave it."

"Thank you, I will be right back."

Last At Bat

As he jogged back to the van to get his equipment, Matt heard Layton bitching, "what a waste of time."

Beck answered, "We need to stretch out ourselves, anyway. This will be a good work out for us…" and some other words Matt could not make out.

Matt jerked his glove, spikes, and bats from the back of the van. He was pissed. He was pissed he had not noticed the age limitation, pissed he had lost his temper, and pissed he acted like a big shot in front of all those guys. Mostly, he was pissed that Sonny and Gwen wouldn't see his tryout. He was also frustrated that all his plans were being messed up by something he could no longer control. He knew that what he was about to do on the field could change his life.

Matt realized what scouts looked for and knew he had the kind of ability that would get their attention. He also knew that Layton, even though he was acting like an ass, was a good scout and would recognize Matt's talent. He had to. Matt jogged back to the main field and saw several Mariners' assistants scattered across the field playing catch, stretching, scooping up ground balls, and throwing the ball around the diamond.

"10 minutes, agreed?" asked Beck. Matt nodded and said, "Agreed."

One hour and 15 minutes later, they were still on the field. After 20 minutes proving his speed and arm strength, Matt went to the plate. Hitting an endless series of line drives to all fields, Matt eventually lost all 22 baseballs pitched to him by blasting them over the fences. The two longest were breathtaking shots. One landed in a drainage pond 150 feet beyond the left field fence and one landed in woods 125 feet beyond the right field wall. One of line drives had stayed in the ball park, bouncing three inches in front of the shortstop and nearly took his head off. At that point everyone moved into the outfield for safety's sake, and watched the incredible hitting performance from 300 feet away.

Layton, the last of the four guys who pitched to Matt, tried to strike him out. Matt hit everything hard, even balls out of the strike zone. Strangely, the workout ended when Layton simply nodded to Matt and said "okay." At that point Matt felt he had done all he could.

Matt's body was lathered in sweat even though it was only 65 degrees and overcast. He did not realize until the workout was over how tired he was. While he was focused on crushing every pitch and making every throw perfect, fatigue was the furthest thing from his mind. Now, he was not only exhausted, but he also felt like a kid who had whined, finally gotten his way, and then felt foolish about it. The six scouts and their assistants had moved over to the third base dugout and were talking as they sat on the bench, leaving Matt without a clue about what to do next.

Tired of waiting, Matt gathered up his equipment and began walking toward the first base dugout.

"Hey, I thought you wanted to play baseball for the Mariners," yelled Beck as he walked across the pitcher's mound toward Matt.

Matt knew he had performed at a major league quality level and was still pissed at Layton' treatment ninety minutes earlier.

"I said I wanted to play baseball and that I was better than anyone you would see tomorrow. I don't remember saying I wanted to play for the Mariners," Matt said calmly.

"Fair enough. I think we need to start over from the beginning. My name is Greg Beck. I am the chief talent scout for the Mariners and I admit you're right; you are better than anyone we are likely to see tomorrow. I feel pretty confident saying that since I have been doing this for thirty-six years. And what is your name?"

Matt almost said his real name and hesitated. To his ears, it sounded like he was making up a name. "Matt...Wolf."

"Glad to meet you, Matt," Beck offered a handshake. "That was quite a show you put on. Obviously, you have played some ball somewhere. Have you ever signed or been under contract with a major league team organization before?"

Matt's brain froze. He suddenly forgot all the "past" that had been created for him back in Blossom. His hesitation made it seem that either he was dense or trying to hide something. Maybe both. "Not really," was all he could think to say.

"What do you mean 'not really'?" asked Beck. "Either you signed with someone or you didn't. If you did sign and are still under contract to some team or even if you are retired, another organization may have your rights and I can't even talk to you."

Matt was shaken at the sudden turn of events and realized that he was not prepared for these questions. Playing baseball was going to be the easy part of the rest of his life. Lying would not be.

Trying to get a grip on the situation Matt said, "Sorry, I'm not trying to be evasive. I have never signed with anyone. I did play a lot of amateur baseball back in South Carolina but was hurt in a hit and run accident several years ago and have been working out the last two or three years getting back in shape. I came to this tryout camp and will be going to the Padres', Giants', and Dodgers' camps over the next two weeks to see if I can latch on somewhere."

Matt felt like crap because he had just told several lies in the course of 30 seconds. He realized that if he was going to reach his dream of playing major league baseball again, his entire life would be based on lies. Not only would he have to lie, but dozens of other people including Sonny, Gwen, Doc, and the rest of his "Team" from Blossom would be lying for all they were worth, as well.

The plan seemed so simple in Blossom, but in a two hour span, he realized how complicated it would be. Implementing the plan would change him on the inside as much as the plane crash had changed him on the outside. Maybe more.

For the next hour, Matt lied his ass off. What was perplexing and somewhat troubling was how easy it was to do. The more he did it, the more he embellished information. At the end of the question and answer session with the six scouts, he had created a persona and history that he knew he would have to remember in detail. He was certain many of the questions would be asked time and again over the next several months and years.

During the Q and A, Glen Layton had remained quiet. There was something about Matt Wolf that was familiar. His mannerisms rang a bell, but Layton just couldn't put his finger on it. All he knew for sure was that Matt Wolf was one of the most talented all round players he had ever encountered. He wondered how in the hell someone this good could go un-noticed in the computerized video world of professional baseball scouting.

The only thing that really bothered the group of scouts was Matt looked like he was about forty years old, as if he had been "rode hard and put to bed wet" as one scout put it. But his body was different. He was chiseled without a weightlifters bulk. His speed, even with a slight limp, and arm strength were big league caliber as was his switch hitting power. Beck later kidded Layton, "Maybe Matt is the reincarnation of a dead guy: The Mick."

Beck was up front with Matt. "I know talent when I see it. I also know the business of baseball, and we won't get into a bidding war with other clubs to sign you. If you are looking for mega-bucks, it won't come from the Mariners, especially after a try-out camp."

Matt was beginning to like Beck.

"If you could stay in town for two or three days," Beck said, "I would like to bring in a few more of our scouting staff and our General Manager to see you work out again. If that goes well, we would sign you as a free agent if your background check comes up OK. With the Internet we can get those things done very quickly these days. Any skeletons in your closet we should know about?"

"No skeletons," lied Matt, again.

"Good." Beck said. "How about an agent. Is there someone representing you?"

Matt was able to say truthfully, "The folks who raised me are the closest thing to my agents and are the only ones I would trust."

"Do they have experience in these kinds of negotiations? After all, this is the business of baseball and you need someone who can get you the best deal. I work for the Mariners, but I don't want you coming back to me in three years thinking I somehow got you into an unfair deal. That's not how I work." Beck's candor again impressed Matt.

"I appreciate that," said Matt. "But if I decide to sign with the Mariners, I have a pretty good idea what I'm worth. If you are prepared to offer me a contract, I would have to think the Dodgers, Giants, and Padres would also be interested in me. If what you offer is what my folks and I think is fair, there is really no need to go to the other camps and start this process over again. I guess the ball is in your court."

Beck realized that he was not dealing with a star struck teenager who would sign a major league contract for a Clark Bar and a Coke just for the long shot of making it to the big leagues. He wondered again; where had this guy been hiding?

Beck knew the Mariners would do their homework on Matt Wolf just like they did on all draft choices and free agents. If there was something troubling in his past, they would find it. Before he went out on a limb and recommended someone he had seen only once, he wanted to be damn sure the guy was not a convicted felon, drug user, wife beater, or even worse... under contract to the goddamn Dodgers.

27.   Randy

Matt agreed to return to the same field in three days for another workout so long as Beck's office gave a thumbs up to Matt after some background checks. If the checks came up with something they shouldn't, Beck would call Matt and cancel the workout. Assuming the workout came to pass and Matt performed as he had the first time, the Mariners would offer him a free agent contract. If Matt accepted, the Mariners would then decide where Matt would be sent to begin his pro career.

It sounded simple. It never is.

Matt entered Sonny and Gwen's room after his initial impromptu workout and announced: "I have decided to forego all this baseball crap and become a country music singer. In fact, I just came from that country western joint down the street. They invited me to come to their Karaoke Night, and if I sound as good as I told them I was, they're going to offer me a full time position as a singer. Did I ever tell you guys that I play guitar and sing?" Not waiting for an answer he launched into an accapella version of The Eagles' "Tequila Sunrise" complete with 100% recall of the second verse.

A red flush crept onto Sonny's face, and he said, "Matt, if we had known you wanted to sing we could have stayed in Blossom and gotten you some work down at Ellie's Bar and Grille. They have a little band there, and I am sure Ellie would have hired you on the spot."

"Well, it's too late for Ellie. Portland could lead to a shot on American Idol or a recording contract down in Hollywood."

"Son, are you serious about this? What do you mean this baseball 'crap?' he asked with increasing volume. "You have worked your tail off to get to this point, and I think you have a real good chance to get signed by one of these clubs out here. Let's face it, you may not make it all the way back to the major leagues, but you can't give up now..."

Sonny and Gwen were stunned into silence when Matt jumped onto the bed and started hammering a mean air guitar. Soon Matt was doubled over with laughter and finally confessed up to what had transpired that afternoon.

"No, you didn't just tell us that enormous lie," Gwen sputtered and slammed a pillow against Matt's head. Attacking with laughter, they three fought a full-fledged pillow war until Gwen called a truce, and they all went out for pasta, wine and more uproarious laughing.

Over the next two days Sonny and Gwen researched the Internet as if they were the Mariners. They found articles about Matt's baseball exploits, his high school graduation and Dean's List recognition and the story about a hit and run accident that left him nearly dead. There were also a few stories about his trying to make a baseball comeback. There was even an unsmiling picture of Matt taken two years earlier with his missing ear, looking far less robust than he was at that moment in Portland. The look in his eyes in that picture made them all realize how far he had come.

They were satisfied that, at least in print, the "Team" back home had done its job. "Matt Wolf" read like a real live person who had spent his life in Blossom, South Carolina, raised by Gwen and Sonny Cook after his mother had died in child birth and his father had disappeared. They crossed their fingers.

They also looked up the major league baseball drafts over the previous years, researching both free agents and amateur draftees. They were shocked at the money major league teams spent on unproven talent. Especially when, statistically, only three or four percent of drafted players make it to the big leagues. Even fewer become the caliber of star that the huge bonuses appeared to justify.

Most players got as far as Double A, got hurt or realized the competition was just too much for them. That fact gave Sonny and Gwen a real understanding of how great Matt must have been when he was with the Reds.

They also knew the biggest enemy for getting Matt back to the big leagues would be time. Even though he was only 27, he could not afford to waste several years in the low minors, where it was likely any team would want him to start, especially when he had been signed as an unknown from a tryout camp.

Gwen came up with a strategy based on one very big assumption: that the Mariners would indeed want to sign Matt to a contract and would be willing to pay him a significant bonus to do so. If the Mariners didn't feel he was worth the risk or the money, they agreed to jump back into the van and head south.

The plan was a huge risk, but they agreed sensible under the unspoken assumption that they did not need money. They hoped that position would give them the leverage they needed with the Mariners. They decided that all three of them would go to the tryout with their bags packed and the van loaded. If things went well, they could always unpack. If things did not go so well, they would simply head down to Sacramento and see what the Giants thought.

Privately, Sonny and Gwen were not as enthusiastic about Matt's chances of being signed as he was, or, of his getting an offer he would consider fair. And, should he even take the first offer he got? But, given Matt's enthusiasm and confidence, they decided to keep their doubts to themselves and see how it played out.

****

Last At Bat

Unlike the cool, cloudy weather of the tryout three days earlier, warm sunshine bathed the field when the three of them walked from the parking lot onto the practice field by the first base line. The large Mariners' contingent had been there an hour earlier reviewing reports and doing other odds and ends.

There were at least ten men in Mariners' uniforms. There were also a half dozen west coast scouts dressed in team polo shirts. Two more were from the east coast doing a "cross check" evaluation; a common practice when evaluating talent. There were also three members of the Mariners' front office including General Manager, Joe Valle.

Greg Beck extended his hand to Sonny. "Nice to meet you folks," he said, sincerely hoping the day would go well for everyone.

The rest of the Mariners' group made their way to the field with the exception of Valle. He walked alone up several rows behind the backstop and sat down in the bleachers. He opened a binder that had a stop watch at the top of it and several sheets of paper inside.

"This is gonna be a 'flat open' work out, Matt. Get stretched out and loosened up because we want to see you at your best," Beck cautioned.

"Already spent an hour stretching," Matt explained. " Give me a few minutes of throwing and I'll be ready to go."

For 15 minutes Matt shagged fly balls in the outfield and made strong throws to all the bases. Then he was surprised by Beck when he was asked to take ground balls at third base. Did the Mariners see a weakness in his outfield play? Was he too slow? His arm too weak?

At first Matt was unsure of himself at third even though the grounders hit to him were at first easy one and two hoppers. He fielded them well and lobbed them back to one of the scouts who was catching the balls at home plate. As the difficulty of the grounders increased, Matt got to each ball. But, when asked to throw to first, he pulled the first baseman off the bag several times with throws that moved left to right. After he made one more errant throw, a scout whom Matt had not seen at the previous tryout walked down to third base and said quietly, "you're throwing three-quarter arm, which is making your throw sail. Come straight over hand after you do your crow hop and aim for the first baseman's eyes."

That 45 second lesson was all Matt needed to straighten out his throws. As he gained more confidence, he began firing the ball with more speed. Of the 50 or so ground balls hit to him, he misplayed only one. Matt was then asked to run the bases as he was timed from home to first, then home to second. Next he had to "steal" second a half dozen times to see how he read a pitcher and reacted to pick-off moves.

Finally, Matt had to hit. Unlike the previous workout, Matt would be hitting off someone a bit more imposing than a fifty- year-old coach, throwing 65 mph cream puffs. Randy McDonald, former runner up for an American League Cy Young award only three years earlier, was going to be pitching to Matt.

McDonald had undergone Tommy John surgery the year before and had been pitching in Triple A ball for the Mariners Tacoma club on a rehab assignment. He was waiting impatiently for his recall to the big club. At 6'5" and 240 pounds, McDonald threw hard and claimed that his fastball, once clocked at 94 miles per hour, was even faster after his surgery. He also had a cutter, a slider, and a nasty disposition, which he made obvious at being asked to pitch batting practice to some yahoo he never heard of. Everyone, including Matt, knew exactly how he felt.

Beck worried that Matt would be pissed off and intimidated about the change of events, especially since Matt would have to perform against a major league-ready pitcher in front of so many of the Mariners' brass. But, he had little choice. Beck knew it would have been nearly impossible to get this many of the Mariners' staff in one place on such short notice to watch someone he had discovered at a tryout camp, no matter how glowing his report was. So, Layton and Beck came up with a little white lie. They had convinced everyone to secretly come to Portland out of the media's eyes to watch McDonald throw and collectively decide if he was ready to be activated and recalled by the Mariners.

Matt's presence and the "informal" tryout was based on another tall tale. Layton and Beck claimed to have seen Matt play in South Carolina and were doing an old friend a favor by giving Matt another "look see." In any case, they needed someone to hit against McDonald, and Matt was a switch hitter, so they only needed one batter. Since everyone wanted McDonald's work out to be confidential, the fewer involved the better. That was their story. Beck knew this would make it tougher on Matt, but they both needed to know if he was for real.

For the first time in four years Matt was up close and personal with a major league pitcher. As McDonald finished his warm up throws, Matt took practice swings a few feet away from the left hand batter's box. He could hear the sizzle of McDonald's fastballs as they plowed into the catcher's mitt. It was a sound he had forgotten, and he wondered if he had made a very serious mistake. After only a few weeks of playing in an amateur league, swinging bats in a batting cage and hitting off a high school kid, could he seriously face a major league caliber pitcher, especially one trying to prove something to his team?

While McDonald completed his warm-ups, Matt thought about all he had been through. About all the people who had helped him. About Cara. Ready or not, this was his chance.

After getting a nod from McDonald that he was set, Matt stepped into the batter's box and decided to bunt the first few pitches to try and get his timing. After laying down the first pitch a few feet in front of the plate he squared around to bunt another, and found a McDonald fastball coming straight for his chest. Twisting out of the way and landing on his ass, he heard McDonald yell, "Swing the fucking bat, asshole."

Back on his feet, Matt's face turned a deep red. He moved back into the box and glared out at McDonald. Glaring back, McDonald threw his next pitch as Matt suspected, head high. Matt was already out of the batter's box as the ball sailed to the back stop. "Randy, if that's as good as your control is, we have all wasted a lot of time," Beck yelled from the bench.

"My control is perfect. I missed him didn't I?" McDonald yelled back.

Matt swung on and missed the next four pitches. Each one was a fast ball that Matt guessed was in the 95-96 mph range. The fifth pitch was a slider that Matt grounded weakly back to the protection screen in front of the pitcher. That was followed by another slider on the outside corner of the plate. Matt laced it into left field. From that point on Matt did not miss another pitch.

Using a format of 10 pitches per "inning," McDonald was scheduled to throw 90 pitches in a simulated game that included a three minute rest period between each 10 pitch segment. As the innings wore on Matt adjusted to McDonald's speed. He also detected a flaw in McDonald's wind up that let Matt know when he would be throwing his slider or cutter. After the fourth inning, Matt was slamming the breaking pitch nearly every time McDonald threw it. Even hitting right handed against the right hander, Matt was able to line the breaking pitch to right field and pull the fast ball.

As the work- out wore on, it became clear McDonald was becoming frustrated with his inability to get his pitches past Matt. While not every pitch was hit hard, McDonald was not able to make Matt swing and miss. As a result, he began over throwing his fastball, and as he did so, they straightened out. While maintaining their velocity, the pitches became easier to hit and Matt deposited several over the fences in left, center, and right fields.

By the eighth inning it was clear that Matt had figured out McDonald. His swings were gaining in quickness and when he was unable to pull the pitches, he ripped them to the opposite field. In the ninth and final inning, McDonald, now dripping sweat, threw two sliders that Matt crushed far over the 385' mark into a grove of trees beyond the right field wall. When the second one cleared the fence, Matt turned to the catcher, said something and the catcher nodded.

McDonald yelled in to his catcher and asked, "What the fuck is he saying to you?"

The catcher yelled in reply, "He said you're tipping off your slider by how you grip the ball."

Saying nothing, McDonald went back to the rubber and began his delivery to the plate. The fastball came straight at Matt's head, but this time, he was unable to get out of the way. The ball hit him flush on the ear hole of his batting helmet and knocked him flat. Stunned for several seconds, Matt finally rolled over on his back and found himself looking up at the catcher and four of the scouts who had run onto the field to see if Matt was unconscious or maybe dead. Long moments passed before Matt could get to his feet.

"Hey asshole, did I give anything away on that pitch?" McDonald yelled.

Matt calmly replied, "With the crap you're throwing, I could be Stevie Wonder and take your ass deep."

It was hard to say who made the first move. But the work-out ended and morphed into something else somewhere between home plate and the pitcher's mound. Perhaps again telegraphing his intentions, McDonald threw a wild round house right at Matt's head that had the look of a quick knockout punch. But Matt ducked under the swing and threw a powerful left upper cut that landed somewhere between McDonald's stomach and lungs, emptying all the oxygen from McDonald's body in a loud rush.

As McDonald doubled up in pain, gasping for breath, Matt laid the Cy Young runner-up out cold with a right to the left side of McDonald's jaw. It was a punch that many a middle weight would have been proud of.

Too late, several of the scouts grabbed Matt for fear he would do further damage to McDonald. Clearly, the fight was over. McDonald was either unconscious or, finally, just had the good sense to pretend he was. In any case, it was safe to say the work out was officially over.

Looking down at McDonald, Layton asked, "damn, is he dead?"

Beck replied, "nah, he's too mean to die."

Turning to Matt, Layton said," I think you better go."

Matt was already picking up his equipment.

Sonny and Gwen came running over just as Matt crossed the first base bag. "Are you hurt?" cried Gwen.

Before Matt could say no, Sonny said laughing, "Is he hurt? Are you kidding, that's the guy you should be asking," motioning over his shoulder toward the now slowly moving McDonald.

"California here we come," Matt sang as the three South Carolinians headed for the parking lot.

As he closed up the rear door of the van Matt heard someone ask, "Do you always smack pitchers around the field like that?" It was Mariners' General Manager, Joe Valle.

"Only when they try to take my head off with a 95 mph fast ball," Matt laughed.

"Actually, he was throwing 97-98 today, and you hit him like you had done this before. Is that true? Have you faced that kind of pitching before in amateur ball back in South Carolina?" the general manager asked.

Again Matt smiled, "We had some pretty good pitching in that league."

"Not that good, Matt," Valle became serious. "It doesn't add up that you could be this advanced at twenty-seven years old with no information on you in the scouting combine and no one, including seven or eight general manager friends that have never heard of you. I saw on your background check that you played high school ball and tore up the league. Then, eight years go by and there is nothing at all about you until you show up on some amateur team in Greenville and tear up that league."

"I was in an accident and lost several years. I gave up baseball for a long time and decided a couple of years ago to try to play again. Here I am, trying to catch on with a team," Matt repeated his rehearsed story.

"Oh, you'll catch on alright. You are what we call a five tool player, even though those kinds of players seem to fail more often than not. But you've got the kind of talent that's easy to see," Valle freely complimented him.

After several moments Matt said, "Sorry about that thing with McDonald but…"

"Forget about it. He's needed an ass kicking for a long time and I would rather have it happen here than on national TV," Valle interrupted Matt's apology.

"Well, thanks for the opportunity," Matt said, a little more relaxed. "We are heading down to Sacramento to the Giants' tryout camp. I'll see if I can stay out of another fight."

"What's your hurry?" Valle asked.   "I thought you wanted to play for the Mariners?"

Matt countered, "That's the second time someone has said that to me in the last few days. Like I said before, I just want to play. I just want to get a fair deal and to begin playing as soon as I can."

"Matt," Valle said, "I would be willing to offer you a contract to sign with the Mariners for what we paid our fifth overall pick in the amateur draft last year. That was a $475,000 with an annual salary of $42,000. We would start you in our rookie league down in Mesa and take it from there."

Gwen stuck her head out of the van's open window and said, "Your fifth overall pick was a bust. He was a twenty year old left-hand pitcher from Scottsdale Community College. He threw hard but had no control, and you traded him to Milwaukee for a player you have already cut. Your fourth and third picks signed for over $600,000 each and are still in instructional ball. Your second round pick, who you gave $960,000 is a shortstop hitting .238 in Double A. Your first round pick..."

"I know where he is...and what he is hitting, I am reminded every day," Valle scowled. "But that's the nature of the business. Most draft picks don't pan out, though some, like an Oswald or Pujols who were low draft choices become superstars. It is an imperfect science to be sure."

Gwen was now out of the van. She gently looped her arm through Valle's and walked with him in the now deserted parking lot. Sonny and Matt watched as Gwen did most of the talking and Valle nodded from time to time, saying little. They wandered aimlessly around the parking lot for nearly twenty minutes with Gwen's right arm inside Valle's left. Finally, they stopped walking. Gwen was looking up at Valle, and both of them then looked back at Matt. They then both turned and walked back to the van.

"Matt, Mr. Valle and I have come up with a plan that is a little different and may not be something you want to accept. If you don't, we can all get back into the van and head down to California and that's that. But if you like what we are going to propose to you, then Mr. Valle will have a contract prepared today and faxed from his office to our hotel. You can be part of the Seattle Mariners by dinner time tonight. Here's the deal," Gwen explained.

The plan was designed to save the Mariners some up-front money but also move Matt quickly through the Mariners system. Matt would be trading money; getting only a $200,000 signing bonus instead of the $475,000 offered. In exchange, he would be added to the Mariners' 40 man roster immediately and sent to Triple A rather than rookie ball. The risk for Matt was simply financial. If he bombed in Triple A, he would be cut and lose $275,000. But by playing at Triple A in Tacoma he would be only one step from the major leagues. With the year the Mariners were having, he could be called up by the end of the year if he played well.

The Mariners were at risk from an organizational perspective. If they added Matt and McDonald, who was scheduled to come off the disabled list in a week, they would then have to take two players off their current 40 man roster. The deal was also predicated on the proviso that Matt would remain on the Mariners roster for two full seasons or on the 40 man roster of any team he would be traded to. That meant the Mariners had to keep Matt around for two years and had to release or trade two major league ready players, but they saved nearly $275,000. While chump change in the baseball world, it was meaningful none the less. The plan had risks for both parties but only if Matt failed.

In less than two minutes after hearing the proposed deal, Matt and Valle both agreed it was worth the risk and shook hands. By 6:30 that evening Matt was a Seattle Mariner and had three days to report to the Mariners' Triple A affiliate in Tacoma. It had all happened so suddenly that Sonny, Matt, and Gwen sat in stunned silence for almost the entire ride back to the hotel. Finally it was Sonny who quietly said, "I knew you could do it."

"Not alone, I couldn't have," was Matt's quiet but emotional reply.

Last At Bat

28.   Two Grands

After showering, Matt called the front desk and asked if they could recommend a good restaurant nearby.

"Well, if you like steak and some good music there is a place called *Two Grands* about 15 minutes away," the young man replied. "The food is good and it can be a fun place."

"A good steak, fun, and music sounds just about right," Matt said.

Minutes after entering the restaurant Matt, Sonny, and Gwen realized they'd been given good advice about *Two Grands*. The place was busy, but they were seated after only a few minutes wait by a friendly young hostess. Waiters and waitresses dressed in tuxedos carried tray after tray of thick, juicy t-bones, prime ribs, and sirloins, accompanied by generous portions of baked potatoes, onion rings, fresh tossed salads, warm dinner rolls and red wines retrieved from a wine cellar. From the other side of the building, a singer could be heard from far enough away so as not to interfere with dinner. In short, it was just about spot on perfect.

Matt was suddenly famished as he scanned the menu. He ordered a 16 ounce medium rare porterhouse with three or four side dishes and a glass of Merlot. Waiting for the dinner to arrive, he felt a sense of calm and contentment he had not felt in years. Sonny and Gwen were also quietly pleased though they did allow smiles of satisfaction to flash between each other from time to time.

After dinner, awaiting a single piece of fresh apple pie ala mode the three of them had decided to share, Matt pulled out a copy of the contract he had signed only two hours before. He silently re-read the legalese with the Mariners' logo at the top of each page. Individually, none of them had believed it would work, but didn't want to voice their doubts to the other two. But, now, Gwen smiled when Sonny winked from across the table; their farfetched, outrageous, unlikely plan had actually worked.

But the day's overwhelming success was also laced with a sad bit of reality. Matt was being sent to Tacoma, Washington, about as far away from Blossom, South Carolina, as you could get and still stay in the country. He was soon going to be on his own for the first time in two and a half years. Gwen and Sonny would leave and head back east. It was a reality they all recognized, but at least for this night, no one mentioned.

29.   "The Great One"

Sitting at his LA Times desk at 10: 40 PM, gnawing on a ham sandwich after a long day, Arthur Robbins got a call from Nat Baker, an old friend of his who worked in the Seattle Mariners' organization.

"This is Robbins."

"So, what did you think?" asked Baker who had days before invited Robbins to the "secret" simulated game in Portland that took place earlier in the day.

"I think the asshole can still pitch, but he is still an asshole," opined Robbins.

"So, are you going to do a story?" Baker asked.

"Why should I?" Robbins replied.

"Because the world is waiting with bated breath to see if Randy McDonald, former Cy Young runner-up, can come back from Tommy John surgery and lead his team to victory. God, I'm getting a chubby just thinking about it."

"So what you are really saying is if I write a story about how amazing the "Great One" looked today, you guys might sell a shit load more tickets."

"Arthur, I am deeply hurt. How could you say such a thing?"

"Because I've known you for twenty five years and you are a mercenary little shit who invited me to go all the way to Portland to write a story about the biggest prick in baseball just so you can sell a few thousand tickets," Robbins suggested.

"So?" asked Baker.

"I wrote your fucking story. By the way, who was that middle-aged guy who ripped McDonald all over the field then kicked his ass?" Robbins continued.

"Damned if I know, but Valle signed him right after the workout."

"You mean he wasn't in the Mariner's organization before today?"

"Nope," said Baker. "Son of a bitch just showed up looking for a tryout camp. McDonald was throwing the shit out of the ball today, and that guy hit him like he was A-Rod. Bastard can hit," Baker said.

"Where did they send him?" Robbins asked.

"Tacoma."

"Triple A? Now?"

"Yep. Valle thinks he can help. Only thing was the guy looked like he was about forty. Bastard could hit though."

"Yeah, that bastard could hit", agreed Robbins. "With the way he decked McDonald maybe he was a boxer at one time. Enjoy the article and get me laid next time I'm in Portland."

"I couldn't get you laid with a gold card in a cat house. Those ladies have too much class for you."

"Good night, asshole."

"Good night, prick."

Putting down the phone, Robbins looked at the pictures he'd taken of McDonald earlier in the day. In several, Matt Wolf could be seen.

Muttering to himself Robbins said, "He does look like he's forty. Bastard can hit though."

Los Angeles Times - April 16

Randy McDonald can be a "pain in the ass," says a former teammate. Others say they don't know him all that well even after playing with or against him for years. Other descriptions include "unfriendly," "aloof," "a loner." But no one says the big man can't still pitch.

To confirm that fact, I went to Portland yesterday to see for myself if the former Cy Young runner up and two time 20 game winner had returned to his All Star form from three years ago.

As far as baseball is concerned, the big right hander was throwing his fast ball 97. His slider, though a little flat, was nasty. His split broke a foot. And perhaps most importantly he looked like a grizzly bear with a tooth ache on the mound.

In short, it looks like McDonald will soon be headed back to the Mariners even though he will not likely help that moribund team, at least not this year. But he could make life miserable for some American League West teams he will face the rest of the year.

Randy McDonald is an enigma in baseball. Talented to be sure, but based on the previous descriptions, for lack of a better term he is, well, "different." He once told me that he had no friends in baseball which was quite a statement from a guy who virtually lives with 35 other players and coaches eight months a year.

I have interviewed McDonald a few times and it is clear he is very intelligent, soft spoken, and even polite in a distant sort of way. And unlike most baseball players, he reads, witnessed by the fact there are always several New York Times best sellers in his locker. I know he went to Princeton on an academic scholarship so it is fair to say that he is no dope. It was widely reported he got kicked out of school his junior year for getting into a fist fight with his catcher on the bench over pitch selection. He would never confirm or deny that accusation.

Rumor had it that McDonald was throwing better than ever and my trip confirmed that rumor. Mariners GM Joe Valle, when asked if McDonald would return soon said, "If Randy feels good after today's simulated game, we will probably send him out for one rehab start. He could be ready as early as next week to start against the A's in Oakland."

While that is good news for Mariners' fans, there was another story that came out of my trip to Portland. The young man McDonald was pitching to in a simulated game also looked like he was ready to help the Mariners. A switch hitting infielder named Matthew Wolf was discovered at a Mariners' tryout camp earlier in the week and looked impressive facing McDonald. Of note was Wolf's impressive bat *speed, reminiscent of Carlos Beltran, Griffey Jr., Dylan Michael, or Albert Pujols. On the other hand, if young Mr. Wolf can't cut it in the big leagues he might make it as a professional boxer --the rest of that story some other time.*

Arthur Robbins.

30.   *Anything you can do...*

After finishing the warm pie and melting ice cream, Matt leaned back in the soft leather booth, listening to the music and singing coming from the upstairs bar. He was relaxed and mellow after a second glass of Merlot. Despite a sore, swollen right hand compliments of McDonald's hard jaw and two semi–aching legs caused by bending over to pick up scores of ground balls, Matt concluded that he felt pretty much right with the world. The fatigue and soreness felt good, even familiar. It had been a long time since he was a tuned professional athlete, and he tried to remember if he had felt this way when he had played with the Reds. In the back of his mind, he knew what he was feeling now was much more acute than the normal fatigue and pains he used to feel.

His body was not only four years older, now, it had also been beat to hell in the accident. He wondered how long it would hold up in a world of eighteen to twenty-five year olds who were strong, in shape, determined, and did not have x-rays that showed a bunch of broken bones. And, why had the Mariners worked him out at third base so long? Did they see something in his outfield play they did not like or were they just curious how he would field ground balls? He decided he would just show them he could play the outfield when the time came and not worry about it now. He also began thinking about Cara. Again.

His thoughts were interrupted when Sonny, obviously neither sore nor tired said, "Let's go upstairs and listen to some music. Hell, the night is young and we need to celebrate a little bit."

"Sonny's right," Gwen concurred. "C'mon, Matt, let's go up and sing some songs."

Matt would have rather returned to the hotel and gone to sleep. But, he did not want to disappoint Sonny and Gwen so he faked it and said, "Damn right, let's go celebrate a little bit."

As they made their way up the narrow staircase to the upstairs bar, the music became louder, and the off-key singing a bit more noticeable. Reaching the top step, they saw a huge circular bar with two grand pianos facing each other. Next to the pianos were a bass player, drummer, and guitarist. They were at the ready to back up any pianists who wanted to take a seat at one of the grand pianos or who wanted a chance to sing just by picking up one of the many microphones that were strewn around the elevated stage.

Gwen, Sonny, and Matt sat down at the nearest table. They ordered a pitcher of Bud and listened to Portland's uninhibited citizenry try their luck at piano playing and singing greatness. From where they were sitting, the group from Blossom could only see part of the stage. They could hear, but not see the performers. Though none of the Portlanders were totally awful, it was clear these folks should not consider leaving their day jobs.

After forty - five minutes, the three from Blossom called for their check. They had pushed back their chairs to leave when a very solid rendition of Chuck Berry's *Nadine,* with its signature bass line and lead piano part, caught Matt's attention. The voice was strong, on key, and had just the right amount of "down home" that old Chuck may have actually approved. *Nadine* was then followed by an even better *Georgia* and then topped off with another Ray Charles hit, *Unchain My Heart.* It was sung in a Joe Cocker kind of voice which had the bar patrons dancing and singing at the top of their lungs.

"Damn, whoever is singing and playing now, is good," said Sonny.

"Let's go take a look on our way out," said Matt as they all made their way around to the other side of the bar. As they moved into position to see the second piano, they stopped dead in their tracks. Randy McDonald was at the piano. He was wearing his Mariners' baseball cap and holding a glass of beer. A shapely red head sat next to him on the piano bench, and a blonde stood behind him with her arm around his neck.

"Oh, my God," said Gwen, tugging Matt's sleeve, "I think we should leave now."

But Matt had already made eye contact with McDonald and was not too thrilled at what he saw. An ugly red and blue welt ran down the left side of McDonald's jaw line. Pronounced swelling made it look like Randy had recently spent time in a dentist's chair. When he saw the look on McDonald's face, it appeared the afternoon's boxing event may have been only Round 1.

Despite McDonald's baleful glare, Matt held the eye contact, reasoning that if he backed down now, there would surely be more trouble to follow. Without looking away from McDonald, he said, "Sonny, Gwen you guys go on downstairs, and I'll join you in a few minutes."

McDonald also held the stare as he shrugged off the blonde and the redhead, emptied a nearly full bottle of Heineken and began playing Joe Cocker's *You are so Beautiful.*

At first, Matt paid no attention to the tune. But then, he saw Randy get a bemused look on his face as he sang the romantic lyrics . Suddenly Matt heard the words, got the joke and both men broke out in wide grins.

Matt joined the rest of the crowd in giving Randy a round of applause. He then jumped on the stage and took a seat at the other piano. He cracked his knuckles and launched into a better than average *Piano Man* by Billy Joel. Randy answered with Jerry Lee

Lewis' *Great Balls of Fire* only to be countered by Matt with *Benny and the Jets* by Elton John. Randy retaliated with a knocked out rendition of Little Richard's *Lucille.* The musical battle went on for several more songs, getting the beer filled crowd on its feet yelling, "More. More!"

After chugging another Heineken, Randy winked at Matt and began playing Chopin's Nocturne Opus 22 in F. At first, the noisy crowd did not hear the soft melody. Then as the notes filtered through the bar, people stopped talking, waitresses stopped waitressing, and everyone listened. The incongruity of the large, unshaven, beer guzzling, bruised pitcher playing such a beautiful piece of art moved even the normally loud drunks into silence. Matt was also taken by Randy's mastery of the piece and the emotion with which he played it.

After a surprisingly civilized round of applause for Randy's effort, the crowd looked at Matt to see what his rejoinder would be. At first he appeared stumped. He started to play, then stopped and appeared to change his mind. After a dramatic pause, he played a nine minute version of *Rhapsody in Blue.* While not perfect, it was very good. The audience cheered. Randy bowed his approval. Sonny and Gwen were stunned at what they witnessed when they returned to the bar after hearing the cheering crowds and music.

As the applause died down, Randy walked over to Matt's piano, stuck out a huge hand, shook Matt's and asked, "Want to get a drink?"

"Sure," Matt said with a smile. He introduced Randy to Gwen and Sonny and the four of them sat down at a quiet table and ordered some more beer.

"Good job up there," said Randy, "maybe we should forget all this baseball stuff, hit the road and play music the rest of our lives."

"Funny you should mention that, I recently had that exact thought myself," laughed Matt as he looked at Sonny and Gwen.

Mark Donahue

Randy moved the conversation to baseball saying, "You hit the hell out of the ball out there today. My stuff wasn't great, but you know what you're doing up there."

Matt looked directly at Randy and replied, "Thanks. If that's not your best stuff , then I would not want to see you when you're back 100 percent."

As the ball players talked, Gwen's eyes were wide with shock. She could not understand how two guys who, only hours before, were trying to put each other into Intensive Care were now having a drink and acting like nothing had happened. She also was taken by just how big Randy McDonald was. He had huge hands, and his arms and shoulders looked more like a professional football player's. His neck was half again as big as Matt's, who looked almost slender next to the right hander.

Soon, all four of them were talking and laughing about everything except baseball, including politics, movies, favorite TV shows, music, books, and cooking. Sonny, Gwen, and Matt were surprised to hear that Randy had attended Princeton University on an academic scholarship for two years before going pro. His wit and knowledge stood in stark contrast to the image he had portrayed on the mound only hours before. Matt almost slipped and told Randy of his college days at Stanford, but that was not part of *his* past. That was part of Dylan Michael's past and Dylan Michael was dead.

Over the next two hours, the four people in the booth became friends. No one mentioned the incident on the field. At the end of the evening, Randy reached out, shook Matt's hand again and said, "Well, I don't think it will be all that long until you are up with the Mariners. They told me today that I would be added to the big club's roster by tomorrow. They said they signed you and were sending you to Tacoma."

185

Matt leaned back as he replied, "It happened very quickly, but I think this is a good situation for me. I hope you're right. It would be great to be playing in Safeco Park someday."

Randy nodded and said, "No question about that. The only questions are: How old are you and how in the hell could thirty ball clubs with hundreds of scouts and bird dogs miss you?" Relying on the story he had told Valle and Beck, Matt retold his "past" one more time. He was getting pretty good at it.

As Matt waited for the valet to retrieve the van, Randy stood next to him, waiting for a cab. Looking up at Randy, Matt wondered what the hell he had been thinking when he decided to fight this guy. He was glad he was now a friend so when the next fight started, they would be on the same side.

31.   Tacoma

Over the next two days, Matt, Sonny, and Gwen played tourists and drove around the beautiful Oregon countryside and shoreline. No one mentioned that they would be saying goodbye in three days. It was something none of them wanted to face.

That second night Gwen and Sonny got on-line and confirmed that Matt's signing bonus of $200,000, minus state and federal taxes, was in a bank in Tacoma where they had opened an on-line checking account.

With the help of a local Tacoma realtor, Matt also found an apartment that was fully furnished and ready to go. He even got a two year lease approved for a Ford pickup from a dealer that would be ready and waiting for him when he arrived in Tacoma.

Sonny and Gwen decided they would drive Matt up to Tacoma and then begin their long drive back east. They had toyed with the idea of heading down to California, but admitted they were actually a little homesick for Blossom and were anxious to head back home.

On the drive to Tacoma everyone was strangely quiet. Aside from the three-day softball tournament in Greenville, the three of them had been together every day for nearly two and a half years. They had become a family by accident, not by design or birth. They loved each other although no one had ever used that word.

Gwen was particularly quiet and clearly upset, knowing they would not be seeing each other for several months. Each mile closer to Tacoma, she seemed more depressed. Sonny could sense Gwen's feelings and was wrestling with his own emotions. He did not want to bring Matt down by saying the wrong thing, so he told jokes for most of the trip.

Matt was flat out depressed. Had he done the right thing by coming all the way to the west coast and leaving behind a new life that had given him so much over the last two and a half years? Blossom had given him everything. Almost. He knew what was left to get was up to him. He would need all the physical skill and determination he could muster to make it happen. He wondered if he could do it alone.

Finally he said kind of off handedly, "You know, you guys could get a little apartment out here for the rest of the summer. You could do some sightseeing when I'm on the road and then we could all drive back to Blossom in the fall." After 15 seconds of silence, Sonny and Gwen said simultaneously, "okay."

****

The Tacoma Rainiers were at the top of the food chain in terms of minor league baseball – beautiful ballpark, great climate, and forgiving fans. They were part of a first class baseball organization that had its share of great players, great moments, great teams, and a beautiful new big league stadium in Seattle, but no World Championships.

Seattle was not like some of the big city teams in Los Angeles, Boston, New York and Chicago ("any team can have a bad century") with a press corps that liked to beat the crap out of their teams and players when they did not win. Seattle was different. It supported its Mariners when they were good or bad. Fans loved the players and made them local heroes. Despite the travel Mariners' teams faced each year being so far removed geographically from the rest of major league baseball, it was a great place to play and live.

Mark Donahue

The attitude of the big league club permeated throughout the organization including its Triple A affiliate in Tacoma. Matt arrived in Tacoma on Sunday night and immediately went to the ball park. It was locked up tight since the Rainiers were on a road trip to Phoenix, but Matt did not care. He wanted to see where he would be playing the next two years.

Walking around the outside of the stadium he could not believe what had happened to him over the last week or, for that matter, over the last four years. It seemed like a dream, but he knew it was real and that everything he wanted to accomplish could start to happen inside the structure he was now walking around.

The next day he got a call from Greg Beck who asked that Matt meet him at the Tacoma Stadium so Beck could introduce him to the Rainiers' manager and team. He wanted to be there because the situation with Matt was, to say the least, unique, and it would be clear that he had replaced someone on that team's roster who was now likely going to be out of baseball.

Mike Mercer was the forty-nine- year- old manager of the Rainiers who knew he was only one step, or one eight game losing streak by the Mariners, away from becoming a big league manager. He had spent 14 years in the big leagues as a good-field, no-hit shortstop who had the well earned reputation of a firebrand competitor. He always played with football intensity and pissed off a lot of people with his habit of sliding hard and not trying to be friends with his opponents on or off the field.

He wanted to win no matter what the cost and saw his players as tools to achieve a goal. He felt his job was to meld players' talents for the good of the team and organization and if the player did not like that, "too bad, go play somewhere else." That attitude did not necessarily endear him to his players, but it achieved results. The Rainiers had been first or second place finishers for the three years

Mercer had managed, despite the fact that Seattle had taken many of his players up to the big club in an effort to get the Mariners in position to compete in the American League West.

"Mike, this is Matt Wolf. He's the player we just signed that I told you about last night," Beck said, introducing Matt.

Shaking hands with Matt, Mercer got right to the point. "Hi Matt, glad you're here. Hear you got a quick bat. What do you play, and where have you hit in the lineup in the past?"

"I have played all the outfield spots and have hit third, fourth, and fifth," Matt answered.

"Well, we got outstanding hitters at three, four, and five, and I don't need another outfielder. What I need is a first baseman. Ever play first?" Mercer needed to know.

"No," Matt said.

"Okay then," the manager said, ignoring Matt's reply. "You will be starting at first tonight, and we'll see how you do. If you stink up the joint, I guess you will have to sit because the only way you crack our outfield is if this guy brings up someone in the next week which I doubt will happen," he said, pointing to Beck.

Matt nodded and said, "Can somebody get me a first baseman's mitt?"

There is a strange Twilight Zone phenomenon that occurs in baseball that the average fan does not realize. It has to do with the fact that wherever you place your weakest defensive player, the baseball will seek out this poor unfortunate bastard and beat the living shit out of him. In most cases the baseball, with a seeming mind of its own, will wait until just the right moment in a game and head straight for the player least likely to field it cleanly.

In Matt's case the leadoff batter of his first game bunted down the first base line. Matt fielded the ball and then proceeded to throw the ball past the covering second baseman down the right field line for an error. The next batter also bunted toward first and Matt again fielded the ball cleanly but then threw in the general area code of second base. The ball ended up in left center field, and the runners moved up to second and third. The number three hitter grounded the ball to first. It hit off the heel of Matt's glove and then ricocheted off his chin and chest. He recovered in time to get the hitter, but the runner from third scored. Matt, glad to have finally gotten an out, lost track of the runner coming from second to third base. When that runner kept coming all the way home, Matt saw him too late, rushed his throw, and it ended up six feet wide of the catcher as the second run scored.

The left handed clean- up hitter then hit a screaming line drive right at Matt's belly button that he somehow clumsily stabbed even though his glove got contorted and in the wrong position. Finally, the right hand hitting fifth batter went the opposite way and hit a sharp one hopper that Matt took off his right knee. The ball then plowed into his protective cup producing a loud "thunk" that could be heard in the upper deck, before it fell to his feet and he was able to crawl to the bag on all fours to get the final out.

When Matt got back to the dugout, none of his new teammates said a word or even looked at him. They were in keeping with an age old tradition of never talking to a player on the bench when he is throwing a no hitter or has done something so remarkably awful on the field that there is a chance he will kill himself with the sharp jagged piece of a broken bat. After a few minutes Matt broke the silence when he calmly said, "Gee, playing first base is a lot easier than I thought." The guys on the bench broke up, and from that moment, Matt Wolf was one of the most popular players on the Tacoma Rainiers.

Matt's popularity was based on a number of unrelated things. He had a low key, droll sense of humor that kept everyone loose on the bench. He seemed to know how to talk to umpires and interfaced well with the press and even the Rainers' hyper manager. And, as someone clearly older than most of the players on the team, his suggestions were respected.

Mostly, he was popular because he could play. After that first game debacle, he worked tirelessly at playing first base. He became a better than average fielder, adept at scooping up bad throws from the Rainiers' cannon- armed shortstop and third baseman. He harnessed his own strong arm and became adroit at the 3 to 6 to 3 double play. He also had three assists acting as the cutoff man on throws from right field to home. He made several good plays on pop ups to short right field that most first basemen would not have caught.

Offensively, Matt got off to a good start average-wise and was hitting nearly .400 after his first 10 games. The only negative being Matt was not hitting for power having only two doubles and one windblown home run in over 40 official at bats. He was happy with his average and the fact he had driven in some key runs for his team. But, he knew that if he was going to get a serious look from the Mariners, he would have to put up some power numbers especially playing the power position of first base.

While things were going well on the field and in the clubhouse, the local Tacoma fans and media became increasingly curious about the older guy with the worn face and quick bat. Soon a "Wolf Pack" fan club sprang up, and Matt was beginning to get requests for interviews from the local media. He was well liked by the fans and media because he was humble, self deprecating, and had a good sense of humor when asked questions about his early success. But when asked about his past, he tried to be as evasive as possible. The vague stories Matt told of his past would have probably worked well for the rest of the season except for some bad luck. Matt caught fire at the plate.

Mark Donahue

The power shortage he had experienced suddenly turned around during a double header in Las Vegas. He went to the plate 11 times over the two games and picked up eight hits including one home run in the first game and three in the second. The third home run in that second game was a mammoth shot estimated at nearly 445', well over the scoreboard in left center. Even with Vegas' thin, warm air, it was a home run that was talked about for weeks throughout the league.

At that point, Matt was moved up to the third spot in the batting order, and an already potent Rainiers' offense began a frontal assault on Pacific Coast League pitchers. The team, only two games out of first place when Matt joined them, put together a streak of 22 wins out of 24 games and moved into first place by six games.

After 54 games with the Rainiers, Matt had 209 official plate appearances, collecting 78 hits for a .373 batting average. He had 15 doubles, 4 triples, 12 home runs, and had driven in 55 runs including five game winners. As his production soared, so did his popularity. He was getting noticed by regional and even national media when a story appeared in *ESPN Magazine* about "Future Stars" in the minor leagues. The blurb about Matt noted that "he seemed to come out of nowhere to dominate the highest minor league level." A writer for one of the local papers said Matt made baseball "look easy" in a feature article about his quick start in Tacoma. It wasn't easy.

Matt told no one, including Gwen and Sonny, that his body was beginning to rebel from the daily grind of games without a day's rest. His legs hurt and he was glad he was at first base and not forced to play the outfield. That would have clearly pointed out that he was losing his speed. The way his legs were feeling, it would have been difficult to play in the outfield and that would hurt his chances to be called up to the Mariners. He wondered more than once if that had been obvious at the work outs with the Mariners in Portland two months earlier and that was why he was now at first base.

Last At Bat

His left arm ached almost daily, and his feet, particularly his heels, which never hurt before, now suddenly required daily ice treatments and padded spikes. The only thing that did not hurt was his back. That irony actually made him laugh, shake his head and wonder if this was God's idea of a joke.

While the aches and pains were bearable, they pointed out to Matt the one thing he did not have on his side was time. He knew his body would not suddenly feel better over the next several weeks and months and realized, in all probability, it would get worse. He had to do everything he could to get back to the "show" as soon as possible. He also knew all too well that he was one injury away from not making it at all, given the normal wear and tear of a long baseball season. His body had been beaten to hell and could fail him at any time.

Life away from the diamond was made much more bearable since Sonny and Gwen had rented a furnished apartment in the same complex as Matt's for the summer. They saw each other almost every day he was not on the road, and it helped having home cooked meals and the company of two people who he viewed as family. The feeling was mutual.

Matt often cranked up his laptop and continued to delve into his past. He would read old articles from games years earlier. He also found a Web site where he could hear radio replays of games and see videos. It was like watching someone else. Someone he did not know.

He also spent endless hours looking at pictures and reading stories about Cara, which became increasingly more painful as time went on. He found pictures of their wedding, of her in beauty pageants, and he would be depressed for days afterward. Though he considered that part of his life as over, he would still sometimes log on to look at those pictures and accept the pain he knew was to follow.

Matt also kept close watch on what the Mariners were doing, and they weren't doing much. They started slowly at the beginning of the year and were never able to get back to .500 baseball. They were in last place in the four team Western Division of the American League. By contrast, the Rainiers were beginning to run away from the rest of their league and had an eight game lead moving into the second week in July.

Sitting in his office with his feet on his desk, Mike Mercer was on speaker phone participating in the monthly organizational meeting with Mariner staff. A voice asked, "How's Wolf doing?"

"He can flat out hit," said Mercer. "He's also improved a lot at first. He's got a gun for an arm. Not sure he is fast enough for the outfield. Looks like he has lost a step since we signed him. Maybe he's sore. Good guy in the clubhouse. He's got a little leadership in him. Good baseball I.Q. I like him because he keeps his mouth shut and plays. And like I said, that son of a bitch can hit. Just not sure what we do with him the way that first baseman we signed last year is hitting in Double A."

With all minor leaguers, hope springs eternal that a call up to the big leagues is only a phone call away and with it, instant fame and glory. In reality, there are few call ups and even less fame and glory. A man can toil eight years in the minor leagues, ride several hundred thousand miles on busses, eat crap food from endless truck stops, play under yellow lights on bumpy fields and then finally the phone rings, and he is summoned to the big league parent. The player then goes 1 for 12 from the plate with one start and eight pinch hitting appearances and he is either sent back to the minors, never to return, or released outright.

The cruelty of such a system was something Matt had not fully appreciated when he was with the Reds' organization. He had been a star at every level he played. Even his early appearances with the

Reds, when everyone said he was too young to stick with the club, were successful. Matt hadn't spent very long in the minors and never realized how tough it is to play seemingly unnoticed for years waiting for the phone to ring.

This time around things were very different. He was much older. At twenty-seven, young in nearly every other career, he was well past the "phenom" stage. Matt presumed the Mariners' organization would project him as a quality hitter at the big league level, but they might question his speed and defensive range. They could be right, he thought. Or they might think he would only be of value as a designated hitter.

Tacoma manager Mike Mercer had grown fond of Matt, mainly because Matt kept his mouth shut, hustled his ass off, and was third in the Pacific Coast League, hitting .358 for the season. Mercer also liked Matt because he was a pro. Even though he had been with the team less than half the season, it was as if he had been in professional baseball for years.

Mercer had heard Matt's story dozens of times and was glad things were working out for him on the field. Had Matt not performed, no matter how sad his tale, Mercer would have gone to the general manger and had him released. Mercer's main concern was performance, and Matt performed.

Two hours before game time, Matt sat in front of his locker reading the newspaper. Two of his younger teammates walked up with some news.

"Hear what happened?" asked the catcher.

"No. What happened?" said Matt, looking up from the business section.

"The Mariners just fired their manager, and Mercer has been named to replace him," announced the shortstop. "We're bettin' the way you've been hitting, and the fact that Mercer loves your ass, you're gonna get called up to Seattle."

As he put down the newspaper, a voice called out.

"Hey Matt, can I see you a minute in my office?" asked Mercer.

Matt's teammates smiled and high-fived him as he walked toward Mercer's office.

Matt's mind raced. In the minute since first hearing the news, he concluded it was his good fortune that Mercer had been named manager of the Mariners. He had put together a good year playing for Tacoma and knew that Mercer respected his work ethic, professionalism, and production. Matt felt good about his chances to end the season on the big league ball club as he walked into the manager's nearly empty office.

Seeing Mercer's packed bags on the floor, Matt felt a sense of anticipation he had not felt since the day he had signed his first contract with the Reds. A nervous excitement took over his body, and whatever soreness he had that lingered from a nine day road trip, suddenly vanished.

"Matt, great job this year," Mercer began. "You played the shit out of first base and hit like a sonvobitch. We just traded you to Cincinnati for two Double A pitchers. We need some young arms to build around, and the Reds are in a pennant race and need a pinch hitter and backup first baseman. Good luck." With that, Mercer picked up his bags and left Matt standing in front of his desk too stunned to move.

Last At Bat

32.   Cincinnati

In less than thirty seconds in Mercer's office, the long held dream to get back to the big leagues had been made a reality. Yet its suddenness was a shock to Sonny and Gwen as much as it was to Matt. They had heard of the trade on *Sports Center* before Matt came home and were elated, stunned, and ultimately a bit concerned about what this all meant. Obviously, the main concern was that he would be returning to the Reds, of all teams. This move could lead to him being recognized by an organization and by fans that had known him so well.

Led by great starting pitching and solid defense, the Reds were only three games out of first place going into the next to last week of July. They would have had a lead in the division if they had even a middle-of-the-road offense. They were second from the bottom in runs scored in the National League and last in home runs. They manufactured runs, and their pitching had kept them in games throughout the season even though they had been shut out a league-high nine times already.

They needed offense and had scoured the major and minor league rosters to help bolster their run production. One of their newest scouts, Glen Layton, over from the Mariners' organization, had recommended they take a chance on Matt. He told the Reds he had seen Matt work out and followed his year with Tacoma. Layton felt he might be able to make an offensive contribution.

To get another opinion, Layton suggested the Reds ask Arthur Robbins, the *L.A. Times* baseball writer, who had seen the same tryout where Layton had first seen Matt. Robbins agreed with Layton by saying, "The bastard can hit."

The trade was made even though Reds' management did not like the contract contingency of adding Matt to their forty man roster for the rest of the current year and the following year. But, being in a pennant race going into late July meant it was no time to play it safe. The Reds decided that Matt would take an early morning flight to Cincinnati and join the team on their current home stand against Houston. Sonny and Gwen would ship Matt's pick up to Cincinnati, pack up all of their and Matt's stuff and drive back to the Queen City in the next four or five days. They would rendezvous in Cincinnati in ten days after the Reds returned from a six game road trip to Pittsburgh and Chicago.

****

Matt gripped the arm rests of the 757 so tightly, his white knuckles could be seen by the flight attendant. "First flight, sir?" she asked quietly.

"No. Just a little nervous that's all."

"Can I bring you anything?"

"No, I am fine. Are we still on schedule?"

"Yes sir. We should arrive in Cincinnati around 3:30."

"Thanks."

Matt was afraid. He had flown on several trips with the Rainiers and was actually surprised at not being afraid before. But this time he was afraid of fate − afraid that he was this close to his dream and somehow it was going to be taken away by having his plane fly directly into the Rocky Mountains. It didn't. For most of the long flight Matt couldn't avoid thinking of Cara. He wondered what she was doing that very second. A more depressing thought was who she was with that very second. He tried not to dwell on the second thought.

The plane landed in Cincinnati's International airport, situated across the Ohio river in Northern Kentucky, at 3:35. Matt headed straight for the Great American Ball Park. In the cab ride to the park, he became nauseous. He tried to write it off to bad food on the flight, but the truth was his nerves were making him sick. He asked the cab driver to pull over on I-275. He got out and walked around and talked to himself.

"What is the worst that can happen, Matt, old boy? You can be found out. You can get re-arrested. You can strike out four times. You can drop a fly ball. So what?" While not exactly filling him with euphoria, the internal pep-talk worked. After ten minutes Matt felt better and re-entered the cab. Within twenty minutes he was at Great American Ball Park. At the entrance of the Reds' clubhouse, he was forced to wait for the clubhouse attendant to clear him through the clubhouse door since he wasn't recognized.

Matt was shocked by how familiar everything was including the "clubhouse smell," a combination of wet towels, sweat, aftershave, shaving cream, and pine tar. It smelled delicious, and he drank in the aroma and the familiar sights that had lived in his dreams for years. The clubhouse boy introduced himself and began showing him around. Along the way they ran into several of the Reds players who welcomed him warmly. Matt did not realize that his teammates had looked up his stats from Tacoma, and more than one said they looked forward to a new "bat."

Reds' manager Frankie Weber, in his fourth year at the helm, had replaced the retired Burt Shelton, the manager under whom Matt had played. Unlike Shelton, Weber had not been able to get the Reds back to the playoffs. As a result, Reds fans were impatient with Weber's "re-building plan" to make the Reds into World Champs again.

If Weber worried about his job, he did not show it. Despite third place finishes in the last two years, he remained popular with his players and the media and seemed sincere when welcoming Matt to the team. "Glad you're here, Matt. We have some great reports on you and need that bat of yours in the lineup. I understand you have played some outfield so you will be starting in left field tonight. Dave Schultz, our third base coach, will go over the signs with you in a few minutes. Good luck. Oh, almost forgot, we just announced another trade with Seattle for a friend of yours while you were in the air today. Randy McDonald will be here tomorrow."

Matt was pleased with the news and looked forward to building on what he felt was the basis of a strong friendship with Randy. They had not spoken, other than by e-mail, since the night at Two Grands. Matt read that Randy had done a good job for the Mariners in his short stint there. Sounded like the Reds were pulling out all the stops to win the division since they gave up pretty good Double A prospects and a wad of cash to get Randy and Matt.

Of greater note was the name Dave Schultz, the Reds' third base coach. Schultz, a guy Matt always liked, was the sole leftover from the Shelton coaching staff. He had spent many hours with Schultz in his first two years with the Reds and had learned a great deal from him about major league life on and off the field. Schultz had been a father figure to Matt, and he was concerned that his old coach may see something in Matt Wolf that would remind him of Dylan Michael.

After meeting with Weber, Matt was shown his new locker with number "29" written in red magic marker above it. He began unloading his travel bag before heading to Schultz' office. As he turned to move across the locker room, he caught a glimpse of the locker directly across the aisle from his. It had Number "21" at the top and the name of Dylan Michael was formed in bronze letters. Below was a matching bronze plaque with an inscription that read:

202

"This locker belonged to Reds' great Dylan Michael who lost his life in a plane crash after only seven seasons with the Reds. His contribution to the heritage and history of the Reds will never be forgotten and this locker will forever remain empty in his memory."

Near the middle of the locker was a glass encased photo of Dylan leaping in joy after hitting "The Double."

As Matt was reading the inscription, Pauly Marazzi, the Red's trainer walked up and said, "One hellava player that one was. Good guy, too. If he hadn't got killed, this team would have won a couple more rings. He was that good. Hi, I'm Pauly, and when you start hurtin', I am around the corner there. Just get your ass in here early if you need something on game days."

Matt smiled, shook hands with the veteran Reds trainer and introduced himself. Damn, he thought, he had even missed Pauly. He had been one of Matt's favorites in the Reds' organization. Pauly was a guy who called "a spade a spade" and took exceptional care of "his boys" as he called Reds' players. He had been the head trainer with the Reds for over twenty-five years, and not only helped make pulled muscles, sore arms, and "strawberries" feel better, he was somewhat of an amateur psychologist in helping the players get through batting slumps, spates of hanging curve balls, girl problems, and even financial trouble. Rumor was that Pauly had the first dime he ever made. After a few minutes of small talk, Pauly pointed the way to Schultz' office and said, "Glad you are here, Matt. We need your big stick in this line-up."

Pauly had done some Internet detective work on Matt, and he told several of the Reds, "It looks like that son of a bitch can hit a little bit." Seeing Matt in person, Pauly was impressed. He looked strong as a bull but sure looked older than 27. As Matt was changing clothes next to his locker, Pauly noticed Matt had lots of scars on his arms and legs as well as what looked like scar tissue on his hair line and under his chin. He knew the story of Matt's car accident. It looked like it had beat the hell out of him. As Matt turned and walked away toward Schultz' office, pulling his t-shirt over his head, Pauly was reminded of something.

When Matt and the coach finished going over the signs, it was clear that there was no recognition in Schultz' eyes of Matt being anyone but who he claimed to be: Matthew David Wolf, first baseman, now left fielder of the Cincinnati Reds. In addition to Schultz, there were only two other players left from Matt's last Reds' team. He said brief hellos to them. They barely looked up, and he was sure he was home free.

After Dylan Michael was injured and then "got hisself killed" as Pauly put it, the Reds team fell on hard times for three or four years. Pauly succinctly described their status as, "we weren't awful like the papers was saying but we weren't real great either. Sort of sucked but not real bad." So the Reds' management decided to start over. They had a "salary purge," as the press called it, and began to re-build the team from the ground up. Now the team was competitive again and was trying to add the final missing pieces with McDonald and Wolf.

The big news revolved around the team getting McDonald.

"A big, ornery son of a bitch who can throw damn hard and isn't afraid to knock someone on their ass if they dig in on him," said one National League scout. "The Reds gave up some solid talent to Seattle, but if you have a chance to win now, you sure as hell better do it. They also got a good hitter in that Wolf guy."

Many fans wondered who the hell Matt Wolf was and why the Reds had not gone after a proven run producer instead of a Triple A no-name. The fact was the Reds didn't have a real deep farm system, and the only thing they had to offer the Mariners for McDonald were young pitchers who were still two or three years away from the big leagues. Matt was a low risk throw-in in the deal. The Mariners got what they wanted, and the Reds got what they needed.

Mark Donahue

When Matt walked from the clubhouse to the field for batting practice before the first game, he wanted to thank someone. He wanted to thank everyone in Blossom for what they had done to bring him to this moment. But the list was too long and now that he was there, he swore that he would make it worth everyone's time and trouble.

He realized he had taken everything for granted when he had originally come up with the Reds. It had all been too easy. The smallest things were now amazing: the sun hanging over the bleachers laying a carpet of gold light on the emerald green field. The smell of the ball park and the murmur of fans entering the stadium. How damned lucky he was to have ever been on the field at all. He felt ashamed that he was the only one who realized how little he had worked on his talent as a young player. He had taken his whole life for granted, every damn thing that he had been given. He swore at that moment history would not repeat itself. He would work every day to be better. He would savor every moment on the field.

Matt hit a few balls out of the park in batting practice but mainly wanted to make sure he was squaring the ball. He felt like a rookie, and in the eyes of everybody there that night, he was. Hanging around the batting cage, he experienced an emotional high while talking to the guys, telling dirty jokes, checking out the good looking women in the stands, and being a baseball player again.

Several of the guys wanted to know if he was nervous before his first game, especially when they heard he was starting in left field. He was not nervous. To his surprise, he was very calm. At first, he was not sure why. But he soon understood. He realized that when that first pitch was thrown at 7:10, he would have reached his goal of officially playing in a big league game again. He was also looking forward to his first at bat.

Last At Bat

As he walked out to the outfield to stretch, he thought of Cara for the tenth time that day and wondered if she was in town or maybe even in the ball park. Over the last few months as his memory had come back, he thought of her almost every day and dreamt of her almost every night. He actually feared going to sleep because he would dream of her and wake up depressed and sad, wondering where she was and who she was with. It was eating at him. He would talk to her in his dreams and even when he was alone and wide awake. He feared he was developing an obsession and wondered if he should go see a shrink, though obsessing over Cara was somewhat understandable. She was not only very beautiful, but he now also remembered how their off-the-wall, senses of humor had clicked. They had become great friends for a year before they married. The love part just sort of happened.

She had never heard of Dylan Michael, and she hated baseball, saying it was too slow. Early in their relationship, he brought her to a game and heard her exasperated yell of "do something" as he was on deck after going 0 for 3 in a tight pitchers' battle. He homered that at bat which made her think her "encouragement" had led the way to the Reds' winning the game. "Do something" became an inside joke for just about everything they did inside and outside of baseball.

Finally, after all the pain, the dreams, the work, everyone's sacrifice, the time had come. He was on the top step of the dugout waiting for the public address announcer to make the player introductions before the team ran onto the field together. That is when he fell for a rookie mistake. On cue, a few of the players started to run from the dugout onto the field, and seeing their movement, Matt started sprinting toward left field. Only problem was, the rest of his teammates had stopped and returned to the dugout leaving Matt as the only Red on the field. His teammates laughed and pointed at him. Matt loved it.

"Well, Weber is wasting little time getting the newest Red into the lineup. Matt Wolf just got off a plane a few hours ago and here he is starting in left field and will be hitting sixth. Wolf hit .357 at Tacoma this year and the Reds hope he can bring some offense to this team that desperately needs it," Mel Bateman, the Reds radio announcer said on the broadcast of the game.

Matt had been around baseball long enough to know one thing: he could and would hit. However, he was concerned about playing left field, a position he hadn't played all year. He hoped that unlike the first game in Tacoma, he would escape being tested early and often in this game. He forgot about the Twilight Zone effect.

On the game's second pitch the leadoff hitter for Houston crushed a line drive down the left field line that Matt got a pretty good jump on. He decided to take a chance. He dove for the ball rather than pulling up and taking the ball on one hop. The ball landed in the web of his glove and stayed there even after Matt belly flopped on the natural grass and slid into foul territory. *"Great catch by newcomer Matt Wolf! He just took extra bases away from Romero on a diving catch!"* Bateman said excitedly.

The next Astro lined a ball to Matt that he almost lost in the setting sun that made left field at Great American Ball Park one of the toughest "sun fields" in baseball. Shielding his eyes with his glove, he fought the sun and won. To complete the tri-fecta, the third hitter sent a routine fly ball to left, and Matt tied a major league record shared by thousands. Rod Serling would have been very proud.

Matt was happy to be back on the bench in the bottom of the first, still trying to get some composure back after his left field adventures. He was dealing with the overload of emotions that were now un-expectantly eating him up inside. His teammates did not give him much time to reflect. The first three Reds reached base, and it was clear, absent a double play, Matt would bat in the first inning.

Last At Bat

As he moved into the on deck circle, he remembered the last time he had been there nearly four years earlier. He remembered "The Double" nine years earlier, the crash, the pain, the work, Cara, all the folks from Blossom, and the dream that he would make it back to the very spot he now stood. He was remembering so much he almost forgot what the hell he was doing.

"You can't hit from there, son," yelled Weber from the dugout. Matt had lost track of what was happening on the field and was inexplicably standing in the on deck circle with everyone in the stadium waiting for him to come to the plate. Jolted by Weber's voice, he lurched toward the plate and dropped one of the two bats he had been swinging in the on-deck circle. Unfortunately, he had thrown away the wood bat and was walking toward the plate with the weighted lead bat.

"Are those the bats they are using in the PCL these days," asked the catcher. Embarrassed, Matt had to retrace his steps and retrieve his Louisville Slugger amid taunts and catcalls from the Houston dugout and many of the home town Reds' fans.

Frank Weber had decided to start Wolf that first night and find out early if Matt would be able to help the Reds. Being in a pennant race, Weber didn't have the luxury of giving an unknown a few weeks or even a few days to produce. This was his chance. The Reds had loaded the bases with no one out in the first inning, but their fourth and fifth hitters had struck out and popped out respectively. Stranding base runners was the repeat of a scenario that occurred regularly to the Reds throughout the year, when missed offensive opportunities seemed to happen almost every game.

The Houston battery, seeing a chance to get out of a tough jam and change the momentum of the game early, decided to take advantage of what they saw as a "rookie" coming to the plate with the wrong bat because he was ready to piss himself. The lefthander fired a

94 mph fast ball down the middle of the plate, and Matt's need to piss was shown to be significantly overrated as he lined the ball to right centerfield for a three run double. Standing on second base he could not help but shake his head at someone's ironic sense of humor. The Reds went on to win Matt's first game 9-3 and Matt went 2 for 5 with 4 RBI. Both hits were doubles.

The next night was more of the same from Bateman. *"Matt Wolf got off to an auspicious start last night with a couple of doubles and four RBI in his first game as a Red and as a result has moved up to fifth in the lineup...here's the 2 and 1 pitch and it's a drive to deep right field. Wolf has struck again...a three run shot and the Reds take a quick three to nothing lead here in the bottom of the first inning."*

Matt's fast start came at a good time for the Reds as they went 8 and 2 in his first 10 games. He made solid contact, got some big hits, and played good if not spectacular defense. Matt's only weakness was he was not quite as fast as the scouting reports said. He had a slight but noticeable limp when he ran hard. Twice he was thrown out on close plays at first that he knew he should have beaten out.

After the initial four game home stand against the Astros, the Reds spent the next six days on the road so Matt did not have a chance to even unpack the stuff from Tacoma that had arrived while he was gone. On the team's return from the two city road trip to Chicago and Milwaukee where they won four and lost two, Matt needed a day off. He had started and played in nearly every inning over 10 consecutive days. He was tired and sore. He spent a lot of time in the trainer's room and in the hot tub. He hoped no one noticed.

Pauly Marazzi had been around long enough to know when a player was sore and when he was just saying he was sore so he could get a day or two off. He knew Matt Wolf was hurting even though Matt never said a word. Pauly almost went to Weber and told him what he was seeing since the Reds were in a tight pennant race. But he decided to keep his mouth shut and see if he could give the kid a little more attention and keep that big bat of Matt's in the line-up.

Pauly was no baseball expert but he could tell Matt was a special hitter. Pauly was also the only one on the team to realize that with all the scars, scar tissue, lumpy bones, and titanium in his body how difficult it must have been for him to play on a daily basis. He wasn't sure how Matt was able to do what he was doing even with "all that yoga shit" which Matt claimed kept him loose and flexible. Something was helping.

At first, a lot of the guys teased the hell out of Matt and called him stuff like "Gandhi," but after watching him hit for a couple weeks, some of them decided to join him in his exercises. They wanted to see if that would allow them to pull a 95 mph fastball like he could. Even yoga couldn't help some guys.

After over thirty years of being a trainer, Pauly had heard lots of stuff from the naked ball players. As they lay there on the table they talked about all kinds of things: like why they aren't hitting, why they threw a pitch the night before that some asshole hit 500 feet to win the game. They talked about their girlfriends, wives, or both. But Matt hardly ever said a word. While friendly, he never spoke to Pauly unless he was asked a question. He would lay there and say nothing. Even if he did answer a question is was usually "yes" or "no."

During one of those long and quiet massage sessions, Pauly saw something he had not seen for a long time; then he saw a couple more things. Then he saw something he had never seen before. He decided to keep his mouth shut again.

Matt decided rather than renting another apartment, he would stay at the Westin Hotel only a few blocks from Great American Ball Park for the remainder of the season. During the day, Matt walked the city streets and refreshed his memory of the beautiful city on the Ohio River. He visited some of his favorite restaurants and the bakeries he had enjoyed in his previous life. Cincinnati had a long list from which to choose.

Reds' fans would recognize him and say hello. But unlike some big league cities, he was pretty much left alone by fans who respected a player's privacy. Despite the crowds, what he did feel when walking the streets was a sense of loneliness he had never experienced before. Even when he spent time with Gwen and Sonny after their long drive from Tacoma to Cincinnati, or when he went out with the guys for dinner after a game, he found himself feeling oddly alone.

Every few days Matt would call Bonnie on her cell just say hello and have someone to talk to. He missed her, their friendship and the time they had spent together. Bonnie had heard of his being traded to the Reds and reminded Matt that the "plan" was indeed working.

To help the situation and in hopes of maybe meeting someone, Matt joined the local health club which featured a great wet steam and sauna along with whirlpool and massage salon. He could have used the facilities at the GABP but decided he wanted a place he could go to around the clock and not get too much attention from Pauly. The plan for the private steam and massage sessions worked. The plan about meeting someone didn't.

After sleeping late on an off day, Matt stopped at Starbuck's on 4th Street around 10 a.m. to read *USA Today,* drink a double mocha latte and nibble on an English muffin. He looked up and she was there. After all the dreams, the thoughts, the memories, and the regrets, she was there standing in line waiting to place her order. He knew she would order a Grande English Breakfast tea with a toasted cinnamon bagel. When she did, he felt the familiar depression grip him. Then she placed a second order, for the handsome middle-aged man who was with her. His depression deepened.

Matt saw the easy banter between the two and saw Cara flash a smile to the man. That smile had a physical impact on Matt. After getting their order, Cara and the man walked past Matt and sat next to the window no more than 10 feet away.

While he could not hear their words, he could tell it was the kind of conversation couples have. The man was doing most of the talking. He seemed to be explaining something to Cara and kept pointing to the newspaper that was folded next to them on the table. From time to time one or both of them would smile or laugh. At one point he put his hand on top of hers and then patted it affectionately.

After a few moments the man glanced over at Matt then turned back to Cara and said something. A few seconds later she turned and also looked in Matt's direction. For a split second Matt was staring into her eyes before she turned away and returned to sipping her tea.

For the next 15 minutes Matt was torn between several possible courses of action. He could run over to her and in front of everyone tell her who he was, how much he loved her, and hope for the best. Of course the best could have been him being arrested for talking like a maniac. Or having her believe him and then spending seven years in jail. Or her saying she was glad he was alive but don't bother her because she had a new life. He could have done many things at that moment. Instead he sat there and did nothing.

The man with Cara was the one who took some action. On their way to the door, the handsome man stopped by Matt's table and said, "Hi, I'm John, just a Reds' fan. I was at the game yesterday and saw you get that big hit in the seventh. Good job, glad you're on the team. Good luck the rest of the year."

"Thanks," was all Matt was able to get out of his tightened throat. Cara had already moved passed Matt's table and did not seem to notice John stopping to say hello to Matt. Then they were gone and Matt was numb.

Outside the Starbuck's, John caught up with Cara and together they walked east on 4th street.

"What did you say to that guy?" asked Cara.

"I told him that I didn't like him staring at my woman like he was undressing you in broad daylight, even if he was the Reds' new player. I also told him that if he wanted to step outside, I just might kick his cute ass."

"You did not!" laughed Cara. "Did you also tell him you were gay?"

"My dear, I would think I would not need to announce such a thing. You know, he was kind of rugged cute in a Charles Bronson sort of way, don't you think? I wonder if he would go out with me?"

"Oh, my God, John. You are incorrigible."

"I know," agreed John.

It took a full 10 minutes for Matt to regain his composure. He kept staring at the now empty seat where Cara had sat next to the window. Then he got pissed. He was pissed that she looked so damn good and that he was feeling what he had felt four years earlier. He realized he had missed her far more than he had wanted to admit. During his memory loss he had seen her in his dreams and wondered who she was. Each time he dreamed of her, he awoke with a pain that he could not explain. That night, for the first time in weeks he could not sleep.

The next day at the ball park, Matt looked at his image in the locker room mirror and understood that such a beautiful woman could not be interested in him. His face, while for the most part free of major scars, was still riddled with scar tissue. He could have easily passed for a forty- year- old man even though his body was probably in better shape than it had been six years earlier. His depression deepened when he remembered how John had patted Cara's hand. He took some of his misery out on the Cardinals when he went three for five, drove in four runs and the Reds won again, pulling to within three games of Houston.

213

Last At Bat

33. It's the Eyes.

Returning to her office after seeing the stranger in Starbucks who had clearly been staring at her, Cara could not shake the feeling that the man looked familiar. It wasn't his face. Or maybe it was. But something looked familiar.

Later that night, Cara was sitting on her couch, wrapped in her Snuggy, reading the latest Stephen King novel when the phone rang. It was Marie.

"Let's go out this weekend," suggested her friend.

"I don't know…"

"Come on," said Marie. "It's my birthday."

"No it's not. Your birthday is in November."

"Okay, so it's a little early.. what's wrong? You sound down."

"No big deal."

"Then tell me," said Marie.

"I saw a guy today…"

"Great, then go out with him. Who is he? Is he cute?"

"I don't even know who he is except he plays for the Reds. I saw him at Starbucks, and he was staring at me," explained Cara.

"That's not news. Men are always staring at you. Was he creepy or something?" asked Marie.

"No, I don't know. He was just, well he, his eyes that is, just reminded me of Dylan's eyes, that's all, no biggie."

"Did you talk to him?"

"Of course not. What am I supposed to do? Just walk up and introduce myself and say, 'Gee, I saw you staring at me, let's go out tonight!'"

"It's been done," confessed Marie.

"I couldn't do that," Cara said. "Besides if I walked up to every man that had some trait that reminded me of Dylan, I would be going up to strange men all the time."

"Well, if you are not going out with this guy, let's go to dinner and a movie Friday night."

"Okay," said Cara. "Call me at the office tomorrow. G'night."

After clicking off her speaker phone, Cara moved to her computer. Going to the Cincinnati Reds web site, she looked up *Matt Wolf, Left fielder.* While she looked at the photo, Carly, jumped up on her lap. Cara grabbed a photo of Dylan from her desk and held it up next to the image on the screen of Matt Wolf. They looked nothing alike.

"What could I be thinking, Carly? He doesn't look at all like Dylan. Am I going crazy, sweetie?"

Cara returned the photo to the desk and clicked off the monitor. For several moments she sat in front of the blank computer screen. Then she clicked on the image again and reached for Dylan's picture a second time.

"It's the eyes Carly. The eyes really are the same. Don't you think?"

For the first time in months she Googled *Dylan Michael Plane Crash.* The now familiar wreckage appeared on the computer screen, and tears welled in her eyes as she realized no one could have survived the devastation she saw. Cara hit "shut down" on her computer and turned off the desk light. She carried Carly to her bed and laid in a fetal position as moonlight streamed into her window.

"Carly, maybe I am finally losing my mind."

Carly didn't exactly respond. But she did look up at Cara with two dark brown button eyes, framed with apricot fur, that seemed to say, "don't worry, you're okay."

216

34.   Milt Pappas

Arthur Robbins was ready to leave the office but couldn't resist making one more call to Nat Baker his friend in Seattle.

"Hey, Nat, it's Arthur. Know what Wolf is hitting now over in Cincy?"

"You called to remind me of that? You're a prick."

"He's hitting .410:   four- fucking- ten. He also has fourteen homers, and forty- nine RBI in only forty-five games. Great fucking trade."

Defending the indefensible Nat said, "How could we know a guy who looks like he is forty could hit like that?   Hell, maybe those kids we got will work out."

"They better, or this trade is going to make the Frank Robinson for Milt Pappas trade look like a steal. Or the Babe Ruth for cash, or...

"Prick," said Nat right before hanging up the phone.

Robbins laughed at his friend's pain, feeling his work day was now completed.

Last At Bat

35. "Oh, by the Way..."

Gwen and Sonny arrived in Cincinnati when Matt was on a road trip. They secured a little furnished condo at the McAlpin near the Westin where Matt was staying for the remainder of the season. They fed him a home-cooked meal when he was in town and hit the sights. The three of them went to movies, the art museum, the German Village called Main Strasse over in Covington, King's Island up in Mason or just down to the river to talk and watch the boats go by. They tried to avoid smothering Matt, although they would have seen him every day if they could.

Sonny knew that Matt had gotten off to a good start with the Reds both with the bat and in the field. But Sonny also noticed Matt looked slower than he looked a few months earlier. He suspected Matt's legs were bothering him. Matt laughed it off when Sonny brought it up by saying, "I'm just getting old."

"Oh, by the way, guess who I saw at Starbuck's the other day?" Matt said with false nonchalance one day before heading to the park. He didn't tell them he had not slept a full night since the encounter or that Cara had been with another man.

After Matt left for the stadium Gwen said to Sonny, "Meeting with Cara tore that boy up."

"I know," said Sonny, "but that is one kind of pain he's going to have to deal with on his own. There's not much we can do."

Matt steamrolled the league with his bat in his first fifty games, and the Reds climbed in the standings. After a big game against the Cubs, a local baseball writer named Eric Patterson, who worked for the Northern Kentucky bureau of the *Cincinnati Enquirer*, made the first connection between Dylan Michael and Matt Wolf in an indirect way in the Sunday paper.

> *"Not since Dylan Michael's last year with the Reds has the team had such an explosive hitter as newcomer Matt Wolf. While not the all around player Michael was in terms of defense and speed on the bases, Wolf hits for average and more power and has a knack for driving in the big runs. He is also good in the clubhouse, a trait he does share with Michael. He seems to be fitting in well with a team up to its neck in a pennant race. When he came to the Reds along with Randy McDonald three weeks ago, he was not considered the most important part of those trades. Yet, even though McDonald has won two of his three starts, it is Wolf who has been the biggest asset to the Reds as this season runs down to the final weeks."*

That afternoon in the clubhouse McDonald came up to Matt's locker and said loud enough for everyone to hear, "Here I am standing next to the Reds 'biggest asset as this season runs down to the final weeks'. Christ, I think I am getting a woody standing next to this man/god."

Matt turned, grabbed McDonald by the cheeks and planted a loud kiss on his forehead and said, "There... you have just been kissed by a man/god. You will go out tonight and pitch a four hit shutout and will return to me before every future start to receive my kiss of ultimate performance." The locker room broke up. That night McDonald pitched a three hit shutout, and the Reds moved to within two games of first place.

While Matt's on field performance was remarkable, he would have gotten even more attention if people knew what his body was going through. He was so sore he could barely walk after most games, particularly when day games followed night games. He spent hours in the hot tub at the spa trying to stay loose during home stints and took every anti-inflammatory he dared. He also spent hours in the trainer's room getting his throwing arm and legs worked on as often as he could without raising too much suspicion as to the pain he was in, for fear of being benched.

The pain got so bad after a 12 inning night game that he asked out of the day game the next day saying he had eaten some bad food and was feeling nauseous. The Reds lost that game 3-2 to Milwaukee, and Matt felt responsible. While he was perfectly prepared to play through the pain, he did not want his lack of speed and quickness in the outfield to cost the team a victory at this late stage of the year.

As the season wore down to the final month, the Reds stayed within two games of Houston but it seemed they could get no closer. When the Reds won, the Astros won, and when the Astros lost so did the Reds. While it was frustrating, it was also exciting. Each day at the ball park meant something, and Matt hoped his "old" body had another month of games in it.

The final 18 games of the season looked to be damn exciting. The Reds were scheduled to play four on the road in St. Louis, then on to Milwaukee for three, and then two games in New York against the Mets. Then, they would head to Cincy for nine straight home games with the final four against Houston to finish out the season.

Matt's performance with the Reds had gotten some attention by the national press, and he was greeted with requests for interviews everywhere he went. The problem the press had with Matt was that he was a boring interview. He seemed to repeat everything he said over and over again particularly when talking about his past.

After the opening game on the road in St. Louis which the Reds won easily 8 to 1, Eric Patterson, the Reds' beat writer from Kentucky, was interviewing Matt who had another outstanding game going 2 for 5 with a double, home run, and 3 RBI. Near the end of the usual series of questions, he suddenly asked Matt, "Many of your mannerisms at the plate and in the field look like those of Dylan Michael. Did you pattern your game after his or try to copy how he played?"

Taken aback, Matt foolishly said, "No, I don't copy anyone. In fact, I never saw Michael play." To have been a professional baseball player or even a sandlot player and to have never seen Dylan Michael play would have been impossible unless you lived in a cave. As soon as he said it, Matt knew he had screwed up.

Sure enough Patterson began to ask more questions. "You mean you never once saw Dylan Michael play? What about the World Series games he played in? You never saw those? Are you saying you never saw him rub the barrel of his bat before stepping into the batters' box like you did in the fourth inning tonight?"

Patterson was about to fire off a few more questions when Pauly Marazzi walked up. "Hey Matt, if you want that hamstring rubbed out, get your ass in the training room. I don't want to be here all night."

Matt smiled at Patterson and said, "Sorry, got to have this leg worked on."

Frustrated, the reporter started to follow Matt toward the trainer's room when he ran into the 6'5" and 245 pounds of Randy McDonald.

"Jimmy Olsen, why don't you leave that man alone. He's sore and needs his hammy rubbed, and he's tired of those questions you were asking." The reporter started to say something else but the cold hard look in McDonald's eyes scared the piss out of him.

"OK, maybe I can catch up with him tomorrow," Patterson conceded.

36.   Fantasies.

They met at Jeff Ruby's on Walnut. Reservations were for 7:00. Marie bounded into the restaurant late, as usual, and waved to Cara who waited at the bar. After several minutes of small talk Marie wanted the scoop.

"Ever see that creepy guy from Starbucks again?"

"I never said he was creepy. And no, he never came back," said Cara.

"Don't tell me you went back there looking for him. That doesn't sound like you. That sounds like me," Marie laughed.

Sheepishly, Cara said, "I kept thinking about him and decided if I ever saw him again, I was just going to walk up to him, brazen as hell and say, 'Hey, guy. You remind me of my dead husband. Are you him?'"

"I am not even sure I would do that. He would think you're crazy."

Cara leaned toward her friend and became animated. "I looked at this guy's picture on line and compared it with Dylan's, and I admit there is no resemblance…"

"So isn't that enough?" asked her friend.

"No," said Cara. "It's not. You didn't let me finish. I said there was no resemblance EXCEPT for the eyes. But then if Dylan had survived a plane crash wouldn't it be likely he could have had some facial damage? Maybe even some plastic surgery? And if so, he would look different, right? That would be logical wouldn't it? And if it was him and he saw me and didn't say anything, maybe he has amnesia. Or even if he doesn't have amnesia, he couldn't just walk up to me and say hello because the world thinks he is dead and he would go to jail and lose his baseball career. That's logical too, isn't it? Right?"

"Honey, are you listening to yourself?" Marie sighed. "You've got to snap out of this. Honestly, like I said before, get some help, please. You really don't sound like yourself."

Cara slowly sat back in her chair. "I know I sound like a crazy woman. But for some reason these kind of..."

"Fantasies?" Marie prompted

"I guess...but whatever they are, they help," she admitted. "I don't know why."

"Honey, you know I am there if you need me." After several moments, Marie reluctantly continued, "I almost hate to say this but one reason that guy never showed up again was the Reds were on the road for a week at the time."

Cara looked up at Maria with a small smile of her face.

37.   Eric Patterson

Eric Patterson had never been an athlete. He was only 5'9" and never weighed more than 150 pounds. Not that there aren't extremely talented 5'9", 150 pound athletes, but Patterson was neither coordinated nor athletic. Though only in his mid thirties, he was already balding, with skin that still erupted with acne at the worst possible times. He also thought wearing large horned rim glasses made him look smarter. They didn't.

Patterson could handle that most of the athletes he covered and grew to know reasonably well never seemed to warm up to him, while others simply dismissed him as a lightweight reporter. What he could not stomach was his fellow journalists. He knew they were jealous of him and his extraordinary writing ability. He suspected that the reason he was stuck in Kentucky, writing stories about the Reds that appeared on page four or five of the *Cincinnati Enquirer*, was just a series of bad breaks and worse timing. He always knew his time would come and he would break the big story, write eloquently about it, and finally be recognized for the talent he knew himself to be.

After watching Matt Wolf play for six weeks, Patterson concluded he might be watching an older, slower, more powerful version of Dylan Michael. Matt's face was different to be sure. His body was much thicker and somehow shorter, but he had that same beautifully balanced and powerful swing that launched a ball like few hitters could. Many young players copied the stances of older players, mimicking their childhood heroes. Eventually, though, they settled into their own hitting approach that matched their strength, skill, bat speed, and coordination. It was true that Wolf held his bat lower than

Michael had, but the follow-through after contact was identical, even to the point of how both players dropped their heads when running toward first base rather than worrying about where the ball went.

Patterson would probably not have thought much more about the similarities he saw in Matt and Dylan except for an abbreviated interview with Wolf after another good game against St. Louis. That was when Wolf said he had never seen Dylan Michael play before in his life. Patterson thought that was a bullshit answer. Later that evening, he got a threatening call from someone telling him to "lay off" Wolf. Patterson wasn't sure what that call meant, but it made him curious.

Later that evening, after the aborted interview and threat, Patterson began checking all the articles he could find about Wolf's past. He found plenty, but they all sounded alike. They sounded as if they'd all been written by the same person since they had the same word structure and used the same adjectives and adverbs over and over again. He did a background check on Matt, and everything checked out except for a single oddity. He had no credit history. He apparently never had a credit card of any kind, no bank loans, not even a car loan or lease until he was twenty-seven. That didn't make any sense.

Another perplexing point was that Matt Wolf was a terrible interview. He sounded like a politician who had rehearsed a series of sound bite answers and kept repeating them time and time again even in response to totally unrelated questions. Despite his curiosity, Patterson realized that absent any definitive proof, the suggestion that Matt Wolf was really Dylan Michael was a good way to get laughed out of press row at the ballpark or lose all credibility with his readers. But if he could prove such an incredible theory, the story would be on the front page of every major paper in the country, maybe the world and so would his name.

38.   Matt

The Reds were hot. Even though they still trailed Houston by two games, the team was confident they would catch the Astros, especially if the Reds' pitching stayed strong and they continued getting the occasional "big hit." Matt had played on championship teams before and knew this team had the right combination of swagger, toughness, and talent to win it all. But he knew they would need help from other teams to catch Houston and, also, some luck.

So would Matt. In his St. Louis hotel room he tried to sleep, but the pain in his legs kept him tossing and turning. And the insomnia inevitably brought thoughts of Cara, making sleep an even more remote possibility. He relived seeing her at Starbuck's and how John had patted her hand. Why such a meaningless gesture bothered him so much he couldn't figure out. But bother him, it did. He could see it clearly and tried to interpret what their body language said. Were they lovers? Friends? Did they work together?

He would change channels in his brain and think of the right hander he would face the next day. That worked for awhile, but then he weakened, and Cara returned to his thoughts. Depression joined the leg, arm, and shoulder pain, and he lay there staring at the ceiling for hours, wondering why the anti-inflammatory medicine Pauly was giving him no longer seemed to work.

At 2:38 a.m. Matt did something he never thought he would. He hit * 67 on his cell phone and dialed the number he'd found weeks before in an on-line search. If Cara answered the phone, it could mean several things; she was sleeping alone; or it could mean the man she was living with was on a business trip; or she was sleeping with someone, and the phone was on her side of the bed. On the other hand, if a guy answered the phone that would probably tell Matt more than he wanted to know. After five rings Matt was about to hang up, left to ponder even more possibilities, when a sleepy Cara softly said, "Hello."

For a few seconds Matt was speechless, and then for some unknown reason he said in a muffled voice, "Hi Cara, it's John."

With a deep sigh, Cara said, "John, you sound funny. Have you been drinking again?" Not answering, Matt held his breath not knowing what to do next. "John, if you need me to come pick you up somewhere just tell me. I don't want you driving if you have been drinking," Cara managed to say, still half-asleep.

Still trying to disguise his voice Matt mumbled "No, that's alright. I'm home now."

"John, you sound awful," Cara said. "Just go to bed, and I'll see you in the office tomorrow."

Matt mumbled, "Awright, g'night. Sorry I bothered you."

Matt pressed "end" on his cell phone and felt like an idiot. For about ten seconds. Then, he felt pretty good. He had learned some stuff with that call: 1. He was probably officially a stalker in several states. 2. She was not likely dating John. At least not that night. 3. John liked to drink, and Matt knew Cara did not like guys who got drunk or guys who used too many over the counter drugs. 4. Cara's voice was still the same. 5. He still loved her. Four out of five wasn't bad, he thought. Matt didn't sleep a wink the rest of the night. The next night against the Cardinals he went two for four and the Reds won 4-2.

After losing the final game of the four game series against the Cards, Matt sat in window seat 5-A looking out at the red and purple hues of a late summer sky on the way to Milwaukee, deep in thought. At first, he didn't notice Randy McDonald sit down in the empty aisle seat. "Hey man, you can't go 3 for 4 every game," Randy said as he smacked Matt on his right knee with a huge left hand.

Matt thought again, *"What in the hell was I thinking when I got into a fight with this guy?"*

"Oh wait a minute," Randy continued. "You did go 3 for 4 didn't you? Ok then, we can't win every game even if you go 3 for 4."

"I know," Matt said. "I just wish we could have won that one today. Then, we'd be only one game out."

"Fuck the Astros, they can't hold our jocks. I think they believe they're chasing us now even though they got a lead," Randy said in pure McDonald fashion. The two friends sat in silence for a few more minutes and then Randy leaned toward Matt and softy said, "Pauly and I are the only ones who know."

At first, Matt thought Randy was talking about how sore he was after playing five or six games in a row. But when he looked at Randy, Matt instinctively knew that Randy and Pauly were on to the ruse. All Matt could get out of his suddenly parched mouth was, "How?"

Randy spoke in a whisper. "Well, Pauly came to me last week and said he had seen something real strange when he was giving you a back rub a couple of weeks ago. He said you had a birth mark under your left shoulder blade that was shaped like the State of Florida and it finally dawned on him where he had seen that birth mark before. He dug through some old x-rays and that pretty much confirmed everything. He said it looked like your body had been through a blender, but he could tell it was you. I guess the final give away was a tiny scar on your right elbow from when you had some bone chips removed six or seven years ago. Pauly remembered it. How in God's name have you pulled this off so far?"

"Damn," was all Matt could say.

Then, after Matt gave Randy the Cliff's Notes version of what had brought him to this point, all Randy could say was, "Holy shit."

Last At Bat

For the first time since Sonny, Gwen, the folks in Blossom, and Matt had hatched their improbable plans months earlier, Matt realized he was in over his head. He was scared, but not for himself. After all, the plan had accomplished its primary goal, and that was to get him back in a big league uniform. Instead he felt fear for those who had helped him and had put their lives and careers on the line to get him this far. He felt guilty as hell that his obsession had put other people, good people, at risk. For the first time in three years he thought he was going to throw up on an airplane.

39.　"Leave the Guy Alone"

Patterson had not forgotten the veiled threat on the night he tried to interview Matt Wolf after the Reds-Cards game. "Leave the guy alone" was the message, and while he was not sure what that meant, the voice sounded gruff and very serious. All he had done was ask Wolf about his past to get some perspective on a guy who seemed to come out of nowhere.

Everyone was talking about him, and both the local and national media were checking the Internet for anything they could find, but there wasn't a lot. The high school star just disappeared until ten years later when he tears up some local South Carolina amateur league and within a year ends up in the Bigs. Great story, but it didn't make a lot of sense.

While the Matt Wolf/Dylan Michael connection would have been an incredible story, the fact remained that the two men looked nothing alike. Michael had been movie star good looking and had a lithe swimmer-like body. Wolf's face looked like a beat-up prize fighter sitting atop a body much larger and more muscled than Michael's. Their personalities were also very different. Michael had been outgoing, talkative, and all-in-all, a great interview. Wolf was just the opposite: quiet, reserved, and more than a little boring. Yet those damn swings of theirs were almost identical.

Last At Bat

40.   Cara

Born in Louisiana, Cara claimed she was a "mutt" when it came to her ancestry. Her dark eyes and skin were Latin in appearance but she had long aquiline facial features reminiscent of European decent. Her eyes were a dark, almost cobalt blue, framed by her shoulder length dark hair. When she put her mind to it she could be "drop dead gorgeous" which intimidated many LSU jocks who were actually afraid to ask her out. At 5'8" she had played volley ball in high school and, while she enjoyed sports, particularly college football, she spent far more time reading in the school library than attending games or playing them.

Cara's beauty was not something that impressed her. But when she heard it might pay for her college, she decided to enter several beauty contests in the South. To her surprise, but to the surprise of no one else, she began winning. Her stunning looks, poise and better than average talent in modern dance combined to insure she would reach the "finals" in nearly every pageant she entered. She worked her way up to the Miss Louisiana pageant, won and headed for the Miss America contest. She may have won that competition as well had she demonstrated more patience for what she announced on national television was a "stupid question" posed to her by the host. Her quote got her a huge round of applause and some major *You Tube* action, but it cost her the title.

After graduating from LSU with a degree in business, she received her Masters in Communications from the University of Kentucky. There, she first met Dylan Michael. Dylan had come to the university to speak to the athletic department. Cara was covering the event for class credit and was very surprised when Dylan sounded reasonably intelligent for a jock.

After several weeks of dating and endless "I told you so's," from Dylan, Cara grudgingly admitted to Dylan, it had, indeed, been love at first sight. Their relationship was based on common interests in literature, movies, politics, and slightly bizarre, marginally sick senses of humor. They felt Monty Python's, The Holy Grail was the greatest movie of all time with Animal House a close second; especially the scene where they crank up the chain saw and to cut up that dead horse.

Even after Dylan's "death", Cara often thought of their nights together, watching a favorite movie with a bowl of buttered pop corn between them. She would laugh out loud, remembering how Dylan used to spontaneously make up his own dialogue to scenes in the movies, making even the most dramatic scenes hilarious. Then she would cry at the memory.

She wanted to believe it was Dylan that first morning at Starbucks. As she waited in line, she had seen his walk as he came in and took his seat. That was the first clue, even though he limped slightly. But, she admitted to herself, over the years she had seen other men who had some characteristic that would remind her of Dylan. Maybe it was their hair, the way they laughed or smiled, but as soon as the memory flashed, she'd quickly turn away. Those moments were too painful.

A few minutes after Cara sat down in Starbucks, she realized Matt was staring at her. That was the second clue, his eyes: a green you could see from ten feet away. But then again, many men had a similar walk, green eyes, and she was used to having men stare at her. Yet there was the *way* he was looking at her – *recognition?* There also seemed to be sadness in his gaze. His stare had so unnerved her that she became dizzy. When John noticed her uneasiness, he nodded toward Matt and said to Cara, "Oh, he's just that new player on the

Reds trying to make eye contact with the best looking woman in town. If he's bugging you, I can go over and beat him up."

Cara said, "No, John, it's no big deal. Let's just head back to the office."

Until John told her who Matt was, Cara had no idea that the man that had been staring at her was a baseball player. She stopped following the team after Dylan's death even though many of the players' wives and girlfriends had tried to stay in touch and keep her involved with the team. Some of the Reds' players even asked her out after a reasonable period of time, but she could not bear to be around anything or anyone that reminded her of Dylan.

As she walked by Matt, heading for the front door, she was so shaken she was afraid she might faint at his feet or fall into his double latte. She purposely avoided eye contact but was concerned when John stopped and said a few words to Matt.

For a year after the crash, she had felt as if she were in a coma. Even though she and Dylan had been separated before the crash and Cara had moved away, she always hoped they were going to get back together. She had even sent him a letter he would have received when he arrived at the prison. In the letter, she told him she would wait for him as long as it took. She told him how much she loved him, how she always would. He never got there to read her letter.

Last At Bat

41.   Road Trip

After Randy confessed to Matt that he and Pauly knew his story, Matt felt a huge relief. He finally had people he could confide in about everything, including Cara. Yet, he also knew that if Pauly and Randy had figured things out, it was likely others may also be close to the truth. Matt hoped his secret would hold until the end of the season.

At breakfast on the morning of the opening game of the three game series with Milwaukee, Matt was more talkative than Randy had ever seen him. "I think I am officially a stalker," Matt confessed.

Randy countered, "I don't think one call qualifies you quite yet."

Matt wouldn't let it go, saying, "What if I call her again? What if I hang out at Starbucks until I see her again? Then I follow her back to her office just to see where she works? What if I hang out in front of her home a couple nights a week?"

"Yeah, that would probably qualify you for "'Stalker Status," said Randy sarcastically. After a few minutes of silence Randy added, "But Matt, you must know what you would be risking if you try to contact Cara. First of all, you don't even know if she would want you back. Maybe she is dating this John dude or somebody else. And even if she did want you and you guys hooked up, the press would be all over it. Someone would make the connection. You could spend seven years in jail. Is that fair to Cara after what she has already suffered?"

"I know. I have thought about all that," said Matt dejectedly. "I've also thought about all the folks in Blossom that have helped me and how my getting discovered could hurt them. That's why I haven't made contact with her. You're right. I don't know how she would react. And I realize the consequences of us getting back together. But, damn, I still love the woman."

"What would happen if she didn't want you?" Randy proposed.

"Well, I guess then I would just have to suck it up and move on. But if I don't at least find out how she feels, it will haunt me for the rest of my life," Matt said.

Hearing Cara's voice after that second game in St. Louis had a curative effect on Matt. Inexplicably, the pain he was feeling in his beat up body vanished. He felt revived. He felt strong.

Those final games were nothing short of miraculous in terms of Matt's performance. No one could remember having ever seen someone hit the ball so hard for such a period of time. No one could stop him. It appeared Matt was trying to cram his four lost seasons and what was left of his baseball career into one 16 game stretch, as if he knew that every game he played would be his last.

The irony was, in his first two at bats in St. Louis in the third game, he was 0 for two. After lining out to left field his first time up, he nearly killed the Cardinal third baseman with a vicious line drive that would have taken out a kidney if it had not been caught.

The next three times to the plate Matt homered, doubled, and homered. The last hit traveled over 470 feet onto the right centerfield walkway. The blast was one of those home runs where the outfielder just turns and watches, making no effort to run after the ball, which really pissed off the pitcher. But the way that Matt had crushed the ball, made it, in Randy's words, a "no fucking-doubter."

The next three games in Milwaukee were unbelievable. Matt was 5 for 5 in the first game with two more home runs and 6 RBI. Then he set a team record of 11 consecutive hits by getting three hits in his first three at bats in the second game. He ended up going 4 for 5 in that game with four more RBI. The Reds pounded the Cheese Heads in three straight games 8-2, 9-1, and 12-4. McDonald won the second game by throwing a five hitter.

While the Reds were dismantling the Brewers, the Astros had lost two out of three to the Pirates and fell into a tie with the Reds for first place. The Reds then headed to New York for two road games while Houston replaced the Reds in Milwaukee.

Matt should have known his current streak was going to get big time press coverage in the Big Apple for the Reds' only trip into New York for the year. But he never expected what he ran into. Matt was on the front page of the *New York Herald*. Not the sports section, but *the* front page of the paper. The *New York Times* had a full page article about him and a four-inch- tall headline that shouted, "Reds Find New Star."

When the team arrived at the hotel, he encountered writers from all over the country who were in town to cover the two division leaders but, also, to find out as much as they could about Matt Wolf.

Matt's oft repeated stories of his past might have worked in middle America, but they were not cutting it with the New York press. The reporters were relentless. How could someone this good come out of nowhere? They all wanted to know. They wanted details, lots of details.

The country was so wrapped up in Matt's story because the numbers he was putting up were stupid. Prior to the Met series, he was hitting .416. He had 23 home runs, 28 doubles, 3 triples and 68 RBI. Only he knew that he could have had a few more hits had his legs not been sore or if he had been a step faster to first base. Even his outs were line shots. His teammates had never seen anything like it.

The writers in New York knew a good story when they saw one and kept after Matt like sharks in bloody water. Matt was pretty cool about it all. Despite the redundancy of the questions, he answered them like he always had, even when some reporters got more than a little testy about what they felt was "the rest of the story" being held back by Matt. He even amazed his teammates with the grace with which he handled the attention.

On the field, Matt was just better than everyone else. It was that simple. His opponents were even in awe of what they saw. Matt appeared oblivious. After he learned that Randy and Pauly knew the truth, he was resigned to the fact that if they knew, it was only a matter of time that others would find out. In a way, that recognition freed him, and his natural talent erupted on the field.

Matt got a kick out of the questions from the New York press like: Did he have a wife or girl friend? "No." Was he gay? "No." Did he take steroids? "No." What was his position on the war? "That's my business." What kind of car did he drive? "Ford pickup." Those were the easy ones.

When the stupid or dangerous ones were asked, Matt would just smile, be really polite, and give his standard answers or say "Guys, you will have to wait until after the season."

Fortunately for Matt, the Reds only had two games with the Mets. He hoped things would quiet down, soon. But the Mets' pitchers, especially the starters, either had no idea what Matt had done or they felt it was all hype. They kept pitching to Matt in situations where they sure as hell should have walked him, pitched around him, or hit him in the back. As a result, he kept up his offensive assault going 7 for 9 in the two games with two more dingers and five more RBI. The Reds won both games 7 - 1 and 8 – 5, and moved two games ahead of the Astros who had lost two of three to the Brewers.

Matt's play took pressure off the rest of the team. Guys who had been struggling all year at the plate started to swing the bats. With their solid pitching, the Reds were the hottest team in baseball. The Reds players had no doubt they were going to hold onto their lead and nail down the division before the home crowd. As they headed back to

Cincinnati, they were a confident team with good reason: They were good.

Last At Bat

42.   The Swings

Eric Patterson had followed the Reds to New York for their series with the Mets, but the games were not all that important to him. Though they looked nothing alike, Patterson had become convinced that Matt Wolf was Dylan Michael. To prove his theory he would need help. In his office after returning from New York, Patterson made a call.

"Mr. Drew Johns? My name is Eric Patterson, and I am a writer for the Cincinnati Enquirer. I wonder if you would mind answering a few questions about your late step son, Dylan Michael."

******

Twenty five hundred miles away, another writer had also become more curious about Matt Wolf. He needed to call Seattle.

"Nat, It's Arthur."

"Yeah, I do know what Wolf is hitting," Nat anticipated.

"I didn't call about that, exactly. But I do have some questions about when you guys signed Wolf," Robbins said.

******

"Mr. Johns, did you actually see your son get on that jet?" Patterson asked.

"No", said Drew. "I left before he went into the terminal with that deputy. But so what? What's this all about?"

243

Last At Bat

******

"Nat, before you guys signed Wolf, what kind of background check did you do on him?" Robbins asked.

"Usual stuff," Nat replied. "Criminal checks, school records, read up on his baseball background. Why? Did the Reds find out he's a terrorist or something? The way he is hitting, we'll take him back for something minor like that."

"Did anybody ever go down to that town he was from… what was it called?" Arthur asked.

"Blossom, South Carolina," he answered. "I don't think so. It's not something we would normally do, especially for a free agent who didn't cost us much money. Why all the questions?"

"Just curious," said Arthur. "I might want to do a story on the guy and thought maybe you could save me some road work."

"You know what I know. But if you go down there and find any more like him, let me know. Hey, by the way, I hate to say this, but Wolf has become sort of an Urban Legend around baseball."

"What do you mean?" asked Arthur.

"Well, I heard it from a good source that he is really the reincarnation of Mickey Mantle," Nat said. "Then I heard from a better source he was partly bionic. And, of course, the old standby that he is really Dylan Michael who somehow survived the crash and is now hitting the shit out of the ball and making us look like idiots."

"So, which one do you believe?" Robbins asked.

"I personally think he is the spawn of one night of intercourse horror when A-Rod and Martina Navratalova decided to breed a superstar athlete, become his agents and split the fees."

Laughing out loud, Arthur said, "Yeah, that sounds the most likely to me, too. Good night you crazy bastard. Thanks, I owe you."

"Anytime, buddy."

After hanging up the phone, Arthur looked at the side by side swings of Dylan Michael and Matt Wolf.

*****

In Cincinnati, Eric Patterson had more questions for Drew Johns.

"Mr. Johns, have you ever heard of a Reds' player named Matt Wolf?"

"Yeah, he's that new guy whose tearing up the league. I wonder if he has an agent?" asked Drew.

"Have you ever seen him play?" Patterson asked.

"No," said Drew. "I don't really follow baseball all that much. Hell, I never really even liked it. Hey, what are all these questions about? You're not one of those crazy bastards sayin' Matt Wolf is Dylan Michael, are you? That shit's been on the Internet for two months. Boy, there are some crazy bastards out there."

"Crazy bastards out there for sure. Thanks for the time Mr. Johns."

Patterson hung up the phone and stared at his computer screen. He wasn't sure how it happened or how he was going to go about proving it, but Patterson was certain that Dylan Michael had survived that plane crash and was playing with the Reds under a different name. The newer version looked older, was bigger and ran with a limp, but in Patterson's mind, that was consistent with someone who had been in an accident, like when a plane crashed.

Eric Patterson firmly believed he was not an average writer. He took pride in how he noticed little things, unlike most of the empty headed fans and lame brained baseball writers who followed the Reds, would not. He put videos of Michael's and Wolf's swings on a computer side-by-side and then overlaid them one on top of the other. While their stances, including the way they held their bats, were different, the swings and follow-throughs were the same. He did admit to himself that throughout baseball there were some swings that are very similar, but these swings were almost mirror images.

But it was more than their swings. It was the mannerisms of how Matt Wolf carried himself on the field. It was the little things that others would not notice. But Patterson noticed. Finally, it was Matt's background. It sounded fabricated to Patterson. It sounded too good to be true.

Patterson concluded two things: 1. Matt Wolf was Dylan Michael and 2. that his evidence was circumstantial and to prove his theory, he was going to have to visit Blossom, South Carolina, after the season. He would stay there until he found out the truth about how Dylan Michael survived a crash that killed nearly 300 other people. It would be a story that could win a Pulitzer, and God knew his career could sure use a Pulitzer. He only hoped that what he knew to be true was something that he alone had figured out.

43.   Arthur Robbins

Until the time Matt came to the Reds in the trade, Arthur Robbins had never heard of Blossom, South Carolina. Yet here he was making a trip to find out what he could about a player who refused to talk about himself. He flew into Greenville, rented a car, and made his way through the beautiful hilly countryside until he found Blossom nestled between two emerald mountains. He felt like he was in another century when things were still very green.

Paraphrasing an old joke, he said aloud, "When it's 2 p.m. in LA, it's 1958 in Blossom." Blossom appeared to have never left mid-century America. But, despite its appearance, Blossom was a bit more hip than many other small towns. This condition was mainly due to the citizens who had built an outstanding school system. They had invested in high speed Internet access and sported a nearly 100% subscription rate. The town had a higher than average college graduation rate compared to surrounding towns, and had a very well stocked public library that nearly everyone used. When one of the large retail book stores came to Blossom with the idea of opening a small store, people asked "You mean we would have to pay for books?"

Blossom citizens, on the whole, were a rather well informed bunch who knew what was going on in the rest of the world. They just didn't care what was going on in the rest of the world.

Robbins went to Blossom because his reporter's instincts said that Matt Wolf was hiding something. Robbins wasn't trying to be a pain in the ass, but everyday that Matt's statistics became more and more unbelievable, so did his story. Several times Robbins tried to have one-on-one conversations, but Matt avoided him as if he owed him money. The few times they did talk, the conversation was always limited to that day's game. Whenever Robbins tried to bring up some details of Matt's life, Matt would clam up and try to change the subject or repeat his standard response. As a result, Robbins decided to take a few vacation days and do some old fashioned investigative reporting. He was actually afraid of what he might find.

Robbins arrived in town late on a Saturday morning and checked into one of the two motels; a nice, clean Fairfield Inn. "Reservation for Robbins, please."

"Here it is," said a pleasant young man after checking his computer. "Only one night Mr. Robbins?"

"Yes, just one night. Actually I'm in town today to do a story on somebody you might know? Matt Wolf."

"Know him! Are you kidding?" he gushed. "We were really good friends and played lots of ball together. He was really good and then he got hit by a car and almost died. But he got better and now he's a damned superstar."

"Yep, that is amazing," Robbins noted. "Did he have any brothers or sisters?"

"You know, ah, well you know, I really don't remember all that much about him. Cept' Sonny and Gwen Cook raised him after his real folks died."

"Where do the Cooks live?" Robbins pressed.

"Hmmm, you know, I think they just moved awhile back, and I don't rightly remember where they moved to. Here's your key Mr. Robbins. You're in room 212. I'm kinda busy here today so I better get back to work."

Looking over his shoulder Arthur said, "Your parking lot is empty."

"Well, you know, paperwork. Look, if you want to know more about Matt, why don't you head on down to the clinic. It's just a few blocks down on your right. Doc Watson is there and he knows all about ole' Matt," he said.

"I think I'll do that. Thanks for all your help."

"No problem. Welcome to Blossom," the desk clerk looked back to his screen.

Arthur walked out of the lobby and grabbed his suitcase from the rental car. Before going to his room, he crossed back in front of the lobby window and saw the young clerk on the phone.

On the 10 minute walk through town, Robbins returned "hi's," "hellos," "heys," "mornin's" to about 20 people who passed him on the street, which was the main shopping area of the town. Blossom was a slice of 1950's America. As the townspeople passed, smiled and offered their greetings, Robbins, uncharacteristically, smiled and spoke right back. He wasn't sure what else to do.

When Robbins got to Dr. Watson's office, four people were in the waiting room. He walked up to the desk and read the name tag on the receptionist saying, "Morning, Annie, my name is Arthur Robbins and I was wondering if it would be possible to spend a few minutes with Dr. Watson."

Smiling, the fifty-something- year- old woman asked what was the matter with Robbins and if it was an emergency. "No, no, I'm fine," said Robbins. "I just wanted to talk to Dr. Watson about one of your former citizens, Matt Wolf. I'm sure you must know Matt."

The woman behind the counter replied casually, "Of course, we all know Matt here in town. We are so proud of him. He is a very nice young man."

"Did you know him well?"

Still smiling, Annie said, "Blossom is a small town. Everybody knows everybody."

"What was he like growing up?" Robbins asked.

"Very nice," she replied.

"I understand he lived with a family named the Cooks. What were they like?" he asked.

"They were very nice too," she answered.

As Arthur readied another question which undoubtedly would have had a "very nice" answer, Doc Watson entered the waiting room. "Hi. I'm Doctor Watson. I understand you have some questions about Matt Wolf."

"How did you know that?" Asked Arthur.

"It's a small town," Doc smiled.

"Yes, I do have lots of questions about Matt Wolf. I was told you might be the man to talk to."

"I will be happy to answer your questions about Matt, but I'm busy with patients now. Why don't I meet you at Millie's Diner up the street across from the Neon Theater around 6:00, and we can talk then," Doc suggested.

"Fine", said Arthur. See you then."

For the rest of the afternoon, Robbins drove around the Blossom area, thinking about 1958. He looked for the old house where Matt had been raised, but could not find it. He did find Matt's high school. He also went to the public library in town and was confused by what he didn't find. While Robbins had made copies of all the Internet info he had found on Matt Wolf, he found nothing about him in the old high school yearbooks where you would have expected his exploits on the field would have been legendary. There were also no pictures of Matt with the team pictures in the year when he was to have graduated. The more Robbins looked for Matt Wolf, the less he found.

Back in town before his meeting with Dr. Watson, Robbins looked up the family, Sonny and Gwen Cook, who had, according to the Internet story, raised Matt after his real birth mother had died during child birth and his father vanished. Robbins called and left a message when no one answered the phone.

Around 5:40 p.m. Robbins walked back to the center of town to meet Dr. Watson. This time the street was empty. As he made his way down to the diner, the entire population appeared to have left town after their shopping sprees in Center City Blossom earlier in the day.

When Robbins arrived at the restaurant 15 minutes early, he took a booth by a window and ordered a cup of coffee.

"Any fresh homemade pie with that coffee?" asked Bonnie.

"Just coffee, thanks," he said. "By the way, do you know a young man named Matt Wolf?"

"Sure do. He's about the nicest young man I know," she smiled.

"That's nice," said Arthur.

As he sipped his coffee Arthur decided to call a friend. Getting no answer he left a message.

"Nat, remember that story I told you I was going to do on Matt Wolf? Well, I am in Blossom, South Carolina, as we speak and all I can tell you is it's just like Mayberry without all the glitz and excitement. I'll call you next week. I may have a story, bye."

As Robbins looked out Millie's window into a deserted Blossom, he did not notice that a scruffy guy in a dirty baseball cap, wrinkled "Tar Heels" sweatshirt, and old Nike running shoes had shuffled up to his booth.

"Doc Watson wants you to come with me," the scruffy man said.

"I'm supposed to meet him here," Robbins objected.

"Not now, you ain't. You're supposed to come with me over to the Neon and meet Doc there."

Overhearing the conversation and seeing Arthur's obvious concern for a repeat of a scene from *Deliverance* , Bonnie interceded.

Last At Bat

"Hi Luke. It's OK, Mister. Luke here is a good friend of Doc's. The Neon is the movie theater here in town, and Doc wants to meet you there."

"OK, then. Luke, lead the way," Robbins waved his agreement.

After crossing the deserted street, Arthur followed Luke into the theater. He stopped short when he saw every seat filled. He then looked toward the stage and saw a dozen brown, metal folding chairs. One was empty.

"Please come on up on stage, Mr. Robbins," Doc invited. "We have a chair waiting for you." At first, Robbins froze in his tracks, not sure what he should do. His mind screamed, *'Head back out the door of this theater, go straight to the motel, get in the rental car and get the hell out of town.'*

"Please don't be nervous," Doc smiled warmly. "We're all friends here. Come on up."

Robbins found his courage and walked up to the stage. As he did so, Dr. Watson said to the audience, "Folks, this is Arthur Robbins. He's a well known baseball writer for the *Los Angeles Times*. He came to town to ask some questions about Matt Wolf."

Robbins' introduction was met with total silence from the audience. For some stupid reason he expected at least some kind of polite applause. This was going to be a tough crowd, he concluded.

"Mr. Robbins, rather than have you go door to door and get bits and pieces of the story about Matt, I thought it would be easier and less time consuming to bring everyone together so you could ask all your questions at the same time," Doc explained.

Doc's next statement made Robbins feel as if he was on the reality show, "Punked," or, in keeping with the 50's theme, "Smile, you're on Candid Camera."

"Mr. Robbins, before you begin your questions, our town has a collective confession to make and we want to make it to you first.

252

Matthew Wolf is dead. He died twenty-seven years ago when he was born. We stole that name and gave it to a young man you once knew as Dylan Michael," Doc confessed, revealing the truth. Robbins looked around for the TV cameras.

"As you know," Doc continued, "Dylan Michael was on the jet that crashed up in Kentucky almost three years ago and was reported as one of 297 people killed on that plane. Very simply, he survived the crash. He was on his way to prison for what we thought were bogus charges. So, as a group we decided we were going to try to save his life, and if we did, we'd welcome him to Blossom and encourage him to live quietly here for the rest of his days. We may have been wrong, but we figured that if we were able to save him, he would be happier here than in jail."

Doc took a deep breath and looked around the theater. "Quite frankly none of us thought he was going to make it, but he did. The crash destroyed his face, and his body suffered 12 broken bones. He lost seven pints of blood, had six transfusions, two dislocations, and needed nearly 300 stitches. He lost an ear and suffered a severe concussion. The decision to work on Matt here in Blossom and nurse him back to health was the decision of those of us here on the stage right now. Matt had no say in the matter because he had total memory loss as a result of the accident."

Doc went on to describe in detail the drive from Kentucky to Blossom. He gave Robbins the whole story. Hearing the sincerity in Dr. Watson's voice and seeing the tears of several of the women on stage, Robbins stopped looking for cameras.

"Everyone you see in this theater, particularly each person on this stage, is complicit in the hoax that is Matt Wolf," he confessed. "We have collectively lied, committed forgery, falsified records, and misrepresented every fact and statistic you have read about Matt on the Internet. We realized then and realize now we could all be in serious trouble for what we have done, but I can tell you right now we would do it all again in a heartbeat." This time the entire audience did applaud, including the people next to Robbins on the stage.

Doc continued, "Dylan Michael may have been a great baseball player, but that's not why we did what we did. We did it because he was such a good young man who we all got to know and care about. The idea that he would, or even could, ever play baseball again was honestly out of the question based on his injuries. Yet somehow, through his unbelievably hard work and sheer determination, he recovered enough to want to play baseball again. We didn't have the heart to tell him he couldn't. So we did what we had to do. We really don't think the federal government or our society as a whole is somehow at risk because Dylan is playing baseball again. If you do, then everything that has happened, everything we have done, what Matt has accomplished, will come out into the open and that's that."

Doc was now moving around the stage and began talking more rapidly and with more animation, using is hands to punctuate the air when making a point. "From the perspective of everyone here, we don't really care what happens to us. Hell, most of us are old farts anyway."

"Speak for yourself, Doc," someone yelled from the back of the theater, and everyone laughed. Doc laughed, too.

"But we do care what will happen to Matt if his story is divulged. Not only will he lose his baseball career, he will lose seven more years of his life serving a jail sentence for something that never would have occurred had he not been under those damned prescription drugs." Doc grew silent, then turned and stared at Robbins as did the entire theater audience.

Seeing and feeling the stares, Robbins shifted nervously in his chair and asked, "Why are you telling me all this? And how do I know what you are telling me is even true?"

Doc didn't hesitate. "First of all, everything we are telling you is true, and we will prove it in just a minute. Secondly, we all figured that sooner or later Matt's story would get out, but by then he would have accomplished his goal of getting just one more at bat in the major leagues. That's all any of us asked for. The only person who seemed to think there would be more to hope for was Matt. He *knew* how good he was.

"We figured we would help him get that last at bat," Doc explained further. "But we wrongly assumed he would not be able to cut it in the big leagues on a long term basis given his physical condition. We thought he would get his last at bat and then come back to Blossom, and his life would go on. Actually, we are all surprised no one has caught on until now. But more surprising, is how successful Matt has become. How great he really is. Ironically, had Matt not succeeded as he has, I doubt anyone would have paid attention to him, and he would be just another player who came to the big leagues, played a few games, and moved on.

"We knew eventually you or someone else would figure out the truth and come to Blossom, asking questions. Actually, after seeing your piece on Dylan on ESPN right after the crash, we even considered going to you then in hopes you might be willing to help us keep the secret awhile longer. But we decided against that and hoped the season would end before any story broke. We almost made it," Doc said with half of a grin.

Arthur Robbins was stunned by what he was hearing. While he never *believed* Matt Wolf was really Dylan Michael, the thought had crossed his mind – not unlike Elvis lovers who would see one of those impersonators and muse "what if that was REALLY Elvis, and he was just pretending to be Elvis because he wanted to escape his old life …," or some pretzel logic like that.

"Mr. Robbins," Doc wasn't finished, "we are glad it's you who came down here because we could tell by your stories and TV interviews that you cared about Dylan as a person. And because of that, we want to ask a favor of you. We want you to walk away from this story and forget about everything you have learned today. In fact, we would like you to consider writing another kind of story that would help stop any further inquiry about the Matt and Dylan comparison." Again the old movie theater was dead quiet as the audience waited for a response from Robbins to the audacious request by Doc.

After nearly a minute Robbins quietly said to Doc, "You are right about one thing, I saw Dylan as more than just another baseball player. But what you and these folks want me to do is to become part of the Dylan Michael lie. And I am guessing you also want me to do an exclusive story on Matt Wolf that would confirm and even elaborate on all the Internet stories. Do some fake interviews, talk to a dozen people in town, take pictures of his home, in short do everything as if Matt Wolf really existed. Is that about right?"

"That's about right," Doc nodded.

Robbins raised his voice and said, "Do you realize what you are asking me to do is a criminal act, and like everyone here, I could be charged with aiding and abetting a felon?" That statement elicited laughter from the audience. It was then Robbins realized that the folks in the theater had already crossed that little ethical bridge with no problem.

"We know there are some risks, but we have accepted them. Everyone in this theater cares for Matt and realizes he is someone who had the kind of bad luck that would have killed many people. And I don't mean just the injuries from the plane crash," Doc said.

Robbins then said something that he immediately realized was just stupid, "Does anyone know what an incredible story this is? What this story would mean to..." The word "me" was not necessary.

Everyone got the meaning without it. A collective whispered murmur rose in the theater, followed by some people getting up, saying nothing and walking toward the exits of the Neon.

"Wait a minute folks, please sit back down," called Doc. "I want to show Mr. Robbins something before everybody leaves. Mr. Robbins, would you mind taking a seat down there in the second row?"

Robbins hesitated, but nodded and made his way to a vacant seat next to Sonny, Gwen, and Annie. Doc pointed up to the projector booth; the theater went dark, and what looked like a home movie began flickering on the big screen. The film started off by showing the shattered remnants of what was once a 757 jet aircraft. More than a crash, what Robbins saw was total devastation. The only recognizable part was the tail section which Robbins later learned was where Dylan was trapped before being rescued by Sonny and Doc.

For several minutes the camera showed why officials had said no one survived the crash. It seemed impossible anyone could. The next images on the screen showed an un-recognizable person. The face was grotesque: swollen, black and blue, misshapen, and missing an ear. The head had no hair and looked like a gruesome mask. The camera panned down the body to plaster casts on the left leg, left arm, and right shoulder. Both knees were wrapped in bandages. Blood seeped from gauze, all over the body and tubes were running into both arms and down the throat.

The next part of the film showed a body in a wheelchair. The face was unsmiling with bandages wrapped around the head. Plaster casts were still in place, and the head was even more swollen than in the first part of the film.

Over the next 30 minutes, each film segment showed a slowly improving Dylan Michael. The last shot was taken from what looked like the high school field Robbins had seen earlier in the day. A

257

familiar hitter was smashing pitch after pitch thrown from some skinny kid who looked shell shocked after seeing his best stuff beaten to death by the batter.

The transformation from the first shot of Dylan to the last was astonishing. What the folks in the theater could not appreciate was the Dylan Michael/Matt Wolf who Robbins had seen only a week earlier, was much further along physically than the one at the end of the film. Robbins could not help but feel deeply touched and impressed by what he saw.

"Dr. Watson, I want you and everyone here to understand that I appreciate everything Dylan, Matt, I'm not sure what name to use, has gone through, and it is certainly not my intent to hurt him. Yet what you are asking me to do is professionally unethical and illegal. I would most assuredly lose my job and even my career if I were to become part of your conspiracy."

What Robbins did not say aloud was that this was also the biggest fucking story in baseball history.

Doc looked down at Robbins and asked him to consider an option. "Mr. Robbins, I realize there are professional ethics involved here, but there is also a person's life and future at stake. In short, if you print a story that does reveal the truth, Dylan's baseball career is over, and he will most likely go to jail. He will lose everything, again.

"What we would like you to consider is what we originally asked. Write an 'exclusive' about Matt as told to you by everyone in this town. By doing so, your story will, in essence, conform to what was written on the Internet and make it far less likely that other writers will come back to Blossom and retrace your steps. I realize that is a huge thing to ask, but please consider it."

Doc scanned the theater and then looked back to Robbins saying, "If you can't find your way clear to write the story as I have requested, then at least wait until after the season to do your own story. As a group, you have our word that we will provide you with an 'exclusive' of the true story. Every detail. Our only request is you wait to print your story. That way, Dylan will have a chance to finish this year and get into the playoffs. What difference could a few weeks make?"

Slowly rising from his seat, Robbins spoke directly to Doc, "I'll need some time to think this over. But I have to say, your request is unfair on a number of levels. You have put me in a no-win position. I am viewed either as a jerk for writing the truth or an unethical felon by ignoring the truth and joining your cabal."

"Frankly, Mr. Robbins," Doc replied, "this isn't about you or the people here tonight. It's about a person we have come to know as Matt Wolf. Everything is about him. Everyone in this theater knows what is the right thing to do. We hope you do too."

After several seconds of silence Robbins said, "I appreciate the situation, and I'll sleep on it. I'll get back to you tomorrow before heading back to Cincinnati."

Reaching out his hand to shake Robbins', Doc said, "Mr. Robbins, we all do understand the terrible position we are putting you in, but we feel we have no choice. No matter what you decide, thanks for coming and at least listening." As Robbins walked out of the Neon, he felt the stares of those who had lingered behind hoping to hear what he was going to do. At that moment Robbins had absolutely no idea what that would be.

Retracing his steps to Millie's, Arthur decided homemade pie was now in order. "What kind of pie did you say you had?"

"Apple, cherry or peach," said Bonnie.

"You pick. You're not going to poison it are you?" asked Arthur, hoping he had not given anybody any ideas.

"Because of Matt? No. You have to do what you have to do," explained Bonnie.

"This is not what I planned for when I came down here," he said.

"Maybe it is somebody else's plan," she observed.

"What do you mean?" Robbins asked.

"Whatever is going to happen is all planned. Now you're just part of the plan."

44.   "Carly…"

The Reds were in first place and Matt was crushing the ball. He felt better than he had all year, and he was headed back to Cincinnati from New York ready to stake out Starbucks like a hunter in a blind. He would be patient and drink as much latte as needed in order to see Cara again.

That Sunday night, he called Cara's number for the second time around midnight just to see if she was in town. He also wanted to see if a man answered the phone. She was in town and he immediately hung up. But, of more importance to Matt, no man answered. He could almost smell the latte.

Monday was an off day and Matt got up at 7. He showered, threw on some jeans with a University of Cincinnati sweatshirt and headed for Starbucks. After ordering his latte and bagel, he bought a *USA Today* and *Cincinnati Enquirer* and took a seat at one of the few outside tables at Starbucks near 4th and Vine. He sat in the warmth of a late summer morning and had a clear view of the inside of the coffee house as well as both doors. He kept a close eye on the table Cara and John had occupied the first time he saw her and hoped it was not "their table." He was prepared to wait all day if need be.

Cara decided she needed a day off…from a lot of things. She got up early, showered, had a bowl of oatmeal, toast, and cup of black pekoe tea.   She put her hair in a ponytail, put on a running outfit complete with new Nikes and set out with Carly for a long walk down into town, over the bridge to Covington and then back home again.

Matt sat quietly nibbling on his bagel, sipping his coffee and looking up from time to time waiting for a woman who thought he was dead. By 9:15, Cara had not showed up, but John, the handsome man Cara had been with earlier, had. He walked in with another man and ordered coffee and apple Danish to go. As Matt watched the two men wait for their order to be bagged, he saw them touch hands. They smiled at each other in a way Matt had never looked or smiled at Randy or any other of his teammates. He felt a sense of relief that made him smile.

As the two men walked out of Starbucks, John noticed Matt, smiled and said "Good morning." Matt smiled back and waved hello, hoping his smile was not *that kind* of smile.

Around 10:15, Matt was on his third latte and second bagel and had just returned to his table with a large orange juice. As he began to take his seat, a cream colored, furry blur with a trailing black leash came out of nowhere, jumped into his lap and uttered a high pitched cry. Matt fell back into his seat and without thinking, buried his face into Carly's feather soft fur. The dog jumped down, bouncing on her hind legs in excitement and repeatedly licked Matt's face, celebrating the return of a lost friend.

A voice from around the corner of the Starbucks could be heard, "Carly, come back here! Carly…!"

As Cara rounded the corner, she stopped short when she saw a large man embracing her Wheaten Terrier his face hidden in her fur. Knowing Carly's deep fear of men, Cara's brain was momentarily addled by what she was seeing. "Oh, I am so sorry, I hope my dog isn't bothering you. She's usually so afraid of men…"

Then the large man lifted his face from Carly, and Cara saw tears running down his face.

"No problem," he said. "I always wanted two dogs and two kids."

Cara began to shake. Her voice came out in a series of barely audible gasps, "Oh my God… oh my God, is it you? Is it really, really you," Cara said in a voice quivering with emotion. Matt slowly rose from his chair and helped a trembling Cara into a seat before she collapsed.

Last At Bat

45. "You Bastard"

After three years of thinking he was dead, and hoping and fantasizing that he wasn't, Cara sat across from a man who was physically unfamiliar to her, yet one she knew and had loved. She had known the truth the second he rose to help her to her seat. Dylan was alive and sitting with her in a Starbucks.

"Are you OK?" he asked quietly as he held Carly in his lap.

"No, no, I am not OK," Cara gasped. "I can hardly breathe. Just let me calm down a second."

He sat in silence and stared at Cara, not knowing what to say or do. Tears streamed down Cara's face and she continued to shake. After several minutes she looked at Matt and in a whisper hissed, "You bastard... how could you put me through three years of hell and not let me know you were alive?"

Taken aback by the anger in her voice, Matt could only utter, "I'm so sorry but I had amnesia for over a year and when I regained my memory..."

"Amnesia?" Cara interrupted," that sounds like a damn soap opera..."

Matt whispered, "I know it does, but it's true." He spent the next three hours telling a spellbound Cara the entire story right up to his plan to come to Starbucks that very morning with the hopes of seeing her.

Every few minutes, Cara would break down in tears. At one point, Matt reached over and touched her hand. That touch made her cry even more.

Last At Bat

After telling his story, Matt waited for a response. But she sat silently looking down at her empty tea cup.

"I never stopped loving you," he said. "I have thought about you for three years even when I could not remember who you were, if that makes any sense. When I did get my memory back it became even harder because I missed us."

Cara was still reeling, "After wanting this to be true so badly for three years, I don't know what to do now."

"I wanted to see you and tell you the whole story, but I never really thought it would happen this way, not in a Starbucks for God's sake. I know I have shocked you, and we both need some time to think things through. But I can't apologize. I did want to see you again, talk to you again and I know by doing so I have opened the door for lots of problems but I could not go through the rest of my life not ever speaking to you again. Even if coming to you means giving up baseball and going to jail, I am prepared for that. Not talking to you would have been worse than jail."

"Dylan, er Matt, I don't even know what to call you," she stammered. "The last time I saw you, we were getting a divorce. But that day at the airport, you seemed like the old Dylan I fell in love with. But we are both different people now. I am thrilled you survived the crash, but we have been through too much to try and rebuild something that was broken years ago."

"You might be right," he said. "All I know is just talking to you at this moment is enough. One last thing. I am a different person now than I was when you left me, a better person. I have learned a lot about myself and other people."

"It's so strange," said Cara, "hearing you talk and seeing a face I don't recognize is bizarre. But there is something so familiar..."

Matt said, "Look, the ball is in your court. I love you as much today as I ever have and that won't change. I can't help how I feel and

I won't apologize for it. Here is my cell number. If you want to see me, even if it's just as friends, I'll understand. But right now, at this moment, I would give up everything to be with you again. But if that doesn't happen, I'll make it. I have a family I love, a career I love and folks who care about me."

Matt stood, laid his number on the table and started to move toward the door. But he then returned, knelt down on one knee and hugged Carly. As he did, Carly strained at her leash now held by Cara, wanting to follow him, not wanting her lost friend to leave.

"Let me know if you ever need a dog sitter," he said, walking away.

Last At Bat

Mark Donahue

46.   The "Issue"

Fans have no idea how long a baseball season truly is. Players start in February, and if they're lucky, they are still playing in late October. A starting pitcher works 40 games and throws over 6,000 pitches including practice and spring training. Pitchers throw another 2,000 pitches just warming up between innings. Hitters see around 10,000 pitches including games and batting practice and maybe another 6,000 practice swings waiting on deck or in the batter box. By the end of the year, players' asses are dragging, unless they have a chance at the playoffs. Then they can't wait to get to the park.

No matter how long the season, some of the best times in a player's career are on the bench or in the bullpen with a bunch of crazy fucking guys. Friends for life are made over the seemingly endless hours talking about such intellectually challenging topics as who would be better in bed - Katie Couric or Laura Bush? These kinds of intellectually and socially relevant topics are not taken lightly and discussions over the three hours of a game are serious and thought provoking. In the above example, Laura won on the presumption that as a repressed Christian Right lady of Texas, there would have been some serious pent up and unbridled desire, that, with the proper encouragement and foreplay, could produce significantly more moaning and violent thrusting than from a left wing member of the media. Actually, that discussion lasted for an entire four game series in Chicago with Randy being the discussion leader.

Another discussion that took place in the bullpen regarded Matt and began when a couple of the guys were commenting on the "urban legend" that was springing up in other dugouts and on fans blogs; the

269

theory being that Matt Wolf was really Dylan Michael. Of course, these same people also heard he was the reincarnation of Mickey Mantle, or Babe Ruth, or Jackie Robinson, which brought up some interesting side-bars. Then there was the enduring bionic reconstruction myth. Of course that discussion inevitably and logically lead to the possibility that Matt's penis was also probably bionic which led directly back to the Katie Couric/ Laura Bush debate. It really did seem to make a great deal of sense in the bullpen during a four hour game in Chicago.

Anyway, the Matt Wolf/ Dylan Michael "issue" was out there, mainly because both had played in Cincinnati and their swings were very similar. No one really took any of those stories seriously, although the robotic tale was the most logical to describe the way Matt was hitting.

The last nine home games included three against the Cardinals, two against Pittsburgh, and the final four against Houston. The Reds had built a two game lead over Houston and were playing their best ball of the year. They had not been in a close game for two weeks, had won 14 of 16 games, and had developed the swagger that all winning teams have.

In the opening game against the Cardinals following a Monday off, the Reds did not slow down. Matt went three for five, had two more RBI and made a great play in left field in the eighth to put the game away. The Reds won 6-3 while Houston lost in Milwaukee. With only eight games remaining, the Reds had a three game lead.

After the game, Randy saw Arthur Robbins from the *Los Angeles Times* having what looked to be an in depth conversation with Matt back near the whirlpool where writers are not normally allowed.

"Good game tonight. Three more hits", said Robbins.

"Thanks", said Matt. "Even though I know what's going to happen now, I feel at peace and am enjoying every moment."

"I hope you understand, that what Doc and the folks from Blossom asked of me, I simply can't do. But I will agree to hold off on my story until after the season ends."

"I appreciate that. I knew it was all going to come out eventually. To be honest, I never thought it would go on this long. If it wasn't for everybody in Blossom, I really wouldn't care that much but I don't want them to get into trouble."

"Well," said Arthur, "I doubt they will arrest a whole town. But those people do think the world of you."

"They're great people."

Robbins then warned, "One other thing you should know. That little prick, Patterson, thinks he knows something. I heard him in the press box showing some other writers 'how similar Wolf's and Michael's swings were'. They all laughed at him, but he made some comment about going down to Blossom at the end of the year."

"Yeah, he's been asking everybody all kinds of questions about my past. I figured he was onto something. Arthur, if you feel he's ready to break the story before the end of the season, I would rather have you do it than him. I'll understand."

"Well, he's kind of a dull bulb, so let's hope he can't prove anything until November. You know if you weren't hitting .415 nobody would be asking questions."

"That wouldn't be any fun," said Matt.

Two hours prior to the second game with the Cardinals, Matt had just emerged from the trainer's room when his cell phone rang in his locker. He recognized the number.

"Hey."

"Hi, Big Red. I've been thinking over the last few days. I've been thinking you owe me dinner after three years of missing your butt."

Last At Bat

Pacing around his locker and trying to hide his excitement, Matt said, "Is that right? Well, maybe I do and maybe I don't."

"Tell you what," said Cara. "I am this minute sitting in the 4th row behind the 3rd base dugout waiting to see you play. You go deep tonight, I buy dinner; you don't, you buy."

"Deal."

The Reds announcers called the first inning action.

"A Reds win tonight and they will maintain their three game lead in the Central with only seven games to play. Here's the pitch to Wolf. Oh my! There is a deep drive to right field and that ball lands just four rows short of leaving the stadium in deep right field. A three run home run. What a blast by Wolf! Reds 3 Cardinals nothing."

As Matt rounded third base he looked toward the third row, saw a familiar face and smiled. He would see that face two more times that night.

Thirty minutes after the game, Matt's cell rang again.

"How about the Golden Lamb tomorrow night so I can collect on my bet?"

"That was kind of obnoxious. Wasn't that over doing it, just a bit?" asked Cara.

"Well, I wanted to be sure I won that bet. You know how you always tried to talk your way out of paying up. Golden Lamb? 7:00?"

"Ok, you big show off. I'll meet you there."

Later, Matt told Randy about his emotional meeting with Cara at Starbucks. Randy could tell Matt was euphoric at what he hoped would be the opportunity to re-unite with the woman he loved. He told Randy they were going to meet for dinner up in Lebanon, Ohio, after the final game of the Cardinal series which was a "Business Person's Special" that started at 12:30 p.m.

"Hey man, don't you think that is risky as hell? What if somebody sees you two together? You've heard all the rumors.

People are already talking about you being Dylan Michael and all. It's all urban legend bullshit, now, but if you guys are seen out together, that will really fan the flames," Randy cautioned Matt.

"That's why she's going to wear a wig and we will be heading 30 miles north for dinner tonight."

Randy was not convinced, "Damn, Matt, they do have TV's in Lebanon, you know. What the hell is a wig going to do?"

Matt smiled and said, "I know, but we have both waited for this for three years, and we can't spend every waking hour in Starbucks."

The dinner bet with Cara called for Matt to hit a home run, but he hit three, just to play it safe. The second one had carried over the Batter's Eye in dead centerfield, bounced twice, and ended up in the Ohio River, last seen heading toward Louisville. According to Mitch Reynolds, the Reds left handed reliever, the hit was "the longest fucking home run I have ever seen, and I have given up a whole shitload of home runs."

After his three home run performance and brief talk with Randy, Matt left the Great American Ball Park and made his way north up I-75 for 20 miles to Route 63, taking him into Lebanon. He arrived at 6:30 p.m. The town reminded Matt of Blossom.

Last At Bat

47.   Golden Lamb

During their five hour meeting at Starbucks on Monday morning, Cara and Matt wrestled with overpowering emotions including utter joy, profound sadness, anger and depression all of which were laced with uncertainty.

Matt had selected the Golden Lamb as a "first date" because six years earlier Matt had proposed to Cara there.   Entering the two-hundred-year-old inn, memories flooded back to him in emotional waves that were palpable. Matt requested a quiet table in the back of the restaurant and was surprised when Cara showed up at 6:35.

"You're early," he said.

"You were earlier."

After being seated, Cara said, "I don't even know what name to use…Matt or Dylan?" Cara asked.

Matt thought for a second and said, "I think 'Matt' is the operative name at this point. But I admit it is hard for me not to respond when I hear guys on the team mention 'Dylan Michael.'"

Three hours later Matt and Cara were politely reminded by their waitress that the restaurant closed at 10 p.m. She asked if they wanted any more wine. That was a very nice way of saying, "We're tired and want to go home, so please drink up and leave."

They got the hint and decided to walk around the nearly deserted historical town doing some late night window shopping. Cara put her arm in Matt's as the two of them walked slowly from store to store looking in at antique stores and dress shops. They even found the bakery that had made their wedding cake.

Matt suddenly asked, "Well?"

275

"Well what?"

"Where do we go from here?"

"Oh, Matt, I don't know. Having you here, it's hard not to want to talk to you."

"So, what's the problem," asked Matt.

"God, Matt, the problems are endless. Are you aware we are still legally married? You could go to jail, lose your career…"

Matt took Cara's hands and faced her. "Are you happy this minute?"

"I guess, I mean, yes, I'm happy being with you but…"

"No buts. Somebody once told me second chances are very rare. We should take advantage of them. We would be fools not to."

"It's not that easy," said Cara.

"Actually, it is that easy," Matt replied as he gently pulled Cara toward him and kissed her.

Back in Matt's pick up in the Golden Lamb parking lot, they plotted like teenagers on how they could sneak back to one of their places and spend the night together. They decided that Cara's place was more secluded. Matt could sneak up the back stairs, and Cara could let him in through the back door near the fire escape.

"Wait a minute, did you say we are we still married?" asked Matt. Cara quickly answered, "I think so, but if we're not, I could never, ever, you know, like fool around with a man I just met a few days ago in a Starbucks."

Matt then said, "You're right darlin'. We probably need to cool it for awhile. After all, we have been seeing just a little too much of each other lately. Maybe we should start seeing other people."

"Oh really," cooed Cara. "Do you think so?" She then slid over on the bench seat of the pick up and put her hand high up on his thigh. This time it was Cara's turn to kiss Matt, and she kissed him like a woman who had not really kissed another man in four years. She flat out just kissed the hell out of # 29.

He was at her back stairs fire escape door in exactly 28 minutes.

The next night the Reds lost the third game of their series against the Red Birds 3 - 2. The bullpen "spit the bit" in the top of the ninth after McDonald pitched eight innings and gave up one run on four hits. "Shit happens," was Randy's explanation. Houston won but the Reds still led the Astros by three games with six to play. Matt was 1 for 3 and walked twice. The pitchers in the league were finally getting smart and pitching around him even with first base occupied, showing unusual respect for a player in the league for only three months.

The Pirates were having a bad year, and the Reds, while not saying it publicly, felt to a man they were going to "seal the deal" against Pittsburgh. The Pirates came into the two game series twenty-one games behind the Reds in the standings, and according to Randy "we should have kicked their asses all over the park." Instead the Pirates scored five in the first inning of the first game and went on to beat the Reds 13-7. It was not pretty. Even Matt was off that night going 0 for 5 for the first time all year.

Houston had won again, and the Reds' lead was now down to two games with five to play. Guys were getting quiet on the bench which was not a good sign. The Reds looked as if they were trying not to lose, rather than trying to win.

The players knew they needed that second game from the Pirates to take some momentum into the final four games against the Astros. So what did they do? They made three errors in the first two innings and the Pirates jumped to a 7-0 lead. The scoreboard also provided some bad news and showed that Houston was leading Milwaukee 6-1 after three innings.

Last At Bat

After 30 years as trainer, Pauly Marazzi developed a philosophy regarding what leadership is on a major league ball team and was never afraid to share an opinion with anyone who would listen.

"Leadership is, in reality, some bullshit writers make up when talking about players. They say 'this guy is a leader' or 'that guy is a leader.' How the fuck do they know? First of all, if a guy hits .220 and plays shitty defense, there is no way he leads any team. He is usually too worried about getting his ass sent back to Triple A and guys would tell him to go fuck himself if he tried to be some loud mouthed rah rah asshole on the bench leading cheers. If you want to 'lead' a baseball team you better be able to play and produce when it counts. Guys on the team know who has 'who cares stats' and who has 'prime time stats.' Hitting home runs or driving in runs when your team leads by 10 runs or trails by 10 runs or your team is 20 games out of first place means nothing and everybody on the team knows it.

If you want to lead a team, hit a two out three run homer in the seventh inning to pull your club to within a run after trailing 9-0 and comeback in the ninth inning to hit a two out two run "Johnson" to win the most important game of the year that set off a home plate celebration that looked like we won the fucking World Series. That's a fucking leader."

That's what Matt did. It was very cool, even cooler when the Cheese Heads came back and beat the Astros. The Reds led by three with four to play. The Division race was over.

After the huge comeback win in the second game with the Pirates, Matt seemed as laid back and just plain happy as he had been in three months. He enjoyed watching his teammates celebrate and knowing it was likely they would not have stayed in the race if not for him. But he was not an aloof star like DiMaggio, Bonds, or Mays; he truly was one of the guys.

The Reds went on to win the first three against the Astros and won the division by five games. Cincinnati went crazy. The local sports radio talk shows talked about the Reds non- stop. The local papers had a contest to come up with yet a third iteration of the "Big Red Machine" moniker dreamed up by Bob Hertzell, a sports writer from Cincinnati who covered the Reds for years. There was the "New Red Machine" that Matt had played on four years earlier, but a new name was suddenly the big question for the fans and media. When Matt was asked what he felt the name should be, he said, "Let's win something first before we start thinking up names."

Matt's response to that question fit perfectly with the "personality" of Cincinnati Reds baseball fans who understand the nuances and subtleties of the game. Reds fans downright love their players based on one condition: they better play hard. During one of his first games as a Red after his trade from Seattle, Matt singled to right center field in a game the Reds were already ahead by a score of 9-1. But instead of being content with a single, Matt saw the centerfielder going after the ball in a lackadaisical way and busted his ass into second base, beating the throw by a whisker with a head first slide. The fans loved it; he played the right way. He played like a real Red.

Last At Bat

48.   Matt and Cara

After their dinner in Lebanon and their "sleep over" at Cara's condo, they saw each almost every night. Matt liked having her at the games and felt a contentment knowing he was going to see her afterwards. Cara added to the "adventure" by wearing a different kind of wig, make-up and sunglasses to each game and by also sitting in a different seat each night "just in case." The night after clinching the Central Division title, Matt, went to Cara's for dinner. She made lasagna served with some outstanding Merlot, and they rented "Vertigo," the Hitchcock thriller, as only part of the evening's entertainment.

The classic movie was as riveting as ever, yet Matt seemed distracted. Just after Kim Novak fell from the roof, Matt rose from the couch and walked out to Cara's balcony. He gazed from the top of Mt. Adams onto the river where he could see the Great American Ball Park and the breathtaking skyline of Cincinnati.

"What's wrong, sweetie?" Cara asked.

Matt continued looking toward downtown and the ballpark and said, "Nothing I was just wondering…"

Cara, with some concern in her voice, said "Wondering about what?"

"I was wondering how you recognized me at Starbucks and how you feel about…" Matt searched for words.

Cara asked, patiently, "How I feel about what?"

"Well, I know I don't look anything like I used to look, and I was wondering if that was going to bother you at some point. You know, I look older and the fact is, my face…"

Last At Bat

"You are an idiot!" Cara blurted. "Sometimes I wonder what planet men are from. How could you think that your face, which is not all that bad at this point I might add, would ever make me stop loving you? Even after I thought you were dead and wanted to forget about you, I couldn't. That's why I could never date anyone, let alone get into a serious relationship."

"Well, Ok, I just thought I would ask…" Matt seemed relieved.

Cara held open her arms and said, "Come here, you dummy."

They lay in bed and talked until the sun rose. There were singular moments when they both felt as if the past five years of agony never happened. They talked about everything. Matt even tried to tell Cara about Bonnie.

Cara said, "Whatever happened, happened. It's in the past now."

Later, they wanted to get up and take a long walk up and down the hills of Mt. Adams before stopping at a small restaurant for breakfast. They thought better of it for fear of being recognized. Instead, they had cold cereal and French Toast, went back to bed, and slept until 2:00 in the afternoon with only two interruptions.

They decided that whatever was going to happen after the season they could deal with. They both knew that jail was likely and that his baseball career was almost certainly over. Cara told him she would be there when he got out, no matter how long it was.

Cara added a bit of good news to the somber discussion, revealing she had inherited a little money from an uncle who had passed away while Matt was in Blossom. While they would not be baseball superstar rich, they would have more than enough money to survive. They would also have enough to hire good lawyers. They would put up a good fight, regardless of the outcome.

49.　Dodgers

The season ended on Sunday. The Reds had two days off before a workout on Wednesday and the first game of a five game playoff series with the Dodgers in Cincinnati. The town was awash with excitement. Everywhere the players went fans came up to wish them good luck. The joke in the clubhouse was even Carlos Mendez, their bad-skinned second baseman, could have gotten laid that week.

While each player was excited to be in the post season, Randy tried to make sure no one thought the team had achieved its goal and made his feelings known in a locker room meeting.

"Winning the World Series should be the only goal for any of us. Just getting to the playoffs doesn't mean shit if you don't win it all. Remember all those Braves teams that won a division every year for about a hundred years? I think they only won one World Series. That's bullshit. I've only been on the team for three months, but I've been on playoff teams before and know what it's like. We should suck in the experience but go out on the field with chips on our shoulders. We should let the Dodgers know right away they are going to be in for a long week."

After his impassioned speech the locker room was quiet. Randy then asked if anyone else had anything to say.

Matt slowly stood, walked up to Randy and put his head on Randy's chest, hugged him, and said, "I love you, man." The locker room rocked with laughter.

The Reds took two straight from the Dodgers in Cincinnati, 3-1 and 5-1. Then, they went to LA and, after losing the first game there in a heartbreaker, 2- 1, they pounded LA 10-3 in game four. They qualified for the National League Championship Series against either the Mets, who had won the East, or the Giants who were the Wild Card team.

In the Dodger series, Matt continued to hit everything hard when he had a chance to hit. But all too often, the Dodgers walked him or pitched around him so he didn't see any pitches he could drive. In addition to having a great swing, Matt had tremendous discipline at the plate. He refused to swing at pitches just off the "black" and would take a walk instead of swinging at something outside his zone. A writer told him once if he swung at more pitches, even the ones two or three inches off the plate, he could still smash those balls and maybe get even more RBI. He just laughed and said he knew that.

On the long flight from LA back to Cincinnati, Matt and Randy talked for three and a half hours. Matt told Randy about his trysts with Cara and about the conversations he had with Arthur Robbins, the sports writer from LA, whom Matt had seen again during the Dodger series.

Randy was mad as hell about Robbins' refusal to "cooperate."

"Well," Matt said, "it was going to come out eventually. I'm surprised I've been able to pull it off this long. Let's face it, if you and Pauly could figure out the truth, anyone could."

Randy burst out laughing. He was mystified by the calmness and serenity Matt was showing. He knew that within a few weeks after Robbins' article ran, Matt would most surely be out of baseball and probably on his way to jail.

"How do you wake up every day and do what you do knowing what's facing you," asked a perplexed Randy.

"Getting back with Cara, coming back to the Reds, and being able to put on a big league uniform again was more than I could have hoped for. I'm ready to get all the bad stuff behind me once and for all," Matt declared.

"Goddamn tragedy," Randy muttered.

Randy later told a reporter that Matt was the most humble "star" he had ever encountered in baseball. Even as far back as Portland, Matt never talked about his accomplishments on the field.

"I really cannot believe how talented this guy is," Randy said. "But you would never know it by talking to him. If I did bring up that he had almost single handedly taken our team to the playoffs with the most unconscious three months of baseball I had ever seen or that he had the most perfect swing I had ever seen, or talked about his stats at all, he would change the subject. He'd tell me I had pitched a good game or some other bullshit."

As the plane landed at the Greater Cincinnati airport on the return flight from LA, Randy finally asked Matt a simple question.

"Matt, do you know how fucking good you really are?"

Matt smiled and said, "Yes. See you tomorrow," and walked off the plane.

The Mets beat the Giants in the Division Series and since they had a better regular season record than the Reds, the National League Championship Series would open in New York. The Reds had secretly hoped the Giants would win since they matched up better with them. The Reds also liked the restaurants better in San Francisco.

Last At Bat

Mark Donahue

50.   Do the Crime; Do the Time

Eric Patterson told himself that his "being sure" that Matt Wolf was Dylan Michael was not enough. He knew he had to get some irrefutable, concrete evidence. He also knew he had to keep his suspicions quiet and make sure no one else, particularly another damn writer, got wind of what could be the biggest story in baseball history.

All his life Patterson had dreamed of an opportunity like this story, something that could get him noticed. A story this big could get him out of Kentucky and maybe serve as a springboard to a major magazine or big town paper. This story was it.

In preparation of going down to Blossom and doing some firsthand digging on Matt Wolf after the season, Patterson also checked on Dylan Michael's past, starting in California and his high school days all the way up to the crash that had supposedly killed him. All in all, Dylan Michael seemed a little too good to be true – great athlete, outstanding student, good musician, good looks. Had he raised the dead, too? "Happy horseshit" was how Patterson phrased it.

Reading the Internet, Patterson discovered Dylan Michael's father had been killed in a car wreck when he was a young kid. Then his mother died of cancer shortly after marrying Drew Johns, with whom Patterson had recently talked. Patterson was sure Johns could be a key to discovering the truth about Dylan. As a result, he was concerned that Johns had not returned his calls over the previous several days.

Patterson also learned that by the time he was seventeen, Dylan Michael was a damned millionaire. Since Patterson was still making less than $40,000 a year, Dylan Michael's early life was hard to imagine. Patterson further reasoned that with the way Dylan looked and the money he had in high school and college, he probably had made it with every sweet young thing in SoCal.

Patterson already knew that a couple years before the plane crash, Dylan married some beauty queen, and they were living life in the fast lane when he got mixed up in drugs, overdosed, and got his rich ass thrown in jail. Patterson remembered writing a story on him, letting the world know what happens to rich spoiled kids who don't know how to handle money and fame.

Dylan's attorney later claimed it was prescription drugs, and Dylan had been hurt and some other sad sack shit, but as far as Patterson was concerned, it was still drugs. To top it all off, Patterson felt that Dylan cheated the government, got caught and all of a sudden, the pretty, rich, superstar was headed for jail. As far as Patterson was concerned, Dylan Michael, Superstar, got everything he had coming to him. Now he was trying to get away without the punishment he deserved.

Patterson had heard some say Dylan was railroaded. Patterson never bought into that crap. Dylan Michael did the crime and had that jet not gone down, he would have and should have done the time.

51.   Sore Arm

More than one reporter commented on how the appearance of Matt's face had improved over the three months since he had joined the Reds. Glen Layton, the former Mariners' coach who had seen Matt way back in Portland, said the improvement was "remarkable." They had all heard the story of the hit and run accident. While he did not look like the "old, young Dylan Michael," he was beginning to look like a reasonably good looking former boxer/football player type. To be sure, his face wasn't pretty, he was ruggedly attractive like a weather-beaten cowboy.

Another thing smoothing Matt's troubled face was the contentment that came with knowing his five year nightmare was nearly over. He was soaking up the last few games of his career to the fullest and hoping the legal system might give him a break with the length of his prison sentence.

An hour after the Reds' last workout prior to flying up to New York the next morning, Eric Patterson cornered Matt near the training room in the nearly deserted club house. "A few weeks ago you told me you had never seen Dylan Michael play. I think you lied to me."

"I did," said Matt matter- of- factly.

"You did? You are admitting that? Why did you lie?" Patterson asked in a high pitched voice.

"I think you know."

"Wait a minute, are you saying you are Dylan Michael?"

"I am saying it to you."

"What does that mean?" Patterson pushed.

"It means you now have to go prove it," Matt smiled.

"Why don't you just let me write an exclusive?" Patterson asked.

"Because I think you are a jerk," came the succinct reply.

"Well, if you are Dylan Michael, you'll get what you deserve and end up in jail where you're supposed to be," he gloated.

"Maybe." said Matt. "But when I get out, you will still be a jerk; a jerk without an exclusive."

Patterson countered, "I will be meeting with Drew later this week, and I'm going down to Blossom right after the season. I also know where your ex-wife lives. I'll be able to prove my story."

Matt stared at Patterson for a few seconds then turned to walk away. As he did Patterson demanded, "Wait a minute" and roughly grabbed Matt's right arm. In a quick move, Matt reached down, detached Patterson's hand from his wrist and latched on to Patterson's skinny forearm. Then he squeezed.

Watching the scene play out from across the locker room, Randy saw a look in Matt's eye he had never seen before. Matt actually had a half smile on his face when he grabbed Patterson's arm and began squeezing it like a banana in a vise. Patterson had a surprised look on his face at first, but that quickly contorted into a look of pain so intense he couldn't make a sound. As Patterson's eyes bulged and his face turned crimson, Randy thought Matt was going to snap off Patterson's arm at the wrist.

Matt said in a low controlled voice, "You can talk to Drew and spend all the time you want in Blossom. But if you call my ex-wife, you will be permanently missing this arm. I promise."

Randy slowly ambled toward Matt and whispered something in his ear. All the while, Matt continued to hold Patterson's arm in his grasp and Patterson, eyes still open wide and gasping for breath, raised up on his tip toes, somehow trying to reduce the pain.

Matt finally released him, turned and walked away from Patterson. Eric Patterson gently cradled his left arm with his right hand. He jumped when Randy laid a hand on his right shoulder and said to Patterson, "Son, if I were you, I would never touch that man again. And I would also suggest you listen to what he told you."

Patterson had tried to extort Matt into giving him an "exclusive interview" to be released after the season. When Matt did not agree, Patterson threatened he would write an article in the next few days telling the world what he knew during the Mets' series to get as much coverage as possible in the New York papers. Patterson believed the timing for his story could not have been better. With the National League Championship Series as a backdrop, combined with Matt's incredible tale and a New York press that would jump all over Patterson's revelations, it would be a perfect storm of events that would catapult Patterson to literary fame and glory, and money − lots of money.

Yet, lingering in the back of Patterson's mind was the concern that if he had figured out the truth, maybe another reporter had done the same and would "scoop" the story before Patterson did. That's why he had gone to Matt, hoping for the exclusive, but if denied, knowing he could get the story printed within a few days. If he could find proof.

Randy had interrupted the encounter between Matt and Patterson for two reasons: 1. He did not want Matt to tear off a reporter's arm in the Reds clubhouse and 2. He didn't want anyone else to see him tear off a reporter's arm in the club house and write a story about it the next day. While Randy knew that Matt had told Patterson to go fuck himself, he was sure that Patterson would become an amputee if he ever tried to expose Cara.

Randy began to understand just how helpless Matt must have felt knowing what faced him in the future. Hell, he might not even get to play in the World Series if the story hit the in the next few days.

Randy walked into the trainers' room.

"Patterson knows", Randy told Pauly.

"Maybe, but if he had proof he would have printed something already. Without proof, he'll look like a bigger ass than he already is."

52.   Big Apple Smack Down

The night before the team flew to New York, Matt told Cara about the incident in the clubhouse with Patterson and about the story he would be releasing in a few days. Like Matt, she was actually relieved that the story was coming out, and, had it not been for Matt's certain prison time, she would have welcomed the opportunity to get everything behind them and just be with Matt like a normal couple. They discussed the possibility of her coming to New York to see the first two games of the NLCS, but realized the media frenzy over the games and what could be a blockbuster press release would make it impossible for them to be together.

After a quiet dinner at Cara's, Matt said goodnight early before leaving to go back to the Westin for the evening to get his bags packed for New York. He kissed her goodnight at her door, and said, in a voice choked with emotion, "Well, this is going to be a very interesting trip."

"I know, honey, and I wish I could be there with you. But we will get through this one way or the other," Cara said, trying to assure him.

Matt gave her a puzzled look and said, "Oh, you mean that jail thing and us? Sure, I know we are going to end up together and things will eventually be fine. I was talking about that big lefthander the Mets are going to throw at us in the first game. I was 1 for 4 against him earlier in the year and he K'd me twice."

Cara laughed and punched Matt in the arm. She then put his face in her hands, kissed him deeply, and said, "I love you so much it hurts.

I refuse to ever lose you again." Matt decided it would probably be all right if he stayed at Cara's maybe another hour longer.

On his way home that night, Matt stopped in and saw Sonny and Gwen at their condo in downtown Cincinnati. "I think we are down to the short strokes here," said Matt.

"Nothing we didn't expect," said Sonny.

"I know, I just hope I will be able to play in the World Series if we get that far."

Putting her arm around Matt's shoulder Gwen said, "When we left last spring and drove all the way to Portland, I don't think any of us would have dreamed things would have worked out like they have. All of us just have to be grateful for everything that has happened and take each day as it comes."

"I worry about you guys and everyone down in Blossom."

"Don't," said Sonny. "Everyone down home is ready for whatever happens. Hell, I think they are all kinda' lookin' forward to tellin' the government to go straight to hell if they come down askin' questions. Like Gwennie just said, look how far you have come. I would have never dreamed all this could have happened."

"By the way," said Gwen, "Doc said 'hi', and Annie told me to tell you it looked like you were letting that big lefthander on the Mets tie you up inside with his slider. She said to keep your hands inside the pitch and pull the ball."

Matt laughed and said, "you know, I think she's right."

The Reds arrived in New York on Thursday afternoon and would open the NLCS Saturday night on national TV and around the world. "A pretty big fucking deal," Randy called it. On both Friday and Saturday mornings, Matt and Randy got up early and checked the Internet and the morning papers to see if Patterson had released his story. Seeing nothing, they knew that barring some big press conference, Matt would at least play one more game.

Over breakfast the day of the opening game against the Mets, Matt and Randy questioned how Patterson could actually have irrefutable evidence of who Matt Wolf really was. Sure, he could suspect, offer conjecture, and point to the similarities between Matt's and Dylan's swings. But beyond that, what could he really have, especially with all the "urban legends" floating around about Matt?

"I don't think he has any proof at all," Randy told Matt. "I think he was trying to bluff you into spilling your guts in an exclusive so he wouldn't have to gather the proof on his own."

"I hope you're right," said Matt."

"Fuckin' A," said Randy. "Remember the reporter who wrote that bogus story about Howard Hughes and got his ass thrown in jail and had his career ruined? I don't think Patterson has the balls to risk something like that without concrete proof. And if he had it, he would have already broken the story."

The friends knew that the major flaw in Matt's story lay in Blossom. There was a distinct possibility, despite everyone's best efforts, that there were some details that had been overlooked by the team and some nosey reporter could turn up and prove the connection between Matt and Dylan. But, if Patterson had already been to Blossom, Matt would have heard that news immediately, and he had not.

They had seen Patterson earlier in the week in Cincinnati and already in New York at the previous day's press conference, although he kept away from Matt. The odds were looking good that he would have to wait until the season was over before going to Blossom to get his proof and release his story. To do it any earlier would pose too great a risk for Patterson.

For the time being, Matt and Randy convinced themselves that Patterson was full of shit about what he claimed to have in terms of proof. He had given it his best shot in an effort to get Matt to give him an exclusive before he had solid evidence, but it had not worked. At least that line of thought made both of them feel better. The idea of Matt being able to play at least in the NLCS against the Mets was "fucking great" according to Randy.

After the first two games of the series, the Mets were hoping they would never see Matt again. He had two hits in each game, and although he only drove in three runs, they were all "prime time ribbies" that tied or gave the Reds the lead in both games. Cincinnati won the first game 4-2 and the second game 6-4.

Randy pitched the second game and left with the scored tied 3-3 in the seventh inning. He later told ESPN, "I had a crap fast ball but my slider sucked." The ESPN host thanked Randy for his insightful and well articulated analysis.

The New York press went ballistic over the Mets losing the first two playoff games to the Reds. The Mets had been favored big time by Vegas and most knowledgeable fans. They were a good team led by an outstanding pitching staff. The press was brutal in saying how the Mets had taken the series for granted.

After returning to Cincinnati Sunday night, Matt snuck over to Cara's for the evening anticipating sleeping in late on Monday morning, the off day between games two and three. They turned off their cell phones, took the phone off the hook and watched Hitchcock's *Rear Window* starring Jimmy Stewart and Grace Kelly.

As usual, Randy was up early on Monday. He opened the *Cincinnati Enquirer* and almost spit up his Fruit Loops when he saw a headline written by Eric Patterson:

"Wolf Reluctant Reds Star"

"The Reds play the third game of the NLCS tomorrow night, far exceeding pre- season expectations for the team. The Reds have come this far due to the incredible play of Matt Wolf over the last three months. Game after game he has come up with big hit after big hit and

taken a team figured to be an also ran in the NL Central, to being just two victories from a World Series appearance.

Despite his and the team's success, Wolf is a rarity in baseball. He seldom talks about himself and is a "bad interview" since he responds to questions posed to him with yes or no answers. As a result, I will be heading to Blossom, South Carolina after the season to visit the small town that produced such a huge talent and hopefully learn more about the Reds' reluctant star."

"That little prick," Randy said to the air.

After getting Randy's call around noon, Matt and Cara read Patterson's article and figured the piece was written directly to Matt and was his "shot across the bow." But it did seem to confirm what Randy and Matt had surmised back in New York. Although he had figured out the truth, Patterson still had no hard proof. Cara agreed. Matt felt sure that he would be playing the remainder of the playoffs. That was a good feeling.

What was not a good feeling, was how badly his left leg hurt. Not only was the pain intensifying, but it appeared some internal bleeding was forming around the metal plates in his lower leg. He called Doc, who wanted Matt to go see a local doctor immediately, to make sure it was nothing serious. But Matt told him that no matter what the doctor found or recommended as treatment, he was going to play the rest of the playoff games and World Series, so why go?

As a compromise, Cara took some digital pictures of the leg then emailed them to Doc. After looking at them he e-mailed back saying it was possible some of the screws and plates in his leg had become loose from all the running and sliding. It was likely they were rubbing against bone causing inflammation and pain. He told Matt that he would need more surgery after the season. In the meantime, Doc wanted to know if he wanted some prescription pain medication. Cara and Matt both laughed. Doc was still a funny guy.

Last At Bat

Matt was getting used to Matt Wolf. Not just the name but the player; the face, the body, the whole thing. Looking at all the old pictures of Dylan Michael was like seeing someone he used to know, but was certainly not him. He asked Cara for about the tenth time if she missed the "old me", and she just smiled, shook her head, and said something about how weird men were. After losing the first two games in New York, the Mets were coming to town needing to win at least two of the three games in Cincinnati to have a real chance. What the Reds had to avoid was having a letdown or getting too cocky.

They did not let down, nor did they allow cockiness to run amuck. After holding the Mets scoreless for the first two innings, the Reds scored six runs in the bottom of the second, three more in the third, and went on to win game three, 12-4. They also easily won game four 5-1 to complete a sweep of the hated Mets, and the Queen City went into a hyper World Series frenzy.

Matt's performance and the overall play of the Reds put both under a media microscope. The questions from the final NLCS press conference, particularly from the New York press, had even more to do with Matt's private life, his past, and other non-related baseball issues. Matt did not want his private life and its major problems to interfere with what was happening on the field. He told the press that after the last game of the World Series he would gladly answer any questions they had on any subject. Until then he would only respond to baseball questions. Matt's position pissed off some of the press, but that was the way he was going to handle it.

During the grilling from the press, Matt noticed he received no questions from either Arthur Robbins or Eric Patterson. Robbins sat off to the side of the press room and seemed almost bored with the proceedings. But Patterson was nervous and fidgety. His face was flushed and he was continually wiping perspiration from his brow.

When the press conference after game four was over, Patterson seemed far more relieved than Matt was. Sonny and Matt figured Patterson was holding his breath on every question for fear Matt would say something that might lead to someone else putting two and two together and blow Patterson's chance for "The Story." Matt was almost tempted to confess everything then and there just to stick it to the guy. Instead, he was grateful the stars had aligned and he would be playing in a World Series.

Patterson also saw an alignment of stars. He planned to drive down to Blossom the day after the World Series and begin his investigation of Matt Wolf. He figured there was some kind of community involvement regarding Matt's true identity but Patterson felt very confident he could get somebody to open up and give him the fodder for what would be the biggest story in baseball history.

Last At Bat

53.　Please Come to Boston

In a best case scenario, Matt's baseball career had only seven games remaining. He knew at any time, Patterson or even Robbins could release their stories and it would be all over. But he was putting everything in perspective. He had re-united with Cara, he had played nearly a full year of professional baseball and he had a support system of people who cared for him who would help him fight to minimize the time he would have to spend in jail. He knew he would survive whatever lay ahead.

From Cara's perspective she realized how much she had lost during the years when she thought Matt was dead. She vowed she would never lose him again. They both realized that severe challenges lay ahead, but they finally saw a future. Together.

Through it all, Matt had remained focused on baseball like nothing Cara had ever seen before. Sometimes at dinner, watching TV, or reading, she would see him drift away. In his mind he was on the field in the middle of a game or an at bat. Seven games, if the series even went that far, was all Matt had left, but he was going to breathe in each second and take those memories with him for the rest of his life.

Randy and Pauly had been baffled at how Matt had handled all the stuff that was going on around him. They expected him to be nervous, depressed, or just plain pissed. He wasn't. Matt refused to let anything or anyone divert him from winning another World Series title.

Boston had the best team in baseball and rightly so with all the money they spent in the free agent market. They had no weaknesses.

301

On a position by position basis, it appeared that Cincinnati was going to get their heads handed to them.

The World Series opened in Boston. In the first game, the Sox' did what all the sport writers said they would do. They handed the Reds their heads 10-3. After the game Randy said that guys were talking in the bullpen about how the Reds' strategy of "giving Boston over- confidence" was really working well. The Reds made four errors in the first five innings, pitching and hitting like they were in a fog. They were lucky the score wasn't 20-3.

Before Game Two the next night, Matt got up in front of the team and made a speech. It was the first time he had done so since coming over from the Mariners in July. Spoken in a soft voice, Matt's words didn't seem to have a whole lot to do with the Red Sox or the Series.

"There are times in all of our lives we should try to hold in our minds; times we should realize how lucky we are to be doing what we are doing at that moment. Because there will be a time when we look back and would give anything to go back and relive them once more, if we could get a second chance. If we don't appreciate what we are living, it all goes away, like sand through our fingers. Yesterday we stunk up the joint because we weren't having any fun. We were nervous and played like it. We were not enjoying the moment, we were fighting it. Let's just relax and have some fun. I'd like to have you guys do me a favor. Just look around the locker room and take in everything you see at this moment."

On hearing Matt's request, some of the guys giggled like twelve- year- olds and looked down at the floor. "C'mon guys, humor me. Just look around. Take a picture of what you see and file it away. Remember it. Live it." Said Matt.

Eventually everyone did look around, and the giggles disappeared.

"All I am saying is to drink in every moment you are on the field for as long as we are in the Series this next week. Do your future self a favor and be able to turn to these moments in your lives like an old movie and relive them. Winning would be great, but if we get all nervous and tight worrying about what some writer might say because we make an error, strike out, or throw a bad pitch, then we'll forget about all the fun. Besides if a writer could do any better, he'd be playing instead of writing."

Then Matt took a serious tone.

"Finally, I think it would help team togetherness and make everyone relax if we leaned over to our nearest teammate or coach and shared a deep mouth- on-mouth kiss to show our love and solidarity for one another."

With his arms open wide, Matt made a bee line for Billy Merrill, a 245 pound back-up first baseman who was one homely bastard, in what appeared to be a sincere effort to plant one on old Bill. Merrill nearly fell on his ass trying to back up from Matt. Merrill finally curled up on the bench in a fetal position like some school girl fighting off her first lip lock. He finally said, "Damn, Matt, I guess I just don't want to win all that much after all." The locker erupted in laughter. It sounded like the whole team was watching the Seinfeld episode where George has "shrinkage."

That night Matt was 0 for 4 although he hit the ball hard. The Reds still won 5- 1 while playing the best defense they had all year. Randy went the distance for his first ever World Series win and vowed he would remember that game for the rest of his life. He would particularly remember how much fun that game was.

Matt called Cara from the Boston airport after the second game and was disappointed when she did not answer. He left a message on her voice mail that he would be coming over to her place to celebrate but he might not get there until after 1:00 a.m.

Last At Bat

Gwen and Sonny had been going back and forth between Cincinnati and Blossom every other week leading up to the playoffs. Everybody in Blossom questioned them, wanting to know how their "boy" was doing. They didn't ask about the baseball, they could read about that in the papers and on the Internet. Instead, they asked about Matt and all the off-the-field stuff they knew he must be dealing with.

They all told Sonny and Gwen to let Matt know that he should just focus on baseball. The rest of it would " all come out in the wash." In addition to Annie's advice on hitting a slider, Irma Bexley, a ninety-four- year- old former Blossom high school teacher and ardent supporter of the team, also had some hitting advice. She told Sonny to tell Matt that he had a tendency to pull off on back door moving fastballs, especially when batting right-handed. Instead, he should just shorten his stroke and take the ball to right field. Irma also knew a little about baseball.

54.   Pressure from Peers

Over the months, the circle of Blossom residents who knew about the real story regarding Matt grew. The circle grew from necessity, practicality, and ultimately, to a defined strategy. At first, it was necessary to bring in the core group who could get specific things done like building a background for Matt. Then, from a practical perspective for those who had committed either crimes of commission or omission. Those people needed to at least tell their spouses or their kids what they had done, in case the police came knocking on their door asking questions.

Finally, after nearly 10 months they decided "what the hell," they might as well bring everybody into the scheme and put community peer pressure on everyone to keep their mouths shut. At first Doc was particularly worried about a leak. But after several months he could see and hear how everybody in town seemed to relish the idea of lying to the state police and/or the federal government if need be. Blossom was unanimous in its belief that Dylan Michael had been flat out screwed by the government years before and it was time the "Blossom Jury" reversed the conviction.

Sonny and Doc heard of folks getting together in small gatherings to rehearse what they would say to a reporter or government cop if questioned. It was not merely that the folks of Blossom agreed to lie their individual and collective asses off to protect Matt, they were actually looking forward to it.

Before the playoffs even started, a test of the Blossom peer pressure had occurred in early September when the Reds had played the Braves at Turner Field on a Saturday night. The Braves brought in a rookie to face Matt with two on and two out in the seventh inning of a tie game. Watching the youngster warm up, Matt thought his motion looked familiar. He thought back to his days in Tacoma but did not remember where he had seen the tall, rangy, lefthander. As Matt stepped into the batter's box, the young man on the mound stepped off the rubber, took off his hat and wiped his brow. At that moment Matt could clearly see his face. He was the young man from Blossom who had signed with the Braves out of high school and had thrown batting practice to Matt months before. The Braves wanted to give their first round pick a taste of the big leagues in an already lost season for Atlanta.

On a 3-1 pitch, Matt hit a 94 mile per hour fast ball to right field that at the time, gave the Reds the lead in a game they eventually lost. As he stood on first base, Matt looked at the rookie, and the young man gave Matt a brief nod. Matt nodded back. He wondered what the lefthander would say to reporters after the game. He said nothing. Had he done otherwise, he might as well have not bothered returning home to face his folks and the rest of Blossom.

Gwen, Doc, Annie, and Sonny all agreed that if the story got out, the four of them would tell the judge and jury that they were the ring leaders of everything that had happened and how everybody else on the team were minor players in the scheme. They also surmised that unless a judge wanted to lock up the whole town, the system would probably prefer to nail the four of them.

Two weeks before the end of the season, they sat in Annie's kitchen over coffee and pecan pie and talked about if they were to "do time" where it might be? They even got on line and checked out all the prisons in the southeast to see what they were like. They also gave Joe Wiley, a local attorney who was also part of the team, a call. They asked him what he felt the prison terms could be. He at first said the gas chamber or life with no parole and then hung up the phone. He called back in two minutes laughing his ass off at what he thought was real funny lawyer humor. After regaining some composure he said that they could get a year or two if they "got the wrong judge." Or he said, they might get shot and began laughing his ass off again.

Right before the World Series, Sonny and Gwen hosted an end of summer barbeque at their place. As usual nearly a hundred folks showed up to eat pork, potato salad, baked beans, and apple pie. The conversations for the most part centered on Matt. Everyone seemed to know all of Matt's statistics and had seen he had won the NLCS MVP award.

The strange thing was even though they all knew his real name was Dylan Michael, the folks of Blossom all referred to him as Matt Wolf. They did so out of habit and design for fear they might slip under future questioning and say the wrong name. At the end of that day in October, the Matt Wolf/Dylan Michael saga was a sacred community secret that would go to the graves of everyone involved. That was just the way things were in Blossom.

Last At Bat

55.   Frankie

On the travel day between Game Two and Three of the World Series, Reds' Manager Frankie Weber talked to a small group of Cincinnati press after a light workout at the Great American Ball Park about what had happened in Game Two. He said his team had listened and taken to heart Matt's comments prior to the game. As a result, the nerves on display in Game One were gone. He said during Game Two, the guys acted as if they were enjoying the moment and played like it. They took chances and played to win, not just to avoid losing. After the game, Weber said the clubhouse was loud, raucous, x-rated, and funny as hell. As the manager, Weber said he knew enough to just stand back and let it happen.

"I decided to be more aggressive that second game," Weber went on. "We kept the Red Sox off balance by calling for stolen bases when we shouldn't have, taking the extra base on their outfielders' arms, playing small ball by bunting, executing hit and runs, and taking walks instead of going for three run home runs. The key to Game Two after that first game blow out was how Randy McDonald stepped up and grabbed the Red Sox' hitters by the throat to shut down their offense."

In the Reds' bullpen, Randy's pitching was described with a bit more color. "McDonald stuck the Red Sox' bats up their asses," was how Bill Merrill put it. That visually challenging description of Randy's performance was universally understood by players on major league rosters. To the rest of the world it meant Randy dominated one of the best lineups in all of baseball.

Randy's dominating performance started in the first inning when he threw a fastball maybe six inches inside to the Red Sox' menacing number three hitter, Adolfo Cruz. It really wasn't all that close of a pitch. Nothing would have happened except that after the pitch, Cruz glared at Randy and took a couple steps toward the mound before being headed off by the ump and the Reds' catcher. At 6'3" and 245 pounds, Cruz looked more like a tight end than a baseball player.

Earlier in the year Cruz had run over a Yankee catcher at home plate and put him in the hospital for two weeks. He had a nasty reputation as someone you didn't mess with. Even his own teammates kept their distance. Randy kept his cool. As a result, many of the fans thought that Cruz had sent a message to Randy and the rest of the Reds' staff to not pitch him tight or he might just come out and kick somebody's ass.

The next pitch from Randy was a 98 mile per hour fast ball that somehow missed Cruz' chin and put him flat on his ass. This time it was Randy who charged the plate and was ready to take Cruz on if he suddenly jumped to his feet looking for a fight. What really pissed Cruz off was as he was heading to the dirt his bat ticked the ball and the pitch, which nearly took off his head and ended up being a strike.

The umps kept the peace by warning both benches that any more close pitches would lead to ejection from the game. Of course that didn't stop Randy from coming inside on the very next pitch. Even though the pitch was, again not all that close, Cruz bailed out and complained loudly to the ump that Randy should have been thrown out of the game. But the ump said the pitch was only three inches inside and told Cruz to get back in the box.

The fourth pitch finally convinced Cruz that he may have been dealing with a mad man. Randy threw a fast ball 101 miles per hour over the catcher's head and hit the backstop on the fly. While not close to Cruz, and, therefore, not a pitch that could get Randy ejected, it was a "fuck you" pitch with a definite warning attached to it that Cruz and the rest of the Red Sox got loud and clear.

Randy came back to strike out Cruz on two straight sliders that had Cruz swinging wildly and bailing out of the batter's box. It was Cruz who then turned away from Randy's glare as he headed back to the bench bat in hand, muttering something in Spanish.

Randy's three hitter gave the Reds that second game, and they headed back to Cincinnati for Games Three, Four, and Five.

After arriving at Cincinnati International airport at 12:30 am, Matt called Cara several times on the way to her condo. There was no answer. That made no sense. A fear seized him that he tried to shrug off as being silly. He tried to think of all the possible reasons for her not answering his calls but while most were plausible, none relieved his apprehension.

Following the usual routine, he made his way around to the back of her condo and entered her screened-in porch. As he did so, two oddities struck him. First of all, the screen door was unlocked. Secondly, the porch light was off. Yet the kitchen light was on, and Matt could clearly see into the kitchen, dining room, and family room. What he saw stopped him in his tracks.

All three rooms were completely empty. All the furniture was gone. Trying the back door Matt discovered it was unlocked. He entered the deserted home and stood in silence in the kitchen unable to control a sense of panic that threatened to overwhelm him. After several minutes he began to roam through the first floor of the condo looking for something, anything. Upstairs he entered Cara's bedroom and found it empty. He moved to her bedroom window, looked out over the night time cityscape, and stood rooted for nearly ten minutes trying to catch his breath. When he finally did, he shook his head and smiled.

After returning to the Westin, Matt saw that an envelope had been slid under his door. He could tell by the writing it was from Cara,

Last At Bat

Dear Matt,

I know what I have done is cruel, yet I hope you will someday be able to forgive me. I desperately need time to think things through. I have decided to move to California, at least for awhile. I want you to know how hard this is for me but I can't go on the way things are.

I have come to the conclusion that my being here in town complicates your life even more than it is. Just know I want what is best for you and always will.

And please never think the way you look today as compared to years ago, had anything at all to do with my decision. After all, would you really care if I looked differently than I do now? If so, I would question if you really loved me at all.

Please don't hate me.

Love always,

Cara

******

In Game Three with the World Series back in Cincinnati, the Reds scored six runs in the first inning and went on to win 8-1. Leading the Series two games to one, the momentum was clearly in the Reds favor. They were feeling very good about themselves. Matt reminded the team of the 2004 ALCS.

******

Matt played well but not spectacularly in the first three games of the Series. The Red Sox pitchers refused to let Matt beat them at the plate, preferring to pitch around him and let someone else come up with the big hit. So far, the Sox had succeeded. While Matt hit .333 in those first three games, he had only two RBI and no extra base hits.

While obvious the Sox didn't want to mess with Matt, it was also obvious that Matt was playing in some pain. Pauly noticed that Matt's left leg, the one which had surgery after his accident, looked terrible and was black and blue from the ankle to the knee. Pauly told Randy he could see and feel the titanium plates and screws through Matt's skin that were holding his leg together. Matt was hurting and his loss of speed was noticeable. He refused to complain and would only take Tylenol for the pain.

Before the fourth game of the World Series, Matt entered the clubhouse in a good mood he should not have felt. His leg ached, and the woman he loved had succumbed to the pressure they had both been living under for weeks.

Matt kept Cara's leaving from Randy and the rest of the team.

The fourth game itself was somewhat anti-climatic. The Reds played good defense, got three timely hits, had outstanding pitching, and won 5-2. Matt was 0 for 3 with a walk. For the first time ever, he was removed for a pinch runner in the eighth after his limp became even more noticeable. The Reds lead the Series three games to one.

After the game, Randy and Matt decided to go out to dinner on the Riverfront in downtown Cincinnati. Even though they would have to bear the crowds they would run into, including all the autograph seekers, Matt wanted to share the city's excitement and in a way say good-bye on his own terms. Without saying as much, Randy could read his friends tea leaves and wanted to be part of Matt's good-bye.

When they walked into the Montgomery Inn at the Boat House for their 9:15 reservation, the place was already packed with Cincinnati and Boston fans in town for the Series. Randy and Matt heard a lot of good natured verbal jousting going on between the two camps of partisans. As they were being led to their table, several fans saw the two Reds and stood to clap as the teammates walked by. Soon the entire restaurant, including both Reds and Red Sox fans were on their feet and applauding. Strangely, no one was hooting and hollering. The clapping seemed almost polite rather than the kind they had heard in other public places. Further, it lasted several minutes, and whatever emotion or feeling was driving the response seemed to transcend baseball.

"I don't think they're clapping for me," said Randy.

"Sure they are," replied Matt. "Big ugly guys are always the fans' favorites." No one came over to their table that evening so they enjoyed themselves knowing that whatever lay ahead was something neither could control. The night was special. The reaction from the fans at the restaurant was warm and emotional. Matt said later, "They were more like friends than fans."

On their way out of the restaurant amid more clapping, Matt looked into the bar and saw Eric Patterson sitting next to a woman that Matt did not recognize at first. He asked Randy to wait and walked over to Patterson, whose eyes suddenly got big as saucers when he saw Matt approach.

Within a few feet of their bar stools, Matt finally recognized the woman as Janet Mason, the State's Attorney who had prosecuted both his tax and prescription drug cases four years earlier.

Reaching out to shake Patterson's hand, Matt calmly said, "I just wanted to say that I saw your article about me earlier this week, and I am flattered you are going all the way down to Blossom just to do a story on me."

Matt then introduced himself to Mason, shook her hand and asked her if she was a baseball fan. Not waiting for her answer, he turned and walked away without a word being uttered by Mason or Patterson. For a reason not all together clear, the encounter felt good to Matt.

******

Randy McDonald later told *Sports Illustrated* that the fifth game of the World Series against the Red Sox was the most fun he ever had in baseball. "We fucking KNEW we were going to win, and the fans were going ape-shit from the first pitch." *SI* printed as many of Randy's quotes as they dared.

Two hours before the fifth game, Great American Ball Park was electric with an energy that had not existed there for nearly a decade. Most of the players had never before experienced something that intense. The game itself was sloppy, with lots of hits, runs, five lead changes, some errors, and some big hits. The uneven play of both teams produced an emotional rollercoaster for fans that left them weak and elated.

Matt, from the first pitch, looked like an eighteen- year-old old rookie. In his first three times up, he went double, double, single, and had three RBI. He was loose on the bench and kept everyone relaxed and laughing. His antics included doing an imitation of the glare that Cruz had given Randy in Game Two. Of course, every time he walked by Billy Merrill he acted like he was going to kiss him. Merrill, playing along, would cover his mouth with both hands and tell Matt "you're not my type" or "winning isn't everything."

With one man out in the seventh inning, Matt came to the plate for his fourth at bat with the Reds down 9-5 and the bases loaded. After taking a strike, then a ball on two fast balls, Matt hit the change-up third pitch on a low line shot into center field directly at the centerfielder. As soon as they saw the fielder take a single step back, everyone in the stadium knew he had messed up big time. On the TV replays you could clearly read his lips when he said to himself, "Aw, shit."

The centerfielder tried to change direction and charge in to get the ball before it hit in front of him. But his arm was too short and his legs too slow. The ball hit six inches in front of the diving outfielder and skipped past him rolling all the way to the centerfield wall.

Matt had taken off at the crack of the bat, unlike some hitters who stay in the box admiring their work. As he gained momentum, he seemed to shift gears and pick up even more speed as he rounded second and headed to third.

The crowd's roar became deafening when it realized that Matt, with his head down and arms pumping in a powerful rhythm, was ignoring the third base coach's "stop sign." When Matt hit the third base bag his stride was long and powerful with no indication of pain or injury. He caught the base just right, on the inside corner with the big toe of his left foot and exploded down the third base line. He had no intention of sliding.

The Red Sox right fielder picked up the ball in right center and made a good throw to the second base relay man who in turn threw a strike to home plate. Waiting at home for the throw, the catcher had his left leg and foot planted on the side of the plate facing up the third base line. His right foot was slightly in front of the plate. He was in a semi-crouched position and at 6'2, 228 pounds, was a tough object to get around.

Seeing the heavily muscled barrier in his path, Matt reasoned if he could not get around him, he would have to go through him. The ball arrived a split second before Matt did at home plate so the catcher had time to brace himself for the collision. He needed a little more bracing.

Matt lowered his left shoulder and hit the catcher around the solar plexus. The resulting sound could be heard even above the screams of the fans. The catcher was knocked onto the back of his head by the impact but sometime before he hit the ground, the ball had been dislodged from his glove. Matt was safe. The game was tied 9-9.

The astonishing thing about the collision was not only the sound it made or that Matt was safe, but that Matt never broke stride after he hit the catcher. He simply ran over him and kept running all the way to the dugout.

The stadium, according to Pauly, went "absolutely fucking bat shit." By any description, the place was up for grabs. Matt got a curtain call. He tipped his hat to the fans for the first time all year. After a pop up ended the inning, Matt was told to take over at first base instead of returning to the outfield. Despite blood seeping through his pants around his lower leg and a decided limp, he headed out to first for the top of the eighth inning.

The Reds relievers finally began to throw the ball as they had done all year. They held the Red Sox scoreless for the eighth and ninth innings and the game remained tied 9-9 going into the bottom of the ninth.

Last At Bat

56.   "The Best I Ever Saw"

The morning of the fifth game of the World Series, Arthur Robbins reluctantly hosted a breakfast at the Westin Hotel in Cincinnati for a group of aspiring baseball writers. They came from a dozen local colleges to gain some insight into the writing profession.

Following the breakfast and according to Robbins, "After some especially inspiring and thoughtful comments" on his part, he agreed to answer some questions. As usual there were the normal technical inquiries, including can you make a living in this field to which the answer was, "barely", and a bunch of other questions that were asked for the most part to show how smart the questioner was.

However, a young man from the University of Indiana asked a rather simple question: "Who was the best you ever saw?" Robbins' answer had to come in two parts: "The best pitcher? Sandy Koufax. During a five year period he was virtually unhittable but had to retire at thirty years old. The best everyday player was another guy who had a short career. Dylan Michael, he was the best I ever saw."

The student then had a short follow-up question. "Why was Dylan the best?" he asked.

Robbins answered, "It seems every year some *phenom* tears up the minor leagues and is tagged a five tool player. Someone who can hit for power, average, run, throw, and catch. Very few can do all five well. Hell, if you could do two of those things well, you could end up in the Hall of Fame. But Dylan could do all five and do each extraordinarily well…"

Earlier on that morning before Game Five, Matt had gotten a call from Arthur Robbins.

"Matt, it's Arthur, sorry if I woke you."

"No problem, I was already up," Matt said. "What's going on?"

"I hear that Patterson has been talking to your stepdad, and they are trying to get something out in the next day or so to take advantage of the World Series coverage. I'm sorry, but I had to release my story early this morning. It's online now. Will probably make some of the West Coast papers later today."

"Oh", was all a stunned Matt could say.

"Like I told you," said Robbins, "I had agreed to wait until after the season to release my story, but I really had no choice. I hope you understand."

"I understand," said a shaken Matt. "It's just kind of a shock. I thought I would be able to finish the World Series if we don't win tonight."

"I'm sorry, but I needed to make sure I beat Patterson to the punch on this," said Robbins.

"I appreciate the call, Arthur. Thanks."

Going to his computer, Matt found Arthur's story.

"Is Matt Wolf for Real?"

"Matt Wolf joined the Reds just two weeks before the July 31 trading deadline and even before tomorrow's fifth game of the World Series, he has become a cult hero of sorts in Cincinnati and throughout the league. Prior to his call-up, he was completely unknown yet has played like an experienced All- Star for nearly three months.

What makes his story all the more compelling is unlike most ball players, who never miss a chance to talk about themselves and their past glories, Matt has refused to talk in detail of his past. What little he does provide is very basic information that he seems to repeat time and again no matter how many times he is asked the same question. The answers never vary nor are they embellished, as if he is reciting from a script. To be honest, he is not a very good interview.

However, despite the loud protests from my employer, (I figured there were more than enough baseball writers covering the Playoffs), I spent a couple days in Blossom, South Carolina, learning everything I could about Matt Wolf.

Blossom is located in the southeastern part of the state and can be best described as similar to Mayberry without all the excitement and glamour. I should also point out that the folks of Blossom choose their friends carefully. They are wary of strangers. They choose their words carefully as well. When asked a question, they pause before answering either being polite, (which is their way), or making sure they respond with care and thought.

Needless to say, Matt Wolf's exploits this season have been followed in minute detail by seemingly everyone in the town. They are able, without the slightest urging, to quote even his most obscure statistics. They know the number of times he failed to advance a base runner with less than two outs (six), or how many two-out game winning hits he had (five) or how many times he talked about himself to a reporter (zero).

However, his success does not seem to be a big surprise to anyone in Blossom. They, as a group, talk fondly of his exploits as far back as Little League, then high school, and on the sand lots around the area. All agree he would have been a superstar far sooner if he had not been hit by a car at eighteen years old and lost five or six years of his career recovering from what had been traumatic, life threatening injuries.

Matt's mother died three days after giving birth to him. He was raised by Gwen and Sonny Cook, a local Blossom couple who had been childless until that time. They raised Matt as their own but did not adopt him on the chance that his real father, who disappeared days after his mother died, would return to claim his son. He never did. The Cooks gave thought to adopting Matt along the way but there never seemed to be a real reason to go through the formality. Blossom is not big on formality.

Being a believer in the theory that when a story sounds too good to be true it usually is, I went to Blossom hoping to crack the veneer of a young man who, from the outside at least, seems a little too good to be true. He is athletically superior, obviously intelligent, (a 3.8 GPA at good old Blossom High), humble, funny, popular with his teammates and damn tough. He plays through pain. On the field he has the knack of being able to come through in the clutch time and time again. I am sure he is able cure the sick and raise the dead as well.

Last At Bat

After four days in Blossom I regret to say I did find the real Matt Wolf. First of all, he is listed at 6'3 ½ inches. He is really 6'2 ½. His weight is supposed to be 223 when he is clearly 221. His waist is 34"not 35." He does swear from time to time although "damn it" seems to be the most often used and preferred oath. The folks in town refer to him as a "real nice, polite boy" and say things like "he never talks about his baseball", "he was always real quiet like" or "you'd never know'd he was a big leaguer, no airs or nuthin'."

It didn't take long to learn that the folks of Blossom care deeply for Matt but not just because he is a professional athlete. No, it isn't the professional athlete part they care about; it is the person part. No jealousy, no talking behind his back, no bringing out the dirty linen. They just really like Matt Wolf. Seemingly, for all the right reasons.

In the few times Wolf has spoken of his past, he talked fondly of Blossom and its people. He once told me that while Sonny and Gwen raised him and he will always love them for all they did for him, it was the town that accepted him and allowed him to grow up. The people of Blossom taught him lessons about what is important in life and what is not. It's clear to see that Matt Wolf is a product of Blossom. He remains a part of the town and a part of everyone who lives there.

Since Wolf's coming to the Reds and his subsequent remarkable success, there have been all kinds of bizarre stories floating around him. It is almost like the Elvis sightings that apparently happen every week if you read the National Inquirer. *In Matt's case, the stories say that he is the clone or illegitimate bastard son of Mickey Mantle. He is the result of alien intelligent design or has bionic body parts thus creating amazing bat speed. He is really Dylan Michael raised from the dead. Or, my personal favorite, that he is the love child of Martina Navratalova and Alex Rodriquez, secretly reared in a laboratory specializing in the creation of high paid professional athletes whose earnings were then invested into diamond mines. Pick your favorite fantasy.*

Unfortunately, I can attest to one of those stories. Four years ago I went several hundred miles north of Blossom to southern Kentucky. I was one of the few reporters given access to that awful plane crash site where Dylan Michael and nearly 300 other people died. I went there the evening of the crash to write a story of the life and death of a truly tragic baseball figure. Early the next morning, I saw the charred remains of Dylan Michael's body. While horrifically burned, Dylan's first World Series ring was clearly visible. It was the same ring I had

322

seen him wearing the day before when I said good-bye to him at the Cincinnati airport the day of the crash.

Sorry to eliminate one of the Matt Wolf urban legends but the vision of Martina and A-Rod creating what could become a sports legend is a very compelling and enticing visual alternative.

As I was leaving Blossom after completing my research, I stopped at Millie's Diner for breakfast. Some of the folks I had interviewed earlier in the week recognized me and came over to say goodbye. Soon there were more than a dozen of us including the town doctor, the high school coach, the mayor, and even Sonny and Gwen (who were headed back to Cincinnati for the World Series,) all talking about Matt Wolf. They were all excited about the World Series and of course they all felt Matt would play a key role in the outcome. In fact, it was more than a feeling. It seemed, in their minds at least, a certainty. In the eyes of Blossom, Matt Wolf can do just about anything. After all, he recovered from an awful hit/run accident and now is getting an opportunity to show the world what he can do. One can only wonder what talent would have been on display for all baseball fans if Matt had not been hit by that car so many years ago?

Even though it's only been three months of major league experience for Matt, the folks of Blossom seem to know the answer to a question I often get "Who is the best player you ever saw?" To the people of Blossom, the answer is easy.

Arthur Robbins

"Did you see it," asked Randy excitedly.

"I saw it," said Matt.

"I can't believe it. Why would he do that?"

"I don't know."

"You know what this means don't you?'

"I think so," said Matt.

"It means Patterson is going to go absolutely fucking out of his mind," said Randy gleefully.

In his hotel in downtown Cincinnati, Robbins answered his cell phone.

"Arthur, I just saw your article on Wolf," said a surprisingly calm Eric Patterson.

"How did you like it?"

Through now gritted teeth Patterson exploded, "It's a bunch of fucking lies, you miserable son of a bitch. You know the truth and you know I was on to that story. What you wrote is unethical, immoral, illegal…

"Does that mean you didn't like it?" Robbins said with uncharacteristic equanimity. "I mean I thought it was journalistically well constructed, had a specific point of view, had some pathos, just enough information…"

"You fucking asshole," spat Patterson. "I know the truth and I'll prove it. I'll also prove you lied in that article to protect Michael. I'll have your fucking job, you…"

"Well maybe you should start on that quest by going down to Blossom," said Arthur calmly. The folks there are very nice and I am sure they will fully cooperate with you. Or talk to Drew. But don't mention the IRS to him like I did. He's a little sensitive someone might question what he did with all the money he stole from Dylan. In fact, good luck in finding Drew. His phone is now disconnected."

"You prick, the next time I see you I am going to kick…"

Arthur hit "end" on his cell phone, sat back in his chair and smiled.

******

In Randy's condo he and Matt sat in front of his computer having read Arthur's article for the fifth time.

"I can't believe it," said Randy.

"Me either," said Matt. "All I know is there is no way Patterson can do anything to refute Arthur's story until after the World Series.

And even then for him to challenge the story, given Arthur's reputation, is going to be tough."

"How will you ever be able to thank him?" Asked Randy.

"Maybe by taking advantage of a second chance. What Arthur may not know at this point is that he is now part of the plan."

Last At Bat

57.   Stupid Advice

As he stood on deck in the ninth inning of the fifth game against the Red Sox tied at 9- 9, Matt knew he would hit the ball hard. His bat was lightning quick that day, and despite the fact the Red Sox pitcher could run it up there around 95 or 96 mph, his pitches didn't have much movement.

After the first Reds' batter reached base on a walk, Matt slowly walked to the plate amid the roar of the Reds' fans, a roar he did not hear. Instead he thought of the "Double." He remembered how nervous he had been at the time. He worried now as he stood there taking a practice swing before stepping into the batter's box, if this time he was too calm. But he reasoned his calmness had more to do with the knowledge that he knew no matter what happened, there was going to be life after his next at bat.

While the Boston infield gathered around their manager on the mound discussing how to pitch to him, Matt was motioned by Dave Schultz, his 3rd base coach. They huddled half way between home and third base where Schultz put his arm around Matt's shoulder. "Five years ago you were a pretty good bunter. Can you still bunt?" Schultz asked.

"I can still bunt," Matt said with a smile.

"Fuck, alright. Tell you what, they probably think you're going to bunt. Why don't you take a hack at the first one if it's a fast ball. If it's a breaking ball take it and bunt the second pitch."

"Okay", said Matt. "By the way, how long have you known?"

"Long enough. Hey Matt, swing hard in case you hit that first one."

Last At Bat

"I'll swing hard, Dave."

On the mound, the Boston pitching coach gave his young right hander specific directions. "Throw the fast ball letter high. That's the toughest pitch to bunt, and you can be sure as hell he will be bunting."

Matt walked back to the plate and looked around him. He sucked it all in like a sponge. Then he whispered to himself, "Pick a zone, inner half, look for the fast ball, keep the arms loose…"

In the radio booth the announcer was hoarse from calling the wild game. *"This stadium is going crazy. You can't hear yourself think. The Red Sox are expecting the bunt from Wolf, the 1ˢᵗ and 3ʳᵈ basemen are in on the corners…*

… it's a fast ball, I see it…"

"…here's the pitch to Wolf, a fastball, Wolf swings and…"

58.　California

The morning after the fifth game, Randy woke up with a splitting headache. His arm hurt, his back hurt, and his mouth had a taste that only drinking twelve beers in two hours can produce. He felt great. Laying sprawled naked in his bed, he smiled at the memory of the previous night. After getting up to pee, he went to his front door and retrieved the morning paper, looking forward to reading how great his team was after dropping the Red Sox like a bad habit in five games.

He wasn't disappointed. The front page plus the entire sports section talked about the Reds victory in the "front runner" way only newspapers can. For an hour he drank coffee, had some Frosted Flakes, toast and orange juice and read about a night he would never forget.

After reading all the articles about the Series, Randy decided to stay in bed awhile and absentmindedly leafed through the rest of the paper, in between repeated calls to Matt's cell phone. In the City Section of the *Cincinnati Enquirer* which focused on local news, he read a blurb near the bottom of page 2.

Wife of Former Cincinnati Reds Star Missing
Montecito, California

Local authorities confirm that 27 year old Cara Lynn Michael of Cincinnati, Ohio, is missing and presumed drowned in the ocean near the Biltmore Hotel in Montecito. Mrs. Michael was the wife of Dylan Michael, the Cincinnati Reds baseball star, who was killed in a plane crash three years ago.

The star-crossed couple enjoyed national media attention during Michael's career with the Cincinnati Reds. Mrs. Michael had recently left Cincinnati and returned to California where she had lived for several years. Local police confirm that a suicide note was found in

Last At Bat

Mrs. Michael's hotel room, although no details were made available. Funeral arrangements will be announced.

******

Matt slept late the day after Game Five. He awoke around 11 a.m., and when he tried to turn over onto his side, his left leg screamed at him. Despite the discomfort, Matt simultaneously felt relief, sadness, and a bit of euphoria that came in waves of emotion rendering him powerless to move. For nearly an hour he stayed in bed trying to think of what he would do next in his life. He decided a ham and cheese omelet would be good for starters. He then thought about taking a trip to California.

After breakfast he checked his cell phone and e-mail. He had 46 voice, 38 text and over 200 e-mails messages. None from Cara. He figured he would begin responding to his messages after he read the morning paper.

******

Randy was shaking after reading the article about Cara. Tears welled up in his eyes as his right fist repeatedly pounded the bed. He knew what Cara meant to Matt and had no idea how Matt would react to the news. Was he even aware of what happened? Had someone called him? But then again why would they? There was no link between Matt and Cara.

Randy decided to get dressed and go to the Westin to break the news to Matt there. Walking to his door he saw the morning paper had not been taken in as yet. He picked it up and deposited it in a trash can down the hall. Just as he was about to knock on the door, it opened.

"Hey man, I was just getting ready to knock", said Randy nervously.

"Hi, come on in. Looks like somebody stole my paper. Want some breakfast?"

"Ah, no, just ate. Hey Matt, I need to talk to you…"

"Give me a minute, said Matt as he returned to his computer. " I was just sending an e-mail to Arthur.

Arthur,

Read your article in yesterday's paper and enjoyed it very much. Was pleased to hear you had gotten along so well with my friends and family down in Blossom. Also hope you enjoyed the World Series. Obviously, it was one of the greatest thrills of my life. I will be eternally grateful for the opportunity that was afforded me to be able to play in such an exciting game.

I have many people to thank for such an opportunity and will be forever indebted for their collective sacrifice, love, and support. Only with time will I be able to repay so many for so much.

My intention is to play baseball next season and for as many years as my body and circumstances allow me to play. I will be undergoing some minor surgery in the off season that hopefully will fix some loose ends in my left leg, right knee, and elbow. In addition, I will also get some touch up plastic surgery that Randy McDonald says I desperately need. I really think he wants the title of homeliest major league ball player all to himself.

Look forward to seeing you in Arizona for Spring Training.

Matt Wolf

PS: *By the way, have recently been approached by a writer from the New York Times about doing my life story. While telling him I was flattered, I also said it was way too early in my career and a bit presumptuous to have any such stories written about me. But after thinking about it for awhile, I might someday be interested in getting my "whole story" down on paper. Since I don't like the NY Times all that much, I was wondering if you knew a patient writer who might be interested in someday writing my story?*

A minute later Robbins e- mailed Matt back, *"Glad you liked the article. By the way, do you really think your life story is all that interesting?"*

Matt smiled after reading Arthur's return e-mail. Then turned to Randy.

"Well, buddy we are World Champs. Feeling OK this morning after all the celebrating?"

"Matt, I need to tell you something…

"What?"

"It's about Cara…"

"How did you find out? Asked Matt.

"You mean you know?"

"Of course, I know. She wasn't home after I got back from Boston. But how did you find out she left?"

"I didn't know she left. All I know is what I read in the paper this morning."

"In the paper? What was in the paper?"

"Matt, Cara is dead. The paper says she committed suicide in California."

"I figured something like that would happen," said Matt.

"What the hell are you talking about?" Randy yelled. "Something like what would happen? Cara's dead, Matt. How can you respond to something like this so unemotionally? I know how you cared for her and the plans you guys had made. What the hell is going on with you? Are you really such a cold hearted bastard?"

Matt offered an explanation. "Earlier this week I went over to Cara's condo and found her gone. The place was cleaned out. At first I was hurt, angry, and disappointed but it dawned on me that wasn't like Cara. I knew how she cared for me and knew she wouldn't just take off without talking to me face to face."

Looking away from Randy, Matt continued to explain, "I figured she was trying to make things easier on me by leaving town. She knew that if she and I were seen as a couple people could put two and two together and come up with Dylan. I know how much she loves me and that she would do anything to keep me out of jail and playing baseball, even if it meant giving me up for awhile.

"I also figured that perhaps someone thinking they were acting in my best interests had gotten to Cara and told her the risk I was running by being with her. Maybe someone threatened her with their knowledge of the truth. Maybe both. I don't know for sure. Anyway, Cara figured to eliminate the risk altogether and leave town," Matt finished.

"But Matt, even if everything you say is true, Cara is dead. Are you saying that is also part of her plan?" Randy questioned.

"Yes, it's all part of a plan," said Matt.

Last At Bat

59.   Patterson's Blog

Two months after the World Series, Randy saw a blog written by former Cincinnati Enquirer reporter Eric Patterson that proclaimed that Matt Wolf was really Dylan Michael. It showed some video of their swings side by side and suggested that Dylan alone had survived the plane crash that had killed 297 other people. It said Dylan had been rescued by Sonny and Gwen Cook, nursed back to health by Doc Watson and his nurses in Blossom, South Carolina, and then made his way back to the Reds where he became a star, re-united with his ex-wife, and lived happily ever after until she was killed in a drowning accident.

The blog was sandwiched between a story on the Loch Ness Monster appearing in Lake Tahoe and Brittany Spears being Marilyn Monroe and Joe DiMaggio's granddaughter.

Last At Bat

60.   "Got It"

When Arthur Robbins came to Blossom to do his story on Matt before the final game of the World Series, Doc Watson wasn't sure what to expect. He knew Robbins was a fan of Matt's by the story he had written right after the plane crash. But beyond that, there was no way of knowing how he would react to what the town of Blossom was going to ask of him.

The day Doc had Robbins come over to the Neon and tried to explain what the town wanted him to do, Robbins said, with good reason, he could not do it. They wanted him to fabricate a story, to lie, to mislead, to sacrifice his ethics, and to risk his career all for a person he really hardly knew. The town wanted Robbins to trust them and become part of their team and that by doing something wrong, join them in doing something right. The folks of Blossom didn't think he got it.

He got it.

Last At Bat

Mark Donahue

61.   McDonald's Autobiography

Randy was the first Reds' player in decades to write his own life story. It became an editorial challenge that required a warning in advertisements regarding "earthy language," "real baseball," and "outspoken candor," including the following excerpt:

> *In the six years after we beat the shit out of the Red Sox in the World Series, Matt and I each signed long term deals with the Reds, won four more World Championships, five national league pennants and the team averaged more than 102 wins per year. I actually got a Cy Young Award and won over 20 games three times. The Mariners are fucking idiots.*

> *Matt on the other hand, was simply the best all round player on our planet, maybe any planet. After some surgeries to his legs, his speed and defense significantly improved from that first year. Yet, at the plate, he was nothing short of astonishing. He was so good that at the All- Star games the other superstars would watch him take batting practice and ask him about his hitting theories. Actually his theory was pretty simple; "see the ball-- hit the ball."*

> *I know he tried to help some of the younger guys on the Reds over the years when they were having troubles at the plate, but it was like Mozart giving piano lessons to a 10 year old or Renoir teaching an art class to senior citizens. Both Matt and the player he was trying to help would get frustrated because the player simply could not do what Matt did.*

> *They say that male singers get better with age and I guess you could look at Sinatra and Bennett and understand that point. Hitters also get better with age. They get naturally stronger, their bat speed increases, they learn the pitchers in the league, and they know what the hell to do at the plate. I know I would have much rather faced some 22 year old stud who would swing his ass off trying to hit everything 500 feet no matter the score, than some 37 year old bastard who would look for his pitch and if he didn't get it, foul off about ten fucking pitches and wear my ass out.*

339

Last At Bat

In his seventh year with the Reds and at 34 years old, Matt put together a season unlike any other player in history. On July 5 he was hitting .404 and was leading the league in home runs, RBI, runs scored, total bases, and walks. Even his outs were absolutely crushed. The stars truly aligned and every bit of bad luck that had happened to him years before was being made up in an almost mystical season.

The general wisdom was he would melt down in the July and August heat and come back to earth. Instead he went to outer space. He finished that season with an average of .414. He hit 63 home runs, drove in 174 runs, scored 131, and walked 194 times. Sports writers called it the greatest season of all time. It surely was for one whole year, until Matt bettered each statistical category the following year. He was MVP both of those years in addition to winning back to back Triple Crowns. It was fucking amazing.

After those back to back miraculous years in which we won two more World Championships, his statistics began to sag just a bit only because pitchers refused to face him, preferring to walk him two or three times a game. And he was, by his own admission, getting older.

The Reds moved him to first base permanently when he was 40 and began giving him more days off during the season. The less stressful position and the rest, even though he would bitch and moan about sitting out a game or two here and there over the season, seemed to give him a boost mentally and physically. For the next four years Matt continued playing at an All Star level before retiring when he was 44 years old. His last year he hit .337 with 29 home runs and 104 RBI.

I once asked Matt how he kept his concentration for all those years, all those at bats. He said every time he went to the plate, every single time, he told himself it was his last at bat. His last career hit was a double.

Randy's autobiography became a best seller. He became a regular on TV talk shows and radio interviews. He even had a stint on FOX Sports Network as a color commentator until he pointed out the obvious one afternoon by saying a young third baseman had hit a "cock high fast ball" out of the ball park. It was Randy's last broadcast.

62.   Cooperstown

Of all the awards and recognition Randy won over the years, the one he treasured most was when Matt asked him to formally introduce him at Matt's induction to the Baseball Hall of Fame in Cooperstown.

Thank you, Ladies and Gentlemen.

The first day I met Matt Wolf he beat me up. Not that I didn't deserve it, mind you, but I wasn't used to having someone lay me out with two punches. On top of which he had, only minutes before the punches, ripped every pitch I threw to him at what I will call a very "spirited" practice session.

About halfway through that practice session I could tell I was facing a hitter that was the greatest I had ever seen. Since then, others who have been around the game even longer than I, have said he was the greatest hitter they ever saw. At some point I guess you have to believe Matt Wolf was the greatest hitter ever and let it go at that. And yet one can only wonder what he would have achieved if he had not been hit by a car that night in Blossom nearly 30 years ago.

For some reason I never had a lot of friends in baseball. Not sure why. I am quite lovable in a Genghis Kahn sort of way, but if I was to have only one friend in my whole life, I am proud to say it is Matt Wolf.

I am proud to introduce my friend, Matt Wolf, who also happens to be the best goddamn hitter any of us will ever see.

Matt came to the microphone turned to Randy and said,

"Thank you Randy...for everything."

******

"...Finally, I deeply, deeply appreciate all the kind words I heard today regarding my career. It seems like all those things happened

Last At Bat

just yesterday. I can clearly remember my first game in the majors and all the wonderful things that have happened to me since that time. While baseball has been a huge part of my life, it was not the only part. The friends and family who have supported me over all these years are the reason I am here today.

But in my case, I was blessed to have more than just "support." I had people sacrifice a great deal for me. I had people do things for me I did not deserve. People who took risks because they felt taking those risks was the right thing to do. Those are not the kinds of things you can ask people to do for you. It comes from them. It comes from a place inside them that knows things – the right things.

Over the last several years, a number of the people who are responsible for my being here today have died. Ironically, in each case, they died during the baseball season and I could not be with them in their final days. But I would have, if they had allowed it.

When I heard that my mom, Gwen, was very weak, I called and told her I was coming home to see her. She said, "Don't you dare come back here this weekend. You've got the Cubs coming into town and you know how well you hit those guys. You come down on Monday on your off day. I'll see you then, honey." She passed away that Sunday afternoon after watching our game on cable. I was an hour late.

Two years later Doc Watson and Sonny Cook died within one day of each other. Neither one ever let on to me that they were sick. It was their secret. They were real good at keeping secrets.

There is another friend who perhaps gave up and risked the most in his life for me. He asked that I not acknowledge him by name and that is probably for the best because I am sure it would embarrass him to have me tell him I love him in front of the whole world. But I do.

With all the wonderful things that have happened to me over the years I truly regret that Sonny, Gwen, and Doc along with scores of other friends, could not be here today. I cannot express to each of you how much they all mean to me. But more importantly, I wish all of you could have met them, could have gotten to know them. To see firsthand what they were all about. What good people are all about. What good people are capable of.

My family and I will never forget them. Thank you.

63.   Cooperstown, New York

O'Reilly's Stone House Tavern

The graying man in the Dodger baseball hat, Hawaiian shirt and wrinkled khaki slacks listened to the question from the young man behind the bar and answered, "How would I know? You think I have seen every goddamn ball player since 1869?"

"Well, all my friends and I think he was the best we ever saw and the numbers don't lie. You really think one of those guys from the old days was better than Matt Wolf?" he asked.

"Numbers do lie, kid. In fact they lie like hell," he replied.

"So, who was better?"

For a split second a smile flickered across the old man's face. Then he spoke.

Over the next few hours Robbins told the enterprising young bartender the true story of Dylan Michael and Matt Wolf, every detail. The young man was spell bound but suspicious.

"That's one hell of a story mister, but it can't be true. I think you're full of shit. Something like that would be all over the papers, TV and the Internet. It's like somebody finding Elvis working a lounge show in Atlantic City."

"It's all true," said Arthur.

"If it is, why are you telling me? I could go to the press and make a fortune telling everybody what you just told me."

"I would deny saying anything to you. Nobody would believe you anyway."

"Holy shit, wait until I tell my friends."

"They won't believe you either."

Last At Bat

At the front of the tavern, a group of seven entered. Matt, his wife Rebecca, their twin boys, Annie, Robbins' wife and Randy all waved to Arthur. Arthur waved back. After twenty years Arthur still had a hard time seeing Matt's wife with auburn instead of brunette hair. And how her turned up nose changed her looks so dramatically. Robbins shook his head and smiled when he remembered Sonny saying, "Well, hell, we did it once; we can do it again."

Matt motioned the group into the adjoining restaurant and then walked over to Arthur at the bar. The young bartender was stunned to see Matt Wolf in his tavern only hours after watching his induction on TV.

64.   Last at Bat

All great players know they are great. Robbins always said false modesty was a sign of insincerity or stupidity. Matt knew he was a great player. Hell, all he had to do was look at his statistics to figure out that much. But there were a lot of great players over the years, and it is very difficult to determine who was the greatest. But Matt Wolf/Dylan Michael had accomplished something no one else ever had or would. He/they had been inducted into the Major League Baseball Hall of Fame …twice.

Seven years after his "death," Dylan Michael had been given a rare honor.   Despite his conviction and short career, he had been inducted into the Baseball Hall of Fame by the players over the then Commissioner's objections. The players in the Hall of Fame knew how great Dylan Michael had been and how great he would have been if not for a spate of bad luck that appeared Job-like. At that induction ceremony years earlier, several Hall of Famers got up and talked about Dylan Michael with awe in their voices relating to skills that come once in a lifetime. Or twice.

Matt Wolf did not watch the ceremony that day. Instead he went 4 for 5 in a 7-3 Reds win over the Giants. He seemed particularly focused at the plate that afternoon.

******

Robbins saw Matt motion the group to the restaurant side of O'Reilly's Stone House Tavern and heard him say he would join them in a few minutes. As Matt walked toward the bar, Robbins saw Matt still had that "athlete walk" and at forty-nine-years old he looked like he could have suited up and played a double- header that afternoon. Matt's shoulders were still wide and with 'Becca watching his diet, his waist still thin. His hair was salt and pepper and when Robbins shook his hand it felt like it usually did, in that Matt's hand was huge and muscular and Robbins' was not.

While he liked to tease Matt with his "dumb jock" comments, Robbins knew the truth. He realized Matt now presided over a far reaching philanthropic enterprise that included the Gwen and Sonny Cook Children's Cancer Treatment Center in Cincinnati to which Matt had donated over $10,000,000 and raised millions more serving on the hospital's Board of Directors. In Blossom, the local clinic, after an $8,000,000 donation from Matt and Rebecca, had become the Dr. Walter and Annie Watson Regional Hospital. Matt also made a $5,000,000 donation to the African-American Veterans Association Scholarship Fund in the memory of Doc. In addition, Matt and Rebecca built dozens of baseball fields in both communities and served on various community service boards including Becca's duties as President of *Wheaten's in Need,* an animal rescue organization that was particularly close to Becca's heart.

"The boy and girl have done good," was how Sonny put it before he died.

But in some ways Matt did remain a jock. He started playing golf at 39 and shot in the mid-70's. He was a 4.5 tennis player, played basketball and even competed in the Men's Senior Baseball League over 30 Division up in Cincinnati just for some weekend fun and exercise. In his first game with no batting practice in over three years, he went 4 for 5 with two home runs.

Robbins came back to the present as Matt approached. At first Matt didn't say anything to Robbins. He just sat down, ordered a beer, and began watching the Mets' game. After a few minutes Robbins said without looking away from the game, "Nice speech."

Also staring at the TV Matt said, "Thanks."

For several minutes nothing more was said until Matt casually mentioned, "You remember right after the Fifth Game of the World Series against the Red Sox, I told you that a writer had said he wanted to write a book about me?"

Robbins, still watching the TV, said, "Yeah, I remember. And now, like then, I don't think your story is all that goddamned interesting."

After another minute, still looking at the TV Matt said, "Maybe, maybe not. But since you are older than hell and have been around forever, even though God knows you are no Hemmingway, you might want to reconsider doing a book on me. You know, something awe inspiring and inspirational. Maybe even tell the truth."

"Some people don't like the truth and prefer things just the way they see them. They don't like anything that can change their perception about things," Robbins offered.

"Well if you don't want to write my story, maybe I'll just do it myself. You will have to live with whatever I come up with and whatever I will say about all the people I want to talk about in my book," Matt teased.

Robbins, not fazed in the least, said, "I doubt you could write out a Kroger shopping list, much less a damn book."

Matt laughed and said, "Well then, I guess you had better get to work."

Reaching under his bar stool, Robbins lifted up a beat up yellow envelope and pulled out a 350 page double spaced manuscript then handed it to Matt. Finally looking at Robbins, Matt said, "What the hell is this?"

Robbins joked, "Read it, you dumb jock."

Titled *Last at Bat,* the manuscript was Matt's life story written by the only person who could have written it. It had been created from a series of interviews with the people who had changed his life. As he read, Matt could hear Sonny, Gwen, Doc, Annie, and Randy's voices and see their faces, as their words sprang off Arthur's pages. He could see all the folks from Blossom, his teammates, 'Becca.

As he flipped through the pages he could visualize everything through Arthur's words. He could see all the biggest moments of his career including what he thought was going to be his last at bat ever against the Red Sox in the Fifth Game of the World Series.

As he read the words he remembered floating around the bases and looking for Sonny, Gwen, Annie, and Doc in the stands as he rounded third. He could still hear the crowd's roar and feel his teammates beating him half to death at home plate in their joy and excitement.

"How did you do this? When did you do this?" Matt gasped.

"Hell, I started the process in Blossom nearly twenty years ago with all the folks there," Robbins admitted. "And then over the years I interviewed everybody else including you and 'Becca."

Matt then remembered all those late night conversations Arthur and he had shared over the years. "I never thought I was being interviewed," Matt shook his head.

Robbins laughed and said, "I told you, you're just a dumb jock. By the way, I was never gonna publish this crap until you approved it, you know," Robbins said, almost as a second thought.

"I know you wouldn't," Matt said quietly.

Robbins told Matt the book was certainly about him but more importantly it was about a town. A town which Arthur Robbins now called home. A town where 'Becca, the kids, and Matt spent four months every year living in the house that Sonny and Gwen had left to Matt in their will.

Robbins had never seen Matt break down before. Arthur said quietly as he put his right arm on Matt's left shoulder, "Matt, this is your story. If you don't want to share it with the world, that's your call."

As Matt turned to answer, 'Becca and the rest of the group walked up behind him and she said, "Oh, you saw it."

Matt looked up at her and said, "You mean you know about this?"

"Of course silly, everyone in the book knows about it, even Eric Patterson, although he still thinks you owe him a Pulitzer Prize. He's kind of mellowed in his old age. We all figured it was a gift to you and you could decide who reads it."

"I knew about it too," said Bonnie. "When Arthur moved to Blossom and we got married, we worked on the book together, right honey?"

"Yep, Millie's Chili, apple pie and Bonnie here got me through a lot of writer's block."

"I helped too, said Annie. "It was a team effort."

"It was all part of the plan," said Bonnie.

As he turned the pages and the years rolled by before his eyes, Matt decided the time had come to start paying back his debts. He stopped and read Sonny's words, "*...after Gwen told us about six times, Doc and I finally went outside in that cold rain to get that damn fire wood...*"

He hoped Arthur won the Pulitzer.

Last At Bat

******

EPILOG

As he stood on deck in the ninth inning of the fifth game against the Red Sox tied at 9- 9, Matt knew he would hit the ball hard. His bat was lightning quick that day, and despite the fact the Red Sox pitcher could run it up there around 95 or 96 mph, his pitches didn't have much movement.

After the first Reds' batter reached base on a walk, Matt slowly walked to the plate amid the roar of the Reds' fans, a roar he did not hear. Instead he thought of the "Double." He remembered how nervous he had been at the time. He worried now as he stood there taking a practice swing before stepping into the batter's box, if this time he was too calm. But he reasoned his calmness had more to do with the knowledge that he knew no matter what happened, there was going to be life after his next at bat.

While the Boston infield gathered around their manager on the mound discussing how to pitch to him, Matt was motioned by Dave Schultz, his 3rd base coach. They huddled half way between home and third base where Schultz put his arm around Matt's shoulder. "Five years ago you were a pretty good bunter. Can you still bunt?" Schultz asked.

"I can still bunt", Matt said with a smile.

"Fuck, alright. Tell you what, they probably think you're going to bunt. Why don't you take a hack at the first one if it's a fast ball. If it's a breaking ball take it and bunt the second pitch."

"OK, said Matt. "By the way, how long have you known?"

351

"Long enough. Hey Matt, swing hard in case you hit that first one."

"I'll swing hard, Dave."

On the mound, the Boston pitching coach gave his young right hander specific directions. "Throw the fast ball letter high. That's the toughest pitch to bunt, and you can be sure as hell he will be bunting."

Matt walked back to the plate and looked around him. He sucked it all in like a sponge. Then he whispered to himself, "Pick a zone, inner half, look for the fast ball, keep the arms loose…"

In the radio booth the announcer was hoarse from calling the wild game. *"This stadium is going crazy. You can't hear yourself think. The Red Sox are expecting the bunt from Wolf, the 1st and 3rd basemen are in on the corners…*

… it's a fast ball, I see it…"

"…here's the pitch to Wolf, a fastball, Wolf swings and there is a tremendous drive to right field that ball is gone.. gone… gone!!! It has cleared the bleachers in right field to win the World Series for the Cincinnati Reds!!! The longest home run in this stadium's history!!!